About the Author

Author photo credit: E & E Turton

Originally from Bedfordshire, Nicola currently lives in Hampshire with her overactive imagination. It was whilst researching the Tudor Ruin of Basing House, where she also lived, that she first learned about Joan Larke. This is her first novel. As long as she can recall, Nicola has been fascinated by history and archaeology, two passions that are essential to her writing. Wolsey's Wife was one of the six shortlisted books in the 2022 Aspects of History Unpublished Novel Competition.

Wolsey's Wife

N J Turton

Wolsey's Wife

To Susanne

love from Topsy.

1st Dec. 2025

Vanguard Press

VANGUARD PAPERBACK

© Copyright 2025
N J Turton

The right of N J Turton to be identified as author of
this work has been asserted by her in accordance with the
Copyright, Designs and Patents Act 1988.

All Rights Reserved

No reproduction, copy or transmission of this publication
may be made without written permission.
No paragraph of this publication may be reproduced,
copied or transmitted save with the written permission of the publisher, or in
accordance with the provisions
of the Copyright Act 1956 (as amended).

Any person who commits any unauthorised act in relation to this publication
may be liable to criminal prosecution and civil claims for damages.

A CIP catalogue record for this title is available from the British Library.

ISBN 978-1-83671-004-2

*This book is a work of fiction and, except in the case of historical fact, any
resemblance to actual persons, living or dead, is purely coincidental.*

*Vanguard Press is an imprint of
Pegasus Elliot Mackenzie Publishers Ltd.*
www.pegasuspublishers.com

First Published in 2025

**Vanguard Press
Sheraton House Castle Park
Cambridge England**

Printed & Bound in Great Britain

Dedication

To Henning, my Muse and all those with sunshine in their smiles. And for everyone who has inspired me, whether wittingly or un.

Acknowledgements

Acknowledgements. So many; particularly AJ Lyndon, for saying, "Oh, do get on and write it!" And Gillian Walker Chattell for my forty-year writing apprenticeship and a lifetime of friendship. My first readers: David Hill and authors AJ Lyndon and Penny Ingham. You so skilfully trod the line between firm and kind. I have had many generous teachers, but chiefly the late Sheila Furnell (this time my homework is just too late), and my friend, the gifted historian Alan Turton. I am endlessly indebted to all the historians on whose shoulders I have stood in order to bring as much truth to this book as possible, and I now own some very obscure volumes. Thank you, Jenny Woodward, more than I can ever express. And then there are those who have always had such faith in my writing: Gillian Walker Chattell, David Hill, Penny Ingham, AJ Lyndon, Perry Straker, Henning Wilkens, Carys Wise... (If I've missed you out, you are hereby authorised to insert your name here_____. And of course, first and last, Joan and her Thomas. It has been the greatest privilege to walk beside you. I hope I've done you justice.

Chapter 1

Yarmouth, February 1509

This time yesterday, she had no idea how painful it was to be thrashed across the soles of her feet. But neither did she know how it felt to be held in the arms of Thomas Wolsey and comforted.

And as Joan Larke was young and resilient it was not the memory of the brutal punishment which she carried back to her dreams, but the thought of Henry VII's chaplain, with whom, had she understood, she was more than half in love.

***

For the first time this year, Joan had awoken to birdsong and warmth, making it feel as if spring had arrived. But this was the east coast; within hours the weather could blow in snow from the Russias and they'd be closing their bed hangings and laying furs on the beds.

She pulled on her chemise, wriggled into her stays and pulled the laces tight before tying off the ends. She remembered her grandmother saying that in her day only priests had double-looped bows. So it was Joan's habit to only have single loops, and every time it brought her grandmother to her, even though she'd died when Joan was a small child.

Skirted and gowned, Joan undid her night plait and brushed her hair with such vigour that her scalp and even her forehead glowed a nice pink, but Joan didn't know that, for she no longer had a mirror in her room. Gathering her hair between her hands, she replaited it, catching linen tapes into the braids. Her brown hair had pleasing depths and it was bleached fair in the front, where shorter hairs forever plagued her. She coiled the hair around her head, tied the laces firmly and placed her cap on top just as Little Meg arrived to remove the washing water. Meg was a small girl, but insisted she was strong enough, constantly proving herself as she strained her little muscles hefting the buckets and other heavy items crucial to running the house.

Treading into her backless house shoes, Joan clattered downstairs to break her fast. Unwell, her father was in his room, being tended by James and several other manservants; so, once she had eaten, she would take bread and butter to her father and ensure he took his medicine. But today, there were two places at the cloth, and Joan rolled her eyes and made a face, for her Uncle John was visiting them. John took the joy from every room he entered, and if Joan was honest, she was somewhat frightened of him. Although close enough in age to be her elder brother, he treated her as a recalcitrant child instead of a woman of nearly twenty. Her learning was both too much, and never enough for him, and her heart sank when he took a breath in the evenings and proceeded to discuss the Bible with her. Joan had studied Latin, Greek and French with her brothers, catching crumbs of tuition until the tutor took pity on her and taught her as well, but it had been a secret between them, and her needlework was to hand should anyone come in and ask why she was in the schoolroom. It was a hard day when the kindly tutor left to accompany her younger brother to university before travelling on to another family. At least her father had not minded her scraped education, and to his surprise, he found himself enjoying her company and conversation more and more after they were left alone.

But Joan's sharpened wits and wide reading of her father's library did not endear her to John Larke. His inflexible version of belief left no doubt that a woman's place was to serve the Christ-like males in her family, or even better, live a faith-full life in a nunnery. To realise that his niece had her own thoughts and opinions was a constant thorn to John, and he thoroughly disapproved of her.

Many times, Joan had heard John and her father arguing about her and her place in the world. Her father insistent that Joan was his companion and would marry when he saw fit; John responding that Joan ran wild, was forward and pert, and would bring disgrace to them. Peter would try to end the argument, but John could rumble it along for days, spoiling mealtimes and pleasant evenings till Joan ached to tell him to just leave them alone to live as they wished. But she clenched her jaw, assumed a pleasant little smile and stitched each word she'd like to say into her work, especially if it was a shirt for her uncle, who little knew that each stab of her needle was waxed with venom.

Entering the dining room, Joan's stomach gave a hungry squeak, but she dared not nip a piece of bread. Instead, she waited peacefully, hands folded in her lap, a blank smile on her face, whilst she imagined stuffing one of the fresh rolls into her mouth. She would struggle to chew it because it was such a large piece of bread, but she would manage and the warm bread would hit her stomach and fill it. Then her stomach groaned even more loudly, and she was thankful that John was not here to frown at the uncouth noise. To distract herself, she slid one foot out of her shoe, and wriggled it around the fat leg of their new dining table, feeling the deep and lavish carving.

Finally, she heard his step on the stairs and got to her feet to offer him a morning curtsey. His eyes flicked around the room, but returned the courtesy with a brisk nod, and opened his mouth to speak.

Goodness me, thought Joan, *he's going to apologise for being late.*

'I see you are early for breakfast, niece. You should consider curbing your appetite a little. Spend longer in prayer and seek your reward in less earthly things. And if you behaved a little more sedately, you might find time to wear two shoes.'

Joan ducked her head in another curtsey, this time taking the opportunity to roll her eyes. 'I'm sorry, uncle. I will try harder to bring my prayers more thoughtfully to God. And,' with a bright smile, 'my shoe is just here.' *And now may we eat?* she silently added, and at that thought, her stomach issued its loudest complaint yet and she found that folding her arms across her front made no difference, but resulted in a scratch from a pin tucked into her gown.

John breathed in deeply through his nose, a sign of displeasure. 'Very well. Let us be seated.'

Joan resumed her seat and waited, head bowed and hands clasped, for her uncle to say the Latin grace. It was long, and she felt her mind wandering, especially when a flock of screaming birds swept in front of the window and she heard Pepper barking in the depths of the house. Fortunately, the word 'Amen' caught her attention, and she murmured in response before lifting her eyes which were now watery from suppressed yawns. They ate in silence, which for John was blessed by the presence of God, and for Joan, by the absence of having to make acceptable conversation.

Finishing the last mouthful of bread on her plate and swallowing the end of her warmed small-beer, Joan asked to be excused, but John was not finished. Sitting back, he slowly brushed crumbs from his doublet and looked at his niece.

'This afternoon I would like you to spend a little time in study with me. It is time we start to prepare for your future life.'

Joan felt slightly cold and very panicky. If her father died, as seemed all too likely, her brothers were not equipped to care for her; neither had ambition to follow their father as a merchant, instead joining the church and both attached to the household of their father's friend

Thomas Wolsey. But as good as that was for them, it would leave her in the care of her uncle.

Joan raised her eyes to John, and he felt the familiar wave of irritation within her. If Joan had known, she might have tried to temper it, but since she was born, her eyes had upset John Larke. Even as a baby, Joan would look at him, her eyes seeming to assess him, before looking away as if disappointed. And that continued throughout her childhood; eventually, her eyes settled as a clear blue-grey, but never lost their way of measuring him. John hated the way Joan looked at him as though she was at least his equal, and he sought to subdue her whenever he could.

Swallowing her surge of fear, Joan replied, 'Of course, Uncle John. I have household duties this morning, but I'll join you as soon as I may after dinner.' She paused, then asked again to be excused, adding, 'I would like to go and see how father is and help him with his breakfast.'

John couldn't refuse and watched as Joan placed bread on a plate and poured warm ale into a cup. She added honey, and from the pouch at her belt, withdrew a nutmeg, held in a tiny silver box like a pomander. She heard John's breath drawn in through his nose, and she turned to him with her polite smile.

'I don't know why my Lord Wolsey gave that to you – it's worth a king's ransom and is an unnecessary indulgence. He would have done better to throw his money to a beggar.'

Biting back the many responses *because he knew I'd like it – as it smells so wonderful and why shouldn't he spend his money as he sees fit* – Joan bobbed another obedient curtsey, 'Indeed uncle, but I think he hoped that it might cheer my father. He gave it to us as a curiosity; it came from Italy and before that, from an Arab.'

The only response was more sniffing; so, drawing her knife, she scraped a little nutmeg into the ale and balanced everything on the plate. She shuffled through the door praying that Pepper wouldn't suddenly appear to knock into her and thinking that it would have been kind of John to hold the door for her, she finally escaped and made her way to her father's chamber.

Knocking gently, she heard him bid her enter. The room was still dark, but the gentle glow of the fire gave her enough light. Joan walked to the table by the side of the fire and placed the meal upon it. She moved to the window and carefully drew the curtains. Despite the recent new purchases for the house, Peter Larke preferred to keep his chamber as it was when his wife Jane was alive as if expecting her to return one day and when she did, he would like her to be able to recognise it. Consequently, the curtains were frail and soft with dust, for Joan feared that taking them for a beating in the garden would shred them beyond repair.

The bed was little better, the hangings bagged in the old-fashioned way, but the last time Joan had tried to unbag them, the fabric had started to rip under her fingers, so she dyed linen tapes in the same colour, and now the day-bags were held together with a web of ribbon. At least the constant fire in the room meant he didn't need them drawn at night, but Joan couldn't help but think that her father would feel better if the room was fresh and new.

Peter smiled at her, and Joan noted how his face was more drawn than yesterday, and his lips a little more blue. Inside, her childhood voice cried in anguish, but she ignored it and fetching the food, perched on the side of the bed as her father pulled himself into a sitting position.

They chatted as she helped him to the fresh bread and salty butter and then handed Peter the warm ale and he sniffed, '*Mmm...* is that Thomas's nutmeg on the top?'

Joan nodded, 'Yes...' and brought the silver case out of her pocket and held it under his nose. 'Doesn't it make you long for places you've never been and where people with no bodies live?' She laughed; 'And where the air smells like this, not of fish being smoked!'

Peter chuckled, 'Well... yes... but those fishes were treasure for me – selling them abroad was like boxes of gold. Your mother and I couldn't believe that anyone in the Low Countries would want our red herrings, but we couldn't smoke them fast enough.'

He paused to sip at the ale and Joan continued, slipping into their well-rehearsed family history, 'And the boy from Thetford bought land and houses and entered into the land of milk and honey!'

Peter smiled, 'Yeees, although... to be honest, I never thought that fish went very well with milk and honey.'

'But of course, that meant you met the Wolseys and so, Thomas.' Peter nodded. 'And he was really there when I was born?'

'You know he was,' Peter replied, before continuing Joan's favourite tale, 'your poor mother was with him when you started to arrive. And though he didn't see you born, he was the first person you saw other than your mother, me and Mistress Bray.'

And mother died – the words hung unspoken between them, as Joan bent her head and kissed his hand; then they sat in peace for a while, till the foxglove tincture began to take effect and Peter's lips took on a little colour, and he finally said, 'I'll be having a little sleep now, my lovely, so you go and do tidy things and I'll see you later.'

Joan tucked the sheet around Peter and when she said softly, 'Fa, I think I'll take Pepper for a walk on the beach later. Is that all right?' the only response was a sleepy 'Mm' which she gleefully took as yes and skipped off downstairs to her household chores.

After dinner, which as John was dining with the local priest, Joan was thankful to take alone, the afternoon stretched invitingly ahead of her. In her room, Joan changed her house jacket for a warmer one and tied the ribbons on a pair of thick shoes. Then she whistled through the kitchen door for Pepper who raced to her side with a madly wagging tail, and with an apple stay-piece in her pocket, they slipped out.

Joan kept out of sight of the priest's house, just in case, and they raced along towards the marketplace, before passing down Dog's Leg Row, and winding through Row after Row until the dark little alleys brought them to the town wall, where they left Yarmouth proper through a broken gate. Pepper loved it there and galloped to the top of the sand piled against the outside of the wall, where he dug at the mound, smelling something wonderful in the rubbish dumped there until Joan called him and they continued along the quay to the beach.

The sun was glorious and as soon as they were alone, Joan sat down and undid her leg ties. She rolled down the stockings and took off her shoes until she was barefooted on the sand. Then she tucked up one side of her skirts into her belt and chased Pepper to the water. The damp sand was solid under her feet, and she felt her heels thump as she left scarcely a mark behind her. Reaching the sea Pepper raced in, jumping and biting at the water which Joan scooped up in her hands to throw at him.

Joan and her dearest friend played the afternoon away, stopping only to eat the apple which she sliced with the knife from her belt, and tossing pieces for Pepper to snap at, and sometimes miss, gathering a mouthful of sand when he picked them up from the beach.

Then the tide started to turn and Joan realised how late it was. Her feet and legs were damp and coated with sand, and she knew she didn't have time to go to the water, wash them and stand on one leg at a time to dry and shoe them; so she gathered up her stockings and looped them through her belt. She stuffed the leg-ties into her shoes, before tying the ribbons together and swinging the shoes from her hand and whistling for Pepper. The top of the beach was slightly muddy where the earth and grass met the sand, and there she gathered more dirt on her feet, but once through, she let her skirt down, and with the knowledge of a local girl, threaded her way swiftly and unerringly back through the Rows.

A quick skirt along the edge of the marketplace, now being swept clean following the market, and they were home. As they passed through the gate, Joan could see the candles lit in the parlour and the dining chamber. And her heart leapt, for illuminated in the light was her other dearest friend, Thomas Wolsey. His tall figure in his Dean's robes was a glad sight and she ran even faster to be inside.

Softly opening the front door, she propelled the suddenly rigid-legged Pepper towards the kitchen door, whispering, 'No, you can't see him now, look how mucky you are!' She shot him through the door, hissing 'Supper Pepper, supper' before turning back along the passage. Then surely she felt her heart stop, for there was John standing by the closed parlour door, his arms folded and fury on his face.

After a moment, he spoke, quietly and menacingly. 'Where were you this afternoon?'

'I went to the beach with Pepper.' Her voice was defiant but spoiled by a slight wobble.

'Instead of studying with me.'

As quick as a striking snake, John was by Joan's side, and his hand was around her arm, gripping hard. He pushed her into the dining chamber and silently closed the door. The candles were already lit as the servants were mid-way through preparing a meal for Thomas.

'Slut.'

'No!'

'Slut. Look at you. Where are your shoes?'

Joan held them up, her eyes wide with fear.

'And your stockings?'

She pulled them from her belt, and again John lunged

at her, grabbing the hem of her skirt, and pulling it towards him, causing her to stumble against the table. He seized a whippy piece of kindling wood from the basket and pushed her down on the tabletop, so her forehead met it with a crack. He pulled up her skirts and looked at her legs, mud and sand streaking them, and brought the stick down hard against her calves. Joan squeaked at the sting and wriggled, but John brought the wood down again and again against her skin.

'You are a slut. You will bring ruin to this family. You are worthless. Your tongue is too smart and you will end in the midden.' His words were punctuated by his blows and Joan's arms, flat against the table began to flap frantically as she tried to be free of him. She started to drum her hands against the tabletop, and John grabbed her hair, now unpinned and the plaits coming loose, and rammed her back down. As he did so, she brought her legs up and the switch caught her across the soles of her feet. Joan screamed, and John dropped the stick, swiftly taking his knife from his belt. For a moment, he hesitated, then started to saw at the hank of hair in his hand.

The door opened, and Thomas stood there. For a moment, he struggled to understand what he was seeing, and then he spoke, his voice calm and low.

'John, my dear friend.' John whipped around and stared at Thomas.

'John. Your knife. Away I think, please.'

John didn't move, but Joan worked her way free from the weighty hand pressing her down, and half sat, half stood, staring at Thomas and her uncle, not daring to speak.

In the silence, the nutmeg case fell from Joan's pocket, making them all jump. John looked at it on the floor in front of him, and slowly and very deliberately lifting his foot, he brought his heel down smartly on the little piece of silver. The case crumpled under his shoe, and the nutmeg shot across the floor to knock against the skirting. Joan made a muffled protest but remained where she was.

The two men were motionless for a long moment, then Thomas clasped his hands loosely in front of him, and suddenly it was clear to Joan that Thomas was in charge and that eventually John would obey. And indeed, after a few breaths, John slipped the knife back into the sheath at his belt. He dropped her hair onto the table and seemed to wait for instructions.

'Thank you. Now, John, I would like you to go quietly to your room and I wish you to try and pray and discover what happened here and if it was your will or the Will of God.'

John didn't move, so Thomas opened the door and stepped aside. Then he dipped down and grasped the scruff of Pepper who erupted into the room with his hackles raised and a growl deep in his throat. With a sneer at the dog, John left the room and could be heard climbing the stairs to his chamber. Peering into the passage, Thomas beckoned to Little Meg who was lurking there, eyes wide with excitement. 'Take Pepper and keep him locked up until I tell you otherwise.'

Little Meg nodded, which was often her version of a

curtsey, and dragged Pepper back to the kitchens.

Closing the door again, Thomas held his arms open to Joan who was there in a moment. Thomas had held her as a baby and a child, but in all that time, he'd never felt her so wracked with tears. He simply held her tight, with one hand stroking the shockingly shorn hair which now touched the base of her neck. And as Thomas realised how very pleasant it was to hold a woman close, he was instantly and deeply ashamed of himself. He was a man of God, a churchman, the King's chaplain. He was the friend of Joan's father and trusted to behave with the utmost propriety towards Peter's children. And despite these things, Thomas still felt human emotions. But instead of behaving as any other man, who would have been sorely tempted to bend his head and kiss Joan's tear-blotched face, he concentrated on what he knew to be right. He put her slightly from him and looked at her.

'Your feet – do they hurt terribly?' Joan nodded, her eyes huge and her chin wobbling and Thomas was torn between sympathy and longing to smile at her comical little face.

'Very well.' And he picked Joan up in his arms.

She looked astonished, then helped him to open the door. They crossed the hall passage towards the stairs, but there Thomas stopped. Although Joan was slim, she was still surprisingly heavy, and Thomas doubted that he could carry her up.

'Can you walk? I'll support you. I just think the stairs might be slightly beyond my magnificent powers.'

Joan gave a shaky laugh, 'Of course. Put me down.

I'll be fine.'

She made not a sound as her burning feet touched the ground, but Thomas could see the tendons in her neck tense as she clenched her jaw, and his heart swelled with pity for her. He slipped his arm around her waist and took as much of her weight as he could as she limped up the stairs.

'This is my chamber.' Joan indicated a door and Thomas opened it and helped her in. When they reached the bed, Joan sat down with a sharp sigh, then as the edge of the bed touched the raw stripes on the backs of her legs, she rolled on to her side.

Thomas busied himself with lighting candles and pouring water, then Joan directed him to her medicine box, and he dropped some lavender oil into the bowl and brought it to her.

'And some marigold salve please. It's in the pot with the orange thread around the top…'

As they did these things, Thomas felt a little peace return to him, but his thoughts were busy and disjointed. Joan was only a child and he was very upset by the behaviour of a man whom he had not always liked, but always respected. John Larke's piety marked him out as a man destined for greatness in the service of God, but Thomas was disquieted by the streak of ruthlessness he had seen in him today. But, he said to himself, the church is for *all* souls, and there will be a place for him. Perhaps a place which is more robust and less domestic, but somewhere there is a place. And Joan's brothers? Well, it was hardly Thomas's fault that the boys were in London, and not here with their family, helping their sister deal with this terrible situation – no mother and a dying father. He had no right to interfere; it was not his family, nothing to do with him.

But as he berated himself, he recalled sitting with Jane Larke on that dreadful day. Thomas was seventeen and on his way home, but had broken his journey with a visit to the Larkes. Peter Larke was Thomas's father's fellow tradesman and friend. Both the Wolsey and Larke families were deeply religious and furthermore shared the spirit of enterprise that brought them success and wealth.

Peter's interest in Robert, an Ipswich butcher, had helped both men and linked their families so that although living miles apart, the children of each were as nearly as familiar and at home in one another's houses as in their own. And Jane and Peter Larke had taken great delight in seeing the child Thomas growing into a gracious and formidably intelligent young man.

That afternoon… little Tom Larke was charging around the house and Jane was clearly very tired when Thomas arrived. He scooped the boy into his arms and passed him to the nursery maid, who took him for his supper, leaving Thomas sitting quietly with Jane in her warm little solar. Thomas recalled how the late sun shone through the window and cruelly picked out the lines on Jane's face and highlighted her pallor. He was shocked; at Christmas, just four months before, she'd glowed as if she had swallowed both the sun and the moon.

Thomas had noticed how Jane's hands kept straying to her sides, pinching at her waist, and it concerned him.

His own mother had easily given birth to him and his younger brother and sister, before returning to the household with an almost unseemly show of speed and health. And so, a couple of worrying hours later, Thomas was greatly relieved when Peter returned home. Jane had stood up to greet him, but with a choking cry fell onto her hands and knees and Thomas was horrified at the great bloom of blood on the back of her skirt.

A strong, well-built man, Peter had no difficulty carrying her to her chamber. Thomas remained in the solar, and when Tom appeared, wailing for his mother and pushing snot and tears around his face, Thomas had comforted the small boy, rocking him to sleep and holding him for hours as his ears strained to work out whose cries he could hear above him.

At four in the morning, Peter stood in the door, looking at Thomas, dozing with Tom in his arms. The slight movements woke Thomas and he looked up at Peter, and instantly knew whose cries they had been.

'She's dead.' Peter's voice was bleak and broken. 'She's gone.' And he started to cry again, great roaring sobs that were more like ravaging pain than grief. The noise woke the child who held his arms out to his father, 'Fa! Fa!'

Then the three of them, Peter, Thomas and Tom sank onto the day bed and held each other in their loss and grief. It was some time before Thomas asked about the baby, and Peter whispered over Tom's sleeping head that the baby lived but was not strong.

As dawn began to push grey light into the room,

Thomas stood quietly and tiptoed up to Jane's chamber. There the woman who had been as a second mother to him lay still and pale in the bed. He struggled to comprehend her absence, and in the end all he could do was to pass his hand over her forehead in a blessing and murmur the Nunc dimittis. Suddenly, he realised that in the corner of the shadowy room sat a wet-nurse. She was asleep and against her she held the tightly swaddled baby. Thomas walked over to her and peered at the child, and to his astonishment, she opened her eyes and stared back at him. The nurse woke and looked at Thomas and then at the child,

'Goodness me, she's still alive. Well I am surprised. Here, hold her a moment.' She thrust the baby at Thomas, who held her in front of him and looked again into those astonishingly direct blue eyes.

They called the child Joan, both as a compliment to the Wolsey family and as a name similar to her mother's, but not quite the same, as Peter had felt he couldn't bear to have the name echoing in a house which no longer held his own dear Jane.

Remembering that difficult day and the months which followed, Thomas smiled at Joan as he knelt to help bathe her legs. In the end, her own quirky nature had taught her father to love her, and indeed almost all those who knew her.

Her legs were no longer bleeding and the pain from the strikes across her feet would ease, but Thomas was deeply concerned about Joan's future. Her uncle could be harsh and inflexible, and when her father died, John would direct Joan's destiny.

Joan looked sleepy now and Thomas sat on the edge of the bed. He stroked her hair, that poor ragged head, and pulled the coverlet over her shoulders and body, leaving the weeping legs bare.

'Darling girl, this will pass. Remember that tomorrow God will bless another day, and you and John will come to an accord. He does love you and seeks only to help you…'

'Even by beating me?' Joan was awake now and Thomas realised with a wry smile that he should have left her dozing. 'How does thrashing me show love?' Working herself up to be quite indignant, Thomas made soothing noises and lowered his voice.

'Joan, step aside from this, and look at yourself in a mirror. No, I *know* you don't have a mirror…'

Joan drew breath to start on another pet complaint about her uncle who had removed the mirror from her room to help her with the sin of vanity.

'But *I* know that *you* know how mirrors work…' he looked at her with an eyebrow slightly raised, and Joan gave a little grin.

'Now see yourself as John sees you. He doesn't see a grown woman but a great child, who runs off and plays on the beach and displays her legs for the town to see. He sees a girl who shirks her lessons with him, and above all, he sees you as a reason why he is not in a religious house serving God. You are his cross, and he is trying to summon the grace to accept his burden and learn how to live with it.'

Joan sniffed giving an almost invisible nod, and encouraged, Thomas pressed on. 'Now imagine if you were to just very slightly improve your behaviour. His cross would be lighter, and this house would be a more peaceful place for you all and especially for your father. Yes?'

Joan suddenly curled round Thomas, so her stomach was against his back and she pressed her face against the outside of his thigh. He slipped his arm over her shoulder and hugged her.

'Yes?' He felt her nod. 'Now look at me.' She turned her face up to him and he placed his hand on her forehead and gave her his blessing. For a moment, he found that he was about to bend forward and kiss her cheek, but he stopped himself.

He felt her eyes upon him as he left the room and gently shut the door, where pausing for a moment, he clasped his hands and spent a moment in prayer.

Then he straightened his shoulders and walked to Peter's chamber door, tapping lightly and going in. The room was warm, and softly lit by the glow of the fire, but Thomas only had eyes for the gaunt figure in the bed, who watched him steadily.

'*Well*? What on earth has been going on in my house? If I hadn't known you were here...' Peter stopped, his words interrupted by a gasping cough.

Thomas walked slowly across the room, to sit on the stool beside the bed.

'Oh, my friend, *such* excitement this afternoon!'

Peter subsided gratefully against his pillows, at least partly reassured by Thomas's light words, but then his face darkened and worry gnawed at him as he learned of the clash between his daughter and his brother.

'Oh Thomas, what am I to do? If her mother hadn't died, if I'd married again. Or if I'd married her to someone. Someone kind, but I wanted her here. Selfish old fool that I am.' His breath was ragged as Thomas fetched wine, warm from the fireplace, and gently held it to Peter's lips.

'Peter, I don't know what to say, but I will think and pray about it. It may be that Joan *should* enter a House. She may well find great peace and contentment there.'

The two men looked at each other and Peter's mouth twitched as he gave Thomas his most sceptical look and Thomas burst out laughing. After a moment Peter joined him and they laughed till they were forced to stop lest someone come into the see what was going on, and certainly before Peter completely lost his battle for breath.

Wiping tears from their eyes, they looked at each other and had a hard job not starting up again. 'Oh Thomas, that's done me the world of good. I can't tell you. It's like living in a house of death before I've even died.'

Wolsey nodded, 'My poor friend, I can imagine. But believe me, I will think on it. Somewhere will be an answer and God will provide it.'

They sat together a little longer, as Thomas gossiped about the old King, whose life also seemed to be drawing to a close; another man unable to flourish without his much-loved wife. Although it had always seemed doubtful to Thomas that the late Queen Elizabeth could have loved Henry – the man responsible for the deaths of so many of her family – with anything approaching the passion the King had clearly felt for her.

As Peter slipped into a wine-fuelled sleep, Thomas readied himself for the hardest interview, that with John. He bent his head and asked God to help him find the words to deal with this man for whom life was so black and white.

John's chosen chamber was in the attic, much to the annoyance of the servants whose own rooms were also in the roof space. Having climbed the narrow stairs, Thomas knocked briskly on the door and entered a room which was long and thin, with only a narrow path down the centre where a man as tall as Wolsey could walk without banging his head.

John was kneeling before his little crucifix, nothing between his knees and the floor boards but his coarse woollen stockings. Thomas idly wondered if John employed a rough undershirt, perhaps nettle fibre woven with horse hair, but with a shudder, resolved not to think of that. Thomas was a sensuous man who enjoyed the touch of luxury against his skin. The softest linens and silks were the only materials to be found in the underpinnings of the Dean of Lincoln, and Thomas would have argued that unnecessary discomfort was a distraction which would divert his mind from the service of God and the King.

'John.' His voice was soft and conciliatory, but John leapt to his feet, staggering as his numb legs failed him. 'Please, John, sit down.' Thomas gestured to the bed and John gratefully lowered himself to the low truckle. Thomas sat on the only stool and faced him.

Their eyes met, John's rebellious and hard, and Thomas's as gentle and soft as he could make them.

'Shall we pray for a moment before we speak?' John nodded and Thomas once more asked God for help, though this time out loud, asking that they each be given the gift of understanding and to see themselves as others see them, and silently adding an apology for troubling God quite so often that afternoon.

It was a difficult conversation, for John was torn between respecting Thomas as an older and far more senior churchman, and his thoughts that really, Thomas had no right to be involving himself in the affairs of the Larke family. But he also had the grace to remember that Thomas was a friend and mentor of more than twenty years, loved by all the Larkes and therefore deserving of John's respect.

And for his part, Wolsey wanted nothing more than to punch John's jaw. He was a chivalrous man and to see a woman treated thus stuck in his throat almost beyond bearing. And it was a considerable effort for Thomas to look in the mirror as he'd asked Joan to do, and see all sides of this difficult situation. But Thomas Wolsey was also a natural diplomat and he soothed and calmed John, asking him to be patient with his niece who was about to lose the only parent she'd ever known.

Thomas was conscious of the approach of evening and the pressing need to return to London. He had not time for the luxury of a night in Yarmouth and the small ship would leave with the tide in under an hour, so he gradually brought their conversation to an end, having extracted a promise from John that he would never again strike or otherwise harm Joan. He left John once more kneeling on the wooden floor and returned downstairs.

Peeping in, he could see that Peter was asleep, snoring gently but with a little colour in his face – perhaps it wasn't from the wine, perhaps he was on the mend – and perhaps all would be well. And to his relief, Joan was also asleep, cuddled around Pepper who looked at Thomas and gave a single wag of his tail as if to say, 'I'm here. She's safe.'

Entering the parlour, Thomas went to the table and picked up the hanks of Joan's hair. They felt heavy and cold in his hand, almost like dead things, and for a moment he held them to his cheek, enjoying the softness of the long hair. Then before placing them back on the table, he drew out a long strand and curled it into a circle, which he folded into the pouch at his belt. As he did so, he touched his own nutmeg case, the companion to Joan's ruined one, and took it out and tossed it into the air a couple of times before going into the kitchens.

The rooms were warm and bright with candles and firelight. He stood for a moment watching Mistress Bray as she worked over a pan, then she straightened up and smiled at him, though Thomas could see that she had been crying. Alice Bray had been his ally since Thomas was a young boy so his height and importance as a grown man made no difference to her affection for him.

She shook her head. 'Oh, Master Thomas, what's to do with them all, eh? That was a wicked beating he gave her, and across her feet too!'

'I know Alice, and I don't know what to do to help.' He gave a tiny sigh and closed his eyes for a moment, 'I have to get along now, I'm afraid, the time and the tide will not tarry. Not even for me.'

He smiled at her, and she patted the side of his face. 'Eh boy, I am so glad to see you doing well, and chaplain to the King, even if it is that old usurper, Henry.' Thomas grinned, raised his eyebrows at her and laid his finger over his lips with a '*ssh*'.

'Come along now Alice, we are all loyal servants of good King Henry.'

Alice winked at him, and gave a solemn nod, before turning to the kitchen table, where she had placed a pouch for Thomas, filled with pie, bread and cheese and a flask of warm wine.

'Make sure you put this inside you tonight, and don't give too much to that rogue, William, who has been comfortable in here all afternoon, I can tell you!'

Thomas smiled, he knew that Alice liked the teasing she had from William. It brought pink to her cheeks and light to her eyes. Thinking of sparkling eyes, his fingers tightened around the silver nutmeg, and he held it up to Alice.

'My dear, would you give this to Joan tomorrow? Tell her to keep it out of John's sight, but I would rather not have Peter short of a little comfort if I can help it.'

Alice fixed him with a steady look. 'For Peter. Of course.' *Well you could have left it with me then,* she thought, *no need to send a little jewel to Joan.* But she kept her thoughts to herself and lifting her hand to Thomas's head, she sent him on his way with her blessing.

Thomas stopped in the hall passage, donning his thick cloak and velvet hat, and the soft leather gloves which were a great pleasure to him, and paused for a moment listening to the servants moving quietly about their evening duties. The house around him was warm and bright with circles of candlelight, and he sniffed the beeswax-scented air. But already, the comfort of the house was slipping from him; he was ready for the journey ahead, but also because he knew that soon this place would only be a pleasant memory. The house would be sold or let and all that would remain would be a series of images in his heart.

He gave his head a tiny shake and opened the door. Little Meg was suddenly there, wishing him a good night, and closing the door behind him. Outside it was very dark – the clouds had raced in, calling lie to the early spring day, and he could smell rain approaching. He shivered slightly and set off briskly towards the harbour, cutting across the marketplace rather than through the Rows which always horrified him with their dark and filthy corners. It was fortunate that neither John nor Thomas realised quite how well Joan knew and used the tiny alleys, although Thomas did suspect that his darling girl was something of a ragamuffin when she got the chance. As Thomas headed through the town, William and a couple of his escorts slipped out from somewhere and joined him. It amused Thomas to have a slightly shiftless servant, but William was utterly loyal to his master and it was useful to have a man who knew the shadows so well.

'Well Master Dean, Sir, that was an interesting afternoon, weren't it?' William's odd London accent, touched with hints of so many other places usually made

Thomas smile and would often prompt him to share a little gossip, but tonight he was too tired. 'William, it was. It was altogether *too* interesting for my tastes, and I long to get aboard and close my eyes.'

William nodded; a good servant was sensitive to his master, and tonight he was wise enough to know that silence was the correct response.

Chapter 2

Yarmouth and London

Dawn came to the handsome house in Yarmouth. In the kitchens, Little Meg brought the fire back to life and fetching water from the well, put it on to boil. The boy should have drawn the water, but he was so young and she couldn't bear to wake him; so, she heaved the buckets into the house. She shook drops of rain from her hair and clothes and shivered, rubbing her bony little hands over the flames; then she made a start on the bread for the day, using her hand as a paddle to mix the flour and yeast and water. She bent over the dough, relishing the smell of yeast, before setting it to prove in the oven, still slightly warm from yesterday.

In a tiny chamber, just off the kitchens and kept cosy by being on the other side of the wall to the boiling room, Mistress Bray lay abed a little longer, listening to the servants stirring around the house, and thinking over the day's duties. She frowned as she remembered the upset from the day before, and she felt a familiar nip of worry about her own fate when the Master died. As die he surely would before long. Those blue lips and gasping breaths told that his life was closing, and even Joan wouldn't be able to ignore it for much longer. She had a sum put aside and perhaps the Master would be generous, but this had been her home for so long that she hated the thought of leaving. She'd come to the Larke household as a maid when Jane married the master, and she remembered the day she'd walked through town, going the long way around to avoid getting muddy in the Rows. As such things are often arranged, an aunt had recommended her for the job, and in those first days and weeks, it had seemed that both girls were on approval in the Larke household: one as mistress and the other as servant.

They'd almost clung together at first and certainly had been each other's refuge in the early days of learning their new lives. Jane had been in slight awe of her ambitious husband. Her parents introduced them, and although they liked each other very much, they had never been alone before they agreed to marry. Peter had been a fairly easy-going husband, but hard-working, and the first years of their marriage had been a challenge as they faced hardships, but Peter's intuition that people in other places might like the local smoked herrings had been a wonderful idea, and more successful than anyone could have imagined. The herring fleet could barely keep up with demand, especially in the winter months, when they provided welcome variety in the diet. Then came the birth of Tom and the death of the old housekeeper and Jane decided to give Alice Bray her chance.

But it was a chance which paid off and after weathering the resentment of a maid who thought the position should be hers, Alice had grown to be an excellent person to help Jane run the house. The two women were firm friends, and the saddest day of her life was when she helped deliver Jane's baby and held her hand as life bled away. Then, when Peter had called the servants to the parlour, and in front of them handed Jane's keys to Alice, she thought her heart might break. But all troubles pass, and Joan had grown into a proper little person, and to Alice, it had seemed a wonderful thing to help raise Joan and in time give her Jane's keys. And now this; Peter on his deathbed, John and Joan at loggerheads, and Thomas Wolsey, the one sensible person in all this returned to London to dally with the king. Alice Bray puffed out her cheeks in a sigh and started to get up and begin her day. 'God will provide. Humph. Well, He wants to get a move on.'

In the room immediately above Mistress Bray, Joan too began to stir, her lovely dream of Thomas slipping away. Despite the pain, Joan had slept remarkably well, tired out by the upset. As she woke, it became apparent that the tentative spring weather had indeed retreated, and she could hear a blustery and doubtless cold wind banging on the windows. She peeped around her bed curtains and confirmed that yes, water was running down the panes. Next to her on the bed, Pepper stirred and looked at her, and she leaned over and rubbed her face against his silky head. Pepper nuzzled her in return and yawned, his long pink tongue visible through the gloom of the bed hangings.

The previous evening, Mistress Bray had come to Joan, persuading her to eat supper, then she brought pillows and made a little tent for Joan's legs under the covers. 'You'll have to try and sleep on your stomach, my little duck. Just for tonight, then the scabs will form and you won't stick to the sheets.'

Joan had solemnly nodded her teary face, and Alice was torn between pity and amusement. John and Joan had always squabbled. Although uncle and niece, they were fairly close in age, but as different as a dog and a fish. John was the fish; single-minded, cold, devoted to God and heedless of human frailty, whereas Joan was the dog; warm, sometimes a bit silly but utterly loyal to all who showed her kindness and affection. John could so easily have won Joan's love and respect, but any hope of that now seemed lost forever.

She sat with Joan until the girl fell asleep then she stroked the girl's short hair, kissed her forehead and drew the curtains shut, deliberately ignoring Pepper who wagged his tail at her. He wasn't allowed to sleep upstairs, but most in the house turned a blind eye to the dog who managed to spend more nights with Joan than with the boy in the kitchen.

Despite her legs, despite the rain and wind and her now empty stomach, Joan felt very happy as she woke. She rolled onto her side, and reaching backwards, touched the scabs which were nice and hard and not attached to the sheets. Flexing her feet, she explored the bruised burning which still lingered. Then she went over the events of the previous day; the beach, Thomas, being thrashed, Thomas, her hair, the broken nutmeg case, *Thomas*.

Joan smiled. Thomas. In her mind, he was a tall clean flame of a man; true and steady. Would that Simon

Sutcliffe was like that. Simon was the son of a local man and had been showing interest in Joan since she began appearing with her father at dinners for the merchants of Yarmouth. At Christmas, Simon had cornered Joan and lunged at her, kissing her half on her mouth, half on her chin. The suddenness of it had made her jump away with a cry of revulsion. It hadn't been a nice kiss. She had felt the soft stubble of his sparse boyish beard, and as he'd left quite a lot of wetness on her face, she immediately caught up the corner of her apron and scrubbed it away. The poor boy had blushed the colour of one of the new Flemish bricks and stalked off. But her father had glanced across and seen what was happening, and he smiled. A partnership between the two families would be an excellent thing for both men and more importantly, would keep his lovely Joan safe.

But Joan had hated the kiss, and she certainly hadn't liked the kisser. But she rather liked the general idea of kissing, and again, her mind swung around to Thomas. He wouldn't be bristly – he was always clean-shaven – and he certainly never had a wet mouth or greasy hair and she smiled as sleep claimed her once more.

***

In the little ship approaching London, Thomas lay in his cabin, the tiny crib far too small for his long legs, but still, he reflected, better than sleeping on the floor, as William was doing.

As there was not really room to climb out of the box-like bed and kneel to pray, Thomas apologised to God and quietly said the morning offices from a recumbent position. As he finished, he heard a soft Amen from below, which made him smile. William was such a mixture, savage, shifty, positively dangerous at times, then surprisingly devout and occasionally kind. Thomas could always rely on William, even if he wasn't sure how he'd react. Life with William was seldom dull, but there was no one else he'd chose to accompany him on the long journeys he often made – all those trips between Calais and England when he was chaplain to Sir Richard Nanfan and the seemingly constant travelling to the Low Countries and Scotland. His other men were sometimes a little faceless, but William saw him undressed, both physically and when he was weary and disheartened.

'Good morning, William. What do you reckon?'

'A good few hours yet, sir. Try and go back to sleep. If you're anywhere near as cosy as me, you'll be away to sleep in a heartbeat.' He paused to see if Thomas would respond to his teasing, and was rewarded with a slight snuffle of a chuckle, and taking his cue, his voice changed, taking on a mischievous tone.

'I was just lying here, sir, on the exceedingly comfortable floor and keeping so nice and warm, thinking about Mistress Larke. Now she's a lovely lass, ain't she? Shame she's stuck all the way out in Yarmouth, stinkin' o' fish for the rest of her life. D'ja think she'd look on the likes of me for a husband? We'd have some handsome children between us, and plenty of 'em if I had my way.' He gave what could only be described as a lewd chuckle and waited for his Master's response. In his bunk, Thomas rolled his eyes and grinned but chose not to encourage the man. After a few minutes, he could hear William's breathing deepen again and he was alone once more with his thoughts.

As a conscientious chaplain and royal servant, Thomas turned those thoughts to the King. Henry was only fifty-two, but Elizabeth, his dearly loved queen and if one was honest, the validation of the Tudor regime, had been dead for over five years. And once alone, the King had not prospered – her death came hard on the heels of that of Prince Arthur, their eldest son. Then Henry refused for weeks to see anyone but his mother, and when he emerged, the court was appalled to see how ill he looked. Never a handsome man and with small mean eyes, he seemed to have lost the will to live, let alone be a king, and his gaunt face haunted the court.

Wolsey heard it muttered that the King was suffering from guilt. A fixed and loyal man himself, he never ceased to wonder at the mutability of people, and he observed with astonishment, the rise of mawkish nostalgia for the golden years of King Edward, father of the late Elizabeth. Never mind, Thomas would think with annoyance, that most of the courtiers were scarce even born in 1485, or that their fathers had rejoiced – at least publicly – at the ending of the reign of Richard. People always want what is familiar and what is gone. That was not Thomas's way – he loved people, let them go with little regret, and surged on to his next challenge, the next appointment. The son of a merchant would always have something to prove. And however far he climbed, the whispered insult *Butcher's Cur* would be his constant shadow because the English people resented a successful man. To be honest, that was why he had so much sympathy for the King and understood Henry's bemusement at his lack of popularity.

Perhaps he thought, that was why the court was growing bored with Henry the Seventh. A usurper, albeit king by right of conquest, would always feel like a subjugator, especially if he was constantly pinching pennies and looking sour. Perhaps when Prince Henry was king, the court would become bright once more.

Young Henry seemed almost golden and reminded the older folk of his grandfather, King Edward; known affectionately as the Sun in Splendour. A renaissance was what the country needed – England was a jewel, a wonderful country which should take its place in Europe. Henry needed a beautiful and fertile wife, and the country would adore a litter of blond-haired babies. If only the old King would hurry up…

At this, Thomas stopped his thoughts. He was fond of the old man, who at the death of Richard Nanfan had appointed Thomas as one of his own chaplains, and trusted him as emissary on several trips. But it wasn't easy serving the first Tudor King; Henry questioned every item of expense, queried each trip, doubted everything that was reported to him, and to Thomas, the most dreadful thing about him were his teeth. They were terrible, and his breath stank as a dead thing. He smelled even worse than the fish smoking in Yarmouth. That was at least a healthy smell, and he raised the sleeve of his gown where he could catch a remnant of savoury smoke.

A little over twenty-four hours after leaving Yarmouth, the little ship started to rock, and Thomas guessed they were probably approaching the Thames Estuary. He shifted his long legs, easing them from one awkward bend into another which for a moment was sweet, but would quickly grow to be just as uncomfortable. But at this time of year, the roads would be painfully difficult to pass, and he hadn't been inclined to trail his party of men through the sunken ways or over the hills where footpads would be only too happy to take advantage of the slowing and clogging effect of thick mud. Even now, some of the men would be cursing the bumpy voyage, but Thomas relished the chance to dismount for a few hours and sleep, however badly.

He reached into his sleeve for his handkerchief, before remembering he'd left the large square of silk with Joan. He'd dabbed her legs with it, and the last he'd seen of it was her cuddling it as a child nurses a favourite rag. Thomas's jaw tightened and he clasped his hands below his chin, with a finger thoughtfully against his lips. What to do with Joan. Peter had said that young Sutcliffe was interested in her and that it would make an excellent match. Thomas had nodded and agreed, but then a thought struck him: did Joan agree? Peter made a slight face and described the scene at Christmas.

'Well to be honest Thomas, she looked likely to be sick.'

Inwardly Thomas had cheered, but spoke mildly, 'Peter, you've raised her to have her own opinions, so would you have her married to a man she doesn't like, or at least respect?' Peter looked as if he'd like to say that it had nothing to do with Joan, but Thomas's serious face made him pause.

'No, of course I wouldn't, but really Thomas, what is to become of her? Am I to leave her to the care of my sons? They wouldn't know what to do with any woman, let alone someone like Joan.'

Thomas smiled, no, they wouldn't. To his clerical brothers, women were an unfathomable mystery and one which they had no wish to solve, whereas Thomas had always liked women. He often found them to be good company and if educated he'd sometimes count them as excellent company. And Joan. Joan was indeed an excellent companion, and examining his heart, he found that he delighted in her voice, in her lovely face, her wicked sense of humour and her wit. Thomas gave a little sigh. He could not marry, or he realised, he would happily marry Joan and therefore he should stop thinking about her. But being brutally honest, he realised that for a long time now, Joan was first in his thoughts, even before Thomas himself, he noted wryly. When he travelled, he unconsciously knew how long before he could see her again. If he saw a man selling trinkets, he'd buy some tiny thing for her, whether it be a length of ribbon, aglets for her laces, or the pretty silver nutmeg case.

And if he told this to his confessor, what would he say? Thomas knew full well he wouldn't accept Thomas's explanation that Joan was just the daughter of his oldest friends. He would tell him to guide his thoughts away from

Joan Larke and that he must not see her again. Like a child, he shied away from this solution, his heart sulkily saying no. His hands found his rosary and he began the calming ritual of counting the beads and the familiar prayers which always soothed his mind. But recognising that his words were without heart, he stopped, and turning fretfully in the crib, pressed his face into the pillow in both frustration and despair. As sleep kindly took him, he stepped forward into a sunlit garden and saw Joan and Pepper racing towards him. Her feet were bare and he laughed with delight to see her.

***

The day began well enough, Joan walking carefully down the stairs to breakfast, and Pepper streaking ahead in his eagerness to go outside. She opened the parlour door, and John got to his feet.

'Good morning, Joan.'

'Good morning, uncle.' Joan kept her face emotionless as she bobbed a slightly unsteady curtsey to him.

They both stood for a moment as if frozen in a painting. Then John moved towards her, and Joan fought the urge to flinch from him. She largely succeeded, with only the slightest twitch of her eyelid, but she knew that John had noticed it.

'May I help you to your place, niece?' John offered his arm and Joan was astonished; he'd never made the slightest chivalrous move towards her or to her certain knowledge, towards any woman.

But in the spirit of amending her behaviour, and with Thomas standing tall in her thoughts, she graciously nodded, thanked him and took his arm for the few paces to the table.

It was one of the strangest meals Joan had ever eaten – she made sure to respond politely to everything John said and smiled respectfully where needed, but her appetite was lost and she felt nervous and wary of him. *He means me no harm. He means me no harm.* The words circled in her head, but she still scented danger.

Finally, it came. 'Joan…' he paused to dab his mouth with the napkin.

'Yes, uncle.'

'You are no longer a child, and decisions must be made for your future. Your brothers are not in a position to take you into their household, for they have none, and likely never will, at least not for many years. If the Dean of Lincoln supports my nephews in the church, then it is incumbent on you to ensure that you are a source of pride to your family, not an embarrassment. And what greater source of pride can there be for a churchman than a sister who is equally devoted to serving God in humility.'

Joan heard John's voice rumble on and continued to nod and smile at him.

'…So when the glorious day comes when my brother is freed of his mortal pain, and God pleases, he is transported to heaven, then you will be free to leave here also, and I shall take you myself to the House at Dorchester and we will rejoice together as you take your vows.'

Joan felt sick, but clasping her hands loosely in her lap nodded as calmly as if he'd just told her that she had mistaken the time of day.

'Thank you, uncle, I am most grateful for your care and interest. We should not anticipate my father's death, but I am happy to rest secure in thoughts of my future.'

She spoke with great composure, but her mind was like a butterfly banging against the glass of a window. She could almost see freedom but had no idea how to achieve it. She was trapped. It was too late to even pretend to love Simon, for in the market just this week, she'd seen him arm-in-arm with Abigail Lyndon. Abigail had been all aglow, tossing her fair curls and prancing like a pony showing off on a sunny day as she'd told Joan of the betrothal. Joan had congratulated them with great sincerity and returned home with a light heart. *Ooh* no, Abigail was welcome to those wet lips and spotty face, but she was glad for her too, for she liked Abigail; it was a great match, and Abigail would make an excellent wife for Simon.

So, Simon was no longer a path she could take and there was no one else who'd marry her. Perhaps her brothers *could* set up a household, and she'd keep it for them. But the boys, obsessed with Thomas Wolsey and the church, would tell her not to be silly.

'May I be excused? I wish to take breakfast to my father.'

'Certainly, but then come back down here. We have more to discuss.'

Joan gracefully inclined her head – there was no escape.

After sitting with her father and prolonging the meal beyond all reason, she left him in the care of his manservant and went leaden-footed downstairs to John.

To her surprise, he welcomed her with a smile, and invited her to join him at the table, where he had laid out some books, and standing to help her to her stool, he said, 'If thou wilt receive profit, read with humility and faith.'

Joan looked up at him with slight puzzlement.

'Thus spake Thomas à Kempis – and this morning we will consider some of his works and meditations.'

As they settled to their work, Joan found that she would quite like to cry and that every now and then, the words swam before her eyes. After a tear trickled down her cheek, she brought her bruised foot down onto the stretcher of the stool, hard enough to distract her and stiffen her resolve. She would never again let her uncle see her cry. She was no longer a child and he must not see the effect he had on her. So she tried to profit from his words and to imagine that he was the tutor who taught her and her brothers so much and by this harmless deceit, the morning passed.

At last, Mistress Bray appeared to say that dinner was ready and Joan looked at John.

'Uncle, may I rise and make ready for the meal?'

He gave a little smile, 'Yes, indeed Joan, you may. I am pleased with our studies this morning, and trust that you too feel rewarded by our work.'

'Oh yes, uncle, I certainly do. Thank you for spending so much time with me.'

Gratified, John nodded his head. 'We will eat a light

and brief meal, then continue while there is light to see.'

Her face quite straight, Joan nodded, then turned to Alice still standing in the doorway, and rather astonished at the strange scene before her.

'Mistress Bray, has anyone seen to Pepper today?'

Alice nodded, 'Yes, the boy took him out and now he's asleep by the fire.'

They both turned to look at John, who made a murmuring noise, then added, '*Hmmm*. The dog.'

A dread feeling gripped Joan, and she hurriedly said, 'Thank you, Mistress Bray, we'll eat now.'

Alice curtseyed to them and left the room. She shook her head as she walked back to the kitchen, which was blessedly warm after the chill of the parlour. She shook her head. 'Poor girl. Poor, poor, girl.'

Dinner was indeed brief, and Joan had barely finished when John called the servants to clear the little table. Excusing herself in order to use the privy, Joan slipped into the kitchens, and found Pepper. Kneeling beside him, he hooked his head over her shoulder and made the little comfortable grunt he always made when Joan's arms were around him. The embrace seemed infinite but was over in a few moments. Bravely Joan stood up and called to Alice.

'I think that my uncle will wish to be rid of Pepper, and I can do nothing about it. When the gypsies stole him, he ran away home within a couple of days, so I can't send him somewhere. I have no power over this, and…'

Joan paused for a moment, swallowing her tears, then continued, '…so all I can ask is that he is well fed before…' her voice failed and she whispered '…

before…'

Alice nodded and gave the girl a quick hug. 'I will do all I can.' Then feeling in her pocket, she slipped the silver nutmeg case into Joan's hand. 'From Thomas. Keep it safe and out of *his* sight.'

Joan stared at the small silver ball in her hand and felt a sense of love clasping her heart; then, she closed her fingers over the case, slipped it into her pocket and flashed a fleeting smile to Alice, before giving Pepper one last kiss on his dear head.

Getting up to leave, the dog seemed to sense her turmoil and got up to go with her, whining as Alice grasped his collar and held him back. Joan stood resolutely and left the room, and Alice felt her heart fill with love at her bravery. Then, she took Pepper into her room and fed him as much meat as he would eat.

The afternoon passed a little more bearably for Joan, and she found herself able to speak to John with a degree of intelligence and grace, and when she felt her patience giving out, or fear overcoming her, she pressed her hand lightly against her pocket and felt the hard lump of the nutmeg.

At last, even John ran short of things to say and finding the light insufficient for their work, he concluded his lecture. Fortunately, it was too dim to see how Joan's eyes rolled with weariness, but she took deep breaths to wake herself up.

'Now there is one last thing I wish to discuss with you this afternoon.'

John stood up, laced his hands behind his back and

drew breath loudly through his nose.

Joan spoke, her voice flat and resigned, 'Pepper.'

John nodded but found himself intimidated by her expressionless face and voice. 'I know. He has to go. It is for the good of everyone.' And as she finished speaking, she held her hands loosely in front of her, and lowered her gaze, waiting.

'Good. Yes. Glad you understand.' And John found he couldn't get out of the room quickly enough, away from the blank face of his niece and the strange feeling that hung between them.

Later that evening, John and one of the men came into the kitchens and Alice silently handed the dog's rope to John, who passed it to the servant. Though neither Alice nor John would have put the feelings into words, their actions felt like a terrible betrayal.

Upstairs in her darkened chamber, Joan watched the dark figure of a servant lead Pepper away from the house. He was dragging his feet, and the white splashes on his fur showed up in the night. There was rain on the glass and it seemed as if there was rain on Joan's face as the tears fell from her eyes. After they vanished from view, Joan remained motionless at the window, her mind a weeping blankness.

Chapter 3

London

Landing in London, Thomas was delighted to see his groom waiting for him and holding the reigns of Star, Wolsey's favourite mule. The mule was supposedly an expression of a clergyman's Christ-like humility but Wolsey always felt they were the most handsome of animals and this one swung his head and looked pleased to see his master. The morning was fresh and the full tide covered the stench from the river. Although it wasn't his home town, Thomas Wolsey felt more at ease here than he ever had in Ipswich, Calais, or any of the other places he'd lived. He could hear the city around him, the cries and smells of the traders, the particular London clop of hooves – half ringing metal on cobbles, half thud through the mud and filth. He smiled, here he was free to make of himself what he could.

William followed his master ashore and spoke a few words to the groom before the stable boy handed William the reins to his pony, and in his wake the men staggered off the small ship, their faces showing varying shades of green or occasionally pink with the healthy sea winds. The groom helped his master into the saddle, the men fell into step behind them and the little procession made their way to Thomas's lodgings.

As they passed the buildings of London, Thomas's thoughts were busy with his duties; to pay his respects to the King's mother and finally to the King. But first, back to his lodgings, and he allowed his mind to wander to hot water and the clean cloths and scented soap with which he would wash. He'd shed his robes and don clean ones, robes which didn't smell of fish or tar and he gave a wry sniff. Then a gull cried and for a moment he was in Yarmouth again, seeing Joan's eyes brimming with tears then reluctantly laughing as he coaxed her to smile. Thomas closed his eyes for a moment and brought his thoughts back to the present. He opened them again and looked at the beautiful ears of Star and made himself aware of his mount, of the muscle moving beneath him, of the sweet smell of hay and horseflesh layering the more dubious smells around him. Once again, he apologised to God for his lack of piety and chided himself for his failure to concentrate and smiled, knowing that God would understand, possibly even find his frailty amusing, and he thanked God for His patience.

Finally at his lodging, Thomas tossed the reins to the groom and thanked him. Then he turned to Star and finding a little of the bread from the night before, he gave the mule the crust before motioning to William to follow him into the house.

Bowing, his manservant, James welcomed Thomas home and followed him to his chamber. Thomas relished the honey-scent of fresh rushes and herbs on the floor and knew exactly the face the man would be making at the smell from Thomas's robes. He turned and gave a gentle smile at the raised eyebrows and half-closed eyes which topped James's flaring nostrils.

'I'm sorry, James. I know. But fish and smoke have made many a fortune, and I for one have reason to be thankful for it. But still, I also find myself grateful to shed it, and know that when I next wear these clothes, you will have performed a small miracle on them.'

James graciously inclined his head. A man of few words, he was yet very clear in his opinions, and his eyebrows had whole vocabularies of their own. Thomas delighted in him, and also in his skills with Thomas's wardrobe.

'I fear James, that it is time to shave my tonsure again. When I have washed, would you kindly oblige me?'

'Of course, my Lord. In the meantime, I will remove these.' The woollen clothes were heavy, yet James managed to suggest that he was carrying them between a thumb and forefinger, and as far from his delicate nose as possible.

Thomas stripped and washed, enjoying the hot cloths against his skin. Then James re-entered, and Thomas sat down and held the shaving bowl under his chin as James lathered soap and shaved Wolsey's face and the crown of his head. Thomas hated this mark of his office, and as chaplain to Sir Richard Nanfan, had let his hair grow. But on the death of his dear friend and employer and when the possibility was first whispered of becoming a royal chaplain, it was quietly suggested to Thomas that he once again adopt the tonsure, for Lady Margaret, the King's mother, liked to see a devout household around her son.

Smelling once more of his usual, sweet spicy scent, Thomas remembered that his silk handkerchief had been left in Yarmouth, and asked James to bring one from the coffer.

'Another one lost, my Lord?' The words were so tightly uttered that Thomas wondered whether to point out that James wasn't the person paying for such wastage.

'I'm afraid so, James.'

'May I ask where, or if it can be retrieved?'

'James, you may not. It is beyond recall, but I think we will find we can bear the loss. Try not to mind too much, and comfort yourself with the thought that it has gone to a better place.'

James nodded, his face expressionless, and Thomas mentally shrugged, another point to James in their constant game where Thomas tried to crack a smile from the man, and James resisted.

Loud banging at the door downstairs interrupted their silent sparring and Thomas could hear urgent voices below.

'It seems the world intrudes once more James. Would you ask William to bring me the news? I will finish dressing myself, thank you.'

James nodded and gathering the washing items, hid them away in a cupboard, to be collected later by a far lowlier servant, and Thomas listened to his unhurried tread down the stairs, and the rumble of his voice as he asked William to attend their master.

The door opened without a polite tap and William

entered, a grin on his face showing that he was aware of his cheek in coming thus into his master's chamber, but he did at least pull off his cap and give a slight nod to Thomas.

'The Lady Beaufort has been asking for you because the King has been asking for you.' As he spoke, William picked up Thomas's long, soft travelling boots, folded them together and placed them on top of a chest, before turning to help his master finish lacing points through his hose.

Wolsey gave a slight sigh and a smile, 'How is the King?'

'*Mmm*, apparently not well. I mean worse than when we left.' William lifted the long gown, helped Thomas into it, then bent to ease the heels of Thomas's shoes over his feet as his master settled his black linen coif over his newly shaven head.

'Thank you, William. So let's away.'

William spun around, picked up the square black velvet cap and clapped it on Wolsey's head. The two men smiled at each other and left the chamber.

For a moment the room sat quietly, the boards settling with a slight creak, and the presence of Thomas and William lingering in the disturbed air. Then the door reopened, and Thomas stood for a moment, before walking to a locked box on a chest top, and drawing the key from the pouch at his belt, unlocked it. Opening a small prayer book, Thomas placed Joan's lock of hair between its pages. He held the book for a moment between his hands – his mind was blank, and he couldn't find God, or Joan, or any point to draw him back to sense. He remained there until a shout from the courtyard made him shake his head and draw a rueful sigh before taking the hair and placing it once more in his pouch.

As he left the room, his hand went automatically to the cross on his chest, but it was still against his skin after his wash, and the seeming absence gave Thomas a lurch, as he feared he'd lost it. Then realising where it was, he pulled the cross on its long chain from beneath his shirt, settled it back in place and pulled his black embroidered cuffs slightly into view beneath his jerkin and outer gown. The King's chaplain was ready to attend the King.

Outside, the brief spring sunshine had fled, and they hurried as they made their way to the river and stepping aboard the boat tucked themselves out of the wind. Thomas drew his fur-edged robe around himself and closed his eyes. He intended to contemplate his duties to the King: how to minister to a difficult man who was both weary of life and unwilling to die. But as his mind relaxed, he found himself back in Yarmouth, feeling Joan curled around him and he smiled as he remembered the grin he had finally won from her tearful face.

Thomas sighed, opened his eyes and watched as the small waves licked grey and rough just inches from him. After a while, he noticed William regarding him, a thoughtful look in his eyes and Thomas forced himself to resume a cheerful mask and talk about the weather to his servant who knew only too well that something serious occupied Wolsey's mind.

Reaching Richmond, Wolsey and his escort stepped ashore and made their way through the lower passages of the Privy Lodgings and across the bridge of the moat. Thomas admired the handsome galleries of the middle court but walked outside them. He never walked under them if he could help it as he still remembered when, only three years before, one garden section collapsed just as the King left it. As he headed towards the chapel staircase, Thomas smiled as servants raced or dawdled past. Not for the first time he wondered if they all had a purpose or if it were possible to be on the household payroll, yet never work and simply spend the day passing from one dark corner to the next; look important and people would believe that you are." *Well, why not?* he thought to himself, *I might have been doing that for years*.

Thomas and William paused outside the door to the King's Mother's pew, the small chamber from which she could pray in private and see the elevation of the host in the main chapel.

'William, you're dismissed for a couple of hours. Go and see how the court is feeling, would you please?' William nodded and disappeared.

Thomas tapped very gently on the door. 'What?' came the sharp reply from within.

'Thomas Wolsey, Your Grace.'

'In.'

He opened the door and immediately stooped into a deep bow, waiting until she bade him rise. He cast a quick glance at her and was shocked by the changes in her face. Always tight and gaunt, her cheeks were now impossibly sunken and her eyes gimlet-like in the yellow face. Irreverently, Thomas wondered if she ever removed that wimple headdress or if it held her together and she would collapse into herself if she removed it. Of course, he noted, her nun-like robes were of the finest silk velvet, and casting back the dying daylight with rich softness. You would never mistake her garb for those of a poverty-observing daughter of Christ.

'You've been away.' Not a question.

'Yes, your Grace. To bid farewell to my old friend and bring the relief of God's love to his family.'

'The King has needed you. You seem to amuse him.'

Thomas inclined his head, 'But Your Grace, he cannot have needed anything but the comfort of your love and reassurance.'

Margaret stared at him, trying to detect irony in her priest, but Thomas was a diplomat and she could find nothing but sincerity in his face.

'My Lord Dean, My Son, The King, has no further need of motherly comfort; so, I pray for him night and day.'

Even now, thought Thomas, *she speaks of 'My-Son-The-King' in case I might mistake who she means. After twenty-four years she still cannot quite believe it.* He smiled kindly at her, seeing in her face the lifetime of worry and misery and obsessive love for her son.

'Your Grace, God will hear your prayers and reward your love and piety.'

'Well, of course He will.' She snapped.

Thomas longed to smile. There really was no chink in her armour, no way of reaching her as one human to another. She was after all a creature of her time and she had reached her goal: her son was King and although they had lost their beloved Arthur, there remained Henry – robust and healthy, sweet-tempered and loving. The throne was safe.

Finally dismissed, Thomas left Margaret's chilly presence and returned to the Privy Lodging. The stairs were sorely in need of sweeping and the hem of Thomas's robe passed through more bat and mouse droppings than he wished to think about. Once on the King's floor, he strode through the corridors, and silent empty chambers. Thomas was struck again by the temporary feel of all the King's rooms. Since the death of the Queen, the tapestries had grown dusty; some even dropped from their hooks, the weave rotted through. No one could be bothered to notice if the King himself didn't care.

Thomas grew more aware of the cold and the lack of servants. *For pity's sake*, he thought. *The King of England stuffed away in a room to die?* Clearly, the court was shifting to the bright light of the future King like a swarm of soulless moths.

Arriving at the King's outer chamber, Thomas was astonished to find the door untended. He retraced his steps a short distance and entered the pages' room. The air was warm and stuffy with the scent of wine and overheated young men and he could hear their snores as he opened the door. Standing in the doorway, he watched as the cold air disturbed the sleeping pages and they woke like a litter of puppies; slightly irritable ones at that, as he was quickly bid to 'B'God shut the door, won't you?'

One of the lads – more awake than the others – got to

his feet and snatching his cap from his head tried to scramble his wits together. Thomas smiled at them; he knew the value of sleep to a youngster and the equal impossibility of getting enough.

'My boys,' he said gently, 'where are the King's servants? Who is attending him?'

The more awake lad looked appalled. 'Oh my Lord, I don't know. I'm sorry…' He looked as if he could do with a shave and a good scrub, and Thomas reflected that this was hardly what his parents would have hoped for when they sent their precious son to join the royal household.

'Very well. I am the Dean of Lincoln. I am the King's chaplain and I am going to attend him. I wish you come with me and stand ready should I require anything. Do you understand? Indeed, can you walk straight? There seem to be a lot of empty wine flagons.'

Thomas tempered his words with a gentle tone as the other pages, some barely more than little boys, pulled themselves up and started to tidy each other.

'Are you *all* on duty to the King?' Some of them shook their heads. 'In that case, I suggest that you be about your lawful tasks. And perhaps have someone on watch next time.'

They nodded their heads like a row of puppets then slid past him with hushed Sirs and thank-yous and other grunts as they melted into the shadows of the palace.

The first boy remained, straightening himself and announcing that he was George. Thomas smiled at him. 'Very good, George. A pleasure to meet you.'

He opened the first door and entered, George behind

him. Even two rooms away from the chamber, the air was thick with a shocking smell. Wolsey continued through the dark outer chambers with George so close that when he paused, the lad bumped into him. Wolsey turned and gave George a wide-eyed grin and George stepped back a pace with a whispered 'sorry'.

At the door, Thomas knocked. After a moment, there was a grunt in reply and he opened the door. Thomas advanced slowly, George dogging his heels once more until Wolsey stopped and motioned him to wait.

'Your Grace?'

There was a sigh from the shadowed room and a weary 'Yes?'

'Your Grace,' taking his velvet cap from his head, 'it is Thomas Wolsey, returned from Yarmouth. I deeply regret that you wished for my attendance and I was not here.'

'Ha. The Dean of Lincoln. Kind of you to call upon me.' There was not a trace of humour in the dry, cracked-leaf of a voice and Wolsey formed his lips into the calmest of smiles.

'Your Grace, may I ask the boy to light a candle for you? And perhaps tend the fire? There is a degree of chill in here which may be uncomfortable for you.'

Thomas interpreted the grunt as yes and waved a reluctant George forward. George's young eyes navigated him easily around the dim room and soon the candles were lit and the fire a little more cheerful.

Thomas went towards the King's great carved bed. He was careful not to stand at the foot of the bed, *mustn't loom too menacingly,* he thought with a trace of humour. So, he went to the side and placing one leg backwards, dipped in a bow to his sovereign. For quite some moments, he wondered if the King was asleep, but the King too had a penchant for making people wait, so Thomas contented himself with admiring the silk velvet of his square cap and appreciating the sensuous feel of it between his fingers.

After some long moments, the King coughed; an appalling thick hacking cough, through which Thomas could discern the word 'Wolsey'. Then the King waved at the stool beside the bed and George brought it forward for Wolsey before gliding back into the shadows.

Wolsey sat. 'Your Grace. I am glad to see you again. I do apologise for my absence…'

The King interrupted him, 'Yes, Ipswich, wasn't it? Red herrings? Can smell them on you.'

No, you can't, thought Wolsey, *but thank you for reminding me of my lowly position.* But at least it wasn't a jibe against his butcher ancestry; a bit of variety never went amiss.

'It was indeed, Sire. My oldest friend and sometime patron is close to death. I may not see him again, so I am immensely grateful to you for granting me leave to visit him. His sons are under my patronage, so I will be able to give them news of their father and sister.'

The King gave another grunt but it turned into a terrible cough as he struggled to draw breath and slid further down the bed. Thomas gestured to George who sped to the other side of the bed. 'George, help me to ease the King's discomfort.'

Each of them slipped a hand under the King's arms and carefully heaved him into a more upright position, then the King coughed and Thomas seized a bowl from the small table. It was full of green matter from the King's diseased lungs and Thomas felt his stomach heave.

'George,' he said softly, 'deal with this and fetch a fresh bowl.' The boy left the room with great speed.

He put his hand on the King's back and supported him through his coughing fit. With a degree of resignation, he found his fresh handkerchief and gave it to the King who spat and hacked into it before handing it back to Thomas.

'Move your hand,' he snapped irritably, and Thomas gratefully did so. The King was burning hot to touch and his bones were so close to the skin that it seemed impossible he was still alive.

Henry slumped exhausted against the bolster, wetness round his mouth and in his wispy beard. Thomas felt his heart fill with compassion and pity for the man before him. He was so lonely, so alone. The King's mother should be here, and he thought of her in her chamber praying for the immortal soul of her only son.

Henry's eyes watched him and Thomas tried to think of a topic of conversation. It seemed that Henry did not want him for a specific duty, just his presence. Or perhaps it was simply to show that he still had a degree of control over his household.

'Your Grace, I came straight to your presence and have heard none of the news from court. How is the Prince Henry?'

'His Highness, my son, is well.' Henry's reply was

terse and Thomas wondered if he had not in fact seen his son in recent days.

'I am glad to hear that. We are indeed a fortunate country to have such a dynasty as the Tudors to secure our future.' He smiled at the King and bowed as if in thanks.

'Your Grace,' he continued, 'I often feel that any country, in fact, any father would be blessed to have Prince Henry as a son.'

Henry glowered at Thomas. 'You should indeed be grateful, but do not presume to think that a man of your Butcher's Cur ancestry could ever sire a son like Henry.'

Ah, thought Thomas, *it had to come.* 'Indeed not, your Grace and I meant no presumption. But you know how the Prince is adored throughout the country; the most common of us hold him dear in our hearts.'

At that moment, the Blessed George as Thomas now gratefully thought of him, reappeared. In his hands were a clean bowl and several napkins.

'Thank you, George.' Then turning to the King, 'Your Grace, would you like your bed made fresh?'

The King nodded and George looked at Wolsey, 'Shall I fetch assistance, Master?'

'Yes please, George, and take this with you if you would.' He lightly dropped the handkerchief into the boy's hand. Despite its contents, the boy looked delighted. 'Do you wish to have this back, sir?'

Thomas smiled at the boy, 'No George, you may do with it as you will.' He knew that it would be laundered and pressed and sold on. The page boys were from good families yet always short of pocket money. And the bonus to Thomas was the exasperation on the face of James later tonight. He might even manage to buy it back if Thomas told him where it was.

Moments later, the summoned men arrived and the King was lifted tenderly into a chair and wrapped about with furs. Food materialised and Thomas lowered himself once more to the stool and helped the King to his porridge. The King only took a few mouthfuls before sinking back in his chair. Thomas brought him some wine and reached into his pouch for his nutmeg before recalling where he'd left it. He closed his eyes for the briefest moment and thought for a moment about Joan. He smiled and felt renewed for dealing with his sick and irritable King.

He watched the men strip the sheets and shake and turn the mattresses. At his signal, they forewent the usual rituals of testing for weapons – an assassin would hardly have crept in and concealed dangerous points when he and the King were present. Moments later, the bed was smooth and fresh and Henry clearly ready to return to it.

Wolsey turned away as the King was gently undressed and washed. Thomas listened to the murmur of care and once again drifted away to another room where he washed Joan's cuts and touched them with salve.

Someone moved beside him and he turned to see George there, 'My Lord, the King is ready.'

'Thank you, George. Would you wait outside for me?' The boy touched his cap and left the room.

Returning to the King, Wolsey bowed again. 'Your Grace?'

'I wish to hear Mass. I wish to be able to tell my Lady

Mother that she is not the only person to have care of my soul.' Thomas could not miss the sardonic note in the King's voice.

A little later, Thomas blessed the King and in turn, knelt for the King's blessing. He remained with the King for a little longer until he heard his master's breaths slow and deepen and then quietly bowed from the chamber. The King might seem to be asleep, but he was almost certainly watching his uppity butcher's boy to be sure that he showed him all respect.

Outside, George was waiting, albeit half-asleep against the wall. Thomas calculated – the poor boy must have been awake for several hours now. But growing children, as well as drinking heavily if opportunity permitted, needed more sleep than hours were in the day.

'George. Thank you for your service today. A word of advice if you will allow…?'

George nodded and spoke with feeling, 'I know, Master. I have seldom felt so unwell. I will *never* drink again.'

Thomas allowed himself half a smile. 'My dear boy. I wouldn't go so far as to say never. But try not to drink when on duty. And drink the best you can afford. You'll find you have bought yourself a clearer head and a better career.' He flipped him a coin and George's eyes widened in delighted surprise.

'Oh. My Lord Dean, thank you.' He gave a deep bow and followed Thomas back through the Palace and saw him safely into the care of his escort and looked likely to join his benefactor on the barge until Wolsey's men good-naturedly blocked his path.

The evening was cold, but, reflected Thomas, it was still only February and how fortunate he was to be fit and have a warm robe. Such a long day.

Dozing until they reached home, Wolsey was slightly unsteady as he stepped onto the landing stage. There was no one to meet him and he could hear William shouting.

'William! It matters not. A walk will wake us up and shake the stiffness from us.'

Still muttering, William arranged the men around their master and they walked through the early evening to his house in Fleet Street. Thomas thought longingly of his large and comfortable bed and a good supper beside the fire. He smiled. It wouldn't be the evening he wished for – it never was and never would be for a man such as he; a man with ambition and skill and the capacity to work when other men dropped. Just those thoughts perked him up and he called to the men to pick up the pace, which they did with hardly any grumbling.

Soon enough, they reached the house and Thomas was in his office. Warmed wine and a cold supper stood ready at the pale oaken buffet. He exchanged his outdoor robes and velvet cap for a thick gown and red woollen cap and his leather-soled shoes for velvet-and-felt slippers.

The candles on his desk were lit and the shutters were closed. Thomas sat for a moment and blessed his repast and thanked God for his bodily comfort: the simple but beautiful room and his recent promotion to Dean of Lincoln. And with the greatest pleasure, he turned to the piles of paperwork which awaited his attention.

Chapter 4

Yarmouth and London, Late March 1509

My dear and true friend, Thomas

I send you greetings from Yarmouth, and tidings of my father, who is more ill than when last you saw him. Doctor McCreadie says that there is now nothing to be done. He continues with the foxglove tincture, but the help it affords grows less and less after each attack. I fear you may not see my father again in this life.

I also must tell you that I too am unlikely to see you again, and for this, I am also very sorry. My good Uncle John has explained to me that once my father is with God, the safest and most proper place for me will be in the holy house at Dorchester and he is making arrangements for me to travel there as soon as my father is released from his pain and suffering.

My uncle is staying with us until that time comes and is helping me to run the household, and I am grateful for his guidance. My uncle thought it best that Pepper be sent to another place, and

> *my uncle assures me that Pepper is happy in his new home. I do not know where his home is.*
>
> *My dear Thomas, as I may not have the chance to speak to you again, I would like to thank you for all the kindness you have graciously shown to me and assure you that I will strive to be a dutiful sister in God to you and a credit to you and my brothers and uncle.*
>
> *Joan Larke*

Thomas stood with Joan's letter in his hand. It was on the top of the piles of correspondence which had arrived whilst he'd been at Richmond. It had lain there all day, innocent and quiet. Just an arrangement of ink on parchment until he opened it and it was as shocking as biting into a rotten apple. *Do her no harm*, he'd said to John. Well, he hadn't really, but of course he'd failed to appreciate the feelings and fears of his niece. Actually, he had doubtless fully appreciated them and viewed them as a weakness of her soul which had to be dealt with for her own good.

Joan had nothing to do with him. She was Peter's daughter. Only he, Thomas, would think that she should be otherwise treated. Perhaps Peter was too weak to argue. He would be content to be assured of her safety. But she'd be so unhappy. She'd never flourish. If only Ipswich were closer. If only there was still a Queen or even a real rather than a dowager Princess of Wales, she could be found a place at court. But this court-in-waiting for the King to die was no place to bring her. She'd be ripped apart by courtiers hungry for their own betterment, all experienced and merciless. No forgiveness for a child from a small town.

He lay the letter aside and settled to his evening's work. Over the last few weeks, Thomas had endeavoured to put Joan out of his mind. He had been pleased to realise that his thoughts no longer swerved towards her with the least excuse. In his prayers, he would offer up Peter Larke and his family. Not naming Joan even in the privacy of his mind. His dreams were another matter and the cause of some shame, but he was developing a strength and focus of mind and on his thumb, quite a callus where he'd grip his cross and force his thoughts away from Joan. Yet here was a reminder of her.

He was sorry to hear of the demise of Pepper. The dog had been a fine fellow; Joan's shadow since his puppyhood. He'd comforted and guarded her for all those years since Thomas fished him out of a sack being dunked by a brutish man just outside Yarmouth. The other puppies were dead, their pathetic ratty little bodies still warm. Fury had welled up in him and he rounded on the man who clearly couldn't care less. The man shrugged, 'Well if y'cares that much, 'ave this one.' And with the toe of his boot, he shunted the small creature towards Thomas before wandering off. Thomas bent over and peered at the tiny creature for several moments before seeing the least movement in the puppy's chest. He picked up the dog who sneezed feebly before showing every sign of relinquishing life. Thomas cupped the pup in the sleeve of his robe and rubbed the material vigorously over the baby until it breathed more regularly.

Thomas recalled that puppies cannot drink cow's milk – he and his brother had learned that when the family's bitch died leaving her litter. On his way to Yarmouth to visit Peter, he remounted his horse and tucked the little dog inside his robe above his belt. At least he'd be warm there for the next hour or so. Arriving at the Larke house, thirteen-year-old Joan heard the horse and popped up at a window before vanishing and reappearing at the door.

'Thomas!' She bellowed, belting down the garden towards him. Laughing, he dismounted and fending her off, fished out the-soon-to-be Pepper. The puppy was now dry and waking from a nice warm sleep. He yawned, showing his needle-sharp teeth and cried for food. Joan's wide eyes almost burst open with adoring excitement.

'*Ooh*,' she breathed and held out her hands, 'for me?'

'Well, if your father is content…' Joan didn't wait for Thomas to finish speaking but walked back to the house, her whole body bent over the puppy as if she carried eggs in her hands.

Thomas followed her and saw Peter's amusement as he looked at the scrappy little dog. 'Yes, you can. But he's very little and he might not live. You must be prepared for that.'

'Oh no. He *will* live. I will *make* him.'

The two men caught each other's eye and laughed. And before she disappeared, Thomas just managed to call out, 'Only goats' milk Joan, not cows'.'

And she had made Pepper live and he grew into a handsome and loyal dog. But now Thomas knew that Pepper no longer walked this earth and he was sorry for it.

Many people believed that animals had no souls. Indeed, the Church taught as much, but Thomas could not believe such a thing. To look into the loving eyes of a dog was to be assured of their spirit and be certain that God knew and cherished all dumb creatures.

He shut his eyes for a moment and prayed to God for guidance. God was, to say the least, infrequent with his communications and Thomas was yet again disappointed, but he grew calm. He sat for a long time, once again feeling life returning to Pepper six years ago. And he found he was angry with John Larke. The man was doubtless devout and holy, but he was mistaken. He was wilful and he was tired of his family responsibilities. It would indeed be a tidy solution once his brother had died: Joan in a nunnery and his sons neatly in Wolsey's household. But Thomas couldn't shake the feeling that to force a vocation on Joan was cruel. She ought to have married the boy who kissed her. He would have been kind to her and given her babies. By now, she would have been established and safe.

He couldn't settle, it was like having a toothache. The papers were neglected as he paced the floor. His very legs twitched with the impotence which gnawed at him. Eventually, he flung open the door and shouted. 'William!'

Something in Wolsey's tone alerted William to his master's urgency and he hurried to the brightly lit chamber. 'Sir?'

'We must return to Yarmouth. As quickly as possible. I will seek leave from court and we will go tomorrow if the tides are with us. Arrange that if you would, please.'

'Yes, my Lord.'

Thomas was able to notice and be impressed by the lack of argument from William before he nodded briskly and disappeared. Moments later, he heard doors slamming and saw a shadowy figure leave the house. Reassured there was nothing more to be done for now, Thomas poured some wine and took the whole glass in a couple of gulps. Good. Decision made. Thomas expertly put aside the lack of any actual decision and sat down to his papers and soon managed to make a credible attempt at solving disagreements in the Low Countries and Lincoln.

To stave off his dreams, Thomas continued to work, pausing only to use his close stool after many hours of unconsciously wriggling in his chair. He shook his head at himself and smiled as he eased his bladder. Then he hurried back to his desk and buried his thoughts once more in requests for grants and pleas for patronage. When morning came, it woke Thomas who groaned as he moved his cricked neck. *Really, Thomas, you grow too old to sleep in your chair.*

He opened his chamber door and raising his voice called for breakfast and heard the grumbling as the servants scrambled together the meal from where it was laid in the dining chamber. *Never mind,* he thought, *I am generally a thoughtful master. Won't hurt them for once.*

He closed the door and quickly thumbed through the documents, placing the most pressing in a small, secure case to take with him. There would be many hours onboard the ship. And doubtless, the King's secretary or his office would have more for him when he called at Richmond.

William reappeared as he started breakfast. 'The ship will leave at noon, my Lord.' Thomas nodded.

'Excellent. Summon James to pack for me whilst I eat, then accompany me to Sheen. Tch. I mean Richmond. I will seek leave from the King and with luck, we can be on our way immediately.'

'I know what immediately really means at court, my Lord. But the ship won't wait.'

Thomas nodded impatiently, 'I know William, I know. So, let us speed on our way.'

Within an hour the boat belonging to the Dean of Lincoln was at the water gate of Richmond Palace, and Thomas was taking the familiar route to the office of the Master of the Household. The conversation was brief and William was left assembling another case of paperwork as Thomas headed towards the King's apartments.

Young George was there chatting to the guards on the chamber door and Thomas was pleased to see the boy looking clean and sober. George was thrilled to see him and bowed long and low at the kind dispenser of coins and silk kerchiefs.

'Thank you, George. Please don't sweep the floor with your hair.' The boy looked up with a blush and a grin.

'Have you kept things in order of late? I haven't seen you for a while.'

'No sir, I had leave to return home to Pakenham. But I'm back now. And I'm very excited about the future and yes indeed, things are in order.'

The boy continued chatting excitedly to Thomas who smiled, then gently held up one finger.

'I'm sorry, George. I am in a fearful hurry. You know how it is.'

George nodded, a serious and busy man-about-town appreciating the bustle of an equal. He bowed again with an air of dispensing an honour on Thomas.

'Please, my Lord, accept my apologies.'

Then a boy again, he dug into his pouch, 'Oh, this is for you, my Lord.'

He looked ruefully at the crumpled silk handkerchief in his hand. 'Oh dear, it was ironed as well as washed, but I have carried it for weeks hoping to see you.'

Thomas felt great affection. 'George, my boy. How thoughtful of you. I did give it to you, and you are not required to return it.'

George blushed slightly. 'My mother said it was an expensive item, and I *should* return it. Please allow me to.'

Thomas inclined his head, 'Then George, I will buy it from you and I think my gentleman will judge a crown well spent.'

'Phew!' Another savage blush followed George's appreciative whistle. 'I mean, thank you, my Lord, I too think that a fair bargain. I mean for me.'

Thomas made the transaction quickly to save the boy any more anguish and parted from him, closing the door to the outer chamber quickly to stop George from attaching himself to Thomas's heels.

Thomas gave a little chuckle. It never hurt to win the heart of someone at court. That coin could be a long-term investment. Or at the very least it was a speedy way to bring happiness to a young boy. And of course, it would be amusing to return it to James.

The King's chambers were much improved of late; Thomas had ordered fires to be maintained in all the royal chambers and they were beginning to banish the damp from the plasterwork of the rebuild. The fire in ninety-seven had been bad in parts, and in others, merely cosmetic. The King had quickly rebuilt, but the decoration was still of recent completion and a steady warmth was needed to ensure thorough drying. The tapestries had been cleaned and rehung and no longer tainted the air with rotting wool.

Moving through the outer chambers, Thomas nodded at the guards and noted that the air was fresh and touched with a pleasant scent. Within the King's chamber, the smell of terminal illness was still apparent but it could not be otherwise. But the tang of blood was new and boded ill for Henry. It had been several weeks now since the King had told his attendants to cease knocking at his door, in case he was asleep. So Thomas stepped silently into the room. He paused, listening for the sound of breathing. There was nothing and for a moment Thomas felt his own heart speed up with a surge of alarm.

Then the King drew a long and rattling breath and whispered, 'Thomas? I know it's you. You sound different to the men. Their breaths sound anxious and my mother smells of incense. Hmmp.'

The little grump was one of faint amusement from a man who could no longer laugh without coughing.

'Come here. I can't see you in this dammed dim light. No, don't move the curtains. Too bright. Come here.'

Thomas approached the great bed and bowed. He'd left on his travelling gown so that the King would have a slight warning and it worked. Henry strummed his spidery fingers on the sheet and grunted once more.

'Off again, are you? Fish mongering or butchery?'

Thomas smiled, 'Fish, this time, your Grace. But tides permitting, I plan to be back in three days.'

'Of course, My Lord Dean of Lincoln. Take all the time you need. I certainly have no requirement for you. You forget that I have many chaplains and you are not in the least needed here.'

Thomas silently sucked his teeth whilst keeping what he hoped was a beatific smile on his face.

'Your Grace is forbearing and kind.'

'Hmm. Go quickly then and I'll endeavour not to die without your supervision.'

'Thank you, your Grace. Thank you.'

The King waved him away and Thomas softly blessed the King before bowing out of the room and silently closing the door. He gave a deep sigh. It grew more and more difficult to cheer the King; he knew he was dying but would not admit it. In fact, this was the closest he had drawn to it. Thomas was sorry he had to leave – it might have been the time to speak of death and resurrection and offer comfort. But he would continue to pray for the King and raise the subject on his return.

When he reached the river, William and the escort were waiting in his boat and they raced along the Thames, reaching the ship at Billingsgate with only minutes to spare. The master looked relieved. If he missed the tide whilst waiting for Thomas then they wouldn't sail for hours and he might lose the work and the fees, and if he left without Thomas, William would never hire him again. It was valuable work, but nerve-wracking and he always wondered if it was worth it. Then he would be paid and Wolsey would tip him handsomely and all would be well until next time.

Thomas stepped aboard and after sharing a few words and a laugh with the master, remained on deck watching London slip past. The Tower – Thomas felt slightly sick to think of the souls in there. William de la Pole had been there since 1502. Cousin of the late Queen he may be, but nonetheless, a potential rallying point and a prize for disaffected Yorkists who had plotted against Henry. It was debatable whether de la Pole had been involved in the plot but Henry took no chances and de la Pole looked likely to spend the rest of his life in the Tower. Thomas had met Elizabeth of York and marvelled at the peace and composure in her face. Of course, that could be attributable to her pregnancies – she'd always carried and birthed easily – but she had seemed to find happiness in marriage to the triumphant Tudor. Perhaps when her Plantagenet family had been taken from the world, it was almost a relief to be free of the constant tussle for power. But then a final pregnancy had brought her death and compounded the tragedy of the loss of Prince Arthur the year before.

Thomas thanked God that he was not a husband or father – the constant worry for their welfare must be intolerable. He gave a little smile, and weary after his wakeful night, went below to his tiny cabin thinking to sleep. But William was laying out papers and eagerly told his master which pile was which. Thomas looked at one document and was immediately seized by the work. William excused himself and Thomas barely grunted as the man left. William on the other hand was delighted to see the Dean of Lincoln deep in paperwork; with luck, Wolsey would sleep well and they might have a peaceful night.

It took almost twenty-four hours to reach Yarmouth and the ship's crew were pleased; the weather and winds had been favourable and those not on duty looked forward to a day and more importantly a night ashore. Once they were safely moored in the mouth of the Yare, William gathered his men and surrounding Wolsey, they headed into the town and towards John Larke's house. Wolsey looked at the splendid church of St Nicholas. He found his thoughts wandering to the many chapels in there and how peaceful they were. His spirit almost failed as he considered Joan and how she was no responsibility of his. But before he could seek refuge, they reached the gate of the house. The tread of the feet of his escort had surely alerted the household to his arrival, but for the first time, the door did not fly open to reveal Joan standing there, delight on her face at his arrival.

William and Thomas walked towards the door, Thomas noting that the herb beds seemed untended. Even in winter, they were always tidy and ready for the awakening that would come with spring, but now dead leaves lay mouldy on the soil. He caught his lip between his teeth and with a slight frown, caught William's eye.

Before they reached the house, Meg appeared, peeping out with huge eyes. 'Oo!' she said and vanished. Thomas pushed open the door and stepped inside. The house smelt stale and was cold and dark.

He halloed and heard a door open above. The stairs creaked and Joan came down towards him.

Thomas felt his world dislocate. His dear Joan had lost all trace of childhood. The girlish round cheeks were thin, and sour new creases marred the skin around her mouth. She stopped on the last step; her hands folded in front of her and nodded to Thomas. 'My Lord'.

Between her palms, Thomas saw that Joan was clasping a rosary which she wore looped through her belt.

'I do not think that we were expecting you?' Thomas ached at her tone; she spoke as if to a stranger.

'No Mistress Larke. I have come in response to your letter. I trust your father yet lives?' Thomas looked at her cautiously and spoke with care. She seemed like a cracked glass which would shatter irredeemably if carelessly handled.

Joan thought for a moment as if his words were being translated from a far-away place. 'Yes. My father still breathes. Sometimes he recognises me. But I believe God will not allow his suffering to continue for very many days.' She stood motionless and looked at something far beyond Thomas.

Thomas felt at something of a loss – what on earth had happened to her – when John Larke opened the parlour door and stepped out. Thomas turned to him. It was apparent that John had come from an unlit and unheated chamber, for in the dim passage, his lips and nose seemed touched with blue.

'My Lord Dean. You honour my brother's house with your presence. Is the King recovered that you were able to travel to us?'

Thomas felt that John was very slightly annoyed to see him there, so with his warmest smile, he held out his hands to John who reluctantly placed them in Thomas's. John's hands were like cold damp fish but Thomas retained them firmly in his own warm grasp as he spoke.

'No, I am deeply grieved to say that the King's illness continues. But he graciously granted me leave to travel here in order to minister to Peter." With a little squeeze, he let go of John's hands, having re-established his seniority. Admitting to himself how much he had come to dislike John and his type of zeal, he made his smile even more warm and turned to Joan.

'Joan, may I send William and my men to the kitchens?' Her eyes flickered towards John who hastily answered in her stead.

'Of course, My Lord. William, you may tell Mistress Bray to send out for food.' He turned to Thomas. 'We keep a poor house these days. Peter wishes to leave his earthly wealth to the church, not waste it on the wages of servants. And of course…' He seemed to warm to his theme, '…it's not only their wages but the bills for fuel and food were ruinous. We run a tight ship now and I flatter myself that Peter is comforted by the reductions.' He ended with a long, self-satisfied sniff and outside a gull gave a screaming laugh. With difficulty, Thomas managed not to raise an eyebrow.

'William. You have sufficient in your purse I think?' William nodded. 'Very well. I can rely on you to arrange suitable supplies to make us comfortable.' William stepped backwards and rolled his eyes at John's back before heading towards the kitchens.

'Joan, would you please take me to your father?' Without a word, she turned and started up the stairs. John made to follow, but Thomas stopped him. 'Thank you, John. I would not tire my friend with too many people.' He spoke gently but firmly and John bowed his head for a moment in acquiescence.

As Thomas followed Joan, he heard John return to the parlour, but he did not hear the click of the door being fastened. He was terribly shocked; Joan was so thin and her spirit quite extinguished. John may not have physically harmed her, but she was greatly diminished and Thomas was furious.

Entering into Peter's room, he was comforted to see a small fire. *Another death-bed,* he thought, advancing slowly. Peter's eyes opened and his face cracked into an enormous smile. 'Thomas! By all that's marvellous! My dear boy.'

The effort of speaking drained him and he closed his eyes and gasped for breath, still trying to utter words, 'Thomas, so pleased. Are you real?'

Thomas laughed, 'Yes, and all too solid. Glad to see you, Peter. Just you hang on until spring and you'll enjoy another year!'

Peter's eyes looked towards Joan who stood silently

with her head bowed and he glanced meaningfully at Thomas.

'Joan my dear. Would you leave us for a few minutes?' She turned and left the room like a shadow passing across the floor.

'Peter. What on earth has been going on here?'

The sick man shrugged. 'What can I do?' he whispered. 'I am surprised to see each new day. I can do nothing for Joan except trust John to keep her safe.' He gave a barely audible laugh, 'There was a time when I hoped you and she might make a match. Jane would have liked that, and so would I. You would be a good merchant.' He half-shrugged and closed his eyes. After a moment Thomas realised that Peter was asleep. Despite creaking floorboards and shoes, he went as softly as possible across the wooden floor and left Peter's chamber.

Presuming that Joan was still in the same chamber, he tapped gently on the door. Her voice returned a flat, toneless 'Yes.'

And he opened the door. Joan sat at the window, gathering the last of the daylight to read the pages of the book in her hands. The room was stale and cold. It seemed like another place from when he'd turned at the door just over a month ago to see Joan's grin and hear Pepper's tail banging away.

He drew a deep breath and joined Joan in the window seat. She regarded him with dead eyes and he gestured towards the book in her hand.

'I gather you and John have been studying.'

A nod and a flat reply, 'Such devotional works can

bring you closer to an understanding with God.'

'What are your thoughts on this?' Thomas picked up the work and immediately felt the deadly boredom of the words. 'Don't worry. I can imagine. Perhaps a little dry for you?' The slightest of shrugs.

Suddenly Joan spoke. 'My uncle says I think too hard about things. A woman cannot think and understand. She needs only to know that God's love is all around.' She cast her eyes all around and looked faintly sick. 'I have given up thinking, for I do not understand why God has brought me to this. It certainly passeth all *my* understanding.' Then she shut her mouth again and it was as if she had bolted her lips.

Oh ho, thought Thomas, *you're still in there then.* 'Has your hair grown a little?'

Joan drew her gaze back from the window and looked at Thomas and she raised her hands to her head. Without unpinning it, she pulled the wimple-like bonnet from her head and Thomas struggled to be silent as he looked at her shorn scalp. Then he forced himself to give a little chuckle and pulled off his own hat to reveal his tonsure. 'See, it's all the fashion now.'

Thomas had not thought it possible but her lips grew even tighter. 'It is suitable for my new life and it pleases my uncle to be able to free me from the sin of vanity. I am happy to be able to please him.'

Thomas was at the end of what to say to Joan. His eyes fell on her hand resting on top of the book on her lap. Her nails were bitten and bloody, the skin torn and they looked so sore that he felt his stomach clench. What was really terrible was the memory of those hands when Joan was a child. She'd been a committed nail-biter and Thomas, Peter and Mistress Alice had bribed, chastised and pleaded with her. Nothing worked until one day she simply stopped. They'd all been so proud of her, yet now here, they were once again tender and ripped. Thomas lost his composure.

He leaned forward and took her hands in his. 'Joan. Your poor hands. This is no good.'

She gave that tiny shrug again as if to say *It doesn't matter. Nothing matters.* Thomas lifted her fingers to his lips and to his astonishment, watched himself kissing them. He was close to tears as he looked up at Joan, shorn and damaged. God's truth, she was only nineteen, she shouldn't look like that, so without hope or joy. This wasn't the love of God in her face, it was deathly despair.

'Joan' he began scarcely knowing what he was saying. 'I am Thomas Wolsey, the Dean of Lincoln. I am a priest. I cannot formally marry you. But we could contract to each other and I would love and protect you for the remainder of our lives.'

His throat was dry and he stopped and tried to swallow. God help him, what *had* he just said? But he was also filled with elation. God had led him to this. He would rescue her and she would be as his wife. Many priests had concubines and they lived discreetly, and if they were careful, they could avoid offending anyone. His mind raced ahead, as if he were playing a chess game. Joan could be his housekeeper. People might suspect but they'd never know. And in the eyes of God, it would be a proper, honourable arrangement. It would be fine. They would be happy and she would be saved from a life which would stifle and ultimately kill her.

Joan snatched her hands from his.

'What?' she demanded, 'Thomas as you have ever been my friend, you must not toy with me.'

'If you would marry me. If you would consent to let me care for you, I will arrange this. I will speak to your father right now and you will never again be subject to John's authority.'

Still trying to clear his dry throat he paused and realised that he sounded like a foolish boy. 'Joan, marry me. Come with me now and speak to Peter.'

Joan looked sceptical but even that was better than the broken oppressed girl who met him earlier.

'Have you a better bonnet to wear? Yours rather reminded me of Lady Margaret, the King's Mother.' He tried a tentative smile and to his great relief, Joan smiled back. Of course, it was barely a smile, but it was a relaxation of her stern face.

Joan got up from the window seat and felt suddenly faint. This was certainly a dream and as with all her dreams, she would soon wake up to another day of grinding criticism and subjugation from her uncle in a house which smelled of death and misery.

The bonnet fell from her lap. It might be a dream but it would still be satisfying; she lifted her foot and stepped on the carefully starched and old fashioned thing. She ground it with her heel and grinned at Thomas. Gracious of him to come and lighten her sleeping thoughts. Thomas stood, stooped and picked up the hated bonnet. He went to her close stool, lifted the lid and dropped it inside. Joan clapped her hands and gave a croaky laugh.

'*Thomas*. Is this real? Shall I marry you? Shall I be safe?' She gave a funny little grunt, half laugh, half disdain. 'My love. I wish this *were* real, for God knows, I do love you.' And she sank down on to the floor and rested her head on her knees waiting to wake.

He went towards her, raised her up and before she could pull away, wrapped his arms around her. She fitted so nicely against him *as if she were made for me*, he thought. He felt her sigh and lean into him, her head sideways on his shoulder, her bristly hair against his jaw. Thomas wondered who had cropped her hair. He could easily imagine John doing it. If they were ever able to speak again, he would warn the man of the sin of power. And being Thomas, he raised his own eyebrow in amusement at himself and considered the plank in his own eye when assessing the mote in John's.

He dipped his head to Joan. 'May I kiss you?' he whispered.

But it failed to be the loving moment he had hoped, for she looked up at him, and said 'We had raw onions at dinner. Surely you can tell?'

Joan felt Thomas heave with laughter, 'Oh yes, my darling,' he said, 'and that will ever after be the smell of love for me.'

She smiled and studied his face with great care as she slipped her arms tightly around him and said, 'This is real, isn't it? Really real and not a dream?'

'Yes.' And he kissed her.

His lips were warm and dry against her chill, onion-scented ones and they brushed together only lightly but each felt the blood racing around their bodies and they quickly came together again for a less tentative kiss. He cupped the back of her stubbly head and pulled her against him. They were both considering these new and wonderful feelings when they heard a chair shift in the room beneath them and heard John clear his throat. When the house was very new, the oak boards had fitted together well, but now they were a little older, gaps were appearing in the drying wood. If the house was properly cared for, the carpenter would fit little slips of wood in the gaps, but instead, it almost sounded as if John was there with them.

They parted, suddenly and guiltily. Thomas said, 'This will not be an easy task. But trust in God.' He drew breath, 'And trust me.' Joan's eyes looked steadily at him and Thomas found himself praying silently to God, *Dear Lord. Let this be the right path.* Then he ran out of words and sent wordless pleading to the heavens.

Chapter 5

Yarmouth

Downstairs, John moved restlessly. He was annoyed that Thomas had shut him out of the room of his own brother. He heard Joan give a short laugh and frowned. Wolsey always encouraged her light behaviour. He shook his head. He could spend years training Joan and if Thomas walked in, she'd forget it all in moments. He gave his long disapproving sniff, and then he heard footsteps above and doors opening and closing, and what was surely Peter's door being opened and closed.

His woollen slippers were silent and he knew which stair-treads creaked as he noiselessly made his way to the upper chambers. Yes, both Thomas and Joan were in Peter's room. He heard the soft tones of Wolsey but could not make out any words. He stared blindly as he strained to hear and eventually had to rub his dry eyes.

Inside the room, Thomas and Joan approached the bed. 'Father?'

After a moment, Peter stirred and his eyes rolled as he tried to focus on Thomas and Joan. 'Peter, I'm so sorry to disturb you but I have something of the utmost importance to say.'

'*Mmm?*'

Thomas lit a candle from the small fire and returned to the bed. He took Joan's hand and positioned her as close as possible to her father, then crossed to the other side of the bed and illuminated her face. 'Peter.' But his eyes were closed again.

'Peter.' Thomas spoke more firmly and Joan took her father's hand to awaken him.

The dying man opened his eyes again. ' Thomas. How nice.'

'Peter. Look at Joan.' Peter did so and a slight smile curved his lips. 'Look how thin she is. She is ravaged.' Joan endeavoured to look ravaged which was difficult as she felt as if she were glowing and full of sunshine.

'See how John's regime has worn her out. Her spirit is failing and she will not last a harsh winter.'

Outside the room, John made out his name and clenched his jaw.

'Peter. I will not let Joan pass from us. She is not suited to the enclosed life. PETER. Please listen to me. I have asked Joan to marry me and we will live quietly together with discretion.'

His words sunk in and Peter looked appalled. 'You can't!' he gasped.

Joan spoke, 'Father yes, we can. You must understand – even if it means that I have to become homeless, I will no longer be subject to my uncle's ministrations. Thomas?'

Wolsey looked at her and took her outstretched hand across the bed. Joan held his gaze and quite calmly she spoke, 'Thomas, I take you in marriage.'

Thomas replied as if in a dream, 'I take you in marriage,' he paused for a moment of mixed elation and horror, '…in marriage. Joan.'

From her middle finger, she pulled off the brass ring with a green glass gem which she'd dug up in the garden, and placed it on Thomas's little finger. Thomas looked at it, wondering how she knew the ceremony, then from his own finger, he drew a gold ring mounted with a misty, grey-blue sapphire. The hoop of gold was engraved with the motto *Liebe nicht Angst.*

'Love, not fear' whispered Thomas as he placed the ring on her right hand. He noticed that the stone was the colour of Joan's eyes.

Joan moved to the end of the bed, her eyes holding Thomas as if they were bewitched. 'A handclasp, a kiss and a gift.' She smiled, 'And we are wed.'

Peter had slipped back into sleep and Thomas took Joan's hands and kissed her. It was a formal kiss and for both of them, it contained little passion but much love and the sense of sealing their contract.

The door opened and John stood there, his eyes wide with shock and anger and his mouth open in appalled fascination. In two strides he reached them and seizing Joan pulled her violently away from Thomas. She stumbled and fell against her uncle who shuddered and made a sound of disgust. 'Whore' he hissed, 'concubine.'

'John. No.' Thomas spoke with authority but John rounded on him.

'You. Are. A. Sinful. Priest.' The words were steady

and low and dripped with poison, and once he'd spoken them, he turned to Joan and swung the back of his hand across her face. Almost immediately, blood trickled from her mouth and she made a gulping noise as she fell to her knees.

Thomas stepped swiftly between them. 'I told you to do her no harm. Do not raise your hand again. Strike *me* if you will, but never again will you touch Joan.'

In the bed, Peter cried out and all three heard his distress. They tried to speak all at once then Joan turned on them. 'Get out. Both of you. We will kill him. Out.'

Astonished to hear such authority from Joan, both men hurried to leave. They nearly collided in the doorway but John unthinkingly ceded seniority to Thomas and followed him, closing the door behind them.

Thomas jerked his head at John. 'Downstairs.' In silence, they went down and into the parlour and stood staring at each other.

After a moment, Thomas exploded, 'For God's sake, where are all the servants? Why is it so damnably cold in here? I need a glass of wine.'

John ran his tongue over his teeth and calmly walked to the desk where his papers lay. He sat down with an air of ownership. 'I have dismissed most of them. This is a wasteful, and self-evidently ungodly house. He leaned back, crossed his legs, regarded the man whom he had admired for so many years and continued, 'Your mouth is sacred to God. How could you even consider this?' His mouth formed a sneer as he breathed long and noisily through his nose.

Thomas composed himself. He was indeed in extremely debatable territory. He needed to calm John or all would be lost. His reputation would be gone and with it any chance of preferment at court. John was right, but he was also so heartbreakingly wrong. And if John had more compassion in him, more human love, none of them would have reached this pass. But a zealot is not a person with whom to reason.

He went to the door and called for Meg who appeared rather promptly from the kitchens. Behind her he could see the few remaining servants gathered; eyes wide as they wondered what was coming to pass in this unhappy house.

'Is William returned?' She nodded and stared at John, wondering if she should take orders from Thomas. 'Is there food?' A nod. 'Wine? Ale?' Another nod. 'Good. Please bring them in here. Mistress Joan will join us shortly and we three will dine together.'

John rolled his eyes but didn't gainsay Thomas and in a few minutes, a warm meat pie and ale were laid ready for them. Thomas poured ale and passed a cup to John. 'Drink it, man. We both need it to steady us.'

John took the cup, placed it untasted on the table and pointedly turned away from Thomas. Then he abruptly, and Thomas thought, rather painfully, dropped heavily to his knees. There he proceeded to pray noisily, for the fallen woman and the sinful lost priest. Thomas rolled his eyes but continued to try and reach John.

'John, this regime of yours has broken Joan. Surely you have seen that? She is thin and wasted and her spirit is crushed.'

At this, John looked up with indignation, 'Crushed? How dare you? Her spirit is properly subjugated to God and for the first time in her sinful life, she has learned the bliss of true obedience. God and all heaven are rejoicing at the homecoming of God's creature.'

Thomas felt that familiar anger against John, who could never see an alternative viewpoint and he spoke with heavy irony. 'And there I was trusting that God had created Joan as he meant her to be – a joyous creature delighting in her creation and the glories of the world in which he placed her.'

'My Lord, do you not approve of religious houses?' John looked at Thomas as if he expected the fires of hell to open behind him and suck him in.

Thomas gave a slightly pained smile. 'John, that is not what I believe. Very far from it. But I certainly do not think that someone who is unwilling should take holy vows. That would be a prison and it devalues the sacrifice of those who willingly and with great love dedicate their lives to God. And although you find it impossible, Joan is not one of those people.'

Stiffly, John got to his feet and Thomas almost reached out his hand to assist him, but he was too angry and then immediately felt ashamed by his petty behaviour. But John had no idea of Thomas's struggle to remain compassionate and moved back to the desk. He looked through a small pile of cheaply printed books and flourished one.

'My Lord Dean of Lincoln. I presume that my Lord is familiar with these writings?'

He flourished the pages at Thomas. 'The Exempla! Would you damn Joan? And not only her earthly body but her eternal soul? Look. A woman who became a priest's concubine, who fornicated with him. She died! She died and her coffin could not be lifted for her soul was drenched with all the sin of the world! Her lust and venality condemned her for all eternity. You are both seized by demons and there is nothing to help you. The demons will ride you both to hell!' John's face was alarmingly red and spittle flew from his mouth. Thomas could see veins at his temple pulsing as John gasped for breath. Thomas took the book from John and looked at it.

'Oh John. These are fairy tales to frighten children. To scare those who have not a mature faith and an understanding of God's perfect love. Don't be swayed by such dreadful nonsense. Such silly superstition.' The two men stared at each other, both conscious of the blood thumping through their bodies fed by their anger.

John spoke with deadly calm, 'She is my niece.'

'And she is my wife. And Peter witnessed the hand-fasting.'

'Then I pray God will have mercy on you both, for I fear that no one else will.' John bowed coldly at the man he'd once admired so much and Wolsey gave him a brief nod before turning to leave the room.

At the door he half turned back, but John's face was bitter and forbidding and Thomas shut his eyes for a moment of sadness before softly closing the door behind him. He stood for a moment, blowing out his cheeks in a long, exhausted sigh and briefly wondered if there was any chance this was a dream. Could he open his eyes and find his head resting on his desk, papers stuck to his cheek and his candle burned down? He opened his eyes but all they saw were the newel post and the treads of the stairs. Behind him was John's frenzied murmuring. Along the passage were the voices of Mistress Bray, William, Meg and other servants – buzzing excitedly, he fancied. And upstairs. Upstairs brought no sound to him, merely a solid silence; no movement, no breath or voice.

Sitting by her father's bed, Joan could hear the rise and fall of the men's voices below. She could even hear that horrible disapproving sniff. In the early days of her torment, she would offer him a handkerchief, politely enquire if he had a cold and offer him a tincture to help clear his nose. All in the hope that John would take the hint and stop it. Ideally, before she upended his chair, flipped him on his back and stuffed lumps of bread up his nose. Then she would turn from this violent vision and resolve to be more patient and forgiving. But after a few weeks, she forgot to notice it and be annoyed. She stopped thinking of her misery and lived half a life. Less than half really; the only part of her which remained was that which cared for her father and the tiny secret fragment which was filled with wicked envy for his illness. That last vestige of Joan which longed for the peace of death.

Her letter – written, ironically enough, at the suggestion of John and sniffingly authorised by him – seemed to have saved her. Now she was seated at the deathbed of her father and felt life returning to her. It was like the blood returning to a limb; painful pins and needles and a glad remembrance of life. Oh – terrified swallow – but what had they done?

Of course, she loved Thomas; she had loved him all her life. Never as a brother because she had brothers and no need for another. But as soon as she had thoughts of love and marriage, she had announced to Mistress Bray that she would marry Thomas and that the next time he visited, she would ask him. Mistress Bray had smiled and explained that Thomas would never marry a woman because he was married to God and the church. Joan nodded and simply thought, *Well, that's silly, Thomas can't be married to God. Mistress Bray doesn't understand.*

But she'd learned to keep her thoughts quiet and no young man had a chance to touch her heart because it was safely guarded – though days and nights and dreams – by Thomas. Wonderful imaginary Thomas who'd saved her from many perilous adventures yet never touched her hand or kissed her lips. And when Joan won her first kiss, it was such a damp disappointment. Then today at the bleakest point of her life, a real, warm, quietly-breathing Thomas had ridden through the door and shattered the nasty life of this house. His hands had held hers and his lips kissed her and told her that he loved her.

Holding her father's hand, Joan found it hard to believe that she had been bold enough to take Thomas's hand and marry him. She felt her pulse race at the thought and peeked at the ring on her finger. *Love, not fear* and that beautiful stone. Oh. Whatever had they done? She couldn't marry a clergyman.

Peter gave a little gasp then his breathing stopped. Joan stared at him, her mouth open and dry. She held her breath with him, and then after many long seconds, he took another breath. She relaxed slightly but it was clear that something had changed. Joan spoke softly to her father. She told him that she loved him and thanked him for his care of her. She spoke of her future and that he must not worry, for Thomas would guard her now. His hand twitched in hers and Joan realised that he had not drawn breath for several minutes. She looked at his face. His eyes were slightly open as was his mouth. But there was no flickering of blood passing through the veins in his throat. Joan stood, closed his eyes and removed the pillow from under his head so that he would cool and stiffen in an easier position. She calmly straightened his hand where his fingers had been clasping hers and placed both arms straight by his sides. Her eyes were dry and she moved calmly as if laying out a corpse was an everyday task for her. Then she stood at the foot of his bed and gazed at him. She had reached the end of her resources and had no thoughts left.

The murmur of voices below changed – now she could only hear John and from the rhythm of his voice, he was praying. Still, she stood motionless until the door opened and Thomas entered. He said nothing but immediately understood. With a couple of strides, he was by her side. Then he went to Peter and Joan folded her hands together and closed her eyes as Thomas performed the Last Rites over his friend. For a moment they were disturbed by footsteps on the stairs and the arrival of John, but the priest quietly joined Wolsey at the bedside and they prayed together. The sudden quiet in the house must have caught the notice of the servants and Meg peeped around the door frame before disappearing to take the news down to the servants' areas.

Somebody, she never knew who, brought Joan a stool and a cup of warm wine. Her legs were so stiff with tension that she almost fell onto the seat and sat hunched, elbows on knees, breathing the scents of spice and wine and almost asleep. After a while, Mistress Bray and Meg, the only two remaining female servants, brought up hot water and soap. They roused Joan and together they washed and dressed Peter's body and laid him on top of his woollen shroud. Then they lit candles and prepared to sit with him through the night.

Alice Bray was heartbroken. This was the end of her time with the Larke family. The house would be sold and the servants paid off. It felt like the end of her life too. Once she had nursed a soft spot for Peter, even coyly suggested that he remarry, but Peter had smiled kindly at her and shaken his head. 'No. Not me, Mistress Alice. I'm married to Jane. That was a contract I shall never wish to change.'

Alice had been disappointed but not inconsolable. She was a sensible woman. The soft spot remained and quietly changed into friendship with Peter. In her future, she had either seen her old age in this house with Peter or perhaps as a respected housekeeper in Joan's family. That was the way for a woman who had given true and loving service to generations of a family. But Joan would be taken as a virtual prisoner to a convent and Alice would seek another place.

The three women sat peacefully by Peter's bed. The body before them was not frightening – it was their friend, father and kind master and they had nothing to fear. Meg did jump once when a cooling muscle contracted and Peter moved a limb, but Alice's hand on hers calmed her. Meg alone had noticed the new ring on Joan's hand. And she knew whose ring it was and she sat motionless on her little stool, her thoughts whirling around.

As the day grew dark, they could hear Thomas and John returning. The sexton would be digging the grave ready for tomorrow. Thomas would conduct the service and his mind was already on this sad final duty. The two men entered the house and parted. John returned to his attic room and Thomas knew that he would soon be enjoying physical chastisement and he wearily shook his head.

Entering the parlour Thomas found the now cold meat pie and his stomach rumbled. Shrugging, he sat down and ate. The meat juices had congealed but it was still very tasty. But of course, William would have bought only good food for his master. He left a thick slice and walked briskly upstairs to the chamber where the women watched.

The door was open and all three looked up as he entered. 'Joan' he said softly, 'come with me for a moment if you will.'

Meg looked at the glow in Joan's eyes and thought, *Oh ho*. Then she met Alice's reproving look and returned to studying her own hands. Joan stood and left the room.

'*Ooh!*' said Meg softly, 'Do you think…'

'No,' snapped Alice, 'I don't think anything at all. And neither do you.' Meg nodded and slumped even further forward as if trying to dodge the Mistress's ire.

In the parlour, Thomas seated Joan by the fire and handed her the plate with the remaining pie.

Joan blinked at it, 'Goodness me. That surely isn't meat?'

Thomas looked puzzled. 'Of course it is. It's a meat pie.'

Joan smiled, an ironic twist to her mouth. 'You should know that meat will inflame me. It is only for the weak after a long illness.'

'Oh, is it now? Well, to me it looks as if you need a little nourishment after an illness. Wife, I bid you eat.'

Joan caught her bottom lip between her teeth and looked at Thomas. A faint blush rose in her cheeks and her face blossomed into a cheerful and slightly naughty smile.

'We did! We really did. I was beginning to wonder if I'd made it up.'

Thomas was filled with steady joy at the of sight Joan and her old smile, now touched with something more intimate and every doubt fled. *Doubtless to return*, he thought wryly, *but for now...*

Standing behind Joan's chair, he bent forward and wrapped his arms around her. He rested his head against hers and she leaned back into the warmth of his arms and placed her hands over his. They remained like that for a long moment until under his hands he felt Joan's stomach give a most indelicate rumble and they laughed and parted.

'Will you please eat?' Thomas sat on another chair

and gazed at Joan as she set about the pie. He was so tired and he knew that he should be dealing with any of a hundred things, not least the papers he'd brought with him from London yesterday, or was it years ago? He jerked awake and realised he'd dozed for a moment.

'My Thomas. You look very tired, my dear.'

'Mmm. I am.' His words were slightly slurred and his eyelids dropped whenever he stopped speaking.

Joan finished eating. She felt renewed and with a thrill she thought, *I must tend to my husband.* She rose from her chair in what she hoped was a wifely manner and took his hand. 'Come along.'

She led him to her room and as he sat on the wooden edge of her bed, she ruefully wished she'd taken time that morning to shake up the mattress. She removed Thomas's velvet cap and kneeling, pulled off his travelling boots. Then she stood and gently pushed his shoulders until he fell back into the bed. She lifted up his feet and pulling the covers over him was amazed to see that he was already asleep and he didn't stir as she leaned over and kissed him. His cheek was slightly rough under her lips but she still detected the delicious smell of soap and scented linen against his skin. Suddenly overwhelmingly tired herself, Joan slid to the floor and rested her head against the frame of the bed. *I could get into the bed too. With my husband.* But that was her last thought and her eyes snapped shut on a day of tremendous sadness and extraordinary happiness.

Chapter 6

Yarmouth

Above her head, Alice Bray could hear John Larke moving around. It sounded as if he was pacing, then thumping down on his knees which then signalled a period of prayer. Sadly, not silent. *God must be considerably more patient than I am,* she thought with irritation. And not for the first time, Alice marvelled at the differences between the two brothers – one so gentle and loving and one so zealous and unforgiving. She could scarcely recall a harsh word from Peter. Even when Pepper was a naughty puppy and chewed an expensive slipper, he was exasperated but not cross. A lesser man might have beaten the animal and pointed out that the house was not suitable for a large dog, but he'd spoken seriously to Joan and explained that Pepper couldn't live in the house if he ate their possessions and he'd helped her to train the animal. Her eyes started to tear at the thought of Pepper and for a moment, she pretended that if she dropped her hand, she would feel his silky head under her fingers and his rough tongue licking her. Another crime to lay at John's door. She knew that the dog had been killed and the thought made her very angry.

The wretched man was continually troublesome. His visits had always been tense, even when Peter was well.

Those disapproving sniffs had made her hand itch and she longed to catch him a smack around the back of his head as he worked his way through her food, eating only the burned edge or choking down a piece of gristle and leaving the good meat and the choice parts of the meal.

And now, John was in his attic and evidently suffering from some great anguish. Joan looking as if spring has come, Thomas more exhausted than she'd ever seen him and Peter dead in the bed before her. She thought for a moment, her head on one side and her nose wrinkled in concentration. A cold thought seized her and gripped her heart. Surely not. She drew a deep breath and tried to relax. It would all become clear in time. But dread stirred in her stomach. She absolutely knew and if she was right, it could bring only disaster.

Rising from her stool she crept from the room and along to Joan's. The door was open and she could see Joan asleep, leaning against the bed and Thomas in the bed and also asleep. Joan's head was against his hand which hung over the edge of the bed and rested on her shoulder. The suggestion of complete trust and easy familiarity was almost nakedly intimate. After a moment, Alice felt her anger mounting and strode in. She stood over them before stretching out her foot and poking Joan's knee, probably with more vehemence than was required. Joan jumped and stared up at Alice, a smile curving her lips. One part of Alice rejoiced to see Joan smile and she hesitated a moment. But then she jerked her head backwards in a gesture of command and Joan got to her feet.

As always in timber-built houses, the only place one

could be private was in one's head, so Alice led the way downstairs and into the garden. The air was fresh and Joan immediately started to shiver as sleep finally left her.

'Would you like to tell me why you're keeping watch over the Dean of Lincoln instead of your dead father?'

The corners of Joan's mouth went down and Alice regretted her harsh tone. But Joan stood dumb, her only movement being one hand twisting the gold and sapphire ring on her finger.

'And why are you wearing his ring?'

Alice could see Joan's mouth working as if trying to clear dryness in her throat. She couldn't help but feel the tiniest pang; even from earliest childhood, when in trouble Joan had always looked as if she was rehearsing her excuses.

Alice waited; her brows raised.

'It's an, um, unusual matter. You might not understand…'

'Try me.'

'Thomas… had an idea…'

'Mm?'

'Well, Thomas wished to marry me. But as a clergyman, he may not.'

Alice's face looked as if she wanted to say *Really? Surely not.*

Joan looked slightly mutinous. 'And I do not wish to enter a convent. I will not. And, and, Thomas agrees with me. He thinks it would do no good to me or the House.'

Her gaze slid to one side and the broken, trapped look returned to her face. Alice sighed. Thomas was right. She too had been deeply concerned to see her darling fading away. 'So?'

'And I would like to marry him. He's so kind and we laugh. And he smells nice.' Joan's eyes filled with tears. 'We told father about Thomas's idea and we hand-fasted over the bed there and then. And exchanged rings.'

Alice was astonished though, she recognised, not quite as surprised as she should have been. 'Right. And what is Thomas's great idea?'

'Oh. That *really*, he's just Thomas, the son of a butcher and that as such, he would be free to marry me.'

Alice could only admire the devious plan of her friend. She recalled he was also a demon card player and she'd always suspected he was better as a friend than an enemy.

'But Joan. You can't.'

Joan's face hardened and she shrugged one shoulder, 'Well we have.'

'But you *can't*. You mustn't. What about the practicalities? Will you go to London with him? How and where will you live? For goodness sake, he's the King's chaplain!'

All at once, Joan looked grown-up. Gone was the carefree child who ran barefoot on the beach, who could be sent to her room. *We should have thrashed her, been firmer with her. But those sad blue eyes in that pretty face...*

There was a slight sound from the house and they both turned. The familiar figure of Thomas stood in the dark doorway. He held out his hand and when he spoke Joan's name, she went to him like a sleep-walker. Alice found a touch of jealousy in her heart – for so long she had been Thomas's confidant and Joan's mother in all but name. Now the two people who were most dear to her belonged to each other and she felt the cold dark night foretell her own lonely future. Her eyes prickled with tears and she strode towards the house.

'Don't you think that instead of discussing blasphemous mischief we should be watching over Peter's body?' She spoke with asperity and the two parted as she pushed between them into the house.

The kitchen was alive with the eyes of the other servants staring as they walked through. It was such an exciting day – Master John screaming about whores and lost souls and the poor Master dying. Before long they'd be visiting the fair and looking for new positions and it always paid to have some good tales of old employers to tell their new fellow servants. And having Thomas Wolsey here, fresh from the court where the old King was dying – why it was almost as good as being there themselves.

Mistress Bray swept through with the young mistress at her heels and Master Wolsey carefully closed the door and spoke softly to them.

'My friends. I'm sorry we let the cold air in. Feed the fire again and get warm.' In return, he heard some muffled thank yous and lifted his hand and blessed them all.

At the door, he turned again, 'And I don't want any of you to worry about your next position; places will be found or salary will be paid to each of you when this house is closed.'

From the dark came a familiar voice, 'Why that's very decent of you Master, and I thank you.'

Thomas rolled his eyes and smiled, 'William, you're most welcome.' As he closed the door, he could hear the man's quiet laugh and found it brought him a little comfort.

In the dark screens passage, he paused. His thoughts ran a little wildly, but he forgave himself. Standing there always seemed as if he was in the heart of the house. He placed his hand on the panelling and reached out his thoughts and located the various inhabitants; John in the attic, trying to keep a Godly roof over them. In the kitchens the servants and his own men laying out their palliasses. Almost above him were Peter, Alice and Joan. His wife. His heart lurched with a mixture of alarm and delight. *My wife.*

After a few moments, he returned to the chamber where the women sat, faintly lit by the candles around Peter's bed. Meg silently turned her gaze on him and he smiled at her. Then Joan looked at him and he was lost once more. *My wife.*

The night seemed interminable, Alice rose once to replace the candles and her movement disturbed them from their nodding reveries. But finally, dawn came. It wasn't a dramatic change of light, just a gradual lightening and they could hear the servants below starting their day. Meg shrugged to herself – all the things that she and Mistress Alice would have completed before any of the men rose, would remain undone today. Why, it was almost a holiday.

Soon there would be a knock at the door as the men arrived with the coffin. Alice stood; a night spent hunched on a stool was no help to a woman of her age. Her knees clicked as she tried to straighten. She touched Meg on the shoulder and together they left the room. Thomas was in the only chair, his elbows on the arms and his chin resting on his linked hands. Joan was folded right up with her arms around her shins and her head on her knees. Thomas smiled; it was a long time since his stomach had allowed him to sit like that. His movement was almost imperceptible, yet Joan opened her eyes and smiled at him and Thomas grinned back.

Alice reappeared with breakfast. Thomas found a stool and they used it as a makeshift table. The bread was yesterday's but Mistress Bray made no apology for it, saying to herself, *if they don't like it then it's no less than they deserve.* Her mind still flew around, trying to compass the enormity of Thomas and Joan's unthinkable act and when above their heads they all heard John stirring, she unwillingly felt great sympathy with him.

They ate in silence until Thomas spoke, 'I will go to the church shortly and say Mass for Peter.' The women nodded.

'I have to return to the King as soon as possible. Both he and the King's Mother will expect me.' Alice shrugged and returned to dipping her bread into the small beer, but Joan fixed her eyes on Thomas. His gaze changed as he looked at her. She was desperately tired but she still looked so much more herself than when he'd arrived yesterday. Shadows ringed her eyes, but those eyes were bright and cheerful beneath the swollen lids.

'Joan, if your father is buried this evening, could you be ready to leave on the night tide?'

Her eyes widened and she glanced at Mistress Alice who refused to look up from her plate.

'Yes, husband. Of course.' Her voice held a little wavering defiance and she dared another glance at Alice.

'Good.' Thomas stood, brushing crumbs from his robe. 'William informed the priest last night and the grave should be dug by now. Dame Alice, will you prepare food for any visitors please? William has money to meet all expenses. And will you please let me see the accounts? I wish to ensure the servants are provided for after we close the house.'

Alice ran her tongue around her teeth before speaking, 'I cannot show you the accounts. John took them over.' Her voice was cold and she sounded slightly pleased to be able to thwart her old friend.

Joan joined in, 'It doesn't matter Alice, I can remember. There are so few remaining that it's not difficult to recall.' Alice shrugged one shoulder and continued to eat.

'Mistress Alice… please…'

But her jaw was set and her lips thin as Thomas spoke to her. 'I do not know of any other way around this situation. This is how it must be.' Thomas's words were firm and authoritative.

'*Any other way…* what nonsense. There are a thousand other ways which do not involve both of you descending into sin and blasphemy.'

Joan spoke, 'And yet this *is* how it will be. There is love between us. God created love. God is love. You have been both friend and mother to me. All my life I've loved and depended on you. I love you still and I would not break your heart. But this deed is done. I am Thomas's wife. We will be each other's support and friend. I wish to part from you on good terms, but how we part is in your hands.'

Joan stood and walked over to her father's dressing chest. 'Thomas, help me please?' She started to heave at the chest which refused to budge. Joan felt her authority ebbing with every ineffectual tug at the handle.

Thomas stopped her with a hand on hers. 'I will send the men up to do this.' Joan blinked back her tears of annoyance and with her chin held high, thanked him.

'Thank you, and before you go to say the Mass for my father, if you would.' And she strode from the room leaving Alice and Thomas to look at each other. With pangs of regret, they both realised that no more could they grin and roll eyes at Joan's behaviour. Joan was no longer Alice's equal; she was now her mistress and Thomas could never again be amused by the antics of his friend's little daughter who was quite suddenly his wife. It was one of the saddest moments of their lives and there was nothing to be said. Thomas bowed to Alice and left the room.

Pausing at Joan's room, he watched her for a moment pulling clothes from her own chest. There were pitifully few items.

'Joan. Do you think you will need your father's chest?' She straightened and looked at her work.

'Quite honestly, no. My uncle gave many of my

clothes to the poor when we were preparing for my glorious future with God. I had some lovely things.' She caught her bottom lip between her teeth and shook her head.

'Oh Thomas, how could I let him bully me so? He really is quite deranged. I was powerless. He cut off my hair and I let him. He stole my spirit and I went along with it because it was the easy thing to do. He killed my dog. He killed Pepper and told me he'd gone to a better place. And may God forgive me, I envied him. I wanted to lie down with my dead dog and never again open my eyes.'

Joan's voice rose and tears poured down her cheeks. 'No person should have the power to make another feel like that. And no one will *ever* make me feel so desperate again.' She gasped frantically through the tears and Thomas opened his arms to her.

Dear God, he thought again, *so thin, so lost.* Then his heart sank as, with impeccable timing, John walked into the chamber and with a heart-rending cry, flung himself on the floor, grabbing at the hem of Thomas's robe.

Joan shrank away with a horrified gasp but her skirt was also firmly in John's grasp.

'My Lord, forgive me!' Thomas was unsure if John was appealing to God or to Thomas himself. But John continued to wail and seek forgiveness.

With a sharp snatch, Joan pulled her dress free and retreated to the far side of the room where she watched with horrified fascination as her uncle besought Thomas to forgive him for failing to save their souls. John's hands were bloodied and she could only imagine what horrible punishment he'd been inflicting on himself all night. Her own tears forgotten, she realised that she was longing to laugh, and to save herself from that, she picked up the ewer of water and keeping in Thomas's shadow till the last, she flung the contents into her uncle's face.

'John! Stop it. Leave my room this instant. And as soon as my father is buried, you will leave my house. I wish never to speak to you again.' Then her voice becoming even firmer, and marvelling at her own daring, she continued, 'You have seen how gentlemen behave; I'm sure you can pretend to be one for the last few hours under my roof.'

She walked forward and shoved him with her foot. Speechless and shocked, John scrambled to his feet and staggered from the chamber. Joan closed the door behind him and faced Thomas. Her eyes so wide that he laughed.

'Joan. Close your eyes, my love. They look fit to fall out.'

She drew a deep breath. 'Thomas. Oh. I threw water at him... but it was *clean* water. And he doesn't wash overly often.'

That was the final straw for Thomas. He gave a huge hiccupping laugh and gathered Joan to him. After a moment, she too started to laugh.

'Oh sweetheart. I... that was... I never...' but words were beyond them and clutching each other, they flopped onto her bed, gasping for breath and wiping their eyes and noses and grateful for more of Thomas's silk kerchiefs.

After a while, they lay sniffing and occasionally heaving with laughter at the remembrance of John's face,

Joan turned to face Thomas. 'All shall be well you know, my love. All manner of things.'

Thomas nodded and sat up. 'I know. But this is certainly a novel life we are planning.' His voice petered out as he exhausted his store of reassuring words.

They were saved by knocking at the front door. It was opened and they heard the voices of some of Peter's fellow merchants. Joan sat up. 'They're coming to pay their respects. I don't suppose there is anything to feed them. I can't bear it. My father was famed for his generous board. Now there is nothing but stale bread and old ale.'

'Then that is what they shall have. But perhaps Dame Alice will have managed a small miracle…'

In fact, it wasn't Dame Alice, but William. His purchases last night had included more than one meat pie and smells of food being warmed began to reach them. They could also hear low voices rumbling away and the occasional shout of laughter as ale and wine began to relax the hush of the house.

Joan found a more flattering bonnet, though it was difficult to secure it without her long hair and she was forced to tie a cloth around her naked head to hold the pins. Thomas brought water from Peter's chamber and carried out a perfunctory wash of hands and face and shuddered at the faintly grubby feel of yesterday's linen. He went down to greet the mourners and his arrival briefly suppressed the peculiar atmosphere of celebration. Thomas understood that feeling: it was a sense of relief that death had called on another, and they might be safe for another day. Death was a familiar presence and he well knew the heavy joke that one might easily wake up dead of a sudden sickness.

Joan joined the men and greeted each one. They were gentle with her; she looked so frail and they were afraid to offend with their black humour but she moved easily around the room, thanking each by name for his sympathy. Simon Sutcliffe was uneasy when she reached him. He looked for his father, then straightened his shoulders. It was her loss, not his. His Abby was just the right woman for him – Joan's huge blue eyes with that seductive hint of sadness, that unconscious grace as she smiled at him, none of these tempted him now. Then he found he couldn't see Abby's jolly face anymore and he was about to reach for Joan's hand and try once more when that churchman crossed the room and stood next to Joan. He saw their knuckles brush against each other and watched in astonishment as Joan's eyelids dropped over a faint smile. Well, that was entirely something to think about and in his heart, Abby stepped once more into the light and he ached to slip his arm around her waist and see her adoring eyes looking up at him. Joan smiled vaguely at Simon for the very last time before drifting off to the next man waiting to speak to her. And all at once, Simon was free of her thrall.

The day was long and yet it seemed but a moment till the men came to collect the body. The sad procession followed Peter as he departed his house for the last time, his coffin being carried into the gathering darkness. Joan watched from the window; her eyes dry. Peter had been unwell for so many weeks that she had lived his death a thousand times and the reality now seemed unreal. She turned to her packing and found that Thomas was right, there was no need for large chests. Since John's harsh work, there were hardly any clothes to take. She would rather leave everything and walk naked into her new life, but that would hardly help their pursuit of discretion. Into her own small coffer, she packed her mother's book of simple remedies and as few clothes and shoes as possible. Her mother had owned little jewellery but the pieces went into the pouch at her waist. Then she remembered and raced into her father's chamber. The stripped bed stopped her; it was such a physical shock that she doubled over, her hand pressed to her mouth and her stomach heaving in distress. *My Fa is dead.* It was so unreal. Had she killed him by declaring her intentions? One part of her longed to return to the security of the half-dead life of John's rule but the rest of her remembered that dawn had come and she was rescued, safe and happy. Her father would have died regardless and she must remember that.

She turned her eyes from the bed and went to the desk. The little drawers held many memories for her and her eyes blurred with tears as she saw the familiar items of her childhood; the sparkling ouch jewel with the broken back which she'd found and presented to her father as a real diamond from the sea. His seals, the scraps of paper with the now incomprehensible notes. The piece of faded ribbon, securing a lock of her mother's hair. Then her fingers found their prize, a leather bag of gold coins. John had sought them, wishing to pass them to the priest but Peter had always refused his brother. Now she had them. The house might not fall to her but she went to Thomas with a degree of wealth and independence.

Now enlivened, she flew around the dusk-filled house, picking up little treasures and saying goodbye to the rooms in turn, closing the doors one by one on each chamber and chapter of her life.

When Thomas and John returned with William and the other men-servants behind them, she was seated on the stairs waiting in the dark. Thomas saw her pale face but John jumped as if seeing a spirit.

Joan stood up. 'All done?' Thomas nodded.

'Thank you. I am grateful.'

She turned slightly, 'William, would you and a couple of your men bring down my coffer? I have dragged it to the top of the stairs but could do no more.' William nodded and gestured to one of the men.

Just then, Meg appeared with a lighted candle in each hand and Alice followed with two more. The light showed their white, strained faces. Joan nodded to them and thanked them.

Meg stopped in front of Joan and gave a deep curtesy. 'Mistress Joan.' Her voice was small but firm. 'I will be coming to London with you. It is seemly that you should have a maid to accompany you.'

Alice gasped. If her hands had been free, she would have cuffed Meg and returned her to the kitchens faster than her feet could have carried her. 'You'll do no such thing! Get back in there, or I will send you into next week.'

Joan ignored Alice; it was her only defence. 'Thank you, Meg. I believe we leave immediately, so I trust you have packed?'

Meg nodded and placing the candlesticks on a table, dragged a pitifully small bundle from inside the dining room door and swung her cloak around her shoulders. 'Mistress. I am ready.'

'Good.' Joan nodded and swallowed. 'Mistress Bray. I have insufficient words to thank you. All my life, you have loved and protected me. You taught me to fill my mother's place in this household and it was the proudest of moments when you handed her keys to me.' Joan found there was nothing more she could say and holding out her hand to Alice, returned the keys.

She turned and the men in the passage parted as she walked towards the door. For a moment, Thomas met Alice's gaze. He nodded, then turned and followed his wife.

Outside, the night was moist and chill, the racing clouds covering the faint light of the new moon. Joan felt as if she were dreaming, but she led the group; Thomas, Meg, William and the small company of men through the gates and into the street. With the faintest of smiles, her mind raced along the Rows, tracing the shortest route to the ship. She would never set foot in the Rows again. She would forget the map in her head and revisit it only in her dreams.

If she had looked back, she would have seen the forlorn figure of Alice, faintly lit from behind. She might have seen John standing lost in the darkness. But she didn't; Thomas was by her side and this was no time to do anything but go forward.

It had taken just a day for Alice's life to be dismantled.

Peter in the graveyard and Joan and Thomas walking away from her without a single glance back. Even William had left without his customary twinkle and squeeze of her waist. Faintly illuminated by the candles, she drew a deep breath and sagged slightly. 'Goodbye, my ducks,' she whispered into the night, then closed the door of the empty house and walked to the kitchens to seek her bed and a long night of sadness and worry.

In their little cabin, Joan and Meg lay curled together, their breathing deep and steady. Joan briefly woke up and pressed her hand against the wooden wall. Somewhere beyond was Thomas. She smiled; *they would be so happy.* She saw a bright garden and Thomas and a pile of children all shrieking with laughter in the sunshine. And she slipped back into sleep as in her dream, Thomas grinned at her and held out his hand.

Tucked into the captain's cabin, Thomas prayed for peace at the end of this frantic day. He deeply mourned the death of his friend and thanked God for Peter's delivery from pain and worry. His finger felt bare without his gold ring and the finger wearing Joan's little ring felt heavy and awkward.

'*Mmm*,' he said thoughtfully and William rolled his eyes, 'Oh, go to sleep, My Lord.'

Chapter 7

London

The voyage took nearly thirty hours and it was dark when the little ship landed in London. Joan's eyes were wide with excitement and fatigue. As she and Meg staggered stiff-legged onto the landing stage, Joan was struck by the noise. Although it was not yet dawn, the clamour was astonishing, even to a girl from a busy harbour town; gulls screamed here too, but there was also a thunderous rumble of carts and shouts as traders readied for the day ahead. Dogs barked as they ran wild or protected their owners. And the smell was quite astonishing: dung, piles of rubbish and a terrible stench from the river.

William sent his fastest man to Thomas's lodgings and shepherded his charges together to wait for the escort and horses to arrive. Noting that Joan was shivering violently, he slipped his flask into her hand and made her take a swig of the fierce liquor. She coughed and then smiled as the icy fire spread into her stomach and warmed her limbs. Another man brought a hot meat pie to them, and Joan seized it, breaking it open to share with Meg who stood almost blue with cold but still managed to look steady and reliable.

William raised his eyebrows as they wolfed down the steaming meat and pastry. 'Good, ain't it? One of Perkin's. Mind you, don't buy pies later in the day. They won't be fresh like this and they'll take their time passing through and make you wish you were dead!'

The group stood around in their various slumped and weary attitudes. As so often in life, Thomas was torn; he'd like to be striding through the early morning streets with his men, enjoying the slight bustle they caused and air of importance. He thought of the day ahead and his thoughts touched on the King's Mother, another who enjoyed her rank. That's why he had a degree of sympathy with Margaret Beaufort; when you've come from the bottom you can't help but enjoy your new consequence, although you could never feel secure... Perhaps that was why she was so autocratic and aloof. Only thirteen when Henry was born of her tiny frame, it was no wonder that she bore no more children. Of course, she wasn't from the very bottom of society but the odds of her boy winning the fight at Bosworth had been poor and if he had been defeated it would have been the end of their attempt on the throne. They were only of legitimised stock. Lose a battle, and there would have been a world of difference between legitimate and legitimised – Henry, Margaret and her second husband Stanley would have been supplicants at a Plantagenet court or plotting in foreign exile.

He turned and looked at Joan, thin and huddled but still more hearty and healthy than the King's mother had ever been. As Bishop John Fisher had said of her, it was astonishing that a child could be born of so little a personage. Yet Margaret never ailed and Thomas always thought it was sheer willpower that had carried her through life.

Joan turned and met Thomas's speculative gaze and winked at him. He gave an involuntary grin. *Well*, he thought, *we've done it. Might as well be happy and see what comes.*

Joan was standing close, watching his face and when their eyes met, she looked questioning. 'What are you thinking, Thomas?'

He gave a little chuckle, 'I'm thinking that I'll have to reduce my expenditure somewhat. Having a beautiful wife will cost many fines.' Joan looked her usual mix of wide-eyed horror that he was serious, mixed with a faint scepticism that he was teasing her.

'*Mmm*. Give me your thoughts on buying fewer silk kerchiefs?'

Thomas looked sorrowful. 'No, my dear, you can't ask that of me. Ask anything but that.' He gave an exaggerated sigh. 'The thing is Joan… well, I realise that I can't afford both you and kerchiefs. Look, you seem to be a good sailor. You can be back in Yarmouth in a few hours. John will forgive you if you show true repentance.'

Joan raised her eyebrows at Thomas, 'No. Not for anything!' Then her face fell slightly, 'I will even join a house of ladies. And I don't mean God's House.'

Thomas looked serious. 'Joan, don't talk like that. I promise I will always make sure that you are safe and cared for. And I swear again, that will be so.'

Sad that the moment had turned slightly sour, Joan

smiled brightly at Thomas and then turned, 'Oh Thomas, see!'

To the east, the sunrise was beginning and the sky was briefly a violent pink and red. It lasted only a few minutes before fading, but it had brightened their mood and it was only a few moments later that they heard the hallooing of the little group of horses and Thomas's beautiful mule arriving to take them home.

Joan was instantly in love with Star, reaching up to stroke her. The animal nuzzled her hand and Thomas chuckled, 'Ah, she's waiting for this.' He handed Joan the crusts of bread and she offered them to the mule who gently took them from Joan's palm.

While they petted Star, the men were dealing with their luggage and being bullied by Meg. Finally fed up with her telling them what to do, one of the guards hoisted her in his arms and swung her onto a small pony. The same man helped Joan onto the mare which had been brought for her and finally, they were ready.

William rode in front on his sturdy gelding followed by Thomas, Joan and Meg. The men on foot surrounded them and they set off. Joan was slightly taken aback by all the grandeur of their procession. It was odd to see Thomas as a man of consequence. Her husband sat tall and proud and nodded graciously as people stepped aside and pulled off their caps. She looked boldly around her and smiled at people.

At Thomas's lodgings, candles shone welcomingly through the sparkling windows and servants could be seen moving through the rooms. Within moments they were inside and Joan found herself shivering at the warmth and unexpectedly, her eyes prickled. The house smelled as the house in Yarmouth had smelled before the sourness of illness, neglect and death had pervaded it. Meg was close by and Joan bent to whisper to her, 'Smells like home.' Meg nodded, but unlike Joan, she didn't look weepy; she was calm and pleasurably excited to begin her new life. Joan on the other hand was desperately nervous. Her thin confidence was further eroded by feeling grubby and tired, and thinking of her father brought her close to tears.

Thomas spoke softly to William who nodded and disappeared. In the distance, she could hear him shouting and gradually the servants began to assemble in front of them in the large parlour. She felt curious eyes on her and looked at Thomas.

'Joan, be calm. I am going to introduce you to my household. If we delay, then gossip will start and you will get so nervous that you'll be unable to speak.' He gently grasped her elbow and turned her to the waiting faces. The room fell silent and she heard Thomas draw breath.

'Good morning! Thank you all for your prompt response to our early arrival. As you can doubtless smell, we are 'fresh' from Yarmouth.' There was a light ripple of laughter and Joan heard the word 'fish' several times. She forced her mouth into a slight smile. Thomas continued. 'Sadly, my friend, John Larke, has died and I have returned with his daughter Mistress Joan and her maidservant Margery.' There was utter silence.

'Now. You are my trusted and valued staff, so I shall be frank with you. Mistress Joan and I are married.' He raised his finger to quell their murmuring. 'Yes, it is somewhat irregular. But I am confident that you have all met married priests. We've never quite taken to celibacy in England, have we?' Faint laughter but every eye remained on Joan who had never felt so naked in her life. 'We shall live together with probity and discretion and Mistress Joan will help to run the house.' Thomas looked at a large man, red-faced and Joan thought, very hostile. 'Anthony?'

Anthony stepped forward and bowed to Thomas. William took a step closer to Joan as if to lend her his support. Then Anthony bent his knee to Joan and outstretched his hands to her. Cupped in them were the keys to the house. 'Mistress. It is my great pleasure to relinquish the keys to you.'

Joan acted as if in a play. She stepped forward and laid her hand on Anthony's shoulder and spoke as clearly and loudly as she could. 'Master Anthony. Those keys look very heavy. I wonder if I could prevail on you to help me carry them?'

Anthony straightened and looked at Joan. *Poor child,* he thought, *what has happened here? What a difficult path she faces.* 'Mistress, it will be my honour. It will be the household's honour.' Joan felt warm relief wash over her and beamed at the man.

A brief nodded communication passed between Thomas and William. Thomas offered Joan his arm and they left the parlour, passing into his study and up a narrow staircase to the upper chambers. William closed the door behind them and they could hear him speaking loudly and firmly. Thomas laughed. 'He'll be threatening them with dismissal if there's any gossip.'

Joan looked sceptical 'Will that work?'

'Well, I wouldn't be surprised. William can be very persuasive. And to be honest, I have found that one can buy loyalty almost as readily as one can earn it.'

He went ahead of Joan and opened the door to a bed chamber.

'This is not a situation I've ever had to consider. But I think this can be your chamber.' She nodded.

'And here…' stepping to the next door, 'is mine.'

He held open the door for her and she stepped inside and he closed it. 'We don't have long; the servants will be bringing hot water.'

For the first time, Thomas seemed uncertain and he spoke hurriedly. 'I think you won Anthony's heart. You spoke very well…' his voice faded and Joan gave a small close-lipped smile, her eyes bright. She reached past Thomas and locked the door. She held out her hands and Thomas placed his in them. Then they drew together, slipping their arms around each other and for a moment she rested her head against the front of his shoulder before tipping her head back and meeting his lips. They kissed long and deeply until a knock on the door jerked them apart.

'Will you lay with me tonight?' Thomas's voice was very soft and Joan found her heart beating rather fast, leaving her slightly breathless. She nodded.

'But only after I've had a bath.'

'Me too.'

'Good.'

They both snorted with laughter and Joan unlocked the door to a blank-faced James.

Joan gave a vague curtsey to Thomas and returned to her new room. She entered and closed the door behind her. She was completely at a loss for what to do next, so she sat on the stool by the window and listened to the quiet murmur of James against the slightly louder Thomas. She could hear the humour in Thomas's voice and fancied the disapproval in James and she tried for a time to hear the conversation before losing interest; then, when they fell silent, she guessed that James was shaving Thomas. After a while, she could just detect Thomas's fresh scent once more. She was so weary that she began to doze and jumped when Thomas tapped on and then opened the chamber door. She got to her feet and swayed slightly. Thomas steadied her.

'Dear girl, you're tired. Don't do too much today. Rest and get used to your home. They will all look after you. You need not fear – not with William and Margery on your side!'

Joan nodded, but Thomas could recognise being brave when he saw it. 'But my love, I promise you that in one week's time, you will be comfortable and at ease here. Hmm? Less than that!'

He peered into her over-wide eyes and won a smile from her. He gave her a quick hug then turned and left the room. William was outside and he caught the door before Thomas could close it, sticking his head in and giving Joan a quick wink. She grinned back and waved them away. But her face relaxed and she listened as the two men made their way downstairs. She heard them leave and followed the sound of hooves till she could only imagine it.

She longed for Meg who seemed to have remembered to pack courage for her new life. Well, she could go and find her. She was now the mistress here. She had a perfect right to move about her home. She opened the door, stepping quickly outside onto the landing then just as quickly she shot backwards, and was about to close the door when she saw a maidservant with a brush and pan peering at her from hands and knees on the stairs.

'Ah, excellent.'

The girl stood up and bobbed at Joan. 'Mornin' Mistress. Can I get summing for yer?'

Joan struggled slightly with the unfamiliar accent, then smiled, 'Oh yes, please, I was wondering where my maid is. Could you find her for me? And tell her to attend me.' The girl's lips moved silently as Joan spoke, clearly having her own concerns over Joan's Yarmouth lilt.

'Yes…' she said slowly, 'You wants yer girl?'

Joan nodded and closed her chamber door. She laughed quietly to herself; life in London would be a challenge in ways she hadn't even considered.

It wasn't too long before Meg arrived. Joan could hear her laughter as she spoke to a couple of manservants before clattering up the stairs. Joan drew breath to speak to her before realising that Meg led a small chain of people carrying hot water an oval wooden bath and at the rear, were two men with Joan's small coffer.

The wooden tub was placed on coarse linen sheets and

the water poured in. Each servant curtseyed or bowed to Joan and nodded to Meg with a muttered 'Margery'.

When they were alone, Joan raised her eyebrows at Meg, 'Margery?'

Meg looked slightly defensive. 'Yes. I never liked Meg. And I really hated Little Meg. Now is the time to become Margery.' She softened slightly. 'Actually, Master Wolsey suggested it. He said it would give me more gravi…' She paused, searching for Thomas's word, but failed, 'Well I can't remember it right now, but can you get used to it?'

Joan looked at Meg's face, 'Oh Margery, yes. I certainly can. But only if you'll lend me some of your courage.'

Margery looked sympathetic. 'They're all right you know. They're as puzzled by us as we are by them, and they talk funny. But that girl that come and got me, she seems nice. This'll be a good time for us. Your husband is kind and that counts for a lot. My father wasn't; he frightened me all the time. And your uncle wasn't kind, was he?' She paused, unused to such long speeches then took her mistress's hands. She made as if to speak but then just closed her lips, smiled and nodded. Joan did the same and the two girls stood united and for a moment, Joan felt very brave.

A thought occurred to Joan, 'How did Master Thomas know your name is Margery? I didn't.'

'He asked me. The first time I met him.' Margery turned away from Joan and started to arrange towels and as much fresh clothing as she could find in Joan's coffer.

Joan stared at her back. She felt horrible. Margery turned and looked questioningly at Joan.

'I should have asked. I treated you dreadfully and didn't even ask your name.'

'Come off it! You didn't treat me badly. Nobody treated me badly in your father's house. It was like coming to heaven. I was warm and well fed and Mistress Bray was a good teacher. And,' bravely outspoken now, 'if you feel bad, take it as advice. Always worth getting to know a servant.' Joan nodded. Margery was right, even if it was startling to be spoken to like that.

After her bath, Joan felt considerably more fit to face the world, despite her ragged clothes. Her linen was worn and torn at the seams where she'd grown out of it. If she hadn't lost weight, she would never have been able to fit into her kirtle which was stretched tightly across her shoulders, biting into her armpits, and her gown was old and patched and far too short. It was a great relief when a tailor and his assistant arrived in the early afternoon.

With Margery there as both attendant and supervisor, Joan was measured. The tailor exhibited pieces of fabric – warm black broad-cloth for her kirtles and beautiful shades of tawny and russet fustian for her gowns – whilst the assistant cut and fitted the Kersey for Joan's new hose.

Then greatly daring, Joan spoke casually, 'And of course, clothes for Margery.' Her tone left no room for doubt and the tailor knew Master Wolsey to be a generous man, so Margery too was measured. It was a glorious afternoon, spent choosing the furs and black lambskin for lining and edging gowns and nightgowns and even, with a slightly sickening sense of extravagance, a white rabbit fur night bonnet. Then from the silk-woman, Joan chose the most transparent linens to make the paste-kerchiefs for wearing over her bonnets, and linen as fine as silk for her smocks. For a moment she could fancy John in the room, shaking his head at the worldly extravagance of fur and more than one pair of shoes and she took great delight in imagining showing him from the room and closing the door against his disapproving sniff. Then she ran her fingers through the silk ribbons and forgot all about him.

Making his way to Richmond Palace through the dismal morning, Thomas lost himself in staring at the choppy waves of the river. After the brief sunrise, the day had settled into greyness, but he barely noticed it. William chuckled to himself. As far as he was aware, his master was yet a virgin and on nights when they had travelled together and shared a room or cabin, he'd never heard any private pleasures being enjoyed. For all he knew, Thomas was a eunuch. He studied Wolsey's face. He was a handsome man for sure and his gentle and witty good humour delighted both men and women. The ladies of court especially loved him for his well-built good looks and his slight air of worldliness which made them think that as an advisor and guide, he would understand their slips and weaknesses and judge them kindly.

Indeed, William felt the same about him and there was nothing he wouldn't tell Thomas if he was in trouble. He and Joan would make a handsome couple. Or they would once the effects of months under her uncle's spartan rule had been softened. She was from a prosperous home and should not look as if she were a peasant emerging from a deadly harsh winter. His master preached that God was love, compassion and forgiveness. Yet, he'd also seen John Larke as a wise and steady man of God, respected by his parishioners and peers. Well, he thought, every family has a knot in otherwise smooth grain; after all, didn't he and his brother avoid each other whenever possible? William yawned and scratched his scalp under his cap. With any luck, Wolsey would be keen to get home and they could all have an early night. He looked around with a salacious grin on his face before realising there was no one with whom he could share this and instead amused himself with a few thoughts about Joan.

At Richmond, Wolsey started on his trek though the palace. The damp weather seemed to have seeped into the walls once more and the sea-coal fires made the air humid and unpleasant. No sign of young George today but in the gardens, he could see a small archery party headed towards the butts. A shout drew his attention and he realised it was Prince Henry. The boy would be eighteen in a few months but for now still had the air of a leggy puppy, all energy and sudden exhaustion.

Henry trotted over, his bow in his hand. 'Wolsey! How nice to see you. Just back from Yarmouth, eh?'

Thomas bowed to the Prince, baring his head and exposing his tonsure. Henry laughed, 'Freshly shaved, I see. My grandmother will be pleased, she likes to see piety. And did you know that she has moved her household here to Richmond? I suppose she feels Coldharbour to be too far from my father, now that he is unwell…'

Thomas straightened and replaced his cap and before he could speak, Henry spoke again, 'Ah, though. Thomas! What is this we hear of a little remembrance brought back from the mysterious east of our country?'

Thomas felt there was little point in dissembling, but by Christ, gossip must be the fastest-traveling thing in the world. He met Henry's eyes, a slight blush on his cheeks and a rueful expression on his face.

'Your Highness, yes. I must confess.' Henry looped his arm through his bow-string and laughed and clapped his hands. Then he turned slightly and waved away his attendants.

'Away now, the Dean of Lincoln wishes to confess and seek my advice.' The courtiers reluctantly moved a few feet away and looked as if they weren't listening. 'Go on! Further!' Resentfully, the handsome young men shuffled off.

Henry waited, giving Thomas a questioning look.

'Your Highness, I cannot deny it. Joan is the daughter of my old friend and advisor, Peter Larke, who has now died. Her uncle wished her to join a nunnery. But she is ill-suited to such and I feared for her strength and her very life. We have hand-fasted and I intend to live a quiet and discreet life with her. And I am prepared to pay the fines.'

'Is she pretty?' Henry looked eager. 'I mean, is she as pretty as the Princess Katherine? No, she can't be. She's not of royal blood, so she can't have the bearing and beauty of Katherine. Oh Thomas, when we are married, our children will be so handsome.'

He stopped for a moment, 'But I am glad for you

Wolsey. Keep her at home. Don't let her paint her face, there's nothing as terrible as a woman who paints her face. What did you say she was like? Has she deep velvet eyes like Katherine? Have you seen her hair? Soft honey with hints of red... but tell me about your Joan.'

Thomas considered; he certainly didn't want Henry and half the court arriving at his house to view the infamous Mistress Larke. 'Well, she's about so tall... her hair is brown and her eyes are blue. She's very thin.'

'Oh no,' Henry interrupted, 'you don't want a thin woman. I always prefer mine with a little padding. More welcoming. Are thin women your general taste, Wolsey?'

Poor Thomas looked slightly flustered. 'Well, no, your Highness. I am a celibate priest, I have never, um... you see Mistress Joan is under my protection. In a way I rescued her. I fear that...' recovering his confidence, 'I fear that I was influenced by the old tales of chivalry.'

Henry laughed, a great shout and his companions looked curiously at them. 'I understand that, Thomas. In a way, I rescued Katherine. I have saved her from having to return to Spain. All that beating, terrible sunshine. Pfff. Can you imagine? So much dust and dry brownness. But I shan't marry her until my father... well you know...'

Thomas gave a half nod, a faint acknowledgement of Henry's wish to have his father's deathbed come to an end, but not enough for anyone to accuse him of imagining the King's death.

'Well Thomas, I have dallied enough. I must go on with my archery before this wretched damp makes my bowstring too soggy and I can't hit the target. Ha! That's rather funny, isn't it? After what we've just been saying. You know? Wait too long, soggy string, miss the bull's-eye?'

'Very good, your Highness. But I wouldn't worry. True love will triumph and you will have your Princess and your beautiful children and you will be a byword for golden triumph. You will hit every bull's-eye.'

Henry beamed at Wolsey. 'And don't you worry either Wolsey. No one will hear of your arrangements from me.' The Prince of Wales gave the Dean of Lincoln a lewd wink, clapped him on his shoulder, man to man, then strode off towards his friends who clustered around him, their voices low.

Thomas turned away and he suddenly caught the words, 'bull's-eye' and heard an explosion of laughter. He rolled his eyes and grinned. The boy was so young. He was untrained in the art of kingship yet soon enough he would be the master and father of this country. Let him enjoy himself whilst he could. Thomas remembered many an argument between the King and his second son. The Prince of Wales simply didn't appreciate what his father had achieved. He looked blankly bored when his grandmother and father told him of the days before 1485. Yet he had a passion for the mythical tales of chivalry and could quote vast chunks of the stories. He'd even heard that Henry was something of a composer of pretty tunes and could set poems to music. He really would be a wonderful King.

Thomas ate dinner at Richmond with Sir George Talbot, the Lord Steward of the Household. They discussed court business; the little cogs which kept revenue coming into the King's coffers; the grants of land or import licences, and the bonds for assuring peace and loyalty to the crown. Under the control of Edmund Dudley, these crippling bonds broke family finances and ensured that disaffected nobility could not afford to call on some distant royal claim and try to win support for a chance at the throne. The common people thought that the King inherited, or won a battle and that was that, but in truth, loyalty was bought or enforced and provided employment and income for many. Thomas found the discussion of business a welcome respite from the last few dream-like days. He listened to Talbot and could almost pretend that life had returned to normal.

His later passage through the palace reinforced that feeling and he was delighted to find George bouncing out of a chamber to escort him. 'Not dodging duties, I hope, George?'

'My Lord. How could you think that?' George looked reproachful and Thomas raised his eyebrows. 'Well, not really. Just a spot of rest after dinner. My Lord, really you should rest too. It is unhealthy to strain oneself after a meal. Especially as one grows older.'

Thomas reached out and lightly cuffed George, knocking his cap from his head. 'George, I thank you for your sage advice. I hope I can rely on you to keep your strength, for I might need your assistance before too long when I am aged and infirm. Shall we say next Wednesday?'

George flourished an extravagant bow, all fluttering cap and hair almost touching the ground. Thomas laughed and flipped a coin towards him. 'My boy, if you are training to be a Fool, you are progressing most pleasingly. I may yet have a place for you. Now if you are at my disposal, I am on my way to see Her Grace, the King's Mother and would have your company…'

George looked appalled and cocked his head, hand behind his ear, 'My Lord, I think I hear my name being called…'

Thomas swallowed a smile. 'I do not hear it, George. But that is doubtless my advanced age.' He jerked his head down the corridor and George took the hint and headed off to another dark chamber to finish his after-dinner nap.

Outside the chapel anti-chamber, he paused. The smell of incense was heavy. If Margaret had her way, Henry would fly heavenward on a soft, perfumed cloud of prayers. He knocked softly at the door and heard the King's mother's voice in reply. He touched his cross and went in.

'Excellent. I have need of you.' Margaret Beaufort flicked her fingers at him and he joined her, kneeling at the prie-dieu. He noticed how the gold in the padded fabric was quite worn away where her arms had rested as she prayed or traced the words in her breviary. He stole a glance at the two women, standing behind her. They were upright yet giving the impression of a slight droop towards each other. Their faces were white with fatigue and one raised an eyebrow at him as she rolled her eyes. Few women had the stamina of Margaret, yet she expected so much from them. He wondered how much they hated her and he'd wager they felt their positions at court were hard-earned.

He and Margaret prayed together for approaching an hour, then conversed about the King's health. Thomas, in common with most people, felt judged and wanting when spending time with the King's Mother, yet she also spoke with a degree of frankness to him. Her place at court was assured, but she had never felt at home there. She almost hinted that when Henry died, she would consider leaving and joining a nunnery. The Prince of Wales held no common ground with her, Thomas knew the boy avoided his austere grandmother and his court would doubtless be a merry one with little place for an old woman who wore grief and judgement as her daily garments.

But with a tiny lurch of foreknowledge, Thomas had caught her profile before she turned to speak to him. It was gaunt and hollow; the face of a woman with little time remaining. She had outlived her daughter-in-law, the enigmatic and pragmatic Elizabeth of York; the one successful survivor of the Yorkist dynasty. He'd seen Margaret's grief when Arthur died and this time, she could well surrender to the unbearable sorrow of losing her only child.

When Thomas left the chamber, two more ladies-in-waiting were approaching, ready to relieve their companions. They curtsied to Thomas and he bowed in return. He had performed the Mass for Margaret and felt calm and filled with faith. He smiled peacefully at the women as they rose from his murmured blessing and one of them caught his eye and winked at him. He felt a surge of something in the base of his stomach; a mixture of dread and excitement and struggled to keep it from his face. The other woman elbowed her and they passed on and into the chapel.

He drew a deep breath. Today's news would become old news. Prince Henry was right, keep her at home, live with discretion. He was grateful that at least Margaret would be very unlikely to hear the gossip. She had been known to dismiss people for the mildest of chatter and no one would risk their place when they were so close to change.

Chapter 8

London

William was correct; Thomas headed home as soon as he was free. The King's bed chamber had been filled with his gentlemen, his advisors and the other chaplains. The King had noted Wolsey's arrival and looked sardonically at him, but had no especial conversation for him. Thomas was not surprised to see that the King had rallied. He had attended enough deathbeds to understand that before the end, the patient so often seemed to regain a little strength. It was, he felt, a blessing which allowed the family a final glimpse of the loved one as they used to be. The King's eyes were bright, but mainly with fever and his voice lacked strength and he coughed frequently. There was discussion and argument over the King's Will. There were documents strewn across his bed, the neat secretary-hand in parts almost obliterated with underlining and crossings through. He lingered for a couple of hours until the King's physicians shooed the others from the room. As he looked back, the King sagged against his pillows and one of the doctors held a small cup to his lips.

Thomas passed quickly through the palace; few needed to speak to him today, and he was grateful. They were with the tide and almost before he knew it, he was stepping onto the wet stairs. William and the escort surrounded him and they set off through the streets, picking their way through the end-of-day leavings.

As they passed St Brides, Thomas tried to suppress the sin of envy at the beautiful house of Sir Richard Empson. Behind it, he knew lay many beautiful gardens. On his one visit, it had reminded him of a gold-touched illumination in a prayer book and he had half-expected to see the brilliant blue of the Virgin's gown as she sat sewing in the shade of a fruiting tree. *Hmmm*, he thought, *not only envy but covetousness*.

Inside his own house, he took comfort. *I have more than is sufficient. I have a warm home with fine wall hangings, fireplaces and enough wood to keep the cold at bay.* A servant took his gown and helped him exchange his boots for soft house shoes which had been held before the fire for a few moments.

His parlour door opened and Joan stood there. She beamed at him and dropped a curtsey. 'Husband. I am pleased to see you.'

'And I to see you, Mistress Joan.' His heart fluttered he spoke to her; his wife.

She drew him into the room. 'Come, warm yourself and we shall take supper.' Thomas placed his hand in her outstretched one and William closed the door behind him before turning to face the servants who still lingered in the screens passage.

'Right! Does the Dean of Lincoln pay you to stand around with your eyes wide and your mouths gaping? No.

I don't think he does.' He clapped his hands and the servants scattered.

Joan enjoyed her first evening as Thomas's wife. She didn't count the hours spent travelling when she'd hardly seen him. Despite the thrill of shopping, her day was long. After the departure of the tailor, cordwainer, silk-woman and their assistants, she'd made a start of learning some of the names of the household. Margery had more than proven her value; one might think that she'd been studying for weeks, such was her grasp of the structure. At least, Joan hoped it was a true grasp. Doubtless, there were many mistakes ahead for them both but they were safely through the first day.

Thomas's feelings were not so much of relief than of apprehension. When they retired to bed, he almost struggled to climb the stairs. His heart was beating so fast that he could barely draw enough breath to keep moving. And now he sat motionless in the window, his hands clasped in his lap.

Joan lay quietly. She had said her prayers and now waited patiently for Thomas to complete his and join her. After a long time, she sat up and parted the curtains at the foot of the bed. She could see him both slightly illuminated by the single candle and outlined by the moonlight shining through the window.

'Thomas?'

He stirred, 'Yes, Joan?'

'Are you praying? Are you asking God if it's… if we're…?'

'Oh Joan, no. We're far beyond that. No…'

His voice faded and she waited for a few moments.

'Thomas…?'

'Mm?'

'If you don't know what to do, it's all right. Because I do.' She heard his gulp of laughter.

'Oh, you do?'

'Well. In a way. I have seen animals doing that. But I'm not entirely sure which way round we'd need to be.' She could hear from his breathing that he was smiling.

'No. It's not that.' He paused for a long moment. 'I was trying to dedicate this to the Glory of God. To sanctify it.'

She nodded and then lay back for a moment. Thanks to John, she certainly understood the need to involve God in all things. Then she sat up again, wriggled her night-rail from under her and pulled it over her head. She opened the bed curtains beside her and flung it across the room at the lighted candle.

'Joan! What on earth are you doing?'

'I'm snuffing the candle without getting out of bed.' She spoke as if it was the most obvious thing in the world.

'Well don't. That looks an exceedingly dangerous thing to do.'

Joan huffed and he heard a muttered, 'Never set it alight yet.'

'Well, every night you're shortening your odds, aren't you?'

Silence returned and Thomas continued to sit by the window, so after a moment Joan scrambled out of bed and went to stand by him. She was quite naked and Thomas finally looked at her. She was thin but still womanly and he felt blood whipping round his body. He stood up and took her shivering body in his arms. 'Oh Joan, you'll freeze.' His voice was slightly uneven.

'There's something else, Thomas.'

'Yes?'

'Well, I was wondering.' She spoke into his shoulder and his clothes muffled her voice, so he drew away from her and looked at her face.

'Mm?'

'You've known me since the day I was born. Now this is our wedding night. Do you still see me as a child?'

She felt his body heaving and looked anxiously into his face to see that he was rocking with silent laughter.

'Well. I have to say that I wasn't thinking about that at all, but now you've mentioned it, there's nothing else I can think of. You did have the most appalling clout cloths. There was never a smell like it.' His laughter erupted and Joan looked quite annoyed. She tried to pull away, now suddenly conscious of her bare and very chilly body, but Thomas pulled her back.

He placed his finger over her lips. 'Please stop talking, my love. Or I shall never manage to bed you for laughing.'

He peered into her face and finally, she grinned. 'Well, I was curious.' She lifted her thumb to her mouth and chewed on the nail. It made her look ridiculously young and Thomas felt a pang of love.

He spun her around and pushed her towards the bed. 'Enough. In.' Then he walked across to Joan's nightgown and picked it up, still marvelling at the thought of having the night clothes of a naked woman in his room. He placed it on a stool and after a moment added his own gown.

Joan stared unabashedly at the sight of Thomas's body. She whispered, '*Ooh*. You *are* beautiful. God has made you very nicely.'

Thomas was suddenly shy. But his feet were cold and he saw no reason why he shouldn't join his wife in his bed. He drew the curtains tight and climbed in.

'It's dark,' came Joan's whisper, 'come here so I can touch you.' The mounded feather mattress gradually sank and surrounded them in a warm grasp. Her hands were cold as she reached for him and he shivered. It wasn't yet spring, no time to be dallying without clothes.

Then they spoke no more. Thomas kissed her chilly lips into warmth and felt her breasts against his chest as she clasped her arms around him and pulled him close. It turned out that they did know what to do; she lay on her back and his weight on her was more extraordinary than she could have imagined. If they could only hold each other hard enough, she felt, they could come together, become one flesh, one person. She lost herself in this new awareness and when he finally slipped inside her, the pain was slight. She gave a tiny shuddering breath as though a piece of her had been nipped, and Thomas in turn felt something giving way inside her. But this sensation was lost in his pleasure; this glorious woman under him, around him, gripping him in ways he could never have imagined. He heard her breathing hasten and as she gave a queer lost cry, felt himself reach an absolutely unexpected peak of pleasure.

Their mouths were together in the deepest of kisses and neither could tell if it was their own heart or the other's which beat so hard. Finally, reluctantly, they parted – Thomas rolled onto his back and took her hand.

He felt his senses returning and swallowed. Now he understood what a miracle God had wrought when he brought man and woman together. Joan was quite silent. Even her breathing was imperceptible.

'Joan?' But she didn't reply. Her hand was motionless in his. Concerned now, he parted the curtains beside him and reached for the candle. As he held it close to her face, her eyes glittered as they turned towards him. She bit her lip, trying to speak, to express what she had experienced.

'I don't know what to say.' She paused, then gave him a sleepy smile. 'Can we do it again, please? It was extraordinary.'

Thomas gave a little huff of laughter. 'Yes it was, and yes we can. I understand now why people are so driven by this.' He replaced the candle on the table and drew the bed curtains against the chill creeping over their naked skin. He drew breath to speak again, but Joan's steady breaths told him that she slept, so he pulled the covers over them and slipped quickly into his own oblivion.

It wasn't a restful night; they woke several times to test again God's miracle and find that the experience only improved. Thomas had been true to his vows until that night but now he wondered. He puzzled over the reasons for celibacy when laying with one's wife was such an exquisite pleasure and he certainly wondered how he had reached the age of thirty-six without being in the least tempted by flesh, whether woman's, man's or even his own. At some point, it occurred to him to ask Joan if she was bleeding, but her breathing was deep and steady and there was nothing damp beneath them and he drifted back into sleep once more.

In the morning, Joan woke to the noises of an unfamiliar household. She grinned as she thought about the night before and tried to remember how many times they'd... but then realised that Thomas wasn't beside her. She could hear him moving around the chamber. She heard him use the pot and slide it back into the cupboard. Then she recognised the rustle of papers on his desk.

Joan closed her eyes again and slid her foot over to his side of the bed. She arched her leg and felt the difference in warmth. His side was so much hotter than hers. Then a change in light made her open her eyes, and Thomas was standing at the end of the bed watching her through the curtains.

'Whatever are you doing?'

'Well, it feels different to when Pepper used to sleep on the bed.'

'Right. Well, I should hope it does.'

'Warmer.' Then she grinned at him. 'In fact, altogether much nicer. *In fact*, you should come back. It can't be very warm out there.'

She looked sideways at him and he laughed.

'No, you're right, it's freezing.' And he leaned forward and pulled the bedclothes from her and she squeaked and wriggled away from his cold hands as he reached for her and began to tickle her.

Thomas came round to the side of the bed and grabbed Joan who was trying to get away, gasping with giggles and protesting about the cold. He flipped her over and bent to blow a raspberry on her bottom. She pummelled her fists, and laughing he let go of her. He straightened up and looked at Joan laying across the mattress. She looked so abandoned, so beautiful that he could hardly bear the feelings which surged inside him. *It is possible*, he thought to himself, *that this is the happiest moment of my life.*

Then she looked at him standing over her, his gown open and she raised an eyebrow. 'I really *do* think you had better come back to bed.' And he did.

Chapter 9

London, Monday 10th May – The Funeral of Henry VII

It was approaching dusk and Joan and most of her household joined the hundreds lining the road to London Bridge. Joan regretted they weren't closer to the foot of the bridge, but through the ranks of the members of the liveried companies she could see glimpses of the river and to the south a glow from the hundreds of torches which accompanied the King's funeral carriage. Thomas was in the party which walked alongside the body and she wanted to strike up a conversation with someone and tell them that her husband was there, with the King. Beside her, Margery shivered with excitement. The poor old King had died three weeks ago and that of was of course awfully sad, but neither of them had known a more exciting time.

She stood on the dim and chilly riverside, clad in fur-lined clothes of great quality. Under her bonnet, her hair was growing nicely – as Thomas said, cutting it short was like pruning it and it would grow all the better for it – and not only her hair but her face and figure had benefitted from a good diet, warmth and above all, love. And now here she was waiting to see the King's funeral procession.

As the column grew closer, the members of the Companies lit their torches and the light was passed along the crowd. Children touched their tapers to the flame and above their excited cries, Joan could hear many languages and briefly even recognised the sound of her own countrymen's accents amongst the merchants. It reminded her of the Tower of Babel and she wryly thought that John would be pleased she'd drawn that comparison. Finally, the horses drawing the sombre carriage reached the waiting crowds and almost everyone fell silent. The bier was like a bed, the four posts draped in black cloth-of-gold which sparkled like yellow frost and the orb and sceptre in the King's hands reflected the light of the torches with a thousand flames and flashes. Joan was startled, but of course, it wasn't the King, only his effigy. Thomas had explained, but the figure was so expertly fashioned that it was almost alive. The King's own robes dressed the tall figure which lay above the King's coffin, which itself was shrouded in more of the gorgeous black cloth-of-gold. There were hundreds of torches which completely banished the last traces of daylight and seemed brighter than the memory of the sun. It was fantastic and Joan and Margery looked at each other in surprised awe.

'Y'see,' muttered Margery, 'you don't get this in Yarmouth. Better than anything we'll ever see again, I reckon.' Joan nodded; it was indeed. The nearest thing to this was thunder and lightning or those strange sprites you sometimes saw over the sea at night. But they were otherworldly and more than a little frightening. This was just impressive and really, rather fun.

After a brief pause, the singers took up their dirges again and Joan was thrilled to hear them. Thomas was a fine singer and she fancied she could hear his voice. Then just for a moment, they caught his profile outlined against a torch before he passed along and out of their line of sight. Margery and Joan turned excitedly to each other, 'Oh, *there* he is!'

The procession slowly climbed to the bridge and began to cross the river. Much earlier, before gathering with the rest of the household, Joan and Margery had walked over the bridge and noted the lanterns and torches ready to be lit and seen the dark cloths draped across the shop fronts. It was a solemn day but the city seemed so excited. Many of the inhabitants of London were too young to have seen, or at least remember the coronation of the old King and now they would have a funeral and soon the 'prince-called-king' would be crowned. Then there would be such merry-making. But today everyone wished to see the awe-full spectacle of the old King's funeral and be reminded of the pomp and treasure of the royal family. To be sure, foreigners would take tales of this home and make their own small kings jealous of wonderful England, and that could only be good for trade and prosperity.

William and James were with them and keeping an eye on all the women of the household, but most of all, on Mistress Wolsey who was gaping like a baby bird. They nodded at each other and closed in on Joan and Margery to keep them safe. It was a perfect time for cut-purses and grocunts; those who would molest their charges and spoil the day for them. Taking each of them by the elbow, they steered them towards the steps, through the gates and into the rear guard of the procession. They were impressive and well-dressed enough to deter any who protested and Joan found herself trailing over the bridge in the wake of the torchbearers. She saw a gap in the buildings and glanced through to the river. The dark water was a chilling contrast to the brightness all around her and she was very glad that she and Margery were safe between Thomas's most trusted men.

The remainder of the household would make their own way home, perhaps by way of an alehouse, but they were all Londoners and not tender girls fresh from the farthest part of the country. Both men saw Joan as green as a new-stripped stick and their honour depended on keeping her safe. In fact, thought William, she was as precious as the jewels sparkling on the funeral carriage. He daily delighted in seeing the happiness which clothed Thomas. Not least because a happy master made for a happy servant.

Ahead of them, the torches made a river of fire – the smoke was illuminated by the flames below before drifting into the gathering darkness and Joan could just about see that the head of the procession had already left the bridge as the rear climbed onto it. The trek across the bridge was long and slow and they were weary from hours of standing. The cortege would halt at St Paul's for the night then Joan could be safely delivered home but their Mistress was eager to see all the spectacle and it would be hours before their responsibilities were over.

Winding through the dusky streets, the torches headed

towards St Paul's, itself ablaze with many candles. Above the heads of those in the funeral procession, Joan and Margery could see that the great west doors were open. It seemed like a long tunnel of light, warm and welcoming and Joan began to think longingly of her own fireside, especially as her head was beginning to ache from the constant noise of the hundreds of solemn church bells throughout the city.

The cortege halted and as the horses were unhitched and led away, the crowds pressed in around the carriage and William tucked Joan's arm in his to keep her close. By luck, they were quite close to the King's body. For a moment, the surprisingly small coffin seemed abandoned as the mourners, the great officers of the household, the mayor and other nobles of the court filed into the cathedral. Then the prelates and the chaplains surrounded the bier and with the aid of the King's squires, lifted the casket from the seeming bed. Before entering the nave, they paused for a moment and the crowd fell silent and they could hear the singing of the dirge. Once again, Joan fancied she heard Thomas's fine voice and she caught a glimpse of his face, serious and beautiful in its stern austerity. Suddenly, irreverently, she could see his face as it looked when they lay together, and she was rather ashamed of herself. As the group carried the king's corpse into the church, Joan pulled her thoughts together and said a prayer for Henry's soul.

'Do you want to go in?' Joan looked up at William as he murmured to her.

'To be honest, I'd like to go home to supper, but it

would be a shame to miss anything.'

William smiled, 'It would. Now keep hold of me. Let somebody cut your hand off before you let go.' Joan giggled.

'Truly, Mistress. For my sake if not yours. My Lord would never forgive me if I let something happen to his dearest jewel.' Wide-eyed and rather impressed by his face, Joan nodded and let him lead her into the cathedral. As they moved forward, Joan reached out her other hand and grabbed Margery's to keep her close too.

The space was filled with a mixture of singing and bells and the quiet chatter of hundreds of people. Through the haze of candles and incense, Joan could see the King's body, placed in another hearse and positioned in the choir before the great altar, with his effigy placed below on the chancel steps.

Keeping next to the wall as long as he could, William worked a route through the crowds until he found them a place some halfway along the nave with their backs against a column and they watched as order formed out of the seemingly chaotic milling crowds. After a long day of being elbowed aside by more important courtiers, the chaplains were finally able to assert their places beside the bishops as the Mass began. It was a lengthy service and difficult to hear through the continuing peals of the city churches; only her familiarity with the service allowed Joan to keep pace with it. The censors swung their sweet smoke through the air and she grew sleepy, barely hearing any of the Bishop of Rochester's sermon. She jumped as Margery poked her in the side with a sharp finger.

'Your knees were sagging,' she hissed. Joan nodded a 'thank you' and drew a couple of deep breaths to wake up.

After a while, William started to move and Joan looked at what he was doing. With his knife, he was carving the pillar against which they stood. As she watched, he made four shallow V marks, each couple joined together and forming a W. 'William Wren', he muttered. Then beneath them added two more V marks, upside down, then another W. 'For Mistress Wolsey.'

Joan was thrilled. And once the marks were made William stroked his knife up and down, deepening them. 'Then when you come in here again, you will remember standing here with me during the King's funeral.' Then seeing Margery's soulful look at him, he rolled his eyes comically and added another M.

'I don't have a last name that I know.' Margery said, 'Least not yet...' Joan kicked her.

'Don't flirt in church. It is not seemly.' Margery stuck out her tongue at Joan and both girls started to giggle, stopping only when a matronly woman tutted at them.

The service seemed interminable as each grand person tried to impress his peers with his level of grief and devotion. Joan grinned to herself as she thought that and looked at the effigy as it lay impassively, staring at the hazy roof. Eventually, the crowds seemed to thin and Joan's little party noticed the courtiers slipping away. She looked questioningly at William, 'Where are they all going?'

'I think they're all trying to secure a bed or at least supper in the Bishop's Palace. Imagine that Mistress

Wolsey, supper and a warm fire...'

She arched an eyebrow at him. 'We'll go soon enough, William. But we've waited this long.'

Within just a few minutes, the cathedral was almost empty. The bishops bowed towards the King and processed out and the King's intimate servants, the squires, groomsmen and chaplains were all who remained. Joan could see Thomas's tall figure as with his fellow clergy they assumed their positions for the vigil; the King would not be alone or bereft of prayer through his last nights above ground and she liked the thought of Thomas keeping watch over the King.

'Mistress?' William looked at her and jerked his head towards the west doors.

'Yes.' She said softly, taking his arm and forcing her cold, stiff feet to move. Her servants followed her; Margery, pacing alongside James, and several of the young maids who lacked the confidence to roam tonight in the altogether too exciting city.

The day before Joan had summoned her household and given them a degree of holiday for the King's funeral; as long as there was food for them all and if Master Anthony was content – here he gave a grave assenting nod – they were free to watch the processions and stay out late.

'However,' Joan had concluded with a stern look, 'if you abuse this and bring trouble to Master Wolsey's house, nobody at all in the whole household will join in the coronation celebrations.'

As they left the cathedral, Joan looked back. The majority of the church was now in darkness, but the chancel and sanctuary glowed with golden candlelight like a religious painting and she couldn't help but reflect with awe that Thomas was at the heart of it.

When they reached home, William hurried through the house to see which servants were there. He ordered wine, meat and bread to be taken to the parlour and joined Joan there to report to her. He smiled as he opened the door – she had taken well to the role of wife and mistress of the house and he always felt a little pride when she saw her speak with gentle authority to the servants. Dame Alice had taught her well.

Dame Alice, he pondered. Unfinished business there perhaps. If Thomas had not brought Joan to London, he may well have proposed marriage to Alice. But now it would make an awkward situation for them – for she would not be content or quiet to see her charge happily established as the whore of a priest.

As yet, Joan was fortunate that her quiet presence had not attracted any adverse attention from their neighbours. It could easily become unpleasant and that would damage his master's reputation and career. William was under no misapprehension – Alice would only bring trouble with her. Thomas had assured him that Alice was safe and provided for and Thomas was always truthful and considerate to servants, so William must trust him and forget about the housekeeper with her easy laugh and neat figure.

Joan looked at William as he paused in the doorway. 'All good, William?'

He nodded, 'Yes Mistress. There are some servants

still here and you have Margery.' He nodded at the girl as she knelt to light the fire and she turned and smiled warmly at him. *Well*, he thought, *now that's a surprise.*

Despite the long and exciting day, Joan slept restlessly; all night, bells sent their peals through her dreams. She missed Thomas's comforting presence beside her; he'd been away from his bed for several weeks now, in fact since the King's last days. And having glimpsed his dear face today brought her vivid dreams of longing. Time after time, she woke and felt for his absent hand before sighing and dropping back into another endless dream of searching for him.

The tapping on the door of a servant bringing bread and ale to break her fast was a welcome sound and she answered, her voice cracking with fatigue. But Joan was only twenty and quickly revived with food and drink and was ready when Margery appeared to help her dress.

Deciding not to attend any of the Masses which would be said this morning over the King's corpse, Joan busied herself around the house. The floors looked dusty and the wood seemed unpolished and Joan was ashamed how much she had let things slide in Thomas's absence. Margery nodded when Joan ran her finger along the edges of the stair treads.

'I think you've become too fond of being a gentle mistress to them. They won't love you when Anthony tells them off for a dirty house.'

Joan nodded and sighed. 'It's hard, isn't it? I want their love and loyalty, not their resentment for being harsh.'

Margery chuckled, 'Mistress, you couldn't understand how to be harsh. But you must be firm. Summon the household and instruct them. And be sure to include me; I don't want to be your pet. They'll hate me for that.'

Within a few minutes, the servants were before Joan and without even a consultation with Anthony, she spoke to them. 'Good morning.' There were some muffled responses but far too many of the household looked fragile and exhausted. Joan smiled with a brightness she did not feel.

'I hope that Master Wolsey will return in a few days. He might even come home today if he can be free of his duties. I wish him to come back to a shining and clean house. I know we are all tired from the excitement of the funeral but we must let my lord see that this is an orderly household. At one o'clock the procession will pass along Fleet Street and I wish you all to join me and watch the old King pass to his rest. But there is much to be done before then. Master Anthony, will you direct us all to our tasks please? You know better than I do what has been left undone of late. Margery will join me in sweeping and polishing where ever you see fit.'

Margery nodded and curtseyed to her mistress and Anthony thanked Joan. He'd been happy to let things ride for a while – it was not yet the dustiest time of year and the house would quickly return to its usual bright order – but he was pleased to see his mistress assume her responsibilities once more. He'd grown fond of the girl and was loathe to see her fail, not least because it reflected on him. His large red face nodded brisky at Joan and he started to send the staff about their duties.

At twelve, the household took their rather late dinner in a house which felt renewed and fresh. The smell of clean rushes and beeswax worked wonders and Joan was beginning to wonder about following the procession to Westminster. Once at the abbey, the King would lie-in-state for one more night before being buried at dawn alongside his queen. This would be the last chance for her to see the great spectacle. Running upstairs, she quickly donned a smarter gown and was ready by a window overlooking the street.

The servants made room for her and she could feel the two young girls beside her jumping with anticipation. She looked fondly at them. *Had she ever*, she wondered, *been so young and excitable?* The bells were ringing and in the distance she could once again hear the solemn singing.

She looked down into the street and saw the lines of people waiting for the spectacle to pass. It was interesting she thought, how cheerful they all looked. It really was a holiday for them. Thomas said that people were very sad when Elizabeth died. But then he'd given a mirthless laugh and explained that people could be very sentimental. They'd all been glad when Henry won at Bosworth and brought stability and a royal nursery full of heirs and candidates for profitable marriages. Yet some part of them had yearned for the days of romantic battles and close-run escapes and all the tales which accompanied the late wars.

Joan had frowned and said that surely only people who hadn't smelled blood in battle and seen their friends die would think like that. And now she remembered how proud Thomas had looked when she said that, as though he felt lucky to have such a wise wife. *Exactly*, he'd said with great satisfaction, *well done*.

Joan found a wistful smile on her face. She closed her eyes for a moment, and with something made of both prayer and wishes, said to herself, *Thomas love. Come home soon.*

The cortege made its mournful way along Fleet Street and towards Westminster Abbey and as the tail passed the house, Joan and William joined the procession. This time Joan failed to see Thomas, but ignoring the hundreds of people between them, chose to feel that she was walking right behind him. She was growing bored keeping house without his occasional presence. She was in love and wished to see the object of her love, wanted to show him that she was a good housekeeper and worthy of him. But every small domestic triumph was lost to the unforgiving air and with a wry smile, she'd imagine saving them all up to tell him in one tremendous wave of information.

As usual, when she was a little dissatisfied, Joan would poke a finger under her bonnet, feel the prickles of her short hair, and think that if not for Thomas, by now she'd be confined in a holy house with dozens of nuns who wouldn't care for her or her feelings. That she might have found happiness and fulfilment never occurred to her. She had narrowly escaped imprisonment thanks to the grace of Thomas and just a little bit thanks to God.

After a long slow walk – on a normal day Joan thought impatiently, she could have reached Westminster in a very few minutes – the procession halted, and skirting round the edges, William found them a reasonable view. The hearse was drawn up in front of the west doors and as at St Paul's the day before, the King's charger waited, his hooves stamping impatiently as though he could do with a good leg-stretching gallop. The waiting bishops looked very grand to Joan, and she whispered to William, 'Don't they look like the best-dressed mummers you've ever seen?' earning Joan a wink and a silent laugh. Then the thuribles swung incense over the corpse and it was received into the church. The King's effigy followed the body into the gloom. Later, the dusk would make the interior seem bright, but for now, the sunshine made the abbey a dark glittering jewel, rather like the black cloth of gold, all velvety shade picked out with golden sparks.

Trailing in with the crowds, Joan and William listened to the service but it was hard to hear through the chatter of the people milling around and after the third lesson was read and not heard, Joan nodded her head to William and they left. Looking back once more, Joan tried to paint the picture in her memory.

As they walked home, Joan looked at William, 'He's not coming home tonight, is he?'

'No Mistress, I don't think so. There'll be another vigil and he will wish to be there, both for the old King's sake and so that he is seen to be there.'

She nodded and walked for a moment in silence.

'William?'

'Yes?'

'Can I ask you… What do you think of our marriage?

Do you think it is really a marriage, or do you see me as a whore?' Her chin wobbled slightly as she spoke the harsh word but she resisted the urge to cry.

William was shocked. 'Mistress, please. Don't say things like that. That's not fair to you or Master Thomas. Yes... your position is *slightly* debatable, but you are a decent modest girl. The master didn't pick up some woman for convenience. He married *you*. I used to think that Master Wolsey was without interest in love or flesh. He loves you deeply and you are both so happy. Mistress? Why do you ask? Has someone said something?'

Joan shook her head but continued to look miserable. After a few more paces she seemed to have formed her reply and spoke again. 'It's not a marriage such as I might have had. Thomas will undoubtedly rise in the church and at court. Of course, he will. This time of uncertainty will pass and a man of his great skills will always be needed. I think... well, I fear being left behind.'

William looked at the girl walking beside him and he felt very sorry for her, poor little soul. He'd seen samples of the young men in Yarmouth, all fishy and pimply. No wonder she was in thrall to Thomas Wolsey. The man was all glamour and a powerful presence and Joan had known Thomas all her life. Any man would be found wanting beside Wolsey. Greatly daring, he spoke these thoughts to his mistress and she giggled and nodded.

'But, Mistress Wolsey, I can promise you, he will always look after you. I have known and worked for him for many years and there is not a kinder or more conscientious man. If one day there is no longer a place for you…' here he looked anxiously at her; he really hadn't intended to be quite so frank, '…then he will ensure that you are safe and provided for. I think in your heart you know that. I mean, you know that your path might not always run beside his.'

'No,' she said softly, 'I see how that might be the case. Especially,' she said bravely, 'when he is the pope.' She gave him a brilliant smile and tucked her arm in his. William gave her hand a little squeeze. It was all the comfort he could offer.

Joan was asleep in bed when she heard someone moving around the room. Whoever it was tripped over something and gave an exasperated sigh. 'Thomas?' she whispered.

'Yes, of course it's me. Go back to sleep. And what have I just tripped over?'

'Oh, that'll be my night-rail. And yes, Thomas, I'll just go back to sleep.' He could hear the laughter in her voice and he chuckled as she slumped back onto the pillows with a loud snore.

'But seriously, Thomas, as if I could. You've been away forever and I've longed for you. I've missed you.'

He could hear scrambling noises and spoke, 'No, no. Stay where you are. James will be here in a moment with water. I must wash.' She heard him light the candle and a faint light could be seen through the bed curtains.

'Oh, don't worry about that, just come to bed!'

'Really Joan, I must be clean. I am so sickened by the smell of embalming spices and what they are meant to be masking. I have worn these clothes for days and I cannot bear my own stink.'

Joan did as she was told and soon heard James come in and heard their low voices chatting. The smell of soap reached her and she could hear the rasp of the razer. She was drowsing when at last the door closed behind James. And finally, Thomas opened the curtains and climbed in.

She shivered as his cold hands touched her. Then he sighed and fell back against the pillows.

'Tell me?'

After a moment he moved and leaned his head against her shoulder. Joan pulled the sheets around them and held him to her.

'It's been a long journey. His death was hard.'

Thomas spoke with long gaps as his tired brain sought for the words, 'You'll hear people say it was a peaceful and godly death. But he fought all the way as if the darkness held no paradise for him. The filth in his lungs was choking him and he fought death for every breath. I kept thinking that it was unbearable. How could I endure it? Then I would think, but the King is bearing it. I thought that again and again, endlessly. The gentlemen of the chamber all materialised. All those weeks he was alone, then they landed like carrion waiting for their prey to die.'

Thomas sounded bitter and angry, 'His mother appeared twice. Once when he was still alive. She stood staring at him until he opened his eyes and simply said '*Mother*'. She nodded and said that she would be praying for his immortal soul. He thanked her very politely and she left. Then she came again afterwards. They told her that the Prince was now the King but that they would keep it secret until the banquet on the Day of St George. She nodded and returned to her prayer.'

Thomas shook his head. 'She seemed as ever. Calm and cold and needing no comfort from mere servants. Her faith is exemplary; a fine example to more mortal souls but it does seem to lack compassion.'

Thomas laid his arm over Joan and pulled her towards him. 'I have missed you, my love. I have missed the warmth of you. The world is cold and ambitious.' He gave a mirthless laugh, 'Not that I am blameless. My very blood is ambition.'

They were silent for a while, and then he told her of the weeks of jostling at court as people struggled to secure their places in the new order. He remained a royal chaplain and of course, as Dean of Lincoln, he had hopes of more. The new King had spoken briefly of making him almoner.

There was silence between them then, Joan spoke. 'Tell me of the funeral? We saw parts of it. It was so imposing. I have never seen such pomp.' She smiled. 'I could hear all the foreign merchants talking. It was like the Tower of Babel and I am sure they were impressed. They certainly sounded awestruck.'

Thomas gave a grunt of approval. Then he continued. 'The King was placed in his tomb this morning. One is always reminded that all flesh is not really grass but in fact, just meat which rots like any other animal.'

In the darkness, Joan made a face but held her tongue, Thomas sounded upset and she had nothing of comfort to say.

'I looked into the tomb once it was opened. The

Queen is not yet in there but I fear someone much older was disturbed when they dug the vault, for the stench was terrible. It seemed indecent to lower the King into that darkness, but as they moved him, they released an appalling smell and I couldn't wait for it to be over. I think the lead inside the coffin must have cracked along a seam.' Thomas paused for a moment, sniffing the air as if to refresh himself before continuing.

'The officers of the household snapped their staves and dropped them on top of the King's coffin. As the pieces fell, they were almost soundless against the black velvet. I couldn't see but in my mind's eye, I saw the white rods laying like slashes across the white satin cross and the black of the mortcloth. Behind us, the heralds took off their coats and shouted: *The King is Dead*. And that shout drowned our groans at the smell. One of the other chaplains gripped my arm. He looked ill and I don't blame him. We stepped back; I didn't want him to faint.' Thomas raised his eyebrows and whispered, 'Or me.'

'Then I heard the rustling as the heralds put their coats back on and in French, they proclaimed Henry as king, and wished him a long life and it felt as if we were touched by sunlight. Joan, it feels good, and blessed by God that this Henry should follow his father. The country needs a steady dynasty. I want Henry to take his place in Europe.'

Joan listened with wide eyes as Thomas fed her nightmares with his description of the King's burial, but she was also impressed by his words; talking of the King as a familiar friend.

'The new King likes you, doesn't he?'

'I think he does, Joan. He knows about you and he doesn't mind. He is a good and generous man and I pray God to help me serve him.'

They lay for a while and Joan's arm under Thomas began to go numb, but he seemed comfortable and she didn't like to move him. She had so few things to offer her husband, but then she smiled to herself.

'Thomas?' she spoke softly.

'Mm?'

'Are you awake?'

'Partly…' she could hear a smile in his voice.

She giggled, 'Which part?'

'See if you can guess.'

Chapter 10

London

The next morning, Joan rose early with Thomas. He was likely to be away a great deal as the preparations were now underway for the King's wedding and coronation. Joan sighed but she could see the truth in his words; if he were to secure a place at court then he needed to be visible. And as she constantly reminded herself, it was better to be the mistress of her own household than be under the care of her uncle. But she missed Thomas when he wasn't there and her thumb would rub over the shank of his ring and she'd think of the words graven within; *Liebe nicht Angst*... James shaved Thomas while Joan sat on the bed and watched. Her eyes wandered and she noticed two pieces of ragged-edged fabric on Thomas's desk.

'Thomas, what are those bits of material for?' She knew they couldn't be pieces he was considering for clothing, that sparkly black and gold was not at all his choice.

'Ah yes. Those are for you.' Thomas smiled as much as he could through the soap and razor.

Joan jumped off the bed and picked them up. The blue piece was a thick felted piece of wool and the black one…

she paused.

'Oh! Black cloth-of-gold! She rippled it over her fingers, admiring the gold flashes. 'Goodness Thomas, am I to imagine you taking your knife and cutting souvenirs for me?'

Thomas laughed, 'No, I bought them from the man who did take them. The blue piece is from the carpet in the abbey. Not really a carpet but such a pretty blue.'

'*Thank you*. I shall make a bag from them and keep my treasures in it.'

'Will you indeed? Will it be large enough for all your treasure?'

Joan stuck her tongue out at Thomas and they both laughed and even James allowed a very slight bend of the lips.

'Perhaps I should buy my pretty wife some pretty jewels?'

Joan smiled at Thomas in what she hoped was a charming way but Thomas at first laughed then feigned concern. 'My dear, have you the wind? Are you in pain?'

Joan huffed at him and left the room. Behind her, she could hear the two men chuckling and she smiled.

It was true, for the next few weeks she saw Thomas but once; by the light of a candle when he flew into the house with William in tow. She hovered in the door of the parlour and watched her husband tear through piles of paper before seizing what he sought with a quiet and satisfied 'Ah.'

'What's that, Thomas?'

'*Mmm*? Just a paper I was after, something Foxe asked

me to look over.'

'A fox?

'Ha! A fox indeed! Very good.' Then Thomas was gone, whirling out of the room and leaving Joan somewhat confused and irritated. On the brink of following his master, William took pity on her.

'Bishop Foxe. Of Winchester. Seems to have taken the Master under his wing. Good to have influential friends. Now is the time!' Then with a wink and a grin, William too disappeared.

William was right, Thomas and his patron Richard Foxe were wily and now was indeed the perfect time for all men of talents to make a place. Thomas already knew the King, had laughed and joked with him and was truly very fond of the young monarch. Thomas still smiled when he remembered that awkward conversation with the old King. He *would* be proud to have a son like Henry. And of course, he thought with a slight jolt, he might have his own son one day.

Over the weeks that followed, Thomas's brain was never quiet as he joined the people who surrounded Henry. He tried to be all things to the young man; friend, always ready to laugh at a joke, or wise spiritual advisor. He was a ready helpmeet and would sometimes take papers from the King and return them an hour later with a brief resume of their contents. He once said to Henry that he should read all the papers from the Privy Council and had not forgotten the young King's grimace.

'I suppose my father the King read everything?'

'He did, your Grace. And he signed everything, even

the least wardrobe warrant.'

'Oh. That feels like I've eaten too many unripe apples. Whenever did he find the time to enjoy himself? Or get my brother and all my sisters on my mother?' Then Henry laughed and looked very naughty. 'Oh, well he'd have done that at night. In the dark. That would have been a powerful saving on the price of candles!'

Despite himself, Thomas had laughed. Then Henry spoke again.

'I have had a splendid idea. I think that I should get some of my most trusted companions to read these papers and tell me, briefly, what's in them. Now, isn't that brilliant?'

Thomas hadn't spoken but maintained an open-faced, encouraging expression.

'Yes…' and the King had wandered off, shouting to his friends.

Thomas had great faith in planting the seed of an idea and letting it be till it sprouted and so he quietly collected documents from Bishop Foxe or Dean Hobbes, the ailing Almoner. His quicksilver mind speedily distilled the contents and he would deliver them to Henry between bouts of tilting at the ring or tennis. He prided himself on his speed and succinct speech and it was especially satisfying to see Henry's friends sit with him and heavily explain their version of some matter to Henry's evident impatience.

Now June was here. It was to be the most splendid month of Henry's life to date and Thomas intended to be as visible as possible. He wanted the King to see him there, enjoying the wedding and coronation celebrations. He would be clapping and cheering at the jousts, in direct opposition to the Council who maintained the ban on Henry's participation at the lists. Henry would see that Thomas was a man who loved life. With a smile he realised that Joan would be an asset, not an embarrassment; as long as he and Joan were quiet, the King would still know that Thomas was equally a spiritual and worldly man, a man to whom one could talk about anything.

Then Thomas's mind divided. This was a trait he both disliked and found very useful. The warm passionate side thought lovingly of his Joan, of how it felt when she curled against him after they had lain together. It was easy to recall how he would pass his hand over the firm, warm curves of her waist and hips, the astonishing fact of having a woman lying beside him was still a delightful novelty and how could he ever think of being apart from her?

But the cold part of his brain traced the path he wanted his life to take. He saw himself rising in position and influence to a point where there wouldn't be a place for a wife, for his darling Joan.

Thomas was not a proud or boastful man, but he hadn't been born to privilege or position and he knew it was his native wit and talent that had brought him this far and would take him further. He wasn't a betting man, but if he was, he'd bet on himself.

But he was also pragmatic, and today and tomorrow were not for sad thoughts. This wonderful time was when England and Henry would consolidate the work begun by the old King. They would take their place high above the salt at the table that was Europe. England would be highly regarded and Thomas Wolsey would be there too.

Chapter 11

London

It was the morning of the coronation processions and Joan woke early. She couldn't stay in bed and climbed out with her usual thump onto the floor. Margery had half an ear out for her mistress and arrived promptly. Joan sat whilst Margery brushed her hair. It was growing but still scratched deafeningly against her pillow at night and she'd taken to tying one of Thomas's silk kerchiefs around her head to subdue the bristles.

'By Christmas, we'll be pinning it back. Look how thick and curly it is.' Margery finished by rubbing a couple of drops of some sweet-smelling oil through Joan's hair. 'Lovely.' She wound a length of fine linen around Joan's head; their solution to the cropped hair and gave Margery something to which to pin her bonnet and frontlet.

Joan's gown was a new one, a beautiful russet fustian over an only slightly less-new green kirtle. She ran the material between her fingers, relishing the light smooth feel of it. A smart bonnet with exquisite edging, gloves and ribbons with glittering points at the ends and fine linen – it was moments like this that Joan both enjoyed and felt guilty about. She didn't only love Thomas because he ensured that she was well dressed and happy but she was forced to admit that it often contributed to a flush of love when she looked at her fine new wardrobe. Close association with her Uncle John had trained her to examine her feelings and bring them back to a point where she could thank God for his love. John Larke would not be pleased to realise that Joan now traced all her luck and happiness to the somewhat less divine figure of Thomas Wolsey.

As soon as they had eaten dinner, Joan, Margery and two men of the household ventured out to join the excited citizens of London. The day was bright but scudding clouds sometimes darkened the sun. Joan, now a firm favourite with the traders in her vicinity had spoken prettily to Master Mortimer, who owned a handsome drapery and haberdashery shop on the route of the coronation procession, and he and his wife had invited her to stand with them.

Joan's small party hurried through the streets behind the route. Glancing through the cut-through alleys, they could see the crowds lining the way. Now and then was a ragged cheer, taken up by those who couldn't see properly and thought the King or Katherine had arrived. They reached the wall with the garden gates. Master Mortimer had chalked an M on his gate for Joan's sake and they passed through into the neat little garden. Mistress Mortimer made the most of her little patch and grew herbs, flowers and a few vegetables. A small boy met them and led them down the narrow passage into the shop where Master Mortimer and his wife greeted Joan and made room for her at the wooden counter. Joan was grateful for the slight barrier between them and the crowds and even more grateful when the boy fetched a lump of wood for her to stand on.

Master Mortimer had hung a length of rich yellow linen as an awning and in the sunshine, it almost looked golden, a fact which made him beam when Joan complimented him. It was a lengthy wait and long past 4 o'clock when the boy brought them refreshments and fresh wafers. Joan's purse was thin of coin and fat with new ribbons when finally, they heard trumpets.

The procession was preceded by small groups of excited red-faced boys and Joan saw one hauled off by his embarrassed mother. Then loudly protesting, he wriggled free and raced to re-join his mates. Then followed the fine gentlemen in blue robes, looking proud and Joan thought, just as excited as the hot little boys and she exchanged amused glances with Mistress Mortimer. And finally, the King. Henry was magnificent; stately in his red robes, and the cloth-of-gold underneath was so richly sparkling with precious jewels that Joan could hardly take it all in. Even his horse and his canopy were great expanses of golden cloth and Joan was especially awed as Master Mortimer had explained at some length the whole painstaking process of making this valuable cloth, making Joan feel even more excited about her own small piece.

Then followed more lavishly dressed men; Joan heard the crowd muttering names, and sometimes a noble would hear his name, wink and if the crowd was lucky, a handful of coins would be thrown to them, glittering in the midsummer sun.

At long last, the words, 'The Queen! The Queen's coming!' could be heard and necks were craned to the left. But poor Katherine; Henry had passed in bright blessed sunshine but for her, there was a sudden deluge. The crowds murmured sympathetically as the horses carrying her litter shook their heads and the poles supporting the golden canopy bent inwards with the sudden weight of water. Then as they approached Master Mortimer's shop, the cloth sprang a leak and Katherine, managing not to look too alarmed, drew her feet and skirts out of the small but horribly persistent stream of water which now fell on her.

Joan was nearly jolted off her piece of wood as Mortimer shot past her into the small passage and out of the front door. Joan and the household watched with astonishment as he appeared on the street and bowing very low, stood and addressed the Queen.

'Your Grace!' His tones were clear and loud and only someone who knew him well would note the tiny tremor in his voice. 'I fear you are in danger of a thorough drenching. I beg you to take shelter by my poor shop for a moment.'

Katherine looked faintly surprised but then a warm smile lit her face. 'My Lord,' she said graciously in her charming Spanish-accented voice, 'I would be greatly honoured.' Her grooms steadied the horses and her ladies helped her from the litter and to everyone's astonishment, the soon-to-be-crowned Queen of England took shelter under Master Mortimer's beautiful awning.

The rain quickly eased but whilst Katherine's attendants busied themselves with emptying the rain from the canopy and turning the damp cushions, the Queen unwittingly won the hearts of some of her new subjects. She sweetly agreed to some warm ale and took a small piece of wafer and while they were being brought to her, she asked to be introduced to Master Mortimer's wife. Mistress Mortimer grew very pink and sank into such a curtsy that all feared she might never rise again.

'And may I present to you Mistress Wolsey who has also honoured us today with her presence?'

Joan was conscious only of her pulse beating hard in her throat as she dropped down before the Queen.

The Queen spoke slowly and thoughtfully, 'Mistress Wolsey?' then she raised Joan and looked at her. '*Hmmm*. I wonder. Perhaps I have heard of you at court? The Dean of Lincoln's…?'

Joan was glad that she was dressed so well and so modestly. Her mere existence would be difficult for the Queen to accept, but at least she was outwardly decent, no common drab.

'Your Grace. Yes, I think you may have heard of me.'

Katherine looked slightly sad and tilted her head to one side and in a voice that was almost a whisper spoke to Joan. 'May God keep you safe, my child.' She raised her hand in blessing and Joan found tears gently prickling her eyes at such a kind and gentle reproach.

'Thank you, your Grace. And may God grant you a long and happy life.'

'My dear, God will grant me what is right for me. But

I do thank you.'

And then it was all over. The rain stopped and the sun was bringing out whisps of steam. The awning was free of its reservoir and the ladies of the court helped the Queen back into her litter.

'Thank you, Master Mortimer. I will never forget your kindness!' And accompanied by the cheers of the crowd, the procession was underway once more.

The party made its way inside once more and they all looked at each other in astonishment.

'My love! I couldn't believe it when you shot outside!'

'I couldn't leave her in the rain. And no one else was helping – gaping fools would have seen her drown.'

'And she was so beautiful and so gracious and so ready to be pleased. To think she stood under our awning and spoke to us all.'

Joan smiled at her hosts and was glad for them but she felt a little subdued. She noticed Margery looking sympathetically at her and gave a tiny smile and a slight sideways nod.

'Mistress Mortimer. I think you must excuse me now. I am weary after such excitement and would be in my own bed.'

Joan noticed the woman's eyes flicker over her stomach but she smiled kindly, 'But of course. And I'm glad we were able to let you meet the Queen today. Won't that be something to tell your husband?'

'Yes it will, and she was so lovely, so beautiful and gentle. And I can't thank you enough for inviting me today. I shall never forget it. Let's hope such royal favour brings fortune to you all.'

Master Mortimer was almost too excited to let Joan leave – he wanted to rehearse the Queen's words over and over again and he couldn't be grateful enough to the impulse which had caused him to raise his golden awning over his fortunate shop and wasn't it lucky that the rain had come just then. And his neighbours had laughed to see him raise the golden cloth but he had the last laugh. Joan congratulated them all again and left the household to their supper which was never better earned.

Joan, Margery and the two men made their way home. It was sad, reflected Joan, that Thomas hadn't been there with her. But he'd probably have far greater tales to tell her when he came home. But it would have been nice to talk it over with him and then wander home to supper. Then they could take a walk together in the long midsummer evening. But she thought briskly, this was not the way to be. She turned to Margery and chatted to her, telling her how sweetly perfumed the Queen was. And what a shame that she'd been stuck at the back of the shop, she would have enjoyed seeing the Queen; she was as lovely as an angel. And all that wonderful long auburn hair…

When they reached home, supper was ready and the whole household already knew that their Mistress had met the Queen. The maids especially were keen to hear of it and once they'd eaten, Joan ventured into the kitchens and told them of the great adventure. The men hung around and pretended not to listen but at the end of Joan's story, which could only be very short, they were unanimous in declaring it a good and fortunate thing for both Joan and the entire household.

It had been a good day, Joan reflected as she climbed into bed and shied her night-rail at the candle.

Thomas wouldn't like that, she said to herself. *Well, Thomas isn't here.*

Chapter 12

London

October arrived and England was settling down under the new King. Hardly anyone called him the new King anymore. But then, barely anyone mentioned the old King. If they thought of him, it was as a shadow which had passed over the land, as necessary as night is to bring day. New laws and general pardons gladdened the hearts of the people but few realised that only the most obvious of abuses had been rescinded – the Council had no intention of losing the crown's income and the keenest of minds were always working at ways to make more money for the King who seemed intent on spending his inheritance as quickly as he could. Bishop Foxe loved the logic of Morton's fork – if Henry's people were living humbly, they must be saving money and could afford to pay more tax. If they were families living extravagant lives, then they must have the slack to pay more taxes. It wasn't quite Thomas's way, but he too appreciated the theory.

And now Thomas was the King's new almoner and one of those keen minds; in September, poor Thomas Hobbes, the erstwhile Dean of Exeter, had finally died and Bishop Foxe commended the King's notice to Thomas

Wolsey and the King had been delighted to agree. My old friend Wolsey, he'd said, now there's a man I can trust. He won't be hoodwinked into giving away my money.

Thomas had many things on his mind; not least was being the youngest member of the King's Privy Council and was carefully treading a narrow path between impressing Henry and trying not to irritate the senior men who had nearly as much right to the throne as Henry—certainly several of them came from much more legitimate breeding lines.

Thomas was also closely following the gathering of evidence against Sir Edmund Dudley and Sir Richard Empson. Faithful servants to the old King, no one really doubted that they had done little more than serve him zealously, but their methods of extracting money were universally hated. Many a noble family had found themselves paying enormous fines in order to keep the head of their house from the execution block. These bonds were intended to take several lifetimes to pay off and were both a way of ensuring income and of making sure that no would-be-king could afford to rebel.

In private, Thomas was impressed by their ingenuity, but he also found their methods loathsome; it was not an elegant or ethical way to run the country. Additionally, if the two men were found guilty, their estates would be forfeited and Thomas had long cast covetous eyes on the Bridewell land. The beautiful gardens running down to the river, the orchards, even La Parsonage, the oldest part of the house.

Empson held the lease but leases change hands and if

Empson and Dudley were to take the blame for the shortcomings of Henry's reign, if they were to be the curtain closing on the old and rising on the new, then so be it. And of course, it would be a larger place in which to bring up his family. His family. As usual, he experienced that mixture of excitement, love and sheer panic. He'd almost begun to believe that Joan wouldn't become pregnant, that somehow, he'd get away with having a mistress. *Wife*, he corrected himself. But when she came to him in September, only a couple of weeks ago, he knew what she had to say.

Joan's eyes, always the window to her thoughts, had shown excitement and dread and Thomas had been ashamed that she might not think him unreservedly delighted. But Joan had grown wise in their short relationship – *marriage* – and she clearly had reservations about her news. But Thomas looked at her and once again fell in love with her. Her hair was growing and was endearingly curly; when he held her for a kiss, the curls would seem to grasp his fingers in a feather-light embrace. Her blue eyes were huge with her news and of course, he'd noticed the slight changes in her body. He'd certainly noted the lack of her monthly courses and when he made love to her, there was a slight roundness to her stomach which he found both touching and exciting.

But, Richard Empson's lease. Thomas pulled his thoughts back to his desk. This was really not the time to think of his soft wife, carrying his child, or of her breasts which were already swelling slightly. Thomas shifted uncomfortably and grinned. He must go home more often, sate himself and stop thinking about her. Then his eye fell on her brass ring with the green stone. He smiled and twisted it on his little finger. His darling girl.

Henry was relying on Thomas more and more. The King had lost patience with his friends and their stumbling briefs and all concerned had given up the idea with great relief. But then the King realised that all along, Wolsey had been doing that very job with no apparent effort. He did not of course see the long nights spent studying papers and the endless conferences with Foxe and other important and influential counsellors. Thomas was beginning to know the business of the country as well as anyone. He sometimes felt it a pity that he could not have been trained by the men now known as traitors, Empson and Dudley. But he would learn and be more efficient and competent than any of them.

The King was a notoriously early riser and anyone who wished to have his ear was well advised to do the same, and so more often than not, Thomas found it easier to stay at court. William was always around and they were both ready to shift with the King to a different house or palace. This life with a sole focus suited Thomas very well; he thrived on bending his great mind to a single subject, but then in the background of everything was one little figure: Joan. All she wanted from him was his occasional presence and that was so hard to give. At any moment when Thomas found time in his thoughts for Joan, he would have been touched if he had known that she was invariably thinking of him. In fact, Joan could think of little but Thomas.

The heady days of March and April when Joan was elated to wake every day to a life free from misery had eased. She was learning that the sharpest grief and the happiest moments lose their edges and that everyday life could be a little dull. She had no real friends except Margery and they both tried to avoid too much intimacy. Margery because she knew it would do her little good in the servants' hall and Joan because she did not wish to be too dependent on anyone. Anyone except Thomas of course. And once again she circled around Thomas, who was invariably absent.

When Joan first missed her monthly blood, she thought little of it. Her poor diet in the early part of the year had led her body to behave erratically, but by September she was sure and so was Margery. The girl, far more experienced than her mistress, pointed out the swelling of Joan's breasts, and Joan had touched them and her stomach in wonder.

'It's like being a shell with a pearl inside me.' She spoke dreamily and Margery snorted with laughter.

'Something like that. You wait till it's in your arms, and its clothes are full of stinking mess. Not so pure then.'

Joan had rolled her eyes at Margery. And she concentrated a moment, sensing each part of her body.

'It almost feels hard there, like an acorn.' She sighed happily, 'A little sprouting acorn which looks like Thomas. A tiny face, tiny hands.' She stopped speaking and closed her eyes. Margery, normally so cynical, was touched. Poor girl, time she had something of her own to love.

Margery thought about it; probably early August when he'd been home a fair bit whilst the King and Queen were in progress. The Master may have had a desk in the bed chamber, but he'd also worked hard at other things too. The air had sparked between the two and they'd had many early nights. *Keep planting seeds and one is bound to take root*, Margery thought wryly. She wondered if she'd ever have a family. William was very attentive when he was there and he'd talked almost too sweetly to her on several occasions. But Margery was no fool. One of many brothers and sisters, probably even more than she knew, for her father was notorious, she had no intention of letting a moment of pleasure blight her life and despite William's words and promises, there was only one way to make certain you didn't fall for a baby.

Telling Thomas had made Joan feel sick, though that was also his scent. He'd come in one evening, tired, but elated after a good day's work and the sweet smell that was uniquely him had seemed to press in the soft parts under her jaw and she felt her stomach clench with nausea.

Thomas saw her turn pale and went to her in concern before stepping back with great speed as she suddenly vomited. He called Margery who refused to meet his worried look, but quickly cleaned up after her mistress and helped her to a chair.

When they were alone again, Joan seized her courage. 'Thomas.'

Thomas waited with a gentle smile and Joan weighed her words.

'I believe I am with child. Your child.' She stopped

and made a funny face, 'Well, our child, obviously.' She rolled her eyes in mock exasperation at herself but behind them was pure worry.

Thomas thanked her sickness for giving him a moment's notice and he knelt before her. 'Joan, I am more grateful than I can express. I thank God for blessing our union.'

Joan smiled and sniffed at him.

'It's my scent, isn't it? When I was younger, I once saw your mother in the garden. She rubbed some lavender between her fingers and then brought up her breakfast into the flower bed. She was carrying your brother. She used a ginger infusion, sweetened with honey to ease her sickness.'

Then Joan really did cry, for relief that Thomas wasn't angry and for the fact that her mother would never teach her to be a mother. Thomas braved her sickness and held her tight. When they lay together later that night, he stroked her stomach and listened in wonder as Joan told him about the tiny acorn Thomas growing inside her. He really meant it; God had blessed them with a miracle.

This made the matter of Bridewell and La Parsonage all the more pressing and today, the first day of October, Thomas Wolsey lifted his hand and looked at a small piece of paper which lay under it. It was a bill scrawled by the King in his distinctive hand. Thomas would pass it to Lord Chancellor Warham and it would pass to Bishop Foxe and finally, probably months ahead, a beautiful parchment document would be given to Thomas. Seals would hang from it and confirm Thomas as the holder of the lease to

Bridewell. It was his and next spring and summer he would walk with Joan through the orchards and gardens down towards the river. They would sit peacefully together and their baby son would play at their feet, he'd lift his arms to his father and... the summer sun of his imagination seemed to dazzle Thomas's eyes and he wiped a little moisture from them. Such a small piece of paper to realise his dream and asking Henry had been so easy.

The King was elated and in a bountiful mood, for Katherine was pregnant. Henry could hardly believe the change from a year ago when his father had been ailing and rallying then sickening again and his son ordered around and treated as a child. Now he was King, husband and soon-to-be-father. Of course, Thomas should have Bridewell if he wished. After all, Empson wouldn't want it again, would he? And he'd winked at Thomas who had forced himself to chuckle and agree. That was a hard price to pay for his prize. Thomas could never find amusement in the death of another for doing his duty; *I must watch my heels* he thought. But Henry took a piece of paper from the folder of documents they'd been discussing, wrote the bill and handed it to Thomas. Thomas had leapt to his feet and bowed low to his King, thanking him.

The afternoon was quiet and Thomas decided to go home early. He shouted for William and his escort and they set off. There was still a little light remaining when they arrived and Thomas asked William to collect a couple of lanterns. Going inside he was greeted by a surprised Joan; it was unusual to see Thomas at this hour. She had been dozing by the fire and her eyes were sleepy as she looked at Thomas. But his enthusiasm soon woke her and she happily donned a warm cloak and slipped her hand in his.

Only a short walk along to the Bridewell estate where William opened the gate to them.

'Why are we here, Thomas? Isn't this Empson's house? Oh, but he's in the Tower…'

Thomas smiled at her. 'Joan, this is where we will bring up our family.'

Her mouth gaped. 'Oh goodness. But what will Sir Richard say? Will we share it with him?'

'No, Joan, I fear he won't be back. And even if he is released, this is mine now, the King has given it to me.'

In the falling daylight, they walked around the outside of the old house, La Parsonage. Joan rather liked the patchwork of timber, stone and brick, and in the gloom, she could see the grounds stretching out before them.

'There are orchards and flower gardens and… well, it's enormous, isn't it?' She placed her hands round her stomach. 'What a nice place to be when I bring our child into the world.' Thomas was silent.

'Don't you think?' She pressed on, the slightest touch of anxiety in her voice. 'Thomas?'

He smiled at her. 'Of course. Joan let's go back. It's growing chilly.' He pulled her to him and slipped one arm around her shoulders. In his other hand, he took her hands and in this comforting way, they walked home.

Chapter 13

Ipswich, March 1510

If Joan could have drawn closer to the edge of the ship, she would have got less vomit down her gown but her swollen stomach prevented her. *Still,* she reflected, *if I could have got close enough then I wouldn't be pregnant and I wouldn't be here anyway. And we wouldn't want that, would we, little Acorn?*

She knew this day would come, had known it since that afternoon with Thomas walking around the Bridewell land. By the time they reached home she had worked it out, more or less. The illegitimate sons of priests could not become priests, and in vain did Joan protest that Acorn might not want to enter the church and anyway might be a girl.

So, as soon as Joan had had started to show, she kept out of the way of almost everyone except Thomas and their most intimate servants. Thomas wrote to his sister and brother-in-law who agreed to take Joan and care for her. Then when she returned to London, she would arrive with Thomas's nephew, the son of Agnes and Arthur Wynter. No one could object to the King's almoner bringing up his nephew; the very example of Christian charity.

Personally, Joan thought it a ridiculous idea; as if people wouldn't guess it was Thomas's son. And *as if* word wouldn't get out that Mistress Wolsey had retired to have her child. But she shrugged, Thomas knew best. Each time she thought that she closed her eyes for a moment and smiled.

Only twelve hours since they'd last been together. His face had left a physical pain in her chest. Thomas had looked as if he would die and Joan had had to pull her hands quite forcibly from his.

'I'll be perfectly all right Thomas. I promise. Just think of the huge numbers of women who've given birth since I started speaking. It's hardly an unusual event.' Then Thomas wrapped his arms around her as if to keep her with him forever. 'Don't die.' He muttered.

Now, here they were, Margery cleaning mess from her gown and trying to be sympathetic. Dear Margery; her soul was made mostly of lemons and not quite enough sugar Joan decided. Kind, brisk and impatient, there was still no other person she'd rather be with on this adventure.

Thomas's sister and her husband lived in Ipswich and it was growing dark when the little ship arrived, but Joan was touched beyond measure to see a little group waiting for her. They looked cold and as though they'd been there for a while. William gave an approving grunt. 'Good.' Joan had argued against William attending her but Thomas insisted. Joan might be a slight embarrassment, but she was still the most precious part of his life and if he could not take her to Ipswich then he would trust no one but William in his place. William would stay with the ship's crew and return with them as soon as the tide turned.

Her baggage unloaded, William bowed low to Joan and spoke gruffly to her. 'God be with you, Mistress. Go safely through your travail and come back to us soon.'

Joan was touched. She had no idea that William was so fond of her. Then he'd kissed Margery very affectionately – *Hmm*, thought Joan – and taking Arthur Wynter aside spoke a few words to him. Joan saw the flash of a purse pass between them, then the two men shook hands and parted.

Thomas's sister was very like him, making her a handsome rather than a pretty woman. Agnes had had a life-time to take her elder brother in her stride and if there hadn't been such a family likeness, might have wondered if he wasn't a cuckoo chick. All Robert Wolsey's children were bright but Thomas was exceptional. He looked after his family and now it was their turn to look after his.

But Agnes had not met Joan for many years and had no idea what to expect from this near stranger. Had Joan grown into a rough Yarmouth girl? Was she taking everything she could from Thomas and flaunting herself? Poor Agnes had worried so much about Thomas since he'd taken up with Joan. She had imagined a dozen faces for Joan, a hundred characters, and none of them very nice.

What she hadn't imagined was this poor thing, crusted with vomit and looking deadly tired and quite miserable. She couldn't help herself, any more than Thomas had.

'My sister,' she said, putting her arms around a grateful Joan, 'how very glad we are that you are here.'

Joan gave the slightest sigh of relief and dropped her

tense shoulders into Agnes's embrace. She couldn't remember Thomas's sister and despite his reassurance, had no idea how she'd be received into his family. If Dame Alice's response had been any guide, then she could not expect much kindness.

It seemed a long walk to Joan, but in reality, it was only a few moments later and they were safely inside the warm half-timbered house. Margery and Agnes quickly had each other's measure and Agnes knew that Joan's maid would guard her mistress well. Joan was seated by the fire and fed a little supper before Margery steered her upstairs to bed. Little Acorn stirred and kicked in her stomach and Joan indulged in a few quiet tears before tucking her hands around her belly and falling into sleep. In the darkness of the night, Joan awoke and struggled for a moment to work out where she was. Her body was still looking for the swell and sway of the ship on the water and her hand reached out for Thomas. Swallowing her habitual disappointment, she slipped back into her lonely slumber.

The next morning Margery and Agnes let Joan sleep as long as she could whilst they got to know each other. They both had their territories to protect but their common ground was Thomas, and Agnes was greedy to know how her brother was. How he looked, was he happy? Did he still sing around the house? And she was delighted when Margery told about the story of her name change, how Thomas was the only one who'd asked what her real name was, and she nodded, satisfied that she could still recognise Thomas in that act of unremarkable kindness.

The last days of Joan's pregnancy were peaceful and

she was glad to be safe in a warm home. Daily she traced Thomas's face in his sister and nieces and nephews and found comfort in feeling that she was still close to him. The children were slightly curious, but told that she was a widowed friend from Yarmouth, they quickly lost interest and accepted her as part of the household. Joan spent whole days drowsing by the fire, working her way through Agnes's mending basket and peacefully talking to any who spared time to sit with her a while.

This could have continued indefinitely and certainly the time seemed endless to Joan until the day when needing to use the privy, she hauled herself from the chair to find water running down her legs. For a moment she was confused – her bladder was still full – but then she realised: Acorn was almost here.

Very calmly, Joan visited the privy then wandered around. Never before had the house been entirely empty. There was usually a servant dusting or sweeping. There wasn't even anyone in the kitchens tending a fire or stirring a pot.

Joan shrugged and went to her chamber. Until the first pain came, she wondered if she was dreaming. Several years ago, she had suffered a terrible bout of the gripes, spending hours in the privy as uncontrollable spasms gripped her bowels, making her feel as if she was turning inside out. Now she faced those pains again. She stood by the bed and collapsed onto her arms making a tiny whimpering squeak before realising that if she held her breath it somewhat controlled the pain. As the cramping eased, she grabbed a pillow and placed it in front of her before pacing around the room taking deep breaths and talking to the baby. She smiled to notice that after a year with Thomas, she'd speedily returned to her Yarmouth dialect. Both of them had polished away their accents; Thomas in order to avoid standing out more than he needed to at court and Joan for the simple reason that people didn't understand her.

Then she felt her body gathering once more to squeeze the baby out. Returning to the bed she leaned forward and gripped either end of the pillow in her fists. Again, she took a deep breath – breathing seemed to encourage the pain and she wasn't keen on that. It felt as if the baby was scraping her spine and she pushed and pushed to try and stop him.

Then glory be, just as panic was beginning to gather in her chest, she heard voices downstairs. Still holding her breath, she couldn't call out, but Margery and Agnes had gone into the little parlour and seen the puddle on the floor and were calling her name. As the pain lessened, she shouted and they arrived.

'Oh Lord,' said the usually capable Margery. Agnes turned and told her where the midwife lived and Margery whipped round in the doorway and disappeared.

Joan stood up, grasping the post at the end of the bed, 'I'm so sorry, I left water on the floor.'

'Lovey that's all right! Why didn't you send someone? We were only in the market; it's only a moment away.'

'I couldn't find anyone. And it seems to be going well enough. I think…' she smiled and shrugged at Agnes who gave a nervous half laugh, remembering the demented screaming which brought her own first child into the world. While they spoke, Agnes was undressing Joan until she stood in her linen smock.

'Now, let me help you into bed.'

Joan shook her head but Agnes insisted until Joan pulled away from her and once again held the pillow on the bed, ready to face another spasm.

'Well. All right then. Um, Joan, I'm going to feel between your legs. See if the baby is coming. Yes? Don't jump when I touch you.'

Agnes knelt behind Joan and reached up, but she was the one who jumped as she felt the baby's head, all warm and slippery.

Above her, Joan was forced to breathe, taking a gasping shuddering breath.

'Joan, may God help us! He's nearly here. Push, push!'

Joan, privately thinking that all she could do was push, did so and Agnes held the baby by the shoulders and drew him out. *Now what?* she thought frantically, Joan was facing the wrong way, if she turned to get on to the bed, the cord would get tangled in her legs. Agnes muttered a formless prayer for help which was answered by the arrival of Margery and the midwife, Goodwife Washbourne. They clattered into the room and immediately the air was thick with the midwife's voice as she prayed loudly in order that the child would be born into a room of sanctity. Agnes felt herself relax slightly, Goody Washbourne and the Lord would know what to do.

With Agnes still holding her nephew, the other women manhandled Joan onto the bed and the midwife turned to the baby who was screaming most satisfactorily.

'Good. This isn't her first, I suppose?'

'Well... it is. And she was on her own for quite a while. She wasn't supposed to be but... well, I don't know how the house came to be empty... it's never empty... what if something...'

'Mistress Wynter. *Ssh*. Nothing happened. All is well. Look.'

Agnes nodded and Margery smiled; Joan lay on the bed, slightly pink and sweaty but otherwise sound, and a bonny baby boy lay on her stomach looking utterly furious and uncannily like a miniature Thomas.

'Where's the father? He's going to be very proud.'

Almost imperceptibly, Agnes shook her head and looked sad. The midwife mouthed "*Dead?*" And Agnes nodded.

'Ah well. At least she'll have this fine remembrance. Now you go and warm some wine and a little pottage and I'll tidy up here.'

With relief Agnes turned to leave, but was stopped by Joan's voice.

'Agnes?'

'Yes, my dearie?'

'You have your outdoor shoes on.' Agnes laughed. It was one of her strictest rules in the house.

'So I do. This is a time of wonders.'

Once they were alone, the midwife, who was a kindly woman, turned to Joan, 'Well Mistress, I am mighty impressed by you. It might be your fourth child instead of your first. What're you going to call him?'

Thomas, Joan said to herself, but mindful of the continuing need for discretion, shook her head. 'I don't rightly know yet. I reckon it'll come to me in a day or so.'

Goody Washbourne nodded and continued her chatter. She wanted to keep Joan awake for a while as she needed to deliver the afterbirth. She tied and snipped the cord and wiped baby Thomas clean with oil before wrapping him up and passing him to his mother.

Joan began to feel as though the gripes were returning and through a slight groan, she turned her panicked face to the midwife. 'Another one? More?'

She smiled and patted Joan's hand. 'No, the afterbirth. You give me a couple of pushes and it'll be out as nice as you like.' Joan was so tired, but did as she was asked and Goody Washbourne placed everything in a bowl to be taken away and buried.

When Margery returned with pottage and a flask of warm spiced wine, the midwife settled the baby in the crook of her arm and gave him a spoonful of the wine. 'There my pretty little boy, that'll get the blood moving and set you up nicely for your ma's milk.'

Baby Thomas prepared to cry again and Joan held out her arms for him. She seemed at a distance as she watched herself loosen the neck of her smock, pull it down and expose her breast. For a moment, she wondered how to get Thomas to feed, but when she placed him on her breast, he felt the nipple against his cheek and he moved his head to suckle.

Goody Washbourne smiled too. 'There's a proper little man, knows what to do, doesn't he?'

Agnes drew the midwife out of the room and spoke softly to her. 'Mistress Joan will be returning to London once she is churched and wishes to have passed the child to a wetnurse by then. I wonder, do you know of anyone we can employ? Joan will be returning to quite a grand house so it must be someone quiet...'

Goodwife Washbourne nodded thoughtfully. 'Yes, I might know someone. You let me think on it.'

In time, the servants wandered home to be soundly ticked off by their mistress then to blame each other in an upwards direction till in the end all the servants blamed Mistress Agnes for letting them behave like that. The family spent some time tiptoeing past Joan's chamber door and trying to peep until Joan called them in and the children climbed on the bed to stare at the new baby and marvel at him. Even Arthur stepped in for a moment and congratulated Joan and nodded approvingly at his new nephew.

Joan thanked him for allowing her to be in his house and Arthur looked pleased and embarrassed. He wasn't sure how to react to Joan, for he had always been proud of his link to Thomas Wolsey and this woman somewhat reduced Thomas in his eyes. But on the other hand, she was sweet and lovely. As he repeatedly said to his wife, in the confessional of their bed curtains, 'A priest is a priest and should set an example to us all. Not take up with a woman and have a family like anyone else.' And Agnes could only give a silent sigh and agree with her husband.

Every morning, Agnes looked in anxiously at Joan and each day was rewarded by seeing Joan look well and happy. The baby thrived and there was no sign of childbed fever. It seemed that Joan had taken to motherhood as naturally as anyone could have wished. Once again Joan was adrift in a time of gentle dreaming and once again, she could have stayed like that forever. But Goodwife Washbourne was true to her word and after a fortnight she appeared with a dreadfully plain woman called Anne Godbold whose most recent charge was about to be weaned. Having nursed many healthy children in the town and the villages surrounding Ipswich, Mistress Godbold was in great demand as a wetnurse but as she quietly said, 'I have a fancy now to see the big town.'

Joan and Agnes spent the afternoon with her and found her to be gentle and kind to Thomas and the other children and best of all, once she'd nursed Thomas for a while, he looked very content, burped a little milk and slept in her arms.

It seemed the best for Little Acorn, but Joan found her little paradise had been invaded. She liked Anne but she yearned to feed Thomas. Her breasts ached with the swell of milk and when she heard his hungry cry she reacted physically and had to tie pads of fabric around her to soak up the leaking milk. It reminded her of when her wisdom teeth came, only two years ago. It was an irritating pain that she could only ease by biting on a small twig. Now she would press her forearms hard against the ache in her breasts and try to take away the discomfort by causing a greater one.

As soon as Tom had been born, Agnes wrote a brief note to her brother, informing him that his nephew had safely arrived and that he and his mother were well. After three weeks, Joan was thrilled to have a letter from Thomas.

My dear and most beloved Joan,
I am so pleased to learn of the birth and continuing health of my nephew. I look forward to your return with him. The improvements of La Parsonage go well and there will be a comfortable chamber for you both when you arrive. I have caused to be hung window-curtains at the windows of the bed-chambers, which innovation I think you will like.

Joan was vaguely disappointed; she hoped for his love to be sent, for him to say how much he missed her. But mainly she chuckled at the mention of the window curtains. His brief letter was more news of his building plans than it was about her. Her mind was stiff with disuse but she did remember Thomas showing her the inventories for poor Dudley and Empson. Thomas had been fascinated by the mention of window curtains in Dudley's house. He couldn't get over the convenience of them; how warm they must be, how they could be adjusted against the sun, how cosy the room would feel in the winter, it would be as if the tapestries ran all the way round the room. Joan nodded, and simply added that they'd certainly collect the dust, especially in London during a hot summer. She had given him her mock-exasperated look and they had grinned at each other.

Back in the big town as Anne put it, Thomas had felt the absence of Joan far more than he could have reckoned. He very much missed laying with her; Thomas tried not to think of that act as heavenly, but it surely was. The moment when they became one in that blinding moment of pleasure had been so surprising. Surely God could only have given men that gift as a glimpse of paradise?

But Thomas also yearned for the dear little figure who would meet him at the gate in the dusk or wait supper to a ridiculous hour. Sometimes he found her asleep with food long gone cold and she would never complain. The months of her pregnancy had been very dear to him. Watching his darling girl grow into a woman had been an experience which would stay with him till his last day. Perhaps they had started their lives together in a haze of sadness and mistaken emotions, but between them had grown a true and sincere love.

When he sat down to write to her, Thomas felt the weight of so many words in the quill but found that none would come out without leaving him feeling like a fool. He blushed at some of the things he wrote and with a wry smile quickly burned them. Finally, he settled on prosaic news of the house and the window-curtains. And writing about them brought her to his side once more with her half-laughing, half-weary observation about dust. If Joan could have realised the hidden love in his letter, she would have been well content.

***

Their river-steps came into view and Joan was relieved to see them; it had been a long journey and yet again she had been seasick. Tom and Mistress Godbold had thrived in the fresh air. Both had observed their journey with wide eyes. It had made Margery chuckle but Joan simply groaned and was grateful that someone else was caring for Tom.

After a few minutes on solid London ground, Joan felt a little better, if pale and she looked forward to supper. The small party made their way on foot to Bridewell, but Joan wondered what they would find there. Would they miss the old house, or would Thomas have made La Parsonage their home? How quickly did builders work? Probably as quickly as their pay permitted, she thought ironically to herself. If Thomas paid them too much then they would linger at their work; too little and they would be unwilling. But she knew her husband; he would care for the workmen and make sure they were well-fed. He'd probably even clothe any who looked too threadbare.

It was almost May and the evenings were a little longer and Joan relished seeing familiar faces from their neighbourhood. In Ipswich it was peaceful but here she felt restored to reality, even by the end-of-day smells and noise as traders wheeled their barrows home and small children grubbed about for the cast-offs before the rubbish was swept up for the day.

'Should we get a pie to take home?' The smell was mouth-watering and Joan was ravenous after two days of heaving and gripping the ship's rail.

Margery shook her head, 'Really? A pie at the end of the day? Do you want another night of puking? You're on your own if you do. No, even if my Lord Dean is not at home, there will be kitchen staff. He's hardly a man to neglect physical comfort, is he?'

Joan smiled and shook her head. *Oh, I hope he is home.* Even before they had left London, she was rehearsing their triumphant return. She could see each detail, feel his arms around her, his delight at Tom. She would have stopped to relish the last moments of expectation but Margery nudged her and she heard Tom start to whine and Anne's gentle shushing.

'Come along,' Margery urged her mistress, 'she can hardly feed him here, can she?'

Then rather unexpectedly, there was Thomas, approaching from the opposite direction. He was mounted on Star who saw Joan and gave his little whinny. Wolsey and his men all looked towards Joan and Thomas slowly raised his hand in a mixture of salute and blessing. Joan's party all curtseyed or bowed and as Joan dropped her head, she realised with a pang of painful disappointment that this reunion was not what she had imagined. Then with a strange feeling, Joan led her own tiny procession to the gates and noticed the small group of supplicants gathered there. They raised a cheer for Thomas, especially when William and a couple of the other men threw some coins to them. Then they all looked curiously at Joan and stared hard at Anne carrying Tom.

Joan turned to Margery, 'God's truth, Margery,' she muttered, 'they could close the gates on us and leave us out here begging and waiting for the food dole.'

Margery slipped her arm through Joan's, 'Of course they could, but they won't will they? Now come along, don't be silly. Your husband will be waiting to meet his son.'

And she chivvied her mistress through the gates. It was no good Joan having cold feet now; far too late for scruples and thoughts of what on earth she was doing with a priest. Anne looked calm but was looking around with an air of great interest. Of course, Margery had told her the story of Joan's marriage so she was not surprised but this was going to be tremendously exciting.

Once inside the house, Joan and Margery stood waiting. It seemed odd and unnerving that they didn't know where to go. Almost immediately, William arrived and bowed to Joan. 'Mistress. We are so glad to have you home. I can't recall what stage we had reached when you left, but I am sure you will find many changes and improvements.'

Joan laughed. 'Not the least, the window curtains as I gather from Master Wolsey's letters.' In truth, it had only been one letter and both Joan and William knew it.

'Oh yes. My Lord Dean is *extremely* pleased with the window curtains. Now, let me show you to your rooms.' He winked at Margery and gave a slight nod to Mistress Godbold.

Indeed the house; at one time the parsonage of Bridewell had certainly been improved. Poor Empson – as Joan thought of him – had not changed much during his time, so the modernisations were striking; everything was so clean and fresh. Bright new tapestries ran around the wall and almost into the heavy brocade window curtains which were now closed against the dusk. They did indeed make the rooms cosy but also Joan felt, slightly oppressive. She supposed she'd grow used to it and they would ensure greater privacy.

A smell of over-full clout-cloth began to climb over the scent of new wood and fresh herbs and Tom started to grizzle. William peered at Tom. 'Greetings, Master Wynter.' The baby seized William's outstretched finger and began to suckle at it and they all laughed.

'I believe that our first call should be to the nursery. Mistress, if you'll follow me, please?'

William led them upstairs and along to a large room with a cradle next to the bed. There were linens ready piled on the table and he announced, warm water was on its way. Anne thanked him and as they all left the nursery; Joan heard the door close against them. Against his own mother too, she thought miserably.

Eventually, all were settled and Margery was helping her mistress to wash and change. She smiled at Joan. 'Cheer up, my duck. We're safely home and you have a handsome baby. You are a fortunate woman.' She slipped her arm around Joan's shoulders and gave her a brief hug. What she needed was a demanding household to return to. This pampered life as Wolsey's so-called wife was not, Margery felt, entirely satisfactory; Joan would be better suited as the busy wife of a merchant. But she gave a tiny shrug; things were as they were and so much better than they might have been.

In another part of the house, Thomas was also washing and donning clean clothes. He felt an excited pulse at his neck and if he was honest, elsewhere too but he endeavoured to ignore that. But Joan, even weary and pale was still his love and it had been a long period for a man who'd found himself so well suited to the sport of bed.

As James left the chamber, Thomas paused for a moment. He imagined the house around him and saw a vision of the beautiful gardens embracing the jewel of La Parsonage and with Joan and the baby and himself at the heart of it. He tried to savour the moment and remind himself that only this very moment existed, that the past and the future did not but with a smile he found his mind racing on. The beautiful image of the house and family vanished as he considered the papers waiting for him and the conversations he'd had today. He even saw his son – *nephew* he sternly reminded himself – striding through life as a successful clergyman and courtier. Then his thoughts returned to Joan. He'd seen the flash of disappointment on her face when their eyes met. But really, what did she expect; that he sweep her into his passionate arms and kiss her darling face and… Wolsey gave a mix of cough and laugh and shaking his head, set off through the house to Joan's chambers. He was still undecided if he'd made the right decision having her rooms so far from his. But he couldn't be troubled by the baby crying, or indeed disturb the baby with his own late nights and early mornings.

His mouth was dry by the time he reached Joan's chamber and he felt terribly shy as he gently tapped on the wood. Joan had heard his steps approaching and snatched open the door. A slow smile grew on her face and no longer reticent, Thomas stepped in.

He gave Joan a little bow. 'Mistress, I am very glad to welcome you home. It has been far too long – surely it is a year since you left us.'

'No Thomas, I think not. More like two years and I have missed you very much.'

They stood close together and with a rush of pleasure, Joan noticed that Thomas's scent no longer made her stomach heave. To be certain she lifted her face to his and drew him down to kiss her. Immediately his arm circled her waist and pulled her against him, his lips crushing hers and then there was nothing but their passion for each other.

Hasty lovemaking was not kind on their clothes and Joan laughed as she regarded Thomas's disarray as he lay on her bed. 'Why, my Lord, does James no longer ensure that you are decent and tidy before he leaves you?'

He arched his brows at her with a grin as Joan drew down her skirts and tried to straighten her linen and replace her bonnet. 'Indeed, wife. And I see that you have let Margery's standards slip back into country slovenliness.' Joan stuck her tongue out at Thomas and abandoning her attempts to be tidy, hitched up her skirts and clambered astride Thomas.

'What? What did you say? How dare you be so rude to me?'

'May the dear Lord forgive me, but I've missed you. It was but half a life without you.'

Joan nodded. 'I know,' she whispered, as she bent to

kiss him once more.

It was almost dark by the time they rose from the bed. Joan suddenly and guiltily remembered Tom. 'Oh! The baby!'

Thomas laughed. 'Where did you leave him? No don't worry, we can probably find him. Give me a description.'

Joan smiled. 'Seriously, Thomas, am I tidy enough to go and fetch him?' He leaned over and tugged her gown straight and nodded and she left the room.

Her bare feet pattered along the passage to the nursery and Thomas heard a few words pass between Anne and Joan. Then he listened to Joan's soft voice as she spoke to their child.

'Now then, little Thomas, come and meet your father, big Thomas. If you're as handsome as he is, you'll be a lucky boy.'

Thomas got out of bed and lit some of the candles. The lights seemed to make the room darker, but he positioned one to cast a pool of light on the bed. In a moment Joan returned with the baby in her arms and Thomas realised that he felt strangely excited. That little creature was made of him – of him and Joan. Another of God's miracles. Then he saw the boy and without thinking held out his arms. As he took the baby, he briefly noticed that the child was both heavier than he'd expected and at the same time, terrifyingly tiny and light.

'But he's all done up. I can't see him.'

Joan smiled, 'Yes, to make his arms and legs grow straight. Lay him down and we'll unwrap him.'

Tom giggled and gurgled as his mother undid his

swaddling clothes and once free, waved his arms and legs in delighted freedom. His parents looked down at him.

'Joan, thank you. He's perfect. He's just… he's…'

Thomas was lost for words and in awe of the absolute love which filled him. His baby, his child. He lifted Tom up and cradled him along the length of his forearm, staring into the blue eyes as if bewitched. Thomas cupped the baby's feet in his hand and drew a marvelling breath, 'Oh Joan, his tiny feet, feel those bones in his heels, he's so little, but so solid.'

Joan looked at them and climbed onto the bed to kneel beside them. She wrapped her arms around Thomas and dropped a kiss on each of their heads before resting her own head in the crook of Thomas's shoulder and sighing with utter happiness.

They could have remained in this tableau of adoration for hours, but Tom had other ideas. He began to give his especially irritating cry, the one which made Joan's breasts itch and ache. After a few moments, Anne tapped on the door. 'Mistress? Shall I feed him?'

Joan gathered Tom's cloths and turned to take the baby from Thomas who raised his eyes to Joan. 'This must be hard for you. To allow another woman to have him?'

Joan noncommittally said '*Mmm…*' and gently took Tom before partly opening the chamber door and passing the baby to Anne.

When she returned to Thomas, Joan sat on the end of the bed facing her husband. 'Thomas, it is hard but everything between us is hard, isn't it? If not downright wrong.'

He drew breath to speak but Joan continued, 'When we were at the gate tonight, with all those supplicants, I thought how easy it would be for you to deny me. I wondered where we'd go. I have nothing without your protection and pleasure. My son would be a bastard and I would be a whore. Only you, who have brought me to that, can keep me from that.' Her voice was matter-of-fact and calm.

Thomas, the great statesman in waiting had no idea what to say but he leaned forward and took her hands. 'I promised you and your father that I would always care for you and all I can say is that I will.'

They remained in Joan's room all evening, making love and eating supper, before climbing into bed to sleep. Joan's hand crept across to find Thomas's then she relaxed and was lost in exhausted slumber.

She didn't know what time it was when she was disturbed by Thomas moving. As he rose from the bed, she ran her hand down his back and spoke softly, 'Hurry back.'

She heard Thomas turn to speak, 'Go back to sleep. I have things to do.' But Joan was fully awake now. 'Aren't you just going to use the pot?'

'No, I'm going to my own chamber. I have work to do. Since the Queen lost the child, he has been utterly driven. I need to keep ahead. He relies on me. The poor boy… I want him to feel safe. I want him to feel the happiness in his son that I feel in mine. Joan, I'm sorry, I have to help him.'

Joan sighed. 'Well, open the window curtains before you leave. By God's Wounds, it's too dark in here.'

'Joan. Please! Don't speak like that.' Joan ignored him but Thomas walked to the windows and drew back the curtains and a weak moonlight slightly lit the room. He headed towards the door, eager to leave the company of irritable Joan. He'd never seen her like this and he was worried he might laugh. *I might not be very experienced with women, but I'm sure laughing at her won't help.*

'Thomas?'

'Yes?'

'Were you born in a barn?'

'What?'

'Kindly close the bed curtains behind you.' Thomas rubbed his hand across his face and rolled his eyes.

'Of course. Sleep well.'

The bed hangings closed and Joan huffed. Her blood was racing and she was frustrated and annoyed. Her weary mind circled thoughts. Thomas was tired of her. Of course he wasn't, look how thrilled he'd been with Tom. His lovemaking had been surprisingly passionate, she'd lost count. She smiled. He had a chamber of his own. He didn't want to stay with her. He didn't want to disturb her. He was disturbing her by not being here. She felt sick. Her head ached. Miserable sluggish tears trickled down her cheeks and into her hair. One ran into her ear and was intolerably ticklish. She rolled over and howled into her pillow, all dribble and tears.

After a while, she heard people moving around the house and guessed that dawn was approaching. Thinking about something else calmed her and without realising it, she fell asleep again.

When she woke, Joan's eyes were puffy and sore. Margery said nothing but looked with sympathy at her mistress. Thomas's movements had been noted and she had known before Joan that he now had his own chambers. She helped Joan to wash and brushed her hair. It had grown enough to be annoying yet too short to be pinned back. Margery gently smoothed the hair prior to binding it and pinning on her bonnet, but Joan pulled free. 'I'm going back to bed. I'm too tired.'

She walked to the window and looked out. The May gardens were beautiful; all budding life with leaves growing plumper each day, and spring flowers vivid against the green enamel colour of the grass. Empson had evidently planted daffodils and Joan noted sadly that these were just finishing. She remembered the first one she saw, last year in the garden of the old house. Thomas had encouraged her to kneel down and sniff it. She had fallen in love with the sweet powdery scent and the kiss of the cold flower against her face. And here there were plenty of daffodils and all dying. She sighed and returned to bed.

She could hear her heart beating and closed her eyes, waiting to fall asleep again and cease thinking.

'Mistress, will you break your fast? There is fresh bread and new butter?'

'No.' Joan pulled the covers closer around her neck and was gone.

Margery made a face at her mistress, but she was concerned. She would let her sleep until dinner then she would bring food and baby Tom in the hope he might distract her. Once again, she regretted Joan's situation. It would be all too easy to let her slip into a decline.

Joan's withdrawal from the world lasted for eight days. When Tom was brought to her, she turned her back on him and refused to play. She barely ate and asked the windows to be closed against the birdsong; the cheery spring courting songs irritated her and stopped her sliding away from life.

At first, Thomas was glad not to notice but eventually, Margery caught him late one evening as he returned from court. He'd always been fond of her and willingly listened. His heart sank. He'd never been a man to give way under the weight of life but he could see that Joan could be susceptible to the shadows. With a sick gulp, he realised that he'd nearly lost her once before and narrowly rescued her from the darkness of an enclosed religious life.

Thomas had been working on Henry's great Pardon Roll and reading and commenting on and drafting the endless letters which built the peace treaties with France and Spain. Thomas had seldom felt so useful. He seemed to need less and less sleep and when he lay down to rest, he would leap up to make notes or check details in the ambassadors' letters. He grew lean and his eyes were bright, both with lack of food and with an excess of intellectual delight. His household grew dim around him. James would insist that Thomas be shaved and washed and William would stand in front of him and almost force him to eat. This was indeed an exciting time; never again could they lay the foundations of this strong new reign; every move on the European chess board was carefully planned and executed. To a man who had never felt so alive, the thought that someone in the same house was not infected with the same excitement came as a great surprise.

With great effort, Thomas put aside his work and gave his attention to Margery; she twisted her hands and looked slightly nervous.

'Well, Margery? What can I do for you?'

'It's Mistress Joan, My Lord.' Her jaw shut tightly and she looked sternly at him.

Thomas tried not to laugh. 'What of her, Margery? I have not seen her for a few days. She and Tom are well?'

'Oh, the babe is perfectly well, taking suck whenever he can get it. Like all men…' She looked as if she would like to take those words back and again, Thomas suppressed a smile.

'But Joan. She is fading away and I can't bring her back.'

Thomas was alarmed. At last, she had his attention. 'She is unwell? The sweating sickness?'

'No, sir, but she's like what she was before when her uncle was always preaching at her and telling her how to be. It's as if she goes elsewhere. But I couldn't get her back last time. And I think you can.' She paused and gathered her words and her courage, 'My Lord, she is lost here. She has nothing to be except be your wife. The house is run by your household and the baby is cared for by Mistress Godbold and you are with the King. What is she here for? She doesn't know and I think that she won't be here much longer if we don't call her back.'

Thomas was shocked. As Margery spoke, he remembered the wraith who had met him on the stairs with distant politeness. He remembered the anxious prayers he had spoken, begging God to return Joan to them and the promises he'd made. It wasn't enough to cage his Larke and expect fine food and gilded bars to be sufficient.

With heavy steps, he accompanied Margery to Joan's rooms. Margery had tried to keep it fresh but the chamber still bore the smell of sleep and despair. Across the passage, he could hear the soft voice of Anne as she chatted to Tom and he smiled at Tom's gentle cooing and incoherent responses. He had had no idea that such tiny babies would respond to speech. Perhaps his child was especially gifted. He felt it was more than likely that his son would be particularly clever.

But Joan. Her sleepy eyes blinked at him in the candlelight. She was so thin and he noticed that her pitiful flat breasts had ceased to produce milk. Poor girl. But the Queen did not descend into a fit of the mulligrubs – he smiled at this word from his childhood – no, at least in public the Queen rallied after the loss of her child and her smiles and vigour daily enticed the King to her bed and promised him another child.

Thomas's mind, always debating both sides of an argument spoke firmly. Enough. This girl was not a queen nor bred to be one and he had no right to compare them. This girl was his wife and his responsibility.

'Margery,' he spoke softly, 'please open the window curtains and the windows. Let us have fresh air in here.' Once again, he found himself perching on the edge of Joan's bed, cuddling her to him. But this time he tried to be gently bracing. He made her sit up and when she complained of dizziness, he told her that it was her own fault. Margery, ever useful, was suddenly there with a bowl of warm bread and milk and Thomas fished in his pouch for a nutmeg and with his knife shaved a little onto the slop.

Joan snuffled with weak laughter. 'My Uncle John hated the smell of nutmeg because of you, Thomas. He thought you were ruining me with luxury. It was my only act of defiance against him. Goodness Thomas, I feel drunk with hunger. Where have you been? I thought you had forsaken us.' She looked ready to weep, so Thomas quickly scooped some bread and milk into a spoon and fed it to her.

Her eyes closed in pleasure. Seldom had anything tasted so good. After a few mouthfuls, she held up her hand. 'I don't think I have eaten much these last days. That will do for now, Thomas.'

With a silent sigh, Thomas resigned any thoughts of work that evening and spent the night hours with Joan. He found himself talking and listening to his wife for the first time and it became apparent to them both how childish was their enterprise together.

'Thomas, you are older than me. I trusted you, I thought you knew what was right. But I don't blame you. I would not have done well – all those nuns telling me what to do. Can you imagine? Poor creatures. And there would be no Tom. Our miracle and blessing from God. I think of our marriage as an un-marriage but God smiles on it even if people don't.'

Thomas did not know the hour but as they dozed on

the bed, he was suddenly sickened by the smell of the tired unaired sheets and mattresses. And jumping out of bed, he took Joan by the hands and pulled her with him.

'Come. I know where we will be more comfortable.' He gently placed her fur-lined bedgown around her shoulders and they made their way along the passages to the opposite wing. Joan had hardly ventured here but Thomas's chamber was indeed fresh and sweet and she shivered deliciously as she climbed into his bed between the chilly sheets; then, Thomas pulled her towards him and warmed her as she fell asleep.

The next morning, they were awoken by the birds instead of hungry Tom. Joan felt the loss of that sound but somehow it wasn't as bad as hearing it and not being able to go to him.

She rolled over and smiled. 'I sleep well with you beside me.' She rolled on her back and tucked one arm behind her head.

'Margery says I have the mulligrubs,' she chuckled, 'lots of women get that after childbirth. But I should like to feel better.' She looked at Thomas, 'I should like to feel safe…'

Thomas's heart sank. He'd been thinking about this in the night but he didn't wish to speak his thoughts.

He spoke her name with something of a sigh, 'Joan… would you like to leave?' She jerked into a sitting position and looked rather frantic.

'I don't want you to go, but think on it. I could find you a husband and pay your dowry. Then you would be secure and could build a legitimate family.'

He could have bitten his tongue over the word, for Joan's face was crossed by outrage and resignation. 'Yes, *legitimate*. Of course. *Legitimate* children would be better than our bastard son.'

She turned her back on Thomas. He rolled his eyes. *How does a priest learn to deal with an angry wife,* he thought. Climbing out of bed, he walked round to Joan and knelt on the floor. He took her clenched fists in his and kissed her whitened knuckles.

'Darling girl,' he whispered, 'please don't be unhappy. I want to do what is best for you. I dearly want you and Tom to be here and happy but you have a choice.' His voice broke slightly, and he continued in a hoarse whisper, 'I can't imagine how I'd feel if I had to find a husband for you. You're my entirely beloved wife.'

He rested his head on their clasped hands and Joan, tears in her own eyes, touched her own head lightly against his. 'No Thomas. I don't want to go. The mulligrubs will retreat. No, don't find me a husband. Don't even secretly size them up for me. I'm yours. And you are mine.'

Even in this loving moment of tears and promises, Thomas thought... *and God's and the King's...* and wondered how long he could have all these loyalties and serve them truly.

Chapter 14

London

Summer had come to the magical gardens of La Parsonage and with relief, Thomas and Margery watched Joan return to life as the sun shone on both her and the plants. On bright days, Joan roused her small court and Margery – now in the role of lady-in-waiting and confidante – together with Mistress Godbold carrying baby Tom would settle in one of the pretty gardens, moving around to stay in the shade of hedges or trees. Sometimes they would dine outside, feeling it immensely daring to eat under the wide blue sky. Tom would be unswaddled and wriggle around on his blankets in the sunshine, giggling and sleeping.

Joan ceased to be afraid of the gardeners and sought them out. In Yarmouth, she had only learnt the rudiments of gardening; enough to grow a few household and medicinal herbs, but now she discovered a longing to know more. After a few days spent sighing and brushing muddy hand-prints from Joan's gowns, Margery fashioned her a coverall from coarse linen and James grudgingly found a pair of Thomas's gloves which were plain and slightly worn. James rather resented this even though he would never have permitted his master to wear such a simple pair of gloves.

Joan found the days passed so quickly in the company of Master Laurent and his garden boys. Master Laurent on the other hand was initially wary of his mistress spending so much time in his territory. He was forced to stop the lads from swearing and telling tales of their exploits in the city and as he grumbled to his wife, it was like being always on show to the Master and after all it was the *Master* who was his Master, not her who called herself *wife*. Mistress Laurent was agog, for all had heard of Mistress Joan, but of late few had seen her. News had crept out of her absence and return with My Lord's nephew. The word nephew was always said with a pause on either side and a certain stress on the word and invariably the gossips would then smile and raise their eyebrows.

But before long, Mistress Laurent noticed a change in her husband; each evening he would plan the next day and ponder how he could include Mistress Wolsey – no longer Mistress Joan - and he would wonder out loud what she could learn from this task or that and he'd sometimes say with pride that she was turning out to be quite a nice little plantsman.

One afternoon in late August, Thomas arrived home early. The King and Queen were away on progress and the calm weather called him back to La Parsonage. Sitting in his office, he sighed and longed for Joan and the weight of his child in his arms and the journey home had taken far too long.

Joan heard the light commotion which nowadays announced the arrival of her husband, but she doubted he was home for her, so continued under Master Laurent's instruction. As they worked around the strawberry pots, the scent of them in the summer sun was suddenly too much and she popped one of the warm juicy fruits into her mouth.

Master Laurent grunted. 'If you was one of my boys, I'd clap your head and make you spit that out.'

Joan turned to him and with the pulp deliberately over her teeth, grinned at him. 'I'm sorry. I should have asked.'

He smiled and carried on his work and Joan knew she was forgiven. 'But as they are so good, may I take some over to Margery and Mistress Godbold?'

He gave a hearty sigh but didn't say no, so Joan picked up an old plate which was to be broken and used as crock in pots. She scrubbed it clean on her coverall and picked a few hands full of the juicy strawberries. She stood up and curtseyed to Master Laurent, 'Thank you,' she said politely, *As if they was my fruit* he would later say to his wife, before adding, 'I shall see you again tomorrow, if I may. And I thank you for your time today.'

With her hand cupped over the teetering pile of berries, she followed the sound of laughter to a tiny garden which was cooled by a small pool and a fountain. The fountain wasn't running, but Anne and Margery were dipping Tom's feet into the water and watching his face as he relished the feeling on his toes and screamed with delight.

For a second, Joan paused. It was such a happy scene and she imagined for a moment how it would be when she spoke. All would turn to her with welcome smiles on their faces. Tom would clap his hands and hold out his arms. Joan gave a great shuddering sigh and felt tears of happiness in her eyes. Then she jumped as a hand fell on her shoulder. The plate flew upwards and the fruit went in all directions.

'Oh, *Thomas*!'

'Oh, Joan, I'm sorry.'

They spoke over each other and Joan dropped to her knees to collect the strawberries. Laughing, Margery rushed to help, but Joan stopped her, 'I'll do it, but would you fetch bowls and spoons and cream? For all of us, please.' Margery nodded and curtseyed to Wolsey before heading off.

Thomas carried the fruit to the benches and Joan washed her hands in the pool. Margery soon returned with a page in tow who carried bowls and cream. He licked his lips as he saw the strawberries and Thomas, noticing the hungry look, chose the largest one and tossed it to the boy with a wink.

Thomas picked up Tom and danced him on his knee and the baby laughed and dribbled at his father whilst Joan sat on the ground to hull the fruit before dividing it between the bowls and adding dollops of cream.

As Thomas spooned the first strawberry and thick yellow cream into his mouth, he too experienced a wave of pure happiness. *What joy*, he thought. *If only I could always live in the moment*. But then the thought was lost in a plan for the evening's work.

The family ate the strawberries and cream and Tom soon fell into an exhausted sleep. He was in Joan's arms and when Thomas spoke, she could barely tear her eyes from her baby,

'Joan, what a heavenly dish; the tartness of the fruit and the cream on the back of my tongue.' Joan smiled dreamily at him and raised her brows. *Really? Surely, he'd eaten cream and fruit before?*

'I think I shall offer this to the King when he comes to dine next week...'

Joan simply nodded, she wouldn't be involved in the King's visit and it meant little to her. Thomas would ensure that his mistress and by-blow would be tucked safely away when the court came to play. She understood; she was an embarrassment. Both of them would be uncomfortable to be reminded how fertile the Dean and his lemon were when the King and his Queen grieved for their empty nursery. Joan smiled. *Lemon, what a silly word for a woman of love who was the exact opposite of a sour fruit.*

Just one week later and hanging from the window yet contriving to remain hidden, Joan silently thanked Thomas for the cloaking window curtains as she, Margery and Mistress Godbold watched the King's party arrive in the inner court.

There was a constant jangle and clatter of horseshoes and harnesses and above all, was the clamour of voices. Joan was fascinated to see her husband with the King – they clapped each other on the shoulder and gripped arms with laughter and shouts of greeting as if they were the best of friends parted for many a month. In fact, it was but a day since Thomas had waited on the King. This seemingly impromptu visit had been planned and plotted to the least and finest detail. The nicest strawberries were ready and still scented Joan's fingers as she held the curtains away from her face. As she moved to sniff the sweetness, the King's eyes were caught by the slight movement. His face sharpened and without taking his eyes from hers, turned slightly and spoke to Thomas.

Joan saw slight annoyance cross his face but he smiled and bent his head in obedience. Joan felt a rush of dread and she knew that the King had asked to meet her. *Asked*, as if there was a choice. She slid back from the window and Margery came with her.

'He's coming up here, isn't he?' she hissed. Joan nodded.

'I fear so.' And she stood quite still; both appalled and excited.

'Well then! Get moving.'

At least Margery gathered her wits. Mistress Godbold was banished to the nursery with terrifying threats should Tom make the least noise and all the while she was stripping Joan of her gown and pulling a finer garment from the coffer. Her linen was clean but barely had Margery sprinkled a little scent on Joan, then they heard voices.

'Thomas, please allow me the honour of meeting Mistress Joan. I do after all count us as brothers in the game of marriage, for did you not find your Joan at the very moment I finally won my Katherine?' The King's voice was higher and more strident than she had expected and Joan could imagine Henry raising his voice before a battle to reach the least of his troops. But before she had time to compose herself, there was a knock at the door. Biting down a bubble of hysteria, she wondered what would happen if she refused them entry, but in a low voice, she bade Margery open the door and they sank into their deepest curtseys.

Afterwards, it all seemed so fast. The King entered the room and in a moment his hand was gently under her chin and he softly asked her to rise. Had Joan known it, a pretty blush painted her cheeks and the King understood why his Dean of Lincoln had acted so recklessly. Here was no wanton, but a charming girl who had effortlessly provided Thomas with a son. A nephew, the King silently corrected himself with a smile. Joan was delightful and had he not such regard for Thomas, he would be sorely tempted to see how well this pretty armful would fill his bed.

Then they were gone and Margery stared wide-eyed at her mistress's own wide eyes and before they could stop themselves, nervous giggles quickly had them clutching each other.

'Did he really ask me if I liked herrings?'

'He did. He said that they were well accounted for in the making of healthy young women.'

'His legs. His legs were *so* thin. Did you see? Like little threads hanging from his hose.'

Once again, they burst with laughter and Mistress Godbold peeped around the door to see the girls sitting on the floor wiping their eyes. With a sniff, she withdrew. If it wasn't for their exalted rank, she would pretty smartly take herself home. She loved little Tom but no more than any babe to whom she'd given suck and such immorals –

she silently moved her lips over it; was that the right word? Such poor morals were not right and not what she was used to.

Much later, Joan was blamelessly asleep and didn't hear Henry's confession to Thomas. Tears were edging into his voice as he confided how he envied his friend – she was so soft, so pretty, so fertile. Perhaps he shouldn't have married a highly bred mare, perhaps a little mix in breeding was a good thing? Should he regret the union? But he loved his Katherine. Had loved her since he first sighted her. He was but a boy but even then he knew. Wine showed in his face and the red of strawberries ringed his lips. *All I want Thomas*, he said in a harsh whisper, *all I want is a boy, a son. Of my own loins. My father was blessed, why not me?* And Thomas, his own nursery happily occupied, had no answer for his drink-softened King.

Chapter 15

London, August 1512

As the small boat made its way to London, Joan tried to gather her thoughts. Under her gown, her milk-heavy breasts hung down. She ruefully wobbled her stomach; would it go back into shape again?

She could hear Tom wailing with boredom and Margery trying to amuse him. At least this time she wasn't sick. Their time with Agnes and Arthur in Yarmouth had been so short. This pregnancy had not left Joan in the sleepy misery of last time, instead, she had been a useful member of the household until once more she was blessed with a quick and easy birth. As their eyes met for the first time, Dorothy had looked at her mother with an air of disapproval but Anne Godbold had taken immediately to the new baby.

Margery laughed, 'How can a baby be disapproving after three minutes in the world?' But Joan knew she'd been weighed and found wanting.

Thomas's letters – two this time – had been full of the King. Joan knew of course of Henry's bitter energy following the still-birth of a son. Sadly, his pilgrimage to Walsingham had not yet borne fruit from Katherine's womb and instead, the King turned his energies to the other old enemy, France, which allowed his father-in-law, Ferdinand, to take Navarre. Joan didn't pretend to have the brain of an advisor, but it pleased Thomas to explain affairs of state to her. She liked to listen to him and occasionally interjected with questions such as '*But what will Pope Julius think of that?*' in the hope that it would make her sound wise and thoughtful. It turned out that Julius the Warrior had thought very well of that and stripped Louis of being the Most Christian King of France and tossed that bauble over to Henry. All Henry had to do, Thomas wrote, was relieve the Papal States from being troubled by France. Joan had chuckled when she read that; she could sense Thomas's thoughts behind his words. He would be thinking what rubbish, is the Pope mad? And yet another part of his brain would be racing joyfully to assess the costs and things to be done and could they really do it? Could Thomas Wolsey provision an army and bring France back to England? Could they really stand in Paris and watch the Pope crown Henry as King of all France? *And thank you for asking*, Joan would drily add in her mind, *yes, you have a beautiful daughter*.

Another furious wail brought Joan back to the present, Tom staggered across the deck to her, his face purple with frustration, 'Dothy babs, go!' he screamed, and Joan chuckled and knelt down to him, 'Tom, my sweeting, Dothy is here to stay.' She couldn't yet pick him up, but she sat on the freshly scrubbed deck and pulled him towards her, forcing him onto her lap.

'Noooo.' He bellowed, wriggling hard against her.

Joan quickly wrapped a fold of her skirt around her finger, as if it was a baby and with a fingernail marked a small mouth on the face.

'Tom look, the tiny baby is crying too. See?

She made a wailing sound and bounced the puppet finger around. Tom immediately transferred his interest to Joan's finger and grabbed at it, the tears drying on his face. Sometimes this mercurial behaviour worried Joan – did it indicate a bright mind or a weak one? Would he take advantage of a privileged life or would it spoil him?

Their return home was subdued: Thomas was away, still wondering if the needle-prick actions in France to assist Ferdinand's invasion of Navarre could be turned to greater advantage. He hadn't been home for many days and William and James were with their master, running his almost-household at Richmond or wherever the King settled at this exciting time of war. An army had been sent north against a possible threat from the Scots and the navy was massing in the channel and heading towards Brittany. Joan, with an uneven idea of geography, had hoped to see the fleet and especially the King's new and favourite ship, the Mary Rose, but reached home without fulfilling this ambition.

So it was a quiet and depleted household which greeted Joan but it was good to be home. Wolsey's new niece was exhibited and Tom was much comforted by being taken to the kitchens for treats from the doting cook, so the women were able to head to their quarters in peace. Dotty, as they all called her, was proving to be a peaceful baby and disturbed none of them as they lay on their beds and slept.

Mid-August

The hot day was silent and still and Joan's household had taken little for dinner, preferring a sweet banquet in the privy garden where they could pick at the light food throughout the afternoon.

Two jugs of small beer rested in the pond, and Mistress Godbold slept with Tom in the shade; the wet nurse curled around her charge like a bitch around her puppy. Margery was in the house, supposedly cleaning out chests against the summer infestation of moths but Joan suspected she would find her dozing in a cool place. Joan seemed to be the only person awake. In the crook of her left arm was sweetly sleeping Dorothy and in her hands was Thomas's book of hours. She always marvelled at this curiosity; despite its thickness, it sat neatly in her grasp. She closed it and with a smile knocked her knuckles on the leather binding; it sounded hollow, yet inside were such treasures. Uncle John would be disappointed that the Latin meant so little to her, but she enjoyed the illuminations; the gold bright as it reflected the sun and the domestic pictures reminding her of her own, somewhat less-holy life.

She carefully closed the book and folded it into the leather wrapping – the ground might seem dry but damp could easily damage such a delicate item. The chair was hard under her legs but although tired, she did not want to sleep so she drew some deep breaths and flexed her feet. The heat surrounded her like a hot, thick bath and she longed for fresh air.

After a while, she turned again to the book and was working on the Latin when voices caught her attention. The little garden was like a room with no ceiling but the sky resting on the high hedge walls, and in the doorway stood a small party. The sun on the gold had seared her eyes and she blinked to see past the green phantoms in her vision. One of the visitors stepped forward, a man in his forties, dressed well but not fashionably and he bowed to her.

'Forgive me, Mistress Joan, we disturb you…'

She stood, curtseyed and went towards them. 'My Lord, I fear you have the advantage of me…?'

The two smiled tentatively at each other, and behind the older man stood a boy. Joan's eyes flickered over him and she gave him a vague smile.

'My Lord…?' Joan let her voice tail off but smiled encouragingly, silently urging him to get on with it.

'I am Thomas Legh.' He spoke as if confident that Joan would know who he was and indeed, there was something in the back of her mind…

'My Lord, forgive me. I have been away. I went to Ipswich to my Lord Wolsey's sister to bring her son and daughter to London. My Lord is raising them and I am…' she faltered, how to describe herself to a stranger who was not conversant with the deceit, '…well, I am too.'

As the polite and awkward conversation went on before him, the boy behind Master Legh stared at his father and the beautiful woman. He felt faint and wondered if he was about to fall down a vast bottomless hole.

Only moments before, but indeed a whole lifetime, he had been chatting excitedly to his father in admiration of Wolsey's gardens and they wondered if some of the beauty would transport to their grounds in Cheshire if the climate were not too harsh. As they passed between two hedges George saw a vision, a sight which would remain with him until the day he died and was his ideal of heaven and perfection. In the future, he would forgive his wife every fault because of this day, when he was vouchsafed a vision of heaven.

Reading a book in which he could just see an image of the Virgin and Child, was surely that very Virgin herself. Cradling a baby in one arm and surrounded by the glorious flowers of the privy garden, was the most beautiful woman he could ever have imagined. He would not have been surprised if a unicorn had wandered in and placed its head in her lap.

'Unicorn.' George was appalled to hear the word issue from his mouth and blushed violently, turning the word into a cough. His father and the angel turned to him in surprise.

'My son, George. He is fifteen and I thought it time he travelled and saw London.'

Joan smiled at George and his heart stopped. It jumped and started again and he found the wit to greet her civilly and bow to her. As he bent slightly, the blood returned to his head and he found that he might not die at that moment, but even without putting it into words, he knew he was in love. This beautiful woman, with cheeks softer than a rose petal and her huge blue eyes and luminous smile, made him forget the girls at home with whom he would dally in the stables, gardens and great chambers of the local houses.

His father saw his son's face and his heart sank. He knew exactly who Mistress Joan was and her position in Wolsey's household. Everyone knew that. Few judged Wolsey, for he had a reputation for great kindness, and his growing influence at court and with the King made people treat him circumspectly. And of course, a man needed a woman on occasion. He did not flaunt her and this woman was clearly no strumpet. It was even rumoured that they were married. The boy would get over her, but he had to agree, she was lovely; who could blame Wolsey?

'Is my Lord Dean expecting you?'

'In a manner of speaking, yes. He has been assisting me with a matter concerning some property adjoining my estate in Cheshire. He promised to speak to the King and I thought we would come to town to see how matters are progressing.'

As they chatted, Joan passed Dorothy to the now awakened Mistress Godbold and led her visitors inside to a cool parlour. Thomas Legh was astonished at the riches inside La Parsonage – the gorgeous tapestries and shelves and cupboards displaying the delicate crystal glass from Italy and the soft glow of silver and gold plate, even to his great astonishment, carpets on the floor of the well-proportioned room. He stepped around them and Joan gave her soft chuckle.

'I know Master Legh, such an extravagance, but try it, so nice under your feet.'

Both men were dumbstruck; George Legh continued to feel as if he had been transported to one of the rooms of heaven and his father fought the ungallant feelings of how useful it could be to have a wealthy and influential friend. But even better, one of lowlier origins than himself so he would not feel as if he was a supplicant – even if he was.

After a little polite conversation, wine and cakes were brought to them, and to Joan's relief, as she was beginning to find George's admiring gaze a little wearing, they heard the voices and clatter of Thomas's arrival. But excited as she was, Thomas's men sounded subdued and she felt anxious as she stepped into the screens passage. But her glad greeting died in her throat; her husband sagged against the panelling, he looked ghastly and to her horror there were the traces of tears on his cheeks.

Thomas saw her and straightened up, 'Joan. Of course. You are come home. I am so glad. Did the children travel well?'

'Thomas, whatever has happened?'

Wolsey stepped towards her and she could not help but remark the resemblance between her husband and Tom when he was frustrated or upset. Then she opened her arms to Thomas, who with a sigh of relief stepped into her embrace. He leaned heavily against her and held her tightly as if to break her. Joan longed to know what was wrong but the only movement she could make was to grip him back and rub her hands across his back.

Then all at once, she heard an apologetic cough and Thomas drew away as if pulled sharply by ropes. Joan looked at Thomas's polite smile and whipped her head around to see Thomas Legh standing at the door of the parlour, the very picture of mortified embarrassment.

'Thomas, my friend. How marvellous and unexpected!'

Master Legh bowed deeply but Joan could still feel how uncomfortable the poor man was and not for the first time her soul writhed in discomfort.

Thomas ushered Legh back into the parlour and Joan escaped to her chamber. Climbing the stairs, she could hear the laughter of the three men. Clearly, the King and Queen yet lived. Her children were safe. And she could not imagine what else might so upset Thomas.

Joan was half asleep when she heard Thomas's tread outside her chamber. He was a large man and always walked heavily but even for him it was a slow and weary step. She jumped from the bed and opened the door, holding out her hand and drawing him in. She said nothing but secured the lock. Thomas's face was impossible to decipher; a confusing mixture of grief and what Joan guessed was lust. He pushed her hard against the door, his hand cupping the side of her head and drawing them together until their mouths met. After a while, he lifted her to the bed and they made love with silent passion, rising together to a shockingly intense climax. But then, Thomas collapsed onto Joan, burying his face in the hollow of her neck and to her distress, she felt huge sobs wracking him.

At last, perhaps conscious that he was crushing his wife, Thomas withdrew and rolled to the edge of the mattress.

Joan gave a slight laugh, 'Thomas, you might need to

pull me out of this dip we've made. Or at least send down a rope for me.' But Wolsey ignored her and she wriggled round until she sat beside him and looked into his face.

'Please. Won't you tell me what has happened? Your heart is clearly broken.'

After a while, Thomas spoke and his voice was halting and broken, 'There's a place called Point St-Mathieu.' Joan nodded as if she knew where that was.

'It's near Brest.' Another wise nod and Thomas smiled, 'It's the north-western-most point of France.' He was silent again and Joan waited, lightly laying her hand on his arm to give silent comfort.

'Henry's ships were doing so well. The Mary Rose has proven herself beyond all we could have hoped. Then the French carrick, Cordelière closed with our Regent. I don't know what happened but they became fouled together and Cordelière exploded. And Regent caught the fire and they went down so quickly. They say there were three hundred guests on board the Breton ship, innocents just visiting. Nearly two thousand souls were lost. Joan. I can't bear it. I hear their screams and see their terror. I can't look at the beauty around me without their burnt and lost faces floating in front of me. I feel as if I am drowning alongside them.' Thomas gave a dreadful gasp as if he was indeed seizing his own last breath.

Joan quickly wrapped her arms around Thomas and he pressed his face into her breast and with his arms tightly around her waist, he wept as if the end of the world had come.

They stayed like that for a long time, before Joan

could gently push him back onto the bed and she finished the undressing of him whilst he gazed blindly at the bed hangings.

As dusk approached, Joan brought food and drink and persuaded him to eat, then she fetched Dorothy and gently placed the baby in her father's arms. The new life seemed to revive Thomas slightly and he stared at his daughter's face. Dorothy opened her eyes and regarded him and Thomas gave a small laugh. 'My goodness, Joan. She's inherited your disapproving look.'

Joan was annoyed but at least grateful that he was surfacing slightly from his shock. She sat at the foot of the bed watching the meeting and her mind roamed, trying to find a subject to distract him.

'So, who is Thomas Legh? He seemed to know me.'

'Yes, Legh… He's a nice fellow, good country stock, noble but not ennobled, so seeks friends at court. I think I'm a good friend for him to have; influential but being the Butcher's Cur, never likely to be a threat to his position, such as it is.'

Thomas paused a moment and looked curiously at Joan. 'His boy was rather taken with you. Did you notice?'

Joan smiled, 'Well, actually I did, they came upon me in the garden and he stared at me as if he'd never seen the like. Bless him, it was rather sweet, although a little irritating.' Then relieved that Thomas seemed to be thawing even more, she leaned over and took Dorothy from her father. Thomas leaned over to kiss the baby and asked after Tom.

'Oh, he's all right. Loved playing with his cousins and

has developed a dear little Ipswich accent.'

Thomas gave a little laugh. 'Well, we'll soon knock that out of him. Do you think he's asleep?'

Joan waved at the shrouded windows, 'Well, he might be because it might be dark outside, or it might not. Who can tell with these window curtains?' And with a little flounce, she stepped outside the chamber and called for Mistress Godbold, who appeared so quickly that one might have suspected she was lurking, ready to reclaim the baby.

Joan returned to the room and closing the door jumped partly onto the bed and partly onto Thomas who grunted as his wife landed.

'My husband, I have sorely missed you. My bed is quiet and cold like a grave without you.' Then Joan could have bitten out her tongue at her thoughtless words, for Thomas grew pale once more, and politely excusing himself, left the bed and donned his nightgown. Joan sighed and lay back, regretting the last glimpses of his naked body. For a moment she daydreamed, feeling the grip of his arms around her ribs and looking at the marks of love he'd left on her breasts and feeling heat within her once more. She rolled her eyes; whatever people thought, she loved Thomas with her soul and very much with her body. Then she grinned and jumped as Thomas spoke. She opened her eyes, 'Whatever were you doing, Joan? You sighed and looked rueful and then you shrugged and gave a very naughty grin.'

'Oh, just wishing you were *here*.' Sitting up and patting the bed between her legs. 'Not,' pointing at the desk, 'there. I'm not there. I'm here. And I haven't been here for months…'

She raised her eyes in a pleading way but Thomas refused to be swayed. 'Darling girl, I have letters to write.' He came over to the bed, 'Come along, hop in and cover up. Keep warm for me and I'll be there as soon as I can.' He raised an eyebrow in a suggestive way and with a smile, Joan did as she was told.

After many hours, the flickering of a guttering candle disturbed her, and Joan rose. Thomas was at the desk, asleep with his head resting on his hand. She looked at the letter. It was addressed to the Bishop of Winchester and Wolsey was telling Foxe of the loss of the ships and begging him to keep the news secret. Joan doubted it could be kept secret for long but that wasn't her problem. She gently stroked Thomas's hair and he stirred.

'Without any discussion, my love, bed. Right now.'

Thomas may have been virtually asleep, but once in bed, he stirred and found it possible to make love to his wife once again. And again, before dawn when they finally both slept an exhausted sleep.

Chapter 16

London, 1514

Joan closed her eyes for a moment in an attempt to calm down. Then Tom whooped again and she heard more glass smashing.

'Thomas Wynter. Stand still right now.'

Tom looked slightly taken aback at the fury in his mother's voice and for a moment, he stopped in his delightful game of smashing priceless Venetian crystal and stamping joyfully on it.

'Pretty,' he laughed, 'Sparkles an' spangles!'

Joan put her hands to her face and not for the first time, felt tears in her eyes at Tom's behaviour. Spanking failed, for he enjoyed the drama of screaming like a pig at slaughter. Ignoring him certainly didn't help, for he would shrug and carry on as he wished.

Thomas had no idea what to do; on the odd occasion, he visited his family from his residence at York Place, the new Bishop of Lincoln, soon to be Bishop of York, looked on in bemusement at his son and told the boy to behave. Then he returned to his new love affair, *not God*, Joan thought bitterly, *oh no, not their divine creator*, but the King – seemingly the only provider in this world or any other – of happiness. Thomas spoke of Henry as a girl does of her lover. *For pity's sake,* Joan would think, *you're forty-one. You're a prince of the church and a father, not a green-sick girl.*

Then the impasse was broken by Dorothy who adored her wild brother with a passion only narrowly below that of her love for God. The three-year-old came running into the room and too late did Joan see her small bare feet flashing beneath her gown. The baby, as they still called her, gave an apologetic cry and sank to the ground. Then she cried again and lifted up her hands. Blood poured from hands and feet and shards of glass could be seen sticking out of her innocent pink flesh.

'*Dotty*. My love.' Joan picked her way to the child and lifted her out of the chaos. Tom, for once, seemed appalled at his actions and stood in horror as blood dripped to the rushes.

'Thomas,' Joan hissed, 'this is your fault. You have hurt baby. She might never get better.'

Calling for Margery, Joan took the children to a room which was not full of sharpness and told Tom to stand still. Settling Dorothy on her lap, Joan kissed the child's soft hair and tried to comfort both children. Margery arrived and sighed, 'Oh Tom…' and as she looked at Dorothy, the baby lifted her hands and announced that the blood was from God's Wounds.

Joan let out a shuddering sigh and barely avoided laughing in despair. She gripped the little arms and stopped her from broadcasting holy blood about the room.

Fetching tweezers and bandages, Margery caught

Tom's eye and he tried a wink, but for once he won no response from his usual ally who fixed him with a stony stare. 'No Thomas, I can't talk to someone who would let his sister die just for the fun of being wicked.' And had she not turned away, Margery would have seen remorse and tears crossing Tom's face.

'Mother? Will I go to heaven today?'

'Darling, none of us knows when we will see God. If today is when he wishes to see you, then yes.'

Dorothy looked content and not for the first time, Joan reflected on how much her uncle would love this saintly niece of his.

At his mother's words, Tom was utterly demolished and fell to the floor in floods of tears. The two women ignored the sobbing boy and concentrated on removing the glass from Dotty's palms and soles. She looked pale but determined and when Margery tried to make her take a sip of wine, she turned her face away.

'I can bear it, Margery. But thank you for your kindness.' The brave little whisper almost unmanned Margery who raised her eyes to Joan's, then looked away again as Joan looked equally close to hysterical laughter.

Finally, the tiny hands and feet were safely bandaged and Dorothy settled in her father's chair with his prayer book open on her lap. Tom was asleep with slime and tears drying to a crust on his face and the rushes marking his cheek.

'Dotty, will you keep an eye on Tom, please? Call if he needs us.'

'Yes, mother. Poor Tom. He did *crying*.'

Joan led the way into the room of wrecked crystal. She closed the door and stood staring at her friend with open mouth. Margery wrapped her arms around her waist and doubled over in silent laughter.

'Dear Lord...' Then she was lost for words.

Joan joined her in laughter, 'It was the wounds of Christ. Poor girl, she's going to be so disappointed not to be in heaven this day.'

All at once the door opened and Tom stood there. 'Are you laughing?' he demanded.

Joan straightened up. 'Hardly, Thomas. Margery and I are frightened beyond words that you might have murdered Dorothy.'

Tom looked as if he was chewing stale bread, working his tongue in and out of his cheek and biting his lip. After a few deep sighs, he spoke: 'I'm sorry.'

Joan shrugged, 'I don't believe you, Tom. I think you are a stupid boy who knows nothing. And I am no longer interested in anything you have to say.' She and Margery started to collect the larger pieces of glass and kept their backs to the boy who stood and for the first time in his life, cried quietly and not for show.

As luck would have it, Thomas chose this time to visit his family. They could hear the clatter as his great procession entered the courtyard and Tom jumped up to look out of the window.

Joan looked up from her task and ordered him away. 'Sit down, Tom. Your father will have something to say to you when he arrives.'

Still repentant, Tom obediently sat down and after a

few moments, Margery straightened up and said, 'Tom. Come with me, your mother and my Lord Bishop need to speak alone.' Tom looked worried and again tried to smile at Margery who met his look with hard eyes.

'Tom, your father has heard about his glass being smashed and he has come to see why.'

Tom's eyes widened. 'How does he know?' he whispered.

'Thomas, your father knows everything that happens in the King's realm. Why shouldn't he know what you have been doing?' And with raised eyebrows, she led the awestruck boy from the room.

A little later, Thomas strode into the room and stopped, 'God's Truth, what happened here? Have we suffered an earthquake?' Then he took in Joan's flushed face and the tendrils of hair trailing around her face and thought simultaneously, *Oh. Tom.* And, *how much I want her. My wife. Not my wife.* And cursed the feelings of lust and love and wondered if he could tumble her to the floor there and then. Joan recognised the look on his face and felt an answering flush through her own body. But she ignored it; she was cross with Tom, and angry with Thomas who floated in and out of their lives so infrequently that sometimes she struggled to recall the sound of his voice.

Her face hardened and Thomas found her pink cheeks even more seductive.

'Have you not a kiss for your husband? Not even for a man with the Peace Treaty of London tucked in his pocket?' Despite herself, Joan giggled.

'Hmm,' she said, trailing her gaze down Thomas's front, 'is that what it is?' And in a moment, she was locked in his arms and kissing him back with equal desire.

'Quietly now,' she cautioned, 'Dorothy stood on the glass and if she hears you, you can explain why her wounds are not the Wounds of Christ, and you know how long that will take.' Thomas nodded, a loving smile on his lips.

'I presume that Tom did this,' he waved his hands at the glass, 'and for no particular reason.'

'Precisely. I don't know what to do with *your nephew*. I think he's bored. He should be one of a litter of little boys, wearing each other out all day, but instead, he's confined in a palace with women and a tiny saint.'

'I promise I'll think on it.'

Joan gave him a tight-lipped smile but she knew he would. He did his best for them and his absence was her only complaint.

Walking as silently as possible, nonetheless, Dorothy heard them and called through the slightly open door of the parlour.

'Is Father here? I heard horses.'

Joan stuck her head through the door. 'Sweetheart, that was only the start of his procession. You know it grows longer with each honour from the King. I'll warrant that he's not yet excused himself from the King's presence.' She jumped slightly as Thomas batted her bottom. 'As soon as he arrives, Dotty, he'll come and see you.' Baby nodded, content, and Joan escaped.

Once upstairs, they made love hard and urgently,

Joan's slight cry muffled by Thomas's mouth over hers but when his moment came, he slumped over her and pushed his head hard into the pillow. After a few moments, she wrapped her arms around him.

'What's wrong?' and when he didn't reply, 'Ah. I see. You didn't come to see us, or to do this, or indeed savour the bitterness of remorse.' She pushed him away and he rolled onto the bed beside her. Her fury with Tom now formed into anger at Thomas.

'May I fetch you some refreshment, my Lord? Something to take away the taste? I don't mind waiting on you, after all, you pay handsomely enough for my services. Are you yet made Bishop of Winchester? Then I can officially become one of Winchester's Geese.'

The reference to the prostitutes occupying land owned by the bishop stung Thomas and he sat up.

'Stop it. Don't speak like that. You are my beloved wife. I am your husband. God knows that even if all men disagree.'

Joan stood smoothing down her skirts with trembling hands and astonished that she had finally spoken the words which circled constantly in her head. It was shocking and she found the room was shaking in time with her mad pulse. Her knees gave way and for a moment Thomas thought she was sinking in a low curtsey to him. He leapt up and lifted her to the bed.

'I'm sorry.' They both spoke at once, then Joan continued, 'Nothing is forever, is it, Thomas?'

'No,' he said bleakly, 'it isn't.'

Presently, Joan removed herself from Thomas's

comforting arms. It was as if she was always leaving this safe place, she thought, with no surety that she would ever return but the children needed her and the day had to continue.

As she tidied her hair, Thomas was surprised at how it had grown since he'd last seen her. It was almost its old length and one could imagine that John Larke had not cropped her hair to the scalp. Then remembering why he was at La Parsonage, Thomas spoke, 'Have you seen my illuminated prayer book?'

'Yes, Dorothy has it. It's open on her favourite picture so she may contemplate the Virgin in a heavenly garden. Thomas, it's not only Tom who needs more than I can give… Dotty would soak up instruction like a thirsty sponge. Could they have a tutor? Perhaps my brother would come?'

Thomas looked thoughtful. 'I don't think he would see tutoring our children as advancement, but I really do promise, I will think about it and find a solution.'

Joan nodded; that would have to be enough. Heading downstairs, she left Thomas to comfort or chastise his children as he saw fit and went to the kitchens to discuss dinner and see if it would be fit for the Bishop of Lincoln—if he had time to share it with them.

Returning to the screens passage, Tom bowled into her, 'Mother! Mother! My father says that if I continue to be a naughty boy, I may not be able to stay here! Mother, where will I go? Will there be other boys? Can I take my wooden sword?'

Joan struggled not to laugh at Thomas's great

misjudgement of his son; his threat was now an enticing promise. 'Of course you may take your toys. But we will miss you and Dorothy will pine for you...'

Tom looked slightly thoughtful, uttered a doubtful 'Oh...' and wandered off, chewing his nails and kicking the furniture.

Still smiling, Joan followed the sound of Thomas's voice and stood watching as Wolsey explained to his daughter that actually it was blasphemous to think that one's own injuries were like those of Jesus. Dotty nodded seriously and asked if God might forgive her. 'I think he will, Dorothy, for God is love and he loves you even more than you love him.'

'Even more?' The child's eyes were wide as she tried to encompass that thought. Then Thomas held her little bandaged hands between his and gently prayed for God's protection for his servant Dorothy and that she might become well as soon as it pleased God.

Joan felt her eyes pricking at this tender scene and when Thomas looked up at her, he didn't wink or grin but gave her a gentle smile and blessed her too. Sometimes it was hard to remember that he was a man of God but when she did, she was always struck by his great compassion.

Thomas did not really have time to dine but having entered the house during a crisis and – in his opinion – worsened it, he decided to stay for another hour. The meal was cheerful as a new face helped to ease the boredom and frustration which simmered in the household. As he readied himself to leave, Thomas remembered the purpose of his visit.

'Dorothy, can you help me please?' Baby looked eager. 'I am looking for my prayer book as I want to use it at the marriage of the King's sister, Margaret, to the King of France.'

Dorothy was all eagerness and Thomas carried her around several rooms as she pointed out places where she liked to read it.

'Dorothy. I am proud of you. Our Baby, reading Latin.'

She beamed and then said, 'I like the pictures best though. The words are very hard. Sometimes Tom helps me.'

Tom looked puffed with pride which remained even when she added, 'But he's not really very good at it. But he likes the pictures too.'

Thomas smiled at them both. 'I will only borrow this for a short time then, but I will find some books for you with lots of pictures.' Dorothy nodded and kissed her father farewell.

Within a month, Joan found herself receiving two unexpected visitors, Master and Mistress Richardson. They were prosperous and well-spoken and somewhat taken aback that Joan was surprised by their visit.

'My Lord Archbishop of York spoke to us. Didn't he?' The poor man looked anxious and his wife nodded encouragingly.

Joan smiled and Master Richardson continued, 'I knew Thomas when he was first the chaplain to the old King. Of course that was before we were married.' Then he blushed, 'I mean we,' clutching his wife's hand, '... not we…' gesturing at Joan and the room in general. Joan wanted to laugh and made another encouraging face.

'So I think that he never forgets anyone, and when we were wed,' another faint blush, 'he sent gifts. And gifts when Richard was born and then John. And now he wishes us to have a tutor for the boys… and your boy Tom…'

Suddenly Joan understood and her mouth went dry but she forced herself to smile.

'Oh dear, I think that I must be a letter astray.'

The anxious couple looked relieved and as if summoned, Tom himself crashed through the door, shouting over his shoulder. He continued shouting but the page with whom he'd been chasing around the house had long disappeared. Joan placed her hands on his shoulders and spoke his name in a low voice and eventually he looked at her, laughter still in his features.

'Tom, this is Master and Mistress Richardson.'

Thankfully, the boy made a low bow to them and beamed his impressive smile.

As Joan hoped, Master Richardson took over the conversation with her son. 'Master Wynter. I am glad to make your acquaintance. Your, um…'

'Father.' Joan supplied with a touch of defiance.

'Yes. Hmmm. Well, he would like you to come and spend some time with us at Willesden. We have two boys and we would like you to be our guest for a few days. Of course, if you don't like it…'

Tom interrupted, 'I must fetch my sword. Can you wait?' And he galloped off.

Mistress Richardson looked at Joan with compassion

and that kind face brought tears to Joan's eyes.

'My dear. If he doesn't like it or if you cannot bear it, we will bring him straight home to you.' She rose and knelt by Joan's chair, clasping her hands around Joan's.

Joan sighed, 'I think it is the only way. He can be quite naughty, you know.'

Mistress Richardson smiled, though her eyes remained anxious. 'They are all naughty. It's like having a litter of puppies.'

Her husband laughed. 'I have to make sure they get enough walks. And the dogs!' Evidently satisfied with his joke and the fairly smooth way this potentially awkward interview was progressing, he sat back and crossed his hands over his tiny round stomach and Joan found herself imagining this kindly man in twenty years and hoping he would become the prosperous and gentle man he had promise to be.

'Mistress Joan. You should not pass Tom to us without having seen Master Wolsey's, I mean, my Lord Archbishop's letter.'

At this point, Margery, who certainly hadn't been listening outside, tapped on the door and came in. She gave a theatrical jump and apologised, 'Oh Mistress, I'm sorry. I didn't realise you had guests. I just found this note from My Lord and thought you should see it. I think it was delivered last night…'

Joan took the parchment and cracked the seal. It was indeed a letter from Thomas saying he had remembered his old friend Richardson and with their agreement and of course with Joan's, Tom should spend some time in their household with their new tutor.

Joan looked up at the Richardsons and smiled. 'My Lord is very thoughtful. If he thinks your new tutor is good enough for your sons and his son then I can only agree. I just hope the poor man has a strong character.'

Joan liked the couple and between them, they agreed that Tom would visit the family daily in order to attend lessons and would return home for supper, but he fitted in so well with the family that within three weeks, Joan and Margery stood waving off Tom and a small procession of Richardson servants carrying his belongings.

Suddenly, realising that this was a proper departure, Tom thundered back towards Joan. He slammed into her with his usual enthusiasm.

'Oh, Tom! You've winded me.' But she didn't draw back. Little Acorn was suddenly so grown. He was hard to the touch and always had been; his hair was coarse and unruly but she smoothed it lovingly and held his solid little body to her. His bones stuck out and she felt the angles of his shoulders under her arms and tried to memorise the feeling. His grubby hands – *how* were they grubby, he'd been scrubbed half an hour ago – clasped hers.

'Mother, Richard says that we may go hunting this year. Actually, he said this afternoon, so I need to hurry.'

Joan laughed, 'All right Tom. But say goodbye to Baby and Margery. We will all miss you.'

He impatiently turned to the rest of his little household whom he was leaving so heedlessly. *It doesn't even occur to him,* Joan thought sadly, *that we might never be together again.*

They watched the little party ride away and Joan listened till she could hear them no longer, then they turned back towards the house. Margery was carrying Dorothy who asked to be put down. She looked around and at the door which was being closed and said, 'Tom?' and burst into tears.

She was quickly comforted but Joan too could feel the silent hole in their lives. She tried to remember his thundering footsteps around the building; how he seemed to shake the old floorboards and increase the gaps between them. Now, she thought, she could place one of Thomas's remaining crystal covered-cups in the middle of the floor and it would remain there in peace for all eternity. Then she smiled at Margery who looked with concern at her friend who seemed to be balanced between tears and laughter.

'I may even lose my voice, Margery, for lack of shouting. Oh dear. Can we get him back?'

They hugged each other and Margery said dryly, 'I once took a stone from my shoe. And I found I missed it.'

Chapter 17

London, 1516

Although it was late when Joan returned home, the summer evenings meant that only the slightest suggestion of dusk was creeping in. The western sky held the merest touch of green and as Joan and her attendants walked into the grounds of La Parsonage, she felt very peaceful. She was to all appearances a prosperous gentlewoman. Her gowns and bonnets were of the finest materials and her skin and hair showed a woman who was well nourished. If she saw her reflection, she would give a small smile and wonder if this was how her mother had looked. She might ask Thomas when she next saw him. But Cardinal Wolsey, now also Lord Chancellor of England was an important man. She suspected he had hopes of the papacy and the strictures on the morals and personal behaviour of priests also applied to him.

Tonight she could see their shades dancing around the darkening garden, as they had that evening when he brought her to see the beautiful grounds and tell her that they would live there and always be happy. But she reminded herself, she had no complaints. She was supposed to have spent the day with Tom and she had indeed spotted him a few times. His first gleeful shout of 'mother' had gone slightly awry as he'd seized Constance's hand and not Joan's, but Mistress Richardson had smoothed over it and Joan assured her that she understood. And indeed, she was grateful that Constance was a mother to Tom. And she turned her thoughts away from another woman bathing a scuffed knee or smoothing his hot brow in the night if he woke. Constance and her husband provided Tom with all he needed and that was good.

After those thoughts, which always intruded when she visited Tom, Joan had an enjoyable day. Dotty behaved perfectly even after being trampled by a stampede of boys and dogs and retained her delight in seeing Tom until exhausted, she'd quietly lain down in a sunny window seat and slept.

Thoughts of Thomas's long absence were heavy in her mind and as she passed through the courtyard, she was surprised to see Thomas's mules and she hurried into the house.

The candles were lit through the screens passage, and going into the parlour she saw Thomas by the window, using the last of the day to read and mark some papers. She'd once suggested that he have a little desk fitted to the harness of the mules so he could work whilst travelling. She meant it as a joke, but she had seen him thinking and working out if it was possible.

'My Lord. What a surprise.' Joan curtseyed deeply. She may have known his body inside and out but he was still the alter rex, the other king. She was never sure how he felt about that slightly malicious title; secretly slightly flattered she suspected, whilst vehemently denying it.

'My dear.' Thomas rose and took her hands in his before lightly kissing her cheek. She briefly acknowledged a moment of disappointment. Not that sort of visit then. But then they hadn't lain together properly for several years now and one day she would accept it and put aside her longing and learn to cease her gentle hints which were invariably lost in his busy wake. One day she would learn. But not today.

She spoke brightly, 'I have spent the day with Master and Mistress Richardson. And I am almost sure I saw Tom, but don't press me, for it might have been a laughing whirlwind.'

Thomas smiled. 'I hear he's very happy there. Although his studies could be better.'

Joan shrugged, 'I suppose so, but he is not like either of us, is he? He's a charming boy and will do well enough. And thankfully his tutor is a most patient man. You chose well.'

Thomas nodded and Joan waited. Why ever was he here? He looked anxious and that certainly wasn't in Thomas's nature. Perhaps only on their wedding night had he shown the slightest sign of nerves. Joan smiled; he looked exactly like Tom that time he'd knocked a tooth and spent days wobbling it and rubbing his tongue sore before it finally fell out. Now someone else collected those little teeth and Joan was left with her Thomas who was busily sucking at his own teeth.

Finally, Thomas met her eye and drew breath.

'Joan...'.

She looked questioningly at him. 'I have something to tell you...'

'Is Tom all right?' But she didn't think it was that, he'd have told her very quickly if Tom was ill.

'Oh yes, all the children are very well.'

'All?'

'Well, yes.' Thomas looked sick. 'Joan, we haven't... well... for some time.'

His face was scarlet and he looked at the floor. Joan sat up straight. *Ah,* she thought.

'I was travelling and there was a woman. A lady.'

Joan could scarcely believe what Thomas was saying and she felt the room tilt as dreadful nausea hit her throat. She lifted her hand and touched the points under her chin where she felt sick.

Thomas was still talking and she forced herself to listen. She didn't want to know but knew that later she would need to understand.

'...She looked like you. The curve of her cheek as she turned away from me. I missed you with such force...'

Joan found herself nodding; of course, it wasn't betrayal, it was a compliment to her. He'd done it because he loved her. She laughed and Thomas looked shocked.

She stood up and smoothed her apron. 'My lord. Thank you for telling me.' And she turned to leave the room.

'There's a child.'

Of course there was. There would be no need to tell her if it had been a quick tumble on a lonely night.

'She has called him Thomas. Thomas Minterne because that's where we were. He looks like me and of course, like you because his mother looks like you…' his voice tailed off. 'I was wondering if you could. I mean, she doesn't really want him. So…'

'Really, Thomas? Are my own bastards not enough shame for us both?' To her surprise, tears fell on her clasped hands. 'No. No. I won't take him. You have enough ideas to run the kingdom, I'm sure you can find a place for him.' Her feet managed to carry her out of his reach as he spoke her name and tried to put his arms around her.

'We betrayed God with our union, but you told me it didn't matter, that He would understand. And now you've betrayed *me*. Well.'

And Joan ran out of words. She looked at Wolsey. She saw his entirely beloved face as if for the last time and curtseyed to him. 'Good day, my Lord. Safe travelling.'

Thomas held out his hands to her again, 'Joan, please. I am so sorry. It was the only time and so sweet to think that I was with you…' There was desperation in his eyes but she felt only cold revulsion.

'Oh no, Thomas, you could have lain with me. You didn't have to lay with a version of me. I have missed you and longed and cried for you and you never came because there was never time. Of course, I forgive you. But I cannot…' Joan paused, searching for words to make him understand. 'How can I ever look at you again and not see you with other women?'

He gasped, 'No!'

'Thomas, how many have you lain with? If our union is nothing of value… are you whoring around the kingdom? Do they come to you because you are a man of influence? Are you flattered? Are you so vain that women can simply…?'

Thomas caught her hands in his 'Stop. No, stop. Please.'

He shook his head and struggled for words and Joan looked up into his face. She made that tiny reaching motion with her head which had always caught his attention and brought them together and she ached to lift her hand and cup the side of his head and draw him down to her. Under her fingers she could feel the warmth of his skin and how it felt to her touch. She wanted to feel his lips just once more and she felt sick with yearning, but instead, she stepped away and closed her eyes.

'No,' she whispered, 'no.'

Thomas nodded and bowing to her, he left the room. In the candlelight, tears glistened on his face.

She heard servants calling and the fuss which accompanied Thomas's arrival and departure but she felt as if she had been placed on the other side of a thick wall where none could reach her. She stood motionless for long minutes, feeling her pulse thumping wearily through her body. So, was she still his wife? And if not, then what was she? It had all been a grand deception. What fools they had been. The shade of Thomas Minterne's mother smiled at her with Joan's own face and walked away to join Thomas in his bed and Joan found herself retching into a bowl which miraculously Margery was holding.

Thomas made his way to York Place. He was usually a talkative master and his men would laugh and joke with him, or find a moment to speak seriously but not tonight. They all sensed that the Cardinal was sunk deeply in grief. They progressed in silence and the people they passed in the streets looked in surprise at the normally merry Thomas Wolsey.

That night, both Joan and Thomas might have found a little comfort in the knowledge that the other was lost in torment. Joan cried until she gasped for water to return a little moisture to her aching head and Margery lay beside her friend and mistress and tried to take some of the pain from her.

In his fine chamber, Thomas looked at the bed where no woman had ever lain, but he saw Joan there. Then her beautiful face was cheapened as his treacherous mind painted the Other over it and his papers remained unread as candle after candle burned down and he sought but failed to find comfort in work or in empty prayer.

Chapter 18

London, August 1519

The morning was bright and clear with fresh air, and mist still hung in ribbony shreds across the path. At some point in the middle of England, two messengers passed each other. They nodded briefly in the way travellers do and continued without another thought. One was riding hard to Hatley, near Cambridge to take dreadful news. And the other carried equally terrible tidings to Adlington in Cheshire. The air around them was not heavy with grief but their hearts were and if each had known what the other carried, their burdens would have been more than doubled. But the horses continued and the birds sang in the summer sunshine and nobody yet knew.

September 1519

Joan sang as she worked in the garden. It was now two months since the Clancy family had adopted Dorothy. It had been a hard, heart-breaking decision and Thomas had allowed her to decide, but they were a sweet couple, almost naïve in their godliness and Dotty had immediately taken to them.

In the end, it was Dorothy herself who hesitated. She had cried and cried, refusing for days to tell either Joan or Margery of her trouble. She agreed that yes, she did like the Clancy family very much and that her father had made a good choice. That yes, she could be very happy with them and would once again dissolve into tears and spend hours praying. In the end, it was Margery who won the truth from her. She spoke to her quietly once the child was in bed and had the inspired idea of sitting on the other side of the bed curtain so that Dotty felt she could confess. It transpired that whilst she had come to terms with the irregularity of her parents' relationship, she had also reached the conclusion that she and she alone was responsible for saving her mother's soul. If she should shirk from her care then Joan would be dragged down to hell, the only trace of her being the bloodied marks made by her heels in the dust. This last was such a vivid image that Joan felt tears in her eyes as Margery told her.

In vain did Joan speak to her and Dorothy only grew more hysterical, crying that the devil had told her mother that all would be well and that truly Mother should not trust in anything but God and that the devil would wear a fine robe to deceive. Finally, Joan summoned Thomas and he came, knowing Joan would only call him when exceedingly pressed. It was late but Dotty was still awake, her red eyes the only colour in her face. Thomas sent them all from the room and as he had before with Joan, sat on the bed and comforted Dorothy. Joan never knew what he said to her but he remained late into the night and she heard their voices gentle together.

She sat on the stairs listening. It wasn't that she wanted to hear their confidences, but the sound of their murmured conference together, of Dorothy's questions and Thomas's answers became one of her dearest memories. She couldn't make out their words but in every sound, she heard their love and she constantly wiped tears of gratitude from her cheeks. Her life and her children were not perfect but she would weigh them in the balance and wager they were as close to heaven as she would reach in her life.

She had no idea of the time, but the creak of a floorboard and Thomas's hand on her shoulder roused her. In her room, Thomas and Dorothy explained that most rules were made by man and God was therefore infinitely forgiving of his creation because Man didn't understand everything. He understood that Man was still learning and would make mistakes and a sincere love of God would earn forgiveness. And that each soul was responsible for his own remission and repentance with God. Forgiveness would not be bought with the pain of another's sacrifice. Her daughter sought her eyes and Joan nodded with understanding and thanked Dotty for helping her. After their child was asleep, Thomas and Joan stood together for a long time. They held each other and perhaps for the first time, completely appreciated the privilege and terrible responsibility of having children. Then they parted and once again Thomas left her side.

When Master and Mistress Clancy came again, Dorothy met them with a curtsey and the glad tidings that she would come and live with them. Joan dug her nails into the palms of her hands to suppress her tears and smiled. It was the right thing for Dotty; she would receive a wonderful education. Both Mistress Clancy and her husband were articulate and willing to debate with Dorothy. They were patient and kind and with no children of their own, treated the seven-year-old as an adult, able to understand and deliberate the finest of theological points. Joan could see that her daughter would find life at home dull and stultifying after such rarefied air.

Yesterday she had seen both children; the Clancys brought Dorothy and the Richardson family also made their noisy way to La Parsonage. The day was so happy and it gave Joan great joy to see both her children in what seemed the right place for each of them. Sometimes she dwelt on the thought that she was not the right mother for them, but then she would make herself drop the thought; it was Thomas's fault too that they were not a proper family, but she was grown sanguine and rejoiced to see Dorothy nurtured in a quiet and godly house and Thomas so at ease with his foster brothers and kind parents and about to return to Louvain university. Although that made her laugh, her Tom at university? Poor boy, but he seemed to be having fun, even if that wasn't why he was there.

And me? She thought, *what of me? I will presumably stay here for the rest of my life.* She had a vision of Thomas visiting when they were old and sitting with her by the fire. They would smile ruefully at their mistakes, yet fondly at the passion they once shared. And they might have news of the children. They might even be grandparents, though that seemed unlikely. Both children were surely destined to enter the church. *After all the desperation I felt at entering a holy house and being cloistered away from the world, that's what I will be doing here.* She tweaked her mouth in wry amusement and continued to deadhead the flowers and collect seeds. *At least I live by my own rules and if I choose, I can leave...*

Much later that day, a messenger brought a note from Thomas. To his credit, his notes and letters to her were always in his own hand; he never used his secretary. The Pope's Legate a Latere, Thomas had reached dizzying heights and Joan wondered if she would one day think of Pope Thomas and blush at what she knew of him.

The note asked her to attend him at York Place tomorrow as he had what he hoped would be a pleasant proposition for her. Thomas never left her worrying about any summons. She would be flattered by that but he had the same consideration for the least of his household, which to her amazement, now numbered some five hundred souls.

Arriving at York Place the following day, Joan was expected and escorted into one of the privy gardens where she was greeted by a tall, slightly solemn man who was familiar to her. He took her hand and bowed over it. 'Mistress Larke. Your servant.'

She smiled. Over the years she had shared many cheerful hours with him whilst waiting for Thomas.

'Master Paulet. How very nice to see you again.' Even at their first meeting, she had taken to him immediately, especially when a servant's ill-chosen words had entertained her and catching his eye, she saw he too appreciated the joke and they'd burst out laughing together. To her amusement, she had been charmed by his smile and the way his eyes crinkled in the way of sunbeams. And to her faint consternation, how the sunbeams lit her up inside.

'Are you in attendance on my Lord Cardinal? Or just here to enjoy the gardens?'

'Well, I was here to see Wolsey, but now the blooms have quite won my attention.' He spoke with an amused smile and half a bow to her and Joan gave a laughing smile at his compliment.

She laid her hand on Master Paulet's arm and they slowly walked together admiring the garden. From a distance, they seemed intimate and at ease together and their occasional laughter could be heard across the lawns. After half an hour or so, Joan heard someone call her name and looking up, saw a tall, slightly awkward young man bounding towards her.

'Mistress Joan! I am here to take you to my Lord, the Cardinal.' His voice was breathless and excited and as he raised his hand to secure his hat, he knocked it off and a slight breeze bowled it a short way. As he abruptly folded forward to scoop it up, Joan caught Master Paulet's eye and with her head very slightly on one side, she gave a faintly apologetic smile. He also looked a little regretful and winked at her, which made her silently laugh. But he held her glance and she felt a blush on her cheeks. Then the moment was over and the young man was there, offering his arm and she suddenly recalled his name.

'Master George Legh.' His beaming smile confirmed

her guess. 'How is your father? I so enjoyed meeting you both, well, some time ago. Was it six years?'

'No Mistress, it was seven, and sad to say, my father has recently died. And my mother. On the same day, although many miles apart.'

'Oh, my dear, I am so sorry. What dreadful times you have been through.'

George looked momentarily sad, but then resumed his cheerful face, 'Thank you, indeed. But I hope that more cheerful times are to come to my family. And very soon.' This last was said with a deep look into her eyes and a such degree of emphasis that she could only nod and smile.

George Paulet watched this little exchange with a degree of regret… if only he'd been given a moment longer. But Mistress Lark, for all the spark between them, was not the wife to bring into the family. The star of his elder brother William was beginning to rise and George was to support him, to bring news and useful gossip to his brother's keen ear, not become a source of gossip himself. So, he dropped the thought of Joan and turned to matters of business and some interesting snippets from the city he had gleaned that morning and tried not to hear George Legh's chatter as he took Joan away.

George led Joan as if he were parading his favourite but unbroken colt, with pride and cautious care. They walked through the courts into Thomas's privy rooms and Joan marvelled yet again at the royal splendour in which her husband now lived. Tapestries shimmered on the walls and any spare sunlight glowed warmly on the plate and glass casually displayed on the many shelves along their route. The air was warm and her footsteps barely sounded on the fresh rushes which scented the air. Through a series of rooms they processed, each more gloriously furnished and draped about with young men reading or debating. Thomas's court, for it had the air of a court, was clearly a place of study, not of light pastimes and gambling. In the distance, she could hear the choristers practising and she smiled. Thomas had ever been fond of music, although he preferred the older styles and his choirs did not perform the new fashions of music.

The final door opened and there was Thomas, the glowing heart in the centre of this gilded box. At this thought, Joan realised how far apart they now were. Had they ever really made sport in bed with the delicious abandon she recalled? Surely this stately image before her had never cried out with longing and pleasure in her arms? She gave a silent chuckle which immediately brought her great sadness; part of her life had surely passed forever and she must now live the remainder of her days in quiet seclusion. She must teach herself to be content with less. She, who had once had so much.

Thomas was speaking and she dropped into a curtsey. 'Thank you, George. Perhaps you would leave us?' Joan looked briefly at Master Legh who looked very disappointed but with a humph in his posture which she recognised from Tom's behaviour, he bowed to her and left the room.

Thomas took her hands in his. 'My love. You are well?'

'Indeed, Thomas, thank you. Both Margery and I and

the children are in good health …'

Thomas nodded and silence fell between them. Joan gathered herself to fill the pause and then relaxed her shoulders and waited peacefully.

'Joan…' Thomas crossed to his desk and sat down, folding his hands before him. Then he rose again and returned to Joan. 'Shall we?' He gestured to the window seat and she obediently sat down, her eyes never leaving his face.

Thomas joined her and immediately started to look out of the window. He took a deep breath and spoke in a rush. 'Joan. Would you care to marry?'

She raised her eyebrows, 'Marry again?' She stressed the word *again,* 'Well, I can't say I've ever considered it.' She too looked out of the window. 'Do you have someone in mind for me?'

Thomas linked his fingers together and stretched his arms in front of him. With no emotion, Joan looked at the palms of his hands, hands which had cupped her face and stroked her body and betrayed his vows to Christ.

The quiet fell between them as a solid thing and for a moment Thomas yearned to be a different man in a different life, one in which he would be free to live with and love his beautiful wife. But ever pragmatic, he put the thought from him and continued.

'Indeed, I do. I think that George Legh would make a good and loving husband for you.'

But, thought Joan, *he's such a boy.*

'He is indeed younger than you,' continued Thomas, 'but only seven years and I will pay a handsome dowry.'

Joan nodded. 'May I think about it? I barely know him…' but as she spoke, she could see herself as mistress of his house in Cheshire. He had told her the name but it now escaped her. She could almost smell the clean air of a place far from London where few would know her reputation. There would be no parents to disapprove of her. No one to take away her children.

'Is he kind?'

Thomas smiled, 'I believe he is. I saw him take a puppy who had jumped on him with muddy feet and gently return it to its owner with no cross words. And the puppy now loves him with a great passion.'

'In that case, why ever not?'

Joan fought the urge to laugh. Was she really about to marry again on the strength of a man's gentleness to a dog?

'Or at least, may I have a little time to get to know him? And he to know me? He should not marry purely because he met me for an hour seven years ago. I barely even spoke to the boy. Surely he has not been dreaming of me for all these years? If so, then I'm certain to disappoint him.'

Thomas gave a slight shrug. 'It seems that he has promised his cousin that he will not marry without the cousin's approval, but he counts on my influence to overcome this undertaking. And as for disappointment, I think that no one could be disappointed with you, my dear.'

Joan raised an eyebrow at him and he felt a surge of love at the look on her face. How could he possibly put this woman from him; hand her to another and never in this world see her again? He rose abruptly from the seat and Joan also stood. For a long moment, they faced each other and he opened his arms to her. She stepped into his dear, familiar embrace, scarcely believing that this would be the last time. Never again to lay her head at that spot on his shoulder or feel his arms tightly around her. She lifted her hand to his face and he bent down to her. The kiss lasted forever and was over in a moment. It was as if she saw a dreadful accident happen and was both unbelieving and powerless to stop it.

They stepped apart and outside the room, they heard George clear his throat, clearly impatient at the time he was being forced to wait. Her face serious, Joan nodded at Thomas and he raised his voice and called George to join them.

Afterwards, Joan could barely recall the conversation which followed as Thomas gave her away. Her hands clasped in front of her, she nodded as George agreed to spend some time with her before the marriage was finally settled. She nodded as sums of money and parcels of land were arranged and then kneeling before Thomas, he blessed them both. George helped her to her feet and she felt his hand trembling as he supported her. His eyes were anxious as he looked at her and she forced herself to smile. He seemed a dear boy – man – she corrected herself and she would make him happy. And if she were lucky, he would make her happy too.

Chapter 19

Adlington, Cheshire, Christmas 1519

The great hall at Adlington was strung with ribbons and green garlands and Joan stood silently and alone with a single candle in her hand. The pool of light was very slight but around her, she could feel the hall and beyond it the household. *Her* household. She heard laughter and feet tapping along the wooden floors. Whispers as George's sisters larked about and shared plots and Christmas secrets. And she smiled, for she had been made so welcome at Adlington; they were all like George, eager to love and be loved and somewhat relieved to have an older person arrive and take charge. And someone who was not an anxious and overbearing aunt or uncle. She moved slightly and the ring on her finger – Thomas's ring – glinted softly, the sapphire quite grey in the dim light. And she paused, utterly run through by grief. Her chin trembled and tears threatened and she unwillingly recalled her last moments with Thomas. Contracts were signed and her boxes were packed and on their way. She bid farewell to the children and Tom had seemed briefly concerned but then relieved when she told him that Mistress Richardson had Christmas presents for him. Dorothy looked accepting and perhaps slightly pleased that her mother was at last respectable. She kindly promised her mother that she would continue to pray for her soul and Joan was forced to be content with that.

On the final morning, Thomas had unexpectedly arrived to see them on their way and it had been a cheerful interview. George was tremendously buoyant and chatted loudly and without caring if anyone listened. Then the moment of departure arrived and Joan knelt before Thomas, taking his hand to kiss it. Her thumb ran over the jagged white scar across his knuckles and her eyes flickered up to Thomas's and as a faint grin crossed his face, she saw that he shared the memory. The scar was perhaps ten years old yet she vividly remembered the evening when he'd returned home early, eager to see Joan and chased her around their chamber. She remembered the sound of her breathless giggling, then the thump as Thomas tripped and fell, gashing his hand. Blood had poured from the wound and she stripped off her smock to staunch it, crouching naked in front of him and holding his hand in the linen until he could bear it no longer and the huge bandage around his hand, tumbled her to the bed and made love to her.

Then the moment passed and Thomas had blessed George and wished them a safe and easy journey and they departed. Joan's legs could barely carry her as they left the little house on Fleet Street to which she had returned after the King took on the Bridewell estate. George helped her into the saddle and the steady clip of the horses' hooves carried her away, step by remorseless step. It was as if her heart was being torn from her chest and she could barely speak to George, let alone share his excitement. The journey was long and the boredom of it had calmed her, so that after a few days she could listen with a peaceful smile to George's description of what was before her eyes.

The year would soon change to 1520 and it would be a different year to when she had last seen Thomas. But that was one of the dangerous thoughts to put aside. Nothing could be changed and she was determined to face her new life with a smile. There might even be a child to bring joy to the household. Certainly, her sisters-in-law were keen to have a new baby in the nursery and George was nothing if not assiduous in his attentions. Joan rolled her eyes slightly. He was an eager puppy in all things, including bed-sport. Their first time had been a nervous affair and he had reassured her that he would not hurt her, then repeated his words, several times until she replied that she had every faith in him. Then abruptly, crushing her lip against her teeth, he kissed her. Joan had felt the familiar sweet ache of excitement through her body and said a silent thanks that perhaps all would be well. But then George had clambered on top of her and within a moment was shaking with passion before rolling off her and falling asleep. Joan had opened her eyes wide with surprise and disappointment before giving a slight sigh and joining her new husband in sleep. Sadly, his nightly visits to her bed had retained the same pattern and she could only smile and thank him as he sleepily grinned. At least one of them was satisfied with his performance.

What Joan found most difficult was the thought that

she would change and Thomas would change and each without the other to mark and watch. If she ever saw him again, would she be shocked by a web of new lines on his face? And would he be horrified by her grey hairs if, if they ever came, she thought with a smile. But it cost her such a pang to know that daily his face would age without her there to see it and love him. How could time possibly continue for either of them without the other there? And yet, with pitiless cruelty, it would. But it wasn't cruelty, just unthinking, uncaring remorselessness. She wondered if she was the only one who had such thoughts. These days, her mind was constantly roiling, like the greasy Thames when the tide was turning. Such rubbish would surface then sink again that she almost longed for the black time after Tom's birth. But she didn't really; that had been so dead and so frightening that she prayed never to go there again. In all honesty, this raw, confused and confusing pain was better, even if she imagined that her very footprints left marks of her soul's blood. One day soon, God would draw her feet from the net and He would staunch the constant bleeding. He would. Soon.

Crossing towards the screens passage, Joan placed her candlestick on a side table. Her hand smelled of the metal where she'd gripped it underneath the drip pan. Her candlesticks at home were of silver, she thought before correcting herself. No, *Thomas's* candlesticks in *his* households were silver. This one was engraved with the words, *God in my adversity be my light* and she had taken it for her daily use and improvement. *I'm sorry, Uncle John,* she thought. *You might have been right.*

Standing by one of the two tall trees around which George's father had built his great hall more than thirty-five years ago, Joan placed her hands on the heavy carving, already worn smooth and blackened from the smoke of the central fire. She found building a hall around living trees an odd thing to have done and frequently wondered if anyone had mourned the trees as they silently died. If she continued to smile and serve her purpose here, would anyone notice her soul silently slipping away in this foreign land?

***

At the moment when Joan stood in Adlington's hall looking back over the year, in London, Thomas too stood for a moment of reflection. In York Place, all was clamour as the court enjoyed one of the twelve nightly masques. Christmas was celebrated with great joy in Henry's court and it was hard to win a moment of peace. On his finger was Joan's tiny ring and he twisted it thoughtfully. At his waist hung the beautifully embroidered leather purse which she'd made for him several years before. Opening the purse, he slipped the ring inside the green silk pouch and realised that it came to rest against the lock of hair which he'd carried since that terrible day in Yarmouth. He ought to throw it away. He could toss it in the fire which burned in front of him and his fingers touched the silky curl. Then he closed the purse and in great pain closed his eyes. His grief was so crushing that he could barely breathe but he forced himself to take a steady breath, then another.

He heard the King call his name, laughter in Henry's voice and he opened his eyes and with a cheerful shout, returned to the brightly lit chamber. And in his purse, the ring and Joan's hair remained, safe from the fire for a little longer. But in the flickering of the flames, it seemed for a moment that his figure remained, bent double with unrelenting pain.

Chapter 20

Adlington, Spring 1520

Sitting snug in her solar, Joan heard shouting and horses and when it continued, she walked to the window and peered out. There was a wagon drawn by weary-looking horses and men whom she didn't recognise. Their load was carefully wrapped and seemed to be lengths of wood. It was a miserable day – spring came late in the Palatinate County of Cheshire. Joan always smiled when people gave the county its full title, but it seemed to please them to stress their separateness from London. It was so silent here and at first, Joan had struggled to sleep in the pressing quiet of the night. All her life she had lived in a noisy town or city and it was novel to experience almost complete silence. So to see and hear a team of strangers was almost too exciting. She dropped her sewing onto her chair and left the room, speeding downstairs.

'Ah, Joan! This seems to be for you!' George was flushed from the chill air. He was an early riser and he and the dogs would frequently see dawn from some distant point on his land.

Joan stepped out, holding her skirts high from the mud and dirty dogs who raced to greet her.

'Whatever is it?'

'Good day, Mistress.' One of the men pulled off his cap and bowed to her and she was delighted to hear the accent of the south.

She smiled at him and he handed her a note. 'All right if we unloaded it here? Where'd you like it?'

'Well, what is it?' she laughed, 'because that might make a difference!'

'It's in the letter, Mistress.' He had an air of slight exasperation about him but Joan didn't care; new faces were as refreshing as if spring had suddenly arrived in full bloom.

'Margery…' Joan spoke knowing that her friend would have arrived at her side, 'would you please take the men to have some food and drink whilst I read this letter.'

The men looked pleased and muttered their thanks before following Margery into the house.

'Well?' demanded George.

'Well? Well, I don't know. Let me read the letter and I'll tell you.'

George retreated to prod and peep at the load and Joan turned over the letter. For a moment she savoured the fact that her thumb rested on a seal bearing the impressive arms of Thomas Wolsey, then she cracked it and opened the folded paper.

Thomas sent greetings and apologies that this wedding gift was later than he would have liked, but he hoped that it would bring good fortune and many children to Joan and George. For a moment, tears prickled her eyes; how awful that Thomas should be wishing her a large family with someone else. Then she drew a breath and placed a smile on her lips.

'George!' she called, 'it's a bed from Cardinal Wolsey.'

George redoubled his efforts to see the timbers and succeeded in revealing the end of a bedpost. The wood was pale and golden and Joan crossed to join her husband. Even after such a long journey they could still faintly smell new oak and beeswax.

Joan ran her fingers over the fine carving. 'Goodness,' she breathed, 'how lovely.' Of course, she thought guiltily, she was only thrilled because it was a moment of contact with Thomas and that meant she was still in his thoughts.

By mid-afternoon, the men had dined and Joan had hung around them long enough to know that they hadn't seen the Cardinal and could give her no first-hand news. George, very excited to receive a gift from such an elevated personage, had taken over. Their own bed had been moved into another chamber and Joan was grateful to cease sleeping in the bed of her departed in-laws.

Once assembled, the new bed was indeed a handsome gift; the carving was, as she had suspected, of the finest quality and she traced the knots of the Cardinal's galero and smiled at the lion face peeping from the rose. George ran his fingers over the grotesques and the men fiercely bearing clubs. 'Look, 'he said excitedly, 'in those roundels are my father and there's me.' Joan nodded, but her eye was caught by the birds. They were surely larks and she felt such sweet gratitude to Thomas for the compliment of joining their two symbols on her new bed. It was like a hidden kiss on her cheek. She was not entirely forgotten.

***

As soon as the weather improved, Joan had taken to exploring her new home. It was a flat area surrounded by distant hills which always seemed to have different weather to Adlington. Often their tops were grey and almost invisible. As she grew more accustomed to walking, she roamed further afield and there, far from the house she could at last feel free. The first time she cried she did so secretly as if she were being watched, then one day she found a stream and sat on a fallen log and cried so hard that it felt as if her eyes would explode. Then she calmly dipped her kerchief in the water and bathed her face before returning to the Hall. Some days she would sit doubled over and scream into her knees until she was hoarse but it was such a relief to express her pain. It wasn't only Thomas she missed, but the children; the feel of their heads under her hand or their giggles when she played with them. Dotty was a faithful correspondent and although her letters were dull confessions of her tiny sins, Joan treasured them and would lay her cheek on the paper where that dear hand had passed.

At night, with George asleep beside her, Joan would raise her hands and run her fingers over the intricacies of the carving of the bedhead and then if tears threatened, she would try and recall her journey to Adlington. Much of it was a grey blur, but George so often reminded her of the places they had passed through that it was as if she really remembered them. Poor George, she thought; he tried so hard to create common memories for them and she hated herself for her treacherous thoughts.

She prayed for respite from her pain, but she was also honest with herself that she didn't want to stop missing Thomas. Her memories were so bright they burned, but if they stopped hurting it would mean she was forgetting. As she finally drifted off to sleep, Joan often had the feeling of being lost in a dark forest and sometimes this thought would come to her in the day and she tried to seek a way back to the light. Then she would sit and cry by her stream and the light would fade once more.

***

George flexed his feet and tried to catch more of the heat from the fire. As usual, he was sitting on a cushion by Joan, resting his head against her knees. She was reading a letter from Dorothy, but he knew it was at least the tenth time she'd read it. He never read letters more than once; there was no point. He turned his head to look at his wife just as she drew her hand across her eyes. She looked tired – she shouldn't read by firelight; it was bad for the eyes. She often looked weary these days, but she was always cheerful. She saw his face looking at her and she smoothed his hair with a smile. He wondered if she was with child, but her belly seemed almost hollow when he lay with her and she was growing thinner. Perhaps she was concerned at her failure to produce a child. She shouldn't worry, that wouldn't help.

He moved slightly to look up at her. 'Do you worry that you are barren?' But even as he spoke, he thought that perhaps he'd been too blunt when he actually meant to reassure her, but she smiled and to his confusion, even gave half a laugh.

'Barren? No, of course I'm not worried.' Smiling she shook her head.

Not that then. He changed tack and nodded at the letter in her hands. 'Do you miss those children?'

'But of course.' Again, she looked slightly amused and now also a little confused. 'Why wouldn't I?'

'Well, perhaps you'll have one of your own before too long. And… well… it's nice trying, isn't it?'

She nodded, but there was a little frown on her forehead. 'One of my own?'

'Well, yes. Yours instead of someone else's.' Was she unwell? Was she being stupid on purpose?

'George… they *were* mine.'

'Well obviously they would have felt like yours, but they weren't really, were they?'

On the other side of the fire, one of George's sisters dropped something and Joan realised that they were staring in fascination at them.

Joan felt as though she was falling. *Dear Lord, he doesn't know.*

'George, my dear. They were, *are*, my children. I gave birth to them. I'm not barren. If we don't have children, it is not my fault.'

George looked as if he might laugh. 'How can they be yours? Don't be foolish.'

The dark woods closed around Joan yet again and even the light from the fire seemed to grow dim and draw away from her.

'They are my children,' she said firmly, 'mine and Thomas Wolsey's. We were married and I bore him a son and a daughter. Thomas and Dorothy.'

George stood up and stared at Joan. His world too was growing dark. His darling Joan sat before him. She still looked as divinely beautiful and as if she should be sitting in a heavenly garden as when he first saw her.

'I didn't know. No. You must be wrong.' He laughed and shook his head in disbelief.

Joan was annoyed now. She had no room for another's grief and no patience. 'For goodness sake, George. Of course, you knew. The whole world knew what I was. Even the Pope knew about me. King Henry knew. He thought it a fine joke. Your sisters knew. Didn't you?'

They looked appalled to be brought into this drama but they nodded dumbly.

'See! Everyone knew. Why do you think your cousin didn't want you to marry me? Thomas – the Cardinal – why do you think he was so generous with my dowry and all that land? He knew I was a dangerous bargain for any man and that it was his fault.'

Her hands were slick with icy sweat. He would throw her out. And she would die in her dark forest and no light would ever find her again and she found she didn't care.

All at once, George crumpled, he buried his face in her lap and sobbed. Joan bent over him and wrapped her arms around his shoulders. He was so like Tom when seized by remorse. She kissed his hair and murmured to him. 'I'm sorry, George. I thought you knew. I didn't mean to deceive you. I'm sorry. I'm sorry.'

Her sisters-in-law decided it was time for bed and made a show of leaving quietly and Joan smiled her thanks at them. Then she sat for a long time soothing her husband whilst her own tears darkened his hair.

As they readied for bed, George was irritable and spoke only to Joan in monosyllables. He was undressed when suddenly he burst out with 'Oh, I can't!' And flinging a robe around his shoulders, stalked off into the neighbouring chamber. In annoyance, Joan shrugged to herself and climbed into bed. Her warm, well-aired bed, she thought to herself, shaking her head and preparing for sleep.

In the next room, she could hear George stomping about. The mattress was old and certainly not aired and from the noises she could hear, he was pulling blankets from a press. Then the bed creaked as he flopped onto it. It would also be saggy, for who would bother to tighten the cords on an unused bed?

George was torn between grief and fury. It seemed that absolutely everyone in the world had conspired to fool him. From the Pope to the King and to Cardinal Wolsey, who was only too happy to be rid of his whore. George Legh had been the fool who said yes. Why hadn't his cousin stopped him? It was *his* fault; he should have explained why he wanted George to marry with his consent. George thought he'd been so clever, getting the Cardinal to overrule the agreement.

And now he was cold and not in his bed. Dammit, it was chill and damp and when he lifted his arm, he could feel the faint moisture clinging. He walloped over a few times, huffing and sighing and wrapping the blankets tighter and tighter until he couldn't move. Then in fury, he was forced to roll to the edge and stand up and unravel himself.

Now he was hungry. He flung open the cupboard but there was no ale or wine, no wafers or bread.

He sobbed and returned to bed and wanted to reach out his hand and touch his wife. His wife, he thought in fury. Was she even his wife? But he missed her and wanted to run his hand over her satiny skin and her warm curves. She was such a different shape to him, but his hard bones and angles fitted so well into her. Now he was tormented by passion and the thought that he'd never have her again. And he was still hungry. He got out of bed again, strode towards the door and cracked his toe on a stool which someone had put directly in his way. He swore, hopped on one foot and muttered to himself. Why was there no food in the cupboard and who had moved the furniture? This was his house. He was the master here. She should be sleeping in this cold room and he in the warm chamber with the soft dry mattress. They were all laughing at him. The whole county was laughing at him. The girls he'd courted would have thought they'd made a good escape from George Legh, dupe and idiot. He muttered again, hot blood coursing through him and for pity's sake the only place he could imagine finding comfort was in the arms of the woman who'd so bitterly betrayed him. His despair burst with a sort of cry of pain which sounded like her name.

Joan lay looking into the darkness and listening to George. Suddenly a thought came to her; he sounded like Pepper when he was a puppy and he'd chewed four pairs of shoes. Joan had thrown the shoes down, one by one, in front of Pepper's nose. Not to hit him, but to make him jump and she'd told him very firmly what was wrong. He'd sunk down further and further and looked increasingly miserable. Then she shut the door on him and stood silently outside. Pepper had whined and yapped a few times before sniffing along the bottom of the door and scratching at it. Then he paced and paced, his claws tapping on the floorboards. Eventually, Joan could no longer bear to hear this and his occasional crying and opened the door. His joy at seeing her again made her almost ashamed of her punishment of the dog.

Joan wasn't punishing George, at least not intentionally, but he still sounded remarkably like Pepper and her heart softened. Poor boy. It was such a mess. She could still hardly credit that he hadn't known or that some well-wisher hadn't alluded to her notoriety, but clearly, he hadn't been aware and was suffering a tremendous shock. She got out of bed and slipped on her nightgown. The moon was shining brightly into the room – perhaps we should get window curtains – she thought inconsequentially. It was certainly cold enough in Cheshire.

She left her chamber and stepped along the passage to the little room where George was still muttering. Without knocking, she opened the door and he looked at her. Her beauty in the moonlight was extraordinary and she held out her hand to him like a loving angel.

'My husband, come to bed. All will be well, I promise.' With another sob, he went to her and she led him back to warmth and sanity.

After this revelation, George took weeks to recover his usual manner with Joan. It was as if he was suddenly married to a stranger and had to get to know her again. But one day as he was out with the dogs, with a sudden flash of maturity he realised that he had never known her. From the first time he saw Joan, to the moment years later when he'd brought her triumphantly to Adlington, he was in love with an image. He had no idea of the person he had married. He had never asked about her life before him; in his mind, she was as flat as a painting and it was a slow and painful journey to accept Joan as a person. He came to understand that she had suffered tremendous sadness in her life and he cursed that they were not closer in age; had not grown up together. For he would have saved her from Cardinal Wolsey, from the Holy House threatened by her uncle. A gradually he changed his version of his wife's story from one of debauchery and betrayal to one of heart-breaking circumstance and the failure of a chivalric knight to arrive in time. Her stories became just that, parts of a long saga which finally brought her home to him.

For Joan, that spring and summer were a period of gradually increasing light. Sometimes she would slip back into the dark forest of her soul, but she found the courage to fight the dear, beloved misery and step forward. Now and then, a day came when she didn't think of Thomas and feel her heart's blood seeping away, and that brought her both relief and sadness. She remembered the day when she had wanted to simply fade away, cease to exist and the whispered voice which came to her and breathed the words, *Trust me* into her ear. God was indeed drawing her unwilling feet from the net.

Chapter 21

Adlington, 1525

For five years, George had continued his almost nightly lovemaking but he knew, almost better than Joan when her monthly courses were due and each time, he noticed with sadness that she was wearing the rags once again. His sisters were marrying; his older sister already had children, but there were no tiny voices at Adlington to cheer a man so eager for an heir. But he had also learned to be philosophical and to treasure his wife. He loved to see her blossom and regain her happiness, and even though it took something of her ethereal beauty, it made her seem more real and earthbound and he no longer feared that one day she would simply disappear.

Then, late last year, he summoned the courage to ask her if she should be bleeding. Joan blushed and nodded, then put her finger to her lips to shush him. A dozen thoughts and questions raced into his head but with eyes as bright and hopeful as hers, he grinned and closed his lips.

Now Joan retired to her chamber. Spring, so long in coming was now almost past and summer would bring their first child. Unlike her previous pregnancies, which Joan had sailed through with almost unconscious ease, this one caused her sickness and restlessness. To his credit, George had refused to move into another chamber but tolerated his wife's night-time pacing and vomiting and when she would let him, would stroke her back and try to comfort her. Joan couldn't bear to be touched when she felt ill but allowed George to do this small thing for her even though it made her feel worse. She was huge with this child and thought fondly of the happy times when she could see her feet and fasten her shoes. For once, Margery was of little help; the previous year she too had married; a handsome widower from the village, and was now the mother to a family of six children which was about to become seven. Joan missed her constant presence terribly but could only be glad for her friend.

Joan was whiling away the last days of pregnancy by tidying her chamber. The letters from Tom and Dorothy were today's task and they lay spread on the bed beside her. She picked up the one from Tom which he'd sent in 1522 from Padua when he was twelve and travelling with his tutor.

Mother,
We are in Padua and it is very nice. Master Lupset says I must learn while I am here. I expect I will learn a lot.

I have been sick on the boat crossing the sea. I was sick six times and I didn't like it much. I have learnt that the sea is not my friend and I shall not cross it again. Master Lupset calls for now we must visit somewhere before dinner. I am looking forward to dinner.

Your loving son, Thomas Wynter

Not for the first time, Joan wished she could have seen Tom's reaction when he realised that he would have to cross the sea again. She laughed out loud and kept laughing, even when she realised that her waters had broken.

Elizabeth Legh had proved stubborn and rather unwilling to join the world, but somehow that innocent letter kept Joan chuckling throughout, even when an anxious George had himself brought heavily pregnant Margery from her home in the late evening, his tears convincing her that Joan was dying.

But here at last was their baby. Not a boy, but George was calm about that. His family struggled to have boys and there was always next time. Joan had smiled and considered her age, but kept the thought to herself. She was nearly eight years older than her husband but there was no need to remind him of that.

Cardinal Wolsey sent handsome christening gifts to Adlington and as they sat together one afternoon after dinner, Joan was surprised when Margery saw the beautiful gilded salt cellar and remarked that he had sent an identical one to her new son.

'How did Thomas know you were with child?' Joan asked.

'I told him.' Margery seemed surprised and Joan squashed the very uncharitable thoughts she suddenly had. Margery was just a servant; how could she be in correspondence with the most powerful man in the country?

'He gave me a dowry too.' Margery's voice had the faintest air of defiance. *Poor Joan,* she thought. *She's jealous. Of course, she's jealous.* But she couldn't tell her friend that Wolsey had asked her to keep him informed of Joan's health and happiness. She had not told him of Joan's darkest days, for what could he have done? It would have only made him unhappy. But nonetheless, she had enjoyed the feeling of importance which came from having such a friend in London and it had certainly helped when Jack caught her eye. Margery had been only too conscious that a gentleman like James Griffiths would never have looked twice at Little Meg, but a gentlewoman who corresponded with the Other King? Well, that was a different matter and James had been glad to marry an attractive and competent woman who was the companion to Joan and almost a member of the Legh family.

Little Elizabeth started to cry and Joan crossed the solar to lift the baby. One of the great joys of this baby was being able to nurse her and not be forced to pretend that she was not Joan's own child. It also seemed that still feeding her child was no defence against pregnancy and Elizabeth would not be quite a year old when her sibling joined the family. But that was news she had yet to share with anyone except the ear of baby Izzy. And was a sweet ear it was, Joan thought to herself as she looked adoringly at the perfect soft, warm skin of her child. At that moment it seemed that all unhappiness was wiped away and she existed only for the sight and mostly sweet smell of her baby.

Chapter 22

Adlington, Late Spring 1529

'Leave the baby alone! She's not a dolly!'

Joan swooped down and retrieved Ellen from the melee of children and husband who should have known better, but Ellen screamed in annoyance and waved her arms at her father who seized her from Joan.

'If you break her…'

Elizabeth laughed in delight, 'Break baby? You can't break baby!'

Against her will, Joan giggled, 'Yes Izzy, you can break baby, and don't you come running to me if your legs come off too. Just be gentle with her. All of you,' raising her voice, 'be gentle…'

She sighed and ran her hand across her face. Really, a large family was exhausting; whoever thought it was a good idea to have one a year for four years? They'd all been large babies and Joan had joked it was a good thing that they all came one after the other before she'd had time to shrink back into a normal size. Her litter she called them; Elizabeth, Mary, Thomas and now Ellen. And of course, George – her husband the biggest baby of all. And when his sisters visited with their families, she would pretend that she didn't know whose baby was whose just to see the older children shriek with laughter at her. It was such a joyful household and so different to Joan's childhood. Her brothers had gone early into Wolsey's service, leaving just Joan and her father so that she had felt like an only child and she relished seeing these children grow up free from the cares and fears which had been her constant shadows.

Any minute... yes, there it was, the first howl from someone who was too tired. Dementated laughter quickly turned to tears and soon all four were weeping. Joan sank onto the grass and scooped up the children, comforting and kissing trodden fingers and finding sweetmeats to stop up their mouths.

'Your fault George – you make them so excited.' George just nodded, a grin on his face. He loved to see his Joan with her arms full of her babies. His babies. These days he barely ever thought of her previous life and certainly never wondered if she thought of it. Letters came occasionally from the other children but he shrugged; he wasn't interested and they barely seemed real.

Order restored, Joan sat back down and with her fingers felt the green blades of grass. Such a wet year that it was a joy to come out and enjoy the sunshine but when she moved, she could feel the damp through the thick blankets; she wouldn't stay there much longer but the sun, scarlet through her eyelids, was so delicious. She dozed slightly then stirred when she heard George shout greetings. Her eyes were blurry in the bright light but she could make out the welcome figure of Margery and some of the children.

Sitting by her blinking friend, they greeted each other and Margery made a face 'It's rather damp, isn't it? To be sitting here?'

Joan nodded, 'But the sun is so nice…'

After a while spent in peaceful silence, Margery spoke again, 'Joan, is there anything worrying George?'

Joan made her no-idea face. 'He wouldn't tell me if there was. Such as?'

'Well, Jack seems to be having trouble with some of the land which the Cardinal gave him as part of my dowery.'

Joan moved her head in a way that was neither shake nor nod and Margery continued. 'Perhaps he might not have been quite at liberty to dispense the title to Jack.' She paused, then continued carefully, 'It's not a large piece of land but it's being disputed and if we lose, we must pay the rent for these last few years.'

Joan shook her head decisively, 'No, that can't be right, Thomas is the alter rex. He would only give gifts which were his to give and if there was any confusion then the King would make it right. He holds Thomas dear to him.'

'Joan, may we go indoors? I'm getting too old to sit here inviting aches and pains into my bones.'

'But of course. We'll have wine and wafers. I have a new recipe and would like you to try it.'

Linking arms, the two women waved at the children and headed into the house. Margery was right, Joan did feel quite chilled. Not least because in the back of her mind was the suspicion that this was not the last of the conversation.

That evening, George Legh sat with his head in his hands. Another summons had come from London. He did not read easily and the clerk's hand was very difficult to make out and almost impossible to understand even when he could decipher the words. That parcel of land he shared with Griffiths, their portions butting against each other; he was grateful to Cardinal Wolsey for the gift which had been a marriage settlement but now someone was demanding rent and claiming the land.

Joan tapped at the door and came in and was shocked to see George looking so worried. She crossed to the fire and stirred it up, adding a little more sea-coal.

'George? May I speak to you?' He nodded. 'When Margery was here today she told me that James is being challenged for that land which the Cardinal gave them on their marriage.' Joan never used the name of Thomas when speaking to George, for she hated to see the pain in his eyes. Somehow calling him the Cardinal put him at a remove and they could pretend that he was just a kindly benefactor to them.

George found his mouth too dry to speak and passed her the latest court summons. Joan took the parchment and quickly scanned the contents.

'Oh George, this can't be right. Thom… the Cardinal cannot be aware of this, or he would not have allowed it to happen.'

George was reluctant to admit that he didn't understand the document, so instead he reached into the documents box and found the two previous papers. Joan read them in silence, fear gripping her heart.

Oh, why didn't you show me before, she cried silently, *you fool, you proud, stupid fool.*

Then she smiled at her husband. 'This is all right George, stop worrying. We'll sort it out.' She went to the fire and poured a cup of wine and raised it to her lips, drinking it in one, before filling it again and bringing it to George.

'I know what we'll do. We'll go down to London. I have some money from my father which I've never used. We'll see the Cardinal and he'll put things right. And if that fails, we'll pay whatever needs to be paid and all will be well.' George looked so relieved and Joan inwardly sighed; he thought that the problem was all but resolved, yet he had no idea of the fear she had silently picked up and now bore in her heart.

Within a few days, all was chaos in the Adlington house as George packed endless clothes and shoes and Joan unpacked them. 'If we travel lightly, we can travel more quickly...' She was so frantic to be off that she would go in what she was standing that very minute if she could have done so. The thought of seeing her two oldest children again had given her the energy of a woman much younger. And if she was utterly truthful with herself, the thought of having Thomas before her once more made her feel – well, what did she feel? Sick, excited, nervous? Yes, all that. It was as if the carefully built life of the last ten years was shown to be tawdry and flimsy and she had to keep reminding herself that it wasn't. She was happy. Her life was wonderful. Her Legh children were dear and much loved. And she was wicked and worthless to think of Thomas again. But the thought of seeing him had opened the box in her heart where she'd securely locked away her past and the misery which had dogged her for so long, and it was as if that pilgrimage through pain was for nothing.

Packing her own things, her glance fell on the enamel portrait of Cardinal Campeggio. She had found it in one of her boxes, unpacked months after her arrival in Cheshire. Such a bright and pretty thing, but the eye inevitably fell on the Cardinal's tiny hands and Joan always smiled at the artist's mistake. She ought to take it back to London and return it to Thomas. To be honest, she had no idea how it had come to be with her in Adlington; such a strange thing to have picked up but she had found peace in the eyes of Thomas's friend and had grown rather fond of it. No, she decided, it could stay here. If Thomas had missed it, he could have asked for it to be returned.

Finally, they were ready to leave and Joan went to the large chest in their chamber and in the bottom, found the bag of scraps she kept for patching things. She pushed her fingers deep inside and found the heavy pouch. Carrying it to the bed she tipped out the gold coins, relishing the chink of them against each other. Thomas had kindly increased the number of coins in the purse and told her that they were for her and her alone; nothing to do with George. And over the years they were nothing but a comforting thought, her protection against destitution. But now the time had come to use these pretty golden rounds.

Putting them back into the purse, Joan went to find

George. He had quickly recovered his spirits after confessing to Joan and seemed his usual boyish self, although Joan could see a slight shadow in his eyes. But then he also had a summer cold and wasn't feeling quite as normal.

'Hold out your hands,' she instructed and emptied the coins into his cupped hands. His eyes widened.

'Where did these come from?' His voice was awestruck. Their branch of the Legh family was not overly wealthy and he had never seen such riches.

'They were from my father and I have kept them tucked away.' Now was not the moment to mention Thomas's hand in their increase. 'If we or the Cardinal cannot settle this matter, we will simply pay whatever we need to.'

George nodded; his face flooded with relief. 'Give me the purse and I shall keep them safe on our journey.'

Joan found a degree of reluctance in her, but George looked so much more himself with the money tightly in his hand that she bit down her misgivings. It was solely because the coins had been her comfort for so many years. She must not hoard them; it was right to share this security with George. It was indeed right and her duty as his loving wife to give him what hope and succour was in her power.

The journey south was as tedious as it had been travelling north all those years ago. Their farewells to the children had saddened her. It was almost as if she were bidding goodbye to them forever and her last sight of Adlington brought tears to her eyes. But as before, George was brimming with excitement and she tried hard to share his enthusiasm and nod at his constant cries of 'Do you remember...'

The light rain was endlessly wearing and they grew bored with the nightly routine of trying to dry their heavy woollen cloaks in the inns where they lodged. Joan grew horribly familiar with the weight of wet wool but never entirely accustomed to the smell. Finally, they were but one day from London. She would have pressed on but the horses were exhausted and their servants grim-faced with weariness.

The inn was shabby and the landlord dabbled his fingers in the palm of her hand as he helped her from the horse. His glance into her eyes was so suggestive she wanted to slap his face but she just gave him a cool smile and thanked him. Every instinct was telling her not to stop at this dirty house but their servants had disappeared and the horses were being trailed into the stables. And George. George was coughing hard as his cold was wont to make him do at the end of each day. Even dirt and an unnerving landlord were better than forcing him onward into the evening.

Their chamber made her shudder and she looked around her with distaste. The bed hangings were shredded with age. The silk scarcely more than brittle threads and she was thankful that they were scarlet and so showed the dirt perhaps less than a lighter colour. Above her the ceiling bulged alarmingly; cracks in the plaster showing filthy ancient horsehair and whenever a door slammed dust gently drifted down.

'Well, this is nice, isn't it?' George said, but his

cheeks were worryingly bright with hectic colour. He sat heavily on the bed before falling backwards onto the pillows. 'What a relief. I do believe I have had enough of travel for today.'

Joan put her arms around George and pulled him up. 'For goodness sake, George, help me. I need to get you undressed and into bed.' But he just grinned and putting his arms around her, dragged her on top of him. But she rolled away and tried again, this time making her voice into the one she used to use on Tom.

Finally, he was in bed and she drew the covers over him. Moving to the other side of the bed, she moved the blankets and inspected the sheets and she shuddered. There were countless marks on the sheets from people with dirty feet and there were revoltingly stiff stains which made her feel queasy. Sleeping in her damp cloak was not an option so she carefully lay on the sheets and tucked her feet up inside her skirts praying that she would remember and not stretch her feet out during the night.

She need not have worried, for George coughed all night. He slept heavily and both snored and coughed without waking himself, but time and time again every noise he made dragged Joan back from the brink of sleep. It was with gratitude that she heard the inn begin to stir and dawn, early at this almost-midsummer time of year, crept into the chamber. She watched the room come into daylight and marvelled that it was even more shabby and disgraceful than it had seemed by candlelight. Presumably, it was so close to London that barely anyone stopped there unless driven by direst need, such as their own little party.

Breakfast was not quite as bad as she expected; the beer and bread were not utterly stale and to her immense relief, George woke up clear-eyed and much refreshed. He fairly bounced with enthusiasm to reach the city and enjoy their trip and couldn't understand why Joan looked so tired and worried.

Even the weather was improved and a watery blue sky accompanied their first hour or so. Joan was slightly in front of George's horse, on her mare who also seemed to have enjoyed a restful sleep when George gasped.

Joan looked over her shoulder at him. His face was drained of colour and he was patting his jerkin and looking frantic.

'What…?' she said, raising her eyebrows and shaking her head at him. But really, she thought, she already knew.

'The purse. I can't find it.'

All their faces were deathly pale; the servants knew of the reason for this journey and the three men stood close beside them, helping their master and mistress to check all their bags and boxes and clothes.

'Where did you leave it?' Joan's voice was harsh and angry and George looked panicked at her tone. For a moment, she turned away and closed her eyes in despair and exasperation.

'George, my love,' she said softly, 'try and remember…'

He thought for a moment then his face brightened, 'I *do* remember. It was in my jerkin and I pulled it out and under my pillow was a hole in the mattress. I placed it in there.' He sounded triumphant as if remembering was the same as recovering the purse and having it safely in his hands again.

Joan turned from him. 'John, you do take my mare, she is the fastest of our mounts and return. Ours was the only large chamber. The bed has ragged red hangings and George slept on the right-hand side of the bed, on my left.'

John nodded at his mistress and without wasting further time, was off, retracing their last miles. Joan trusted the man implicitly; his family had served the Leghs for many generations and were as intricately bound as they could be. To be truthful, she would trust him more than she trusted her husband.

Foolish, foolish man. Had he thrown away their last chance of salvation? Foolish, foolish Joan. Why had she let him have the purse? She had kept it safe and hidden for all those years. What did his manly pride matter? That money – a lifetime of money, from her father and Thomas. Stupid woman!

Her thoughts circled for what appeared to be hours and hours until the sound of hooves finally reached them. But one look at John's ravaged face told them that he had not been successful. He started to speak before he reached them, tears in his eyes and his voice breathless. He had found the chamber, found the hole in the mattress. Had even had to pay the landlady to let him look. She had gone with him, but she had surely known the gold wasn't there… but what could he do? The purse would be safely hidden, the wicked-looking manservants would not let him search the whole place…

He was still speaking when Joan realised that her

breakfast which for some time had been greasily rolling in her stomach was now pressing in her throat. She calmly walked to the edge of the track, and placing her hands on her knees, leaned forward and vomited into the grass. George looked at her and followed her, coughing and weeping before sinking to his knees and grabbing at her legs, pleading for forgiveness.

Oh, at least let me stop being sick, she thought exhaustedly. Then she shrugged, grateful that he hadn't worked out that he wouldn't be here at the side of the road, facing ruin if he hadn't married Cardinal Wolsey's whore and accepted a poisoned gift from the King's favourite. The vomit was bitter in her nose and mouth and her eyes streamed.

'Oh George, it's all right. Thomas...' *Not the Cardinal,* she thought rebelliously, *I'm not denying him anymore*, 'Thomas will make it right. Stop crying, George.'

With a degree of calm, they set off once more but the sky had lost its promise and the final trudge into London was miserable. At last, they found the Garland Inn, recommended by Margery's husband and were warmly greeted by the landlady. Joan had money in her pouch so they were not embarrassed to ask for rooms. She was full of chatter but on hearing that they had come to apply to the Cardinal for assistance, Mistress Sheridan raised her eyebrows. 'You'll be lucky,' she said cheerfully, 'he is all took up with the King's Secret Matter.' She looked as if she had said all that needed saying, then looking at the blank faces of her guests, took off again with great delight.

'But surely you know of the King's Secret Matter?' The Leghs nodded vaguely, but Mistress Sheridan continued in an eager half-whisper, her face alight with the delight of sharing with new people, 'The Cardinal is trying to get a divorce for the King, trying to persuade the Pope that the King's marriage was not a true marriage and that our Queen is not our Queen. For he's taken up with a French piece who promises him a son. But I hear, from someone close to her at court, that though she will dally with him, it's only in a French way.' Here, she nodded significantly, certain that her audience knew what she meant, 'In a French way. Well, they have such unnatural ways in France, don't they? And it's so she won't get with his child until she is the Queen. But we have a Queen and we have a princess. And that Bullen woman will not make a good queen. No. But the Cardinal is so busy trying to serve the King and the Pope and keep that woman content and the dear Queen safe. No, he'll be too busy to see you, that I do know.' She folded her arms for emphasis and George and Joan simply stared at her.

After a moment, Joan released the breath she seemed to have been holding since their hostess started and gave a bright smile.

'Thank you, Mistress. We'll see what tomorrow brings, but for now, we need our supper and my husband could do with a good night's sleep. It has been a long and wet journey. Only briefly this morning did the sun shine on us during our entire ride and his summer cold has been very trying.'

Mistress Sheridan clucked with sympathy and took in

the weary aspect of her guests, especially Master Legh. In fact, she harboured suspicions about the man's health and she hoped he wouldn't be taken ill in her house. That wouldn't be good for business. But for tonight at least she would make them welcome.

After years of countryside peace, Joan found the cries and hullabaloo to be surprisingly comforting. *I really am a city maiden*, she thought and the noises made her seem less alone. She could even imagine that Thomas might be listening to the calls of the same hawkers. *Thomas… perhaps tomorrow…*

Despite her worries, Joan dropped off to sleep almost immediately. The bed was warm and blessedly clean and Mistress Sheridan removed their clothes to wash the linen and air the heavy woollen items. Joan could have kissed her for her kindness, although she knew she would be paying for the services. At least Thomas would see her looking tidy and respectable. As sleep took her busy mind, she realised that in not one of her imagined scenes with Thomas was George present. And her last conscious thought was of dry amusement.

When morning dawned, it was clear that George was little improved; his cold had reached the sticky phase but at least she could reassure their landlady that George was not suffering from the sweating sickness. After breakfast, taken in their chamber, Joan began to dress. George climbed heavily out of bed to wash but soon stopped to hold the bedpost whilst he coughed. Joan all but ignored him and continued, fastening her shoes and tidying her hair before pinning her bonnet.

'Joan, can we wait a little? Just a few days? I will soon be well again and we will visit the Cardinal together.' His voice, nasal with the cold had also developed a fretful tone and Joan thought irritably of how annoying children can be.

'No. George.' She lowered her voice. 'We have not money for a prolonged stay here,' then rather pointedly, she added, 'have we?'

George shook his head but continued to dress. 'Very well. But I can't go far. I feel very wobbly.'

Ready to leave, Joan turned back. 'Well stay here then. I shall hardly get lost in London. And once at York Place, I shall easily find Thomas.'

George's face crumpled but Joan had no patience with him and spoke briskly, 'George. You are my husband. The Cardinal is in my past. I shall ask him for help. He will give me help. We shall see my children. We will go home in triumph to our children. But I must go. Please, just let me be.'

George sank onto the bed. 'Very well. Good luck, my love.'

His face was so young and so lost that Joan's heart softened. She gave a gentle smile to George and kissed him. He wrapped his arms around her waist and for a moment clung to her. 'Joan, I love you so much. You've brought me such happiness. Come back quickly.'

She embraced him back and buried her face in his hair. 'Feel better soon, my dear. I'll try and be back by dinner time but don't worry if I'm not. And don't fret about anything. Have a sleep and think of home.'

As she left the inn, Mistress Sheridan was deep in confidential conversation with some of her customers, but Joan caught the words, cardinal and Cheshire. She rolled her eyes to herself and passed the group with a cheerful greeting and a sweet smile. Their conversation restarted as soon as they judged her out of earshot and Joan wanted to call back and say 'I can still hear you!' but today she would see Thomas and nothing could spoil that.

It was not far to York Place, especially not with excitement speeding her feet, and Joan barely spared a glance as she passed the traders and shops along her way. She who had dreamed of the luxuries afforded by London, who longed to taste again a start-of-the-day pie, found her eyes were barely even caught by fluttering ribbons or bright fabrics draped over shop shutters. She was going to Thomas. That was all, her sole bright star.

Afterwards, she could never quite comprehend her good fortune. She walked along the river and in the distance, she could see the York Place privy steps, when drawing level with her was a grand and glorious boat, rowed by liveried boatmen and seated under a gorgeous caparison she saw the longed-for scarlet figure.

A cry broke from her, 'Thomas! My Thomas.' But her voice cracked slightly and as if in a nightmare, she seemed to make no noise. But miracle of miracles, his head turned and his startled face looked into hers.

Then they were past her, the boatmen and the tide conspiring to part them. But Thomas was standing and he looked at her and his hand was raised in reply to her frantic waving. Then he nodded and smiled. He had seen her. Joan gathered her skirts and ran. She thought nothing of being all but forty and a mother of six but simply pelted along. The steps seemed to grow further away and once again she was in a nightmare and she thought helplessly of Tantalus, forever unable to reach what he most needed. But all at once, she was there and Thomas was before her, a crowd of attendants beside him, around him and even someone holding a cross before him, almost as if to keep Joan from him. As if, she thought irrationally, she was a devil come to tempt him.

Her chest heaved and surely she hadn't lost her bonnet? But her searching hands found it, still partly pinned to her hair, although flipped backwards and resting on her neck.

'Joan, my dear! Whatever are you doing here?' Thomas's voice was the same, but she wondered if she would have known him otherwise. He was thin and slightly stooped and his hair almost white against his sunken cheeks. She knew that look, he had been ill and it was without doubt his stomach again and she remembered nights holding the bowl and worrying herself almost to death at the blood he produced.

Then he stepped forward and took her hands in his.

'Trouble?' He said softly.

She could only nod. She wanted to speak but she was lost in his eyes, in devouring his dear face. Her hands were remembering the feel of his hands. How could she have forgotten so much? How was the crinkle of laughter around his eyes a surprise to her, yet so familiar? Her soul cried out, *unfair, oh so unfair*.

He let go of her hands and turned to his attendants. 'Mistress Legh is the daughter of an old friend. We will walk in the gardens for a while. We will be alone.' And he smiled and waved his hands at them, 'Go away, all of you, go as far as…' several of the men laughed and chorused with him, '…as far as one may well shoot an arrow.'

Thomas smiled, 'Exactly. And I thought you were all unteachable.'

Joan was touched at the gentle familiarity and affection between master and servants. He might be George with the children she thought, rather than one of the most important men in England.

Together they all walked into the York Place gardens, Joan with her hand lightly on Thomas's arm and his attendants at the requisite distance, although, she thought to herself, *even I could shoot an arrow further than that. Go away. Go away. Please go away. Give me these few precious minutes with him. Please.*

They sat on a bench and Thomas spoke swiftly. 'My love, I am so sorry, but I can ill spare you much time, yet I know how much longer you deserve. Tell me quickly what I can do. Then I must be about the King's business.' He paused, thinking how much to say, when Joan spoke.

'Thomas, it's all right, I understand. Mistress Sheridan, our landlady at the Garland took pleasure in giving us the latest gossip from court. She has it all from a most excellent person.'

'Oh, I'm sure she does. The least of men across Europe have unimpeachable sources telling them what is happening in the King's most secret affairs.'

Then Joan, her eyes still fixed wonderingly, adoringly on Thomas's face told him briefly of their distress. She wished she had more to tell for she was gradually realising that her time with him was running through her fingers faster than the sun-hot sand on Yarmouth beach and she could not bear it.

Thomas too was stunned by the sight of Joan. She came more frequently to both his sleeping and waking thoughts than he cared to admit and he had often wondered how she would look. When he heard her calling him from the river bank – for a moment he had thought he'd slipped into a dream. He wasn't well. The King was unhappy and so all the court was unhappy, and he, Thomas Wolsey had sworn and promised to make it all well, as indeed he always made things well for the King. Yet, it seemed as if now, in this least wish of the King's, he would fail. He, who had managed armies and forged grand peace treaties could not get this woman for Henry.

And before him was the woman Thomas loved before any other person, whom he'd put aside for the sake of the King and he was powerless to hold her and kiss her and remember all the little quirks which made Joan into Joan. She had indeed aged, but it was as he had always suspected; she had simply grown more beautiful as her years passed, and his soul screamed in agony with the absence of the years that they would never share.

Now she was trying to tell him that his errors had brought both Margery and the Leghs into trouble. His critics, indeed his enemies were always accusing him of mismanaged land deals but whilst they might be wrong –

and he sincerely doubted he had made mistakes – they were not dishonest transactions. Ah, Joan. And now he handed her a handkerchief, for telling of the loss of the gold brought tears to her face. Yet she was half-laughing and saying that oh, he used the same scent and surely her lips were buried too deeply in the silk and he couldn't really be hearing her say that she loved him still. Fortunately, he carried two kerchiefs, for without doubt it was the summer weather, the flowers, heavy with their own perfume which seemed to have brought tears to his eyes too.

'Joan, please, stop worrying, I will arrange matters. All will be well, I promise.' Then he rose and she felt sick; goodbye so soon?

'Walk with me. Have you yet seen Tom? Dorothy? Our children are remarkable. Each time I see them, I marvel at God's creation of two such distinct souls. You must see them before you return home.'

Their steps were slow but inexorable, yet each moment tied her more closely to his side. They continually turned, each to look into the other's face and paint the image into their minds against the long years to come. They knew it was unlikely they would ever meet again and these seconds would have to last them into eternity. As they neared the gateway into the base court, Thomas drew her into the shelter of the arch and for the briefest of moments, held her once more in his arms. Joan lay her head in its place just below his shoulder and it felt as if she had never rested from the last time until this very moment.

'Am I forgiven?' Thomas's voice murmured in her

ear.

She could only nod. 'Are you happy?' Again, she nodded and Thomas reached down to her hand and saw his ring still there. He raised his own hand where her little ring was once again in place.

'I stopped wearing it. For a whole day. But my thumb kept seeking it, so I reinstated it.'

After a moment, he found the words he had wanted to say for so many years. 'My darling girl. Nothing I ever did with you was done lightly. I love you and will continue to when I am no more of this world and that is my whole confession.'

Joan tried but could not speak, so she quickly wrapped her arms around him and held him tight for just a moment, before letting go and stepping back. She swallowed and tried again. 'My love, my husband, thank you.' Then finding strength from some quite unsuspected place, she pushed back her shoulders and turned from him. She walked away and didn't look back, yet she knew that Thomas kept his gaze on her until she was out of sight.

As she reached the river, a man caught up with her, breathless from running. 'Mistress Legh! Wait please.' He gasped, catching his breath. 'Mistress, the Cardinal has instructed me to escort you safely to your lodging and to give you this purse.'

'Thank you. How kind. Would you excuse me a moment, I seem to have dirt in my eyes. It's this dreadfully dry weather. If only the rain would come and lay the dust.'

The manservant drew breath to say, *but you are stepping around mud and puddles* before his thoughts caught up with him and he recognised her tremendous bravery.

'Mistress Joan. Please take my arm. I am entirely at your disposal.' As they walked along, he briefly considered how his comrades would hang on his words tonight when he told them that he had met and walked with the infamous Joan Larke of rumour and malicious rhyme, but then he realised that to speak thus of her would be discourteous to both their kind and beloved master and to this beautiful and heartbroken woman. And that he probably wouldn't tell. Almost certainly not.

Chapter 23

London

As Joan and her companion reached the Garland Inn, the weather was closing in again and Joan hurriedly thanked the man before asking him to return to his master with her gratitude. She stared with naked hatred at the man's blameless back as he hurried away through the rain. *Poor man,* she thought guiltily, *it's not his fault that I envy him his low position, his nearness to Thomas.*

But she had a husband, someone to whom she was so dear. That was not to be scorned and it was more than time she put him at his ease. She turned and pushed open the door. A moment as her eyes accustomed to the gloom of a room with a smoking fire on such a dull day, then she was puzzled at the faces staring at her. Really, had they no manners? Their voices had fallen silent the moment she entered the room and she looked from one to another of the men and women clustered there. Then, finally, Mistress Sheridan pushed through them, flapping her hands at them, or Joan, it wasn't clear.

'Mistress Legh! Oh, such a bother. I didn't know what to do. All day I've been in such a puzzle how to tell you…' she ran on for a moment whilst Joan stood silently, still feeling Thomas's arms around her, holding her safe.

'Mistress Sheridan. I'm sure that you can find a way to tell me your news. Please try. I grow rather concerned. Is it my husband? Is he unwell?'

The landlady, used to dealing with all manner of types, baulked a little at this slight, self-contained woman who stood so patiently before her. She'd been rather hoping for a bout of hysteria so she could show her patrons how admirable she was in a crisis. But that might yet come when she broke the exciting news.

'It is your husband. It most certainly is.' Joan gave a nod and a small smile of encouragement.

'Well, not long after you left but I didn't know where you'd gone so I couldn't send after you.' She finished triumphantly. Joan raised an eyebrow.

'Yes, well, men from the courts came. And they had a ticket to arrest your husband. And they did. Arrest him.' Another triumphant finish.

Joan nodded. 'Thank you. I wonder how they happened to know he was here…'

Then after an awkward pause and a steady look, she continued, 'Do you know where he has been taken?' Her voice was firm; after all, nothing could be as bad or as wonderful as what she had just been through.

Mistress Sheridan felt rather annoyed. Was there nothing that could rouse Mistress Legh? 'Yes, in fact I do!'

Joan waited. She couldn't imagine why James and Margery so liked this woman; she was all gilt-covered wormy wood and at this vivid thought she had trouble hiding a smile.

Was she *smiling*? Wretched woman. All that was said about her was true. The Cardinal's whore. To her core. But at least her customers would be agog and word would spread that she was staying at the Garland. Business would be brisk as people sought to hear about her or even catch a glimpse.

He was taken to the Fleet. And that was no better a place than it ought to be; no good for a man with such a sickness in his chest, but he'd be all right, he'd pay for a private room and firewood and hot food. She wasn't to worry. It wasn't such a bad place if you could pay.

Joan saw the words stream past her and managed to catch them and understand. Then she comprehended that something truly dreadful had happened; George had no money. Still furious with him for losing the gold, when she went out, she had peevishly taken their purse with the ready coins. And right now, it lay in the pouch at her hip, nestling against the money Thomas had given her. George had nothing with him. Nothing but a dreadful cold in this awful summer weather. He would be in a dark, crowded cell with other men, dampness, sickness and hunger all around and no Joan to make it better.

For a moment she was at a loss, then she politely thanked Mistress Sheridan and turned to leave. The Fleet. So close to where she had once lived in such luxury. She hurried along the streets, bumping into countless people with their heads down and earning curses and jostling at almost every step.

Finally, she was there, staring up at the solid gates. Her poor boy was in there. He'd be longing for her, aching for her to come and take charge and all at once, after all the wasted years Joan realised that she did love George. She'd grown to rely on his steadfast passion for her, on his delight in their family and all she had done was accept him and treat him fondly. She had shown Pepper – a dog – more love than she'd shown George.

Oh, I'm sorry, she cried from her heart. *I'll show you love, George. I'll forget the glory of Thomas and I'll love you truly. I'll really try. I promise.*

She pounded on the wicket gate and finally, it opened. The man was grubby but his face lit up when he saw a tearful, well-dressed woman on the other side. This would mean money. Slowly he extracted coin after coin from Joan and in return he promised that George Legh would indeed be moved to a warm room and cared for. So, the Cardinal had an interest, did he? Privately he doubted it; everyone knew that the Butcher's Cur was on the way down. Finally, he gave the woman a last winning smile and one more empty promise before closing the gate and returning to his own small cosy room and his hot supper, whilst deep in the dark and noisome prison, George Legh slipped in and out of a glorious dream of his wife and children who smiled and beckoned to him.

There was nothing more to be done that night; if she went again to York Place, she was unlikely to be allowed to see Thomas, so with weary feet she wound her way back toward the Garland. Her heart sank at the gauntlet she must run of landlady and customers before she could reach her chamber. Their curious eyes would pick her apart, from her muddied shoes and skirts to her strained and tear-stained face but she must seek sleep or she would be unable to fight for George on the morrow. Briefly, she imagined resting on Thomas's bed and what bliss it would be to stir in the night and see his firm profile cutting into the light of the candles on his table. She would smile and gently ask him to come to bed then slip back into her dreams, knowing that she was safe under his guarding watch.

But that wasn't how her night would be spent and never would be again. Her clothes stank; a charming mix of filth, prolonged dampness and a bitter despair. The Legh family would have done better never to have heard of her. If only George had never travelled to London with his father, never seen her and fallen in love with a false image. Right now he could have been happily in bed with a hearty Cheshire lass. Sleeping after a laughing romp with a girl he'd grown up with, who understood him and would never weigh him and find him lacking against another.

A shout pulled Joan from her misery and she jumped back to avoid a barrow-load of rubbish being carted away. The smell was rich, to say the least, and sat ill with the end-of-day pies which were still being sold. Her stomach convulsed and she closed her eyes for a moment. Surely she wasn't with child again? That really would be the cap on this glorious day.

So much later, it seemed, she was at last in bed, shivering with misery and chill and tucking her feet as close to her as she could manage, she did eventually sleep.

The next day arrived, seemingly unaware that it was a new day but instead determined to continue the bleak summer weather. Joan's clothes were stiff but at least they were dry and she brushed dust out of, and life into her hair, before washing and setting off once again to try and find help.

At York Place, she found a much less friendly welcome than before and well-dressed courtiers scurried to and from the river and the great building, trying to remain dry and dignified. Joan was past retaining her dignity and went straight to the gate where yesterday she had bid farewell to Thomas.

The man on duty was sympathetic but he shook his head sadly at Joan. She was one of many with a wish to see his master and he could only tell her what he told the others, that times were not good for the Cardinal and therefore all the worse for his supplicants. She would do well not to count on his help, for he was hard-pressed to help himself in these difficult times.

His face was not unsympathetic and Joan felt sorry for him. She found Thomas's purse and with a small smile gave him a coin to thank him for his help. As she smiled, the man looked closely at Joan. Surely he knew her? Then he had it. 'Mistress Joan?' he asked, squinting at her.

She turned back, 'Mistress Wolsey' he said, more firmly this time.

Joan nearly threw her arms around him. 'Joseph? How wonderful!' She felt quite tearful, not least because he called her by Thomas's name. Yes, she was Mistress Wolsey. They had made those vows, and surely God himself still honoured them, even if they were no longer honoured by the two who made them.

'Mistress. What ails you? What can I do?' Joseph took Joan's freezing hand in his and led her through the wicket gate. 'Let me aid you. Will you write a word to My Lord and I will see he gets it?' Joan nodded and in the tiny guard room took the proffered pen, dipped it in thick and sticky ink and wrote a spluttery few words.

George is arrested and in the Fleet. He is unwell and I fear for his life.

Please Thomas, please help us.

Joan Legh.

Joseph could not say when he would pass the paper to the Cardinal but he gave Joan his earnest word that as soon as may be possible, he would himself press the paper into His Lordship's hand. She could trust him. Joan gave him one more sad smile and her thanks and with reluctance, he opened the gate and allowed her to drift off into the cold wet day. He followed her with his eyes as long as he could and failed to shake off the feeling that the Cardinal would have thanked him if he had kept hold of her and made sure she was safe and warm.

Almost immediately, however, Joan forgot Joseph's kindness. There were hours, perhaps days to fill and she had no idea what to do next. She was bone tired and rather lost and constantly astonished by the way her legs continued to work, placing her feet, each in front of the other. She watched them with fascination, quite hypnotised by the regularity of her paces and their seeming purpose. Where, she wondered hazily, would they take her? Did they have somewhere to go? Well, she might as well go along with them; it wasn't as if she had somewhere else to be.

A tall man brushed past her and Joan looked at his retreating back. Something seemed familiar in the set of his shoulders. She nearly didn't speak, almost couldn't find her voice, yet somehow it was there, whether or not she willed it.

'Master Paulet?'

The man turned and she could see she was mistaken. Yet perhaps not quite. She was confused but the man smiled at her and then lunged forward. Joan wondered what on earth he was doing before belatedly realising that she was about to fall and this someone she almost knew was catching her.

A little later, Joan was seated in a boat and the oarsmen were pulling firmly, their oars easing the craft through the water. There was a fur across her knees and another around her shoulders and the man who wasn't Master Paulet was looking at her.

'Mistress Joan.'

She nodded. 'You know me?'

He gave an odd smile and nodded, his eyes looking keenly at her.

'I know you in several ways.'

Joan smiled politely thinking, *oh be cryptic if you will; I can't be troubled to play this game with you.*

The man was faintly surprised at her lack of interest – any other woman would have eagerly demanded to know how he knew her, been keen to hear about herself. But then perhaps he was not surprised. This woman had troubled Europe all the way to Rome and certainly had ruffled his own brother. There had to be something to her beyond her face, so tired yet still beautiful.

He took her hand, 'I see you still wear Wolsey's ring. That sapphire was famous for its colour and many remarked when he exchanged it for a brass ring set with glass.' Joan felt her fingers curl into her palm as if he had threatened to take it from her and almost snatched her hand away from him. But she resisted and held his gaze. But of course, he was William. Sir William Paulet, elder brother to George Paulet of the compelling eyes. Joan was disgusted with herself; even now, with her husband in gaol, she was thinking fondly of another man. She really was beyond God's love and mercy.

William found her almost unfathomable and he was a man used to assessing people and knowing their price. He thought back four years to an evening at Basing, in the old-fashioned little manor house. It had been but two weeks since their father had died and he and George sat late together.

'George. You should marry.'

George gave his half-shrug and lifted his wine glass to his lips. 'Oh… no… I think not.' He spoke dismissively, but William pressed him.

'You should. A marriage is a good contract if you find a woman like my Elizabeth and get some sons on her. You'll see what your life has been missing.'

Perhaps the drink had softened them, or they felt sentimental over the absence of their father, but for once, George spoke. He was never one to tell of his feelings and William sometimes felt that his brother was in some ways a stranger to him. They worked well together; William with the mind of a tightly secured box and his brother George, content to listen and watch wherever William sent him, feeding information into that steel trap of a brain where it remained till it was needed. And it always was needed in the end.

'Ah, you see William, I should have married. There is a woman. Twice I have not acted and twice regretted it. And now she is safely married and stowed away in Cheshire. That Palatinate County from whence no beautiful woman returns.' He snorted with laughter and drank deeply, his face laughing, but William could see that George was torn with longing.

He too drank, thinking hard and rapidly, and then he had it. 'Ah, the Cardinal's Lark. I hear she is beautiful.' But there was surely more; there were many lovely women in England, and there had to be a better reason why George wanted one of the most notorious in the land.

'She is. And when I last saw her, I almost took her hand and spoke. I wanted to say, *our souls have found each other*. And for a moment the words were there, they were in the air between us. Then a fool lost his hat and I lost the moment.' That don't-care half-shrug again and George changed the subject. But William remembered and here, four years on, the Lark was in his grasp and at last he could try to understand George's feelings.

Joan was watching William. She was silent and he recognised his own way of assessing a new acquaintance. She made a slight face as if working something from a tooth and then she spoke, 'You are remembering all you know about me.' It was not a question and he did her the honour of simply nodding.

She fluttered her brows as if shaking off the thought. 'Do you know that *my husband* George is imprisoned because *my husband* Thomas gave him a bad land contract?' She looked very cross and William felt that was an improvement on her fading-away look of earlier.

'No. I didn't.' But William lied; he knew most things that happened. As a Privy Counsellor, little passed him by and a man of modest family could only climb the rickety ladder of ambition by exercising his wit. Much indeed as the Butcher's Cur had done, although the Paulet family were at least of decent French stock.

'Mistress Legh. I beg you not to worry. I suggest you accompany me to my house. It is modest but I can assure you of its comforts. And I will find out how your husband fares and how he may be released.'

A gust of wind blew rain into Joan's face and made her eyes smart. 'Thank you. You are kind. And I am finding it hard to…' But her voice failed her and she closed her eyes against the tears which slid down her cheeks.

They spoke no more and when in silence they left the boat. William tucked her hand in his arm to guide her up the water stairs. As he promised, his house was well-appointed and she was soon by a fire and warming her stiff hands back into movement.

'Doesn't it seem odd to have a fire lit in mid-June? I fear for our crops these dreadful years, and prices will rise and we shall all starve.' Her eyes were slightly wild and William guessed that she was narrowly containing her panic.

'Mistress Legh. Please rest and I shall send at once to the Fleet to ask after Master Legh. In fact, if you will allow me, I shall go myself... if you are content to remain here?'

She nodded and William set off. To be honest, he had scant hope for George Legh. Wolsey had indeed unwittingly set a trap for the man. It was unlike the great statesman to be so careless but Wolsey had never seen himself on the way down in life, had never imagined that a wronged man would be able to seek redress for land unjustly removed from him so long ago.

It was a damnable situation and William could feel only pity for Joan. She had been Wolsey's bauble and when she became a hindrance to his career, he had carelessly cast her off with a rich dowry to a man besotted and uncaring for her spotted reputation.

Legh had better still be alive, or it might not be long before the Paulet family was welcoming an interesting new thread into the tapestry of their family tree. He hurried his pace and his attendants complained as they sped behind him through the muddy streets.

Joan dozed, waking with horribly regular vicious jumps as she slumped sideways in her chair. She felt sick each time she was jolted from her sleep but lacked the will to move or to awaken herself properly. A manservant peeped in, but the visitor didn't seem to want dinner and he silently closed the door. *All the more for them in the kitchens then*, he thought greedily.

William's return journey to his house was much more measured. He had found things at the Fleet to be as he expected and he had sorrowfully viewed the body of George Legh and left coins to have the man decently wound and placed in a coffin. Sending a note for his brother to meet him outside the house, he found George lounging by the garden wall. The long rows of windows streamed with water as the rain beat down on London.

'There you are, William. Presumably, you have an excellent reason why I am waiting outside, ruining my new jerkin?'

William ushered his brother inside and once they were safely in his chamber, he quickly told George who was in the parlour and why. George stood very still.

'You have Mistress Legh here.' He shook his head. 'So?'

'George. Don't be a fool. Don't treat me as a fool. And do not insult that woman by thinking *she* is a fool. Today is the day to comfort her and support her. Do it well; be her friend and don't let her go for a third time or I shall know that you cannot truly be my brother.'

George nodded and with amused resignation William saw that his brother had taken his words to heart. 'Ah, well,' he thought, 'she will certainly add *something* to life. Pray God she makes George happy.'

Sitting in Lady Paulet's comfortable parlour, in her waking dream, images passed through Joan's exhausted mind. A procession of pictures; sitting on the damp grass laughing at the children and George and watching Margery walking across the lawn to her. She was so pleased to see her, unknowing of the trouble she carried, then the endless journey, those dismal damp inns, all forgettable until that last horrible place. Then each time she lay once again in that bed, she would wake with the dreadful sick jolt and the renewed loss of the gold.

Throughout the long afternoon, Joan heard voices come and go, voices which passed the chamber in which she sat and passed beneath her in the servants' areas, but no one came to her and it seemed as if there was nothing but this existence.

Finally, a quick light step approached and the door opened. A woman in her fifties came in, expensively but discreetly dressed and she paused before speaking softly.

'Mistress Legh? Are you awake, my dear?'

Joan stirred. Her eyes were dry and the lids pulled at her eyeballs as she blinked.

The woman approached and bent slightly to speak to Joan. 'Joan, I am Elizabeth Paulet. My dear?'

Joan licked her lips; she was so dry. She could not recall the last time she had drunk anything. Breakfast. Yes, then. She had a small beaker of ale. Funny she should be so thirsty when the weather was so wet.

Her stiff bones clicked as she moved and spoke, 'Oh Lady Paulet, forgive me. I have been so lost and Sir William gave me refuge.' She started to rise, but Elizabeth stopped her.

'No Mistress Legh, stay there.' The older woman spoke with a smile and pulled a stool over towards Joan before sitting on it and taking Joan's hands in her own.

'Might I call you Joan?'

Joan nodded, 'Of course.'

'Joan. I'm so sorry that I was not here to bear this

waiting time with you. I was visiting my Capel family and had no idea you were here. My husband has been at the Fleet…'

She chafed Joan's hands which were slight and chill between her own. They reminded her of that pitiful bird which had flown in and dashed itself against the window. It lay for hours before being found and Elizabeth had never forgotten the poignancy of the bundle of cold bones in her hands. Bringing her thoughts back, she wondered how to speak to this woman, but Joan supplied the answer.

'He's dead, isn't he? He was too sick when they took him. My poor boy. Oh, George, I'm sorry.' Joan's face grew even more pale and gaunt and Elizabeth could only nod and gaze into the depth of those beautiful blue eyes – expressive and so sad.

'Lady Paulet.' Joan gathered herself together. 'May I thank Sir William? Perhaps he could advise me on what to do. But I wish to be no trouble to you. To any of you. I should take George home if it's possible. I don't know. Do you think it's possible? Can I take a dead man to Cheshire? How do I take him? Oh dear.' Joan looked utterly perplexed and Elizabeth took pity on her.

'Joan, allow me to call my husband. And his brother George is here too and would pay his respects to you. I believe you have met him before?'

Walking to the door, Lady Paulet opened it and softly called her husband's name. Joan heard him walking along the corridor and their soft words, and then a few moments later, both William and George entered. Joan finally got to her feet but she felt dizzy and gripped the back of the chair.

'Sir William. Thank you for your kindness and your efforts on my behalf. Can you tell me? I left money for him to be cared for. Was he? Was he comfortable when he died?'

William had only told George the truth and was not about to share it with Legh's wife. He wanted to forget the tussle he'd had with the gaolers, who weren't even sure where George Legh was. He did not care to remember the state of the corpse when they finally found him, the filth from the floor, the distress on the dead man's face.

'Mistress Joan, please put your mind at rest. I think your poor husband would have died had he been in his own bed, but the bed in which he died was comfort enough. You did right and the gaolers cared for him.'

Joan looked relieved and nodded her thanks. Then George Paulet stepped forward and with a slight bow took her hand.

'Mistress Joan. I am glad to see you again, though I could wish it was a happier time. My brother has told me of the problems which brought you and Master Legh to town. I wish to help. Will you allow me to assist you? To advise you?'

Joan nodded and George continued. 'I think the first thing is to take your husband home. I will put that process underway and if you permit, I will accompany you on your sad journey.'

After a moment she met his eyes and at his own intense gaze, felt her soul writhe. He had always looked at her like that. So few meetings they had had, yet though he was not really known to her, neither was he forgotten. She smiled and her face felt stiff. It was an age, a lifetime since she had smiled and though it was only a tiny smile, she felt just a little better.

'Thank you, Master Paulet, but I cannot allow you to inconvenience yourself on my behalf.'

Elizabeth stepped forward. 'My dear, will you at least allow me to offer you our hospitality for a day or so until you are ready to start your journey? I will send a servant to collect your things and we can discuss matters when you are less shocked.' Certainly, Joan still looked very fragile and George longed to slip his arm around her waist and support her, but instead he allowed his sister-in-law to do that and help her upstairs to a bed chamber.

He went himself to the Garland Inn and gathered up the Legh servants then went into the mean chamber and packed their few items. The landlady was agog to see this and barely managed a protest. George could guess what had happened, her loose mouth had proclaimed her exciting guests and it would have taken word so little time to travel to the right ears and for poor Legh to be arrested.

He sighed as he fastened George's pack. How heartbroken was Joan? And he sighed again. The man was not yet cold and here he was plotting to win his widow. He had no idea of the state of Joan's marriage. But certainly, the times he had met Legh, he had only gained the impression of a good-natured man with little depth. And even today, in extremis she had reacted to him, albeit only faintly. But that still gave him hope.

Chapter 24

Adlington

In the end, Joan agreed to allow George Paulet to accompany her on the long march home. The children had raced from the Hall when they saw the horses approaching, only to stop in confusion. There were the servants but not their father. And who was the tall stranger riding close to Mother? Joan jumped from her mount and pulled them all into her arms, tears running down her cheeks.

They had left Prestbury church only a short while before, leaving behind George's body resting in the Legh chapel and the shocked priest roused from his little house opposite to take charge of the obsequies.

Over the next few days, George Paulet learned to respect the man he had unreasonably disliked for so many years. Legh was loved by his neighbours and servants and the church was full when the time came to place him with his forefathers. Shock and sadness were on every face and his children were inconsolable.

Indeed, it had been a weary journey, yet the weather had cleared and there were moments of clear happiness for George. He relished seeing Joan revive slightly – William and Wolsey had solved the land problems and with that no longer hanging over her, from time to time, Joan found moments of hope. George Paulet was a peaceful companion, speaking only occasionally but always with purpose and she found herself smiling at his gentle jokes. Then she would remember that her dead husband was in their slow procession and she would sag in the saddle and feel guilt and remorse gnawing once more at her soul. But when in later years George looked back at this time, he saw it as a pilgrimage, a time of growing and proving his love. It proved impossible not to fall in love with Joan; unendurable that he couldn't touch or kiss her. He ached to make her smile and bring light back into her eyes. He constantly laughed at himself; all these steady years he had lived with no real idea of love and now here it was and he was helpless.

When they reached Adlington, he saw another side to her. His own parents had been affectionate and proud of their children but she was clearly a friend as well as a mother and his heart melted to see them comfort and love each other. He briefly allowed himself to imagine that he was their father and at last, comprehended the pride and happiness William had found in his family.

Now, with no idea how she felt about him, it dawned on him that he'd inadvertently given a part of himself to Joan and that when he left, he would return to London diminished. It was both irritating and amusing how far he'd relaxed his guard.

He had now spent many weeks in her company and they were comfortable together. They had worked on George's affairs and all was now in order for the estate to run. He had often found three-year-old Thomas at his elbow and had rather taken to the boy, sitting him on his knee and explaining things to him. Thomas listened and picked out words on the documents and George smiled at the child's intelligence. But this time had to end; in London, William was missing his brother and wrote urging his return, for there was no one he trusted like George for confidential matters. And a note from Elizabeth helped him make up his mind. She was a wise woman, he thought as he cast the note on the fire, and she was right. Joan would only miss his company if he removed himself from her side. And if she didn't, well, despite everything, she was not for him.

So tonight, Joan and George sat together for the last time by the fire in the Great Hall. A farewell dinner had been eaten and the guests departed. Joan's sisters-in-law had taken to this gentle stranger who relieved them of much responsibility and sorted out George's problems, and Margery and her husband were likewise grateful, for it was a great relief to stop worrying about the land dispute. Margery had been intrigued by George Paulet; clearly, he and Joan were long acquainted but Margery had never heard of him before. It was immediately apparent that Paulet was in love with Joan and she smiled to see a man of his years gazing so fondly at her friend. But what did Joan feel? As was proper, Joan showed no emotion but gratitude and friendship. It was, after all, such a short time since George Legh had died. But Paulet would be a fine match for Joan and was in every way her equal. She laughed and joked with him in a way she had not laughed with her husband; she was relaxed and calm in his company and never treated him in that motherly way which Margery had noted with George Legh.

Joan looked thoughtfully at George Paulet. This time tomorrow he would be in some cheerless inn and she would be heading to bed and… she stopped and examined her feelings. She would be missing him. His eyes met hers and once again, his glance filled her with sunshine and she smiled.

'George. You have been nothing but kind to us. The children will miss you greatly.'

He nodded his thanks and their thoughts flew unspoken through the fire.

But will you *miss me?*

Oh, you have no idea how I shall miss having you here each day.

George rose and stretched, 'I think I shall seek my bed. My dear, don't rise early. I shall make a good start on the day as the weather seems set fair. Let us part now.'

Joan stood and moved around the fire to stand close to him. She gazed seriously at him, no smile on her lips and her eyes searching his.

'Of course not. I must see you off. But once you have gone, may I write to you? Only if I have any problems, of course, I shall not trouble you. And Thomas would like to tell you things too. He has grown fond of you. I will keep notes of all he wishes to say…'

George nodded. 'Please do. I shall be glad to hear from him. He is a good child and you are very fortunate. In time I shall, if you allow, be happy to be of more substantial use to him.'

Joan offered her hand and he took it. It was icy and her fingers gripped his as he bent to kiss it. Then with a decisive gesture, he straightened and said a brisk goodnight to her. Joan watched his departing back as he vanished into the gloom. She almost offered him a candle, but he was certain of his way to his chamber. If only he was making his way to her bed tonight. Tears prickled her eyes and she silently whispered a blessing after him.

November 1529 – London

Mistress Legh,

I thank you for your letter and the addition from Thomas.

Please tell him to practise so when I may see him again, I will find a worthy opponent.

But between us, my archery skills have always been dreadfully lacking so I hope to encourage him greatly by losing to him with no deceit.

Joan, perhaps I take a liberty but your last gave me hope. You seem to miss me and I can only say that I miss you more than I can bear.

Perhaps I will cast this into the fire and your eyes will never pass over these words. But I might seal it quickly and send it on its way to you before I can call it back.

It seems to me that we would do well together. Will you consider entering into marriage with me?

Send me word. I wish no offence and whatever your answer, will always consider you my dear friend.

George Paulet

George. My love. Of course. Come as soon as you may, but on no account travel if the weather is poor.
I am and will remain,

your
Joan Larke

Chapter 25

Adlington, Late December 1529

Joan paced. If she thought of George and pressed her hand to her neck, she could feel her pulse speeding. Then she touched her hand to her breast but she had done it so many times that the paper hidden there had grown soft and ceased to crackle. All she was able to think were the words, *he loves me. He loves me.*

It was so different to being with Thomas; although she had loved him passionately and completely, there was still the fear that what they were doing was wrong. And her marriage to George had been gentle and familiar but so lacking in the coming together of their souls. Although she often felt that it *had* been that way for George and that was so sad.

But this, this was how it should be. She could barely stay still, she wanted to see him, to devour him with her eyes. He was her first thought on waking. In the night he was there in her mind and she could easily lay awake for hours, tracing his route northwards to her, imagining his hands on the reins of his horse, seeing him in cold beds longing for her as she longed for him. Had she imagined his passion? But no, surely not, no man looked like that at a woman if he didn't want her and she shivered.

George punished his horses and his servants in his race to Cheshire. He had paused only to see Elizabeth who had laughed with delight and kissed his cheeks before wishing him God-speed. What weather? The unusual northerly wind would keep his face fresh as he travelled and the rain softened the roads and saved the horses from injury.

Joan had counted the days to London and added some then counted the days back to Cheshire and added more. He couldn't possibly be here before February and she was a fool to think otherwise. She couldn't see Margery for she would know and Joan wanted to hold this secret as long as she could. She was almost forty, yet a man wanted her as she wanted him and she felt young again.

And so many times each day her steps carried her down to the road and up to her solar and back again until the servants grew tired of the mud she continually carried in and the children bore constantly unsettled expressions on their faces.

Yet now, when at last she'd turned away from the window, to try and be calm, she was called back by the noise of servants and horses; now was the moment he arrived.

She watched from the window as he dismounted and limped slightly. He'd fallen from his horse once in his youth and twisted his left knee and in more mature years it began to trouble him. To know these little things about him felt like possessing a treasure and she wanted to press her fingers into the joint and help ease it. She prolonged the moment of going down and watched the children go out to greet him. He swung Thomas up and hugged him before turning to Elizabeth who lugged Ellen in her arms and kissed them all, not forgetting Mary who always hung back slightly. George looked up at the window and saw her there and as their eyes met, surely her heart stopped for a moment. Then she picked up her skirt and sprinted downstairs. She joined the them in front of the Hall and over the little heads, their eyes met. They didn't need to touch or make physical contact; to stare into each other's eyes was enough.

After supper, the excited children were put to bed and Thomas was promised an archery match on the morrow. He'd fetched his arrows and waved them about excitedly until he'd nearly cut one of his sisters across the forehead and Joan had firmly removed them from his grasp and placed them out of reach on the screen in the Great Hall.

'Tomorrow, without fail, Thomas. I swear on all that is dear to me. Yes, even if it rains. No, I shall not tell you what is most dear to me, but I assure you it is a promise worth having.'

Joan smiled at her son; sometimes, he was so like the other Tom that she could only laugh. Would the brothers ever meet she wondered, but she could not conceive how.

Now, at last, all was quiet. George stood and lifted the wine jug from its warm place by the fire and filled his glass. Joan held out hers but he ignored it and she raised her eyebrows. But she was not forgotten and he pulled a stool to stand next to her chair. Then seated on it he lifted his glass to her lips. She drank, then as she smiled at him, he too drank. 'To you.'

'No. To us.' Then he leaned forward and kissed her wine-wet lips and held her in his arms. He was so tired from the journey, but had the grim reaper called him at that moment George would have smiled at him and asked him to return another day.

They sat peacefully for a while, watching the fire die down, then she turned to him and held his gaze. 'I believe it is time for bed.'

George nodded and in silence, they headed upstairs. Once in bed, Joan threw her night-rail across the room with such abandon that George laughed and pulled her down into his arms. Giggling, she grappled with him briefly until his urgency won and he leaned over to press his lips against hers and he didn't stop kissing her until she cried out with that passion and loss of self which had been lacking for so many lonely years.

They met again and again throughout the night, unable to believe that this was real. George continually woke, anxious that he had dreamed of Joan and sure that he was in fact in London or at Basing and the bed would be empty and cold beside him. Then reaching out his hand he met her warm body and knew from her breathing that she was awake and smiling. He ran his fingers over her face and held her to him whilst she, equally frightened and thrilled lay her hands on him, seeking to know his body and what pleased him.

When dawn trickled through the window and peeped through the bed curtains, George pulled them slightly apart so he could see her face.

'Why, you look exhausted, my love. Did you not sleep well?' She rolled her eyes and snuggled closer into his embrace.

'I kept waking. Oh, the dreams I have had, it seemed to me that I was being crushed repeatedly. Thank goodness, you were here to save me.'

They both gave naughty grins and then George spoke. 'Would you like a new ring?'

Ah, thought Joan, and held up her hand with the blue-grey sapphire.

'Would you *like* me to have a new ring?'

There was silence for a few moments then she spoke again, 'Does it trouble you to see me wearing Thomas's ring?'

George considered. And discovered a new sensation; that he wasn't jealous and here at last was a person with whom he would never dissemble.

'Actually, no, it doesn't. For all the time I have known you, you have worn it. It matches your eyes, which is why I suspect the Cardinal gave it to you. I will give you jewels if you wish, but this is your ring. George didn't mind?'

Joan looked slightly rueful, 'George never asked. He was so taken with the image of me that he didn't even know about Thomas. He… well, it was a great shock for him to understand the truth and that Tom and Dorothy were actually my children. He thought I was an especially fond nurse to them.'

George closed his eyes in sympathy and exasperation. 'The poor boy.'

Then suddenly Joan moved, straddling George and he

grinned up at the delicious view but she was speaking and running her hand across the carved bedhead.

'Thomas sent this bed and even then, George didn't see. He wasn't stupid, just didn't understand. And I thought everyone knew. But it turned out that not everyone did.'

George twisted to see the carvings and smiled, 'Ah. I see. The cunning Cardinal blessing your union.'

Then turning back to Joan, he ran his hands over her shoulders and down her back before gripping her hips. 'Now, while you're there…'

Eventually, they had to rise; the children were running around and calling for George, and as Joan said, 'I am hungry enough to eat you.'

The time before dinner passed so quickly; Thomas demanded his archery match and George put up enough of a defence to make his eventual defeat convincing. And Joan, wrapped up and warm, laughed quietly to herself, George was indeed a terrible shot but it was a joy to see him with the children.

After dinner, Joan stopped them from running off to other pursuits and kept them at the table for a little longer.

'My loves, would you mind if George and I were married?'

Their faces were blank, then Elizabeth, looking at the faces of her brother and sister explained. 'They don't know what marriage means.' And she assumed her eldest sibling role. 'What Mother means is that she and Master George will be like when Father was here.'

Thomas looked – if possible, even more blank – and

looked around the room, 'Who is Master George?'

Elizabeth, already a mature little soul, was thrilled beyond measure to share a look with the grown-ups.

'Thomas, I am Master George but you call me George because we are friends. I am going to marry Joan. *Your mother*,' he added hastily in case the boy was also unsure who Joan might be, 'and I will be father to you all.'

Elizabeth sensed that this was her moment and for the first time, Joan saw Dorothy in her younger sister. She drew breath, 'We,' she said with a sweeping gesture, 'are very happy to hear this news.'

If Joan had not already lost her heart to George, it would have been at this moment, when he stood and with a solemn face bowed low to Elizabeth before taking her hand and kissing it. 'Thank you, Mistress. I am much relieved and very grateful.' Elizabeth nodded graciously and gesturing to the children, led them from the room.

'Phew,' said Joan, 'they are such complete little people. And aren't they funny?'

George pretended to mop his brow. 'I have to admit I was worried there. I thought Thomas was on the brink of forbidding our union and having me escorted from the house and thrown from the county.'

'Well, he might yet, if he can work out exactly *who* he's ejecting.' Joan burst into laughter and flopped forwards, stifling her giggles in her arms. 'Oh, George. I don't think I've ever been happier.' And one look at his face told her that he felt the same.

The days of Christmas never seemed as long as they did that year and Joan did not wish to speak to the priest before February for he was already disapproving of George's presence at Adlington, so much less than a year since she had become a widow. But the date had to be arranged before the weeks leading up to Lent or they would be forced to wait until after Easter. Perhaps, she thought, we should flee to London and have Thomas marry us, but that would be cruel and she didn't think she could bear to stand between the two loves of her life and ask one to give her to the other.

But finally, the day came and Margery arrived to help her dress. Joan wore a new gown, a soft green velvet which she didn't altogether like but George and Margery insisted it was a good colour and an invitation to spring to hurry along. The mink trim was delicious and all day she found herself surreptitiously nestling her neck and chin into its softness. Her mantle was of the same velvet and she was glad of it when the weather proved to be rather fresh. Sitting for a few moments of reflection, Joan and Margery clasped hands. 'We *are* a long way from home, aren't we?'

Margery nodded, 'But was it ever really home? It was where we started, but see where we are now. The first days in your father's house, I would have thought someone possessed by madness if he had told me that one day I would be sitting here as your friend with a family and good husband of my own. And you are about to start on another journey. I am so happy to see you with him. I see such love in his eyes for you. And in yours, for him.'

Joan felt her eyes prickle. 'But poor George…'

'No, don't say that. You gave him all you could; the children and your kindness.' She offered Joan a kerchief and that made her cry again for it so reminded her of Thomas.

Margery laughed. 'Now you are just indulging yourself. And you won't turn the devil away by *pretending* to be unhappy. Come along, my duck.'

And for the very last time, she knelt before Joan and helped her to dress, gently rolling stockings up to her knees, securing them with silk ribbons and easing on the new shoes. She pinned sleeves and fastened skirts before helping Joan into the green gown and swinging the mantle around her shoulders.

Joan drew breath, but Margery spoke over her.

'No, it really *doesn't* make you look sallow. You have a pretty colour in your cheeks and it sits well with your blue eyes. Makes them look less grey. In fact, you look like a bluebell wood. So not another word, please.'

Joan shut her mouth with a jokey snap and sat for her bonnet to be secured. The children were with the Griffiths children in Prestbury, from where they would all walk to the church and there was nothing more to do but to head downstairs and join George. Joan could hear him in the Great Hall where he alternated singing at the top of his voice with shouting for her to hurry up.

They left the horses at the inn and walked the last little way to the church, where although the day was chilly, a watery sun was succeeding in breaking through and in the churchyard primroses and even the occasional daffodil were showing in sheltered spots. When the church came into view, Joan could see hordes of children around the porch. She turned to George and Margery, 'Are they *all* ours? Have I forgotten some of them?'

Margery laughed, 'No, they appear to be village children and our nieces and nephews and I really have no idea which is yours or mine or someone else's. We'll have to see who comes home to bed; see if we can sift them that way.'

So it was that when the priest first saw Mistress Legh's face, she was laughing and he pursed his lips. He knew full well her history, from peasant's daughter to the Cardinal's whore. Then having established herself as a seemingly decent woman she'd managed to rid herself of poor Master Legh. Now she'd ensnared another respectable gentleman. He had tried to speak of his concerns to Master Paulet, to warn him but the man was bewitched by her glamour, ensnared by those eyes. Even today she was laughing and she was only yards away from her husband who had not yet even rotted in his grave. He swallowed his anger and with a hideous smile stretching his lips he welcomed the couple. They stood by the porch and clasping each other's hands, Joan and George made their promises completely unaware of the priest's antipathy.

As George spoke, his hands gripped hers tightly and his eyes held her so close that for a moment she spoke to God. She thanked Him for her blessings and added that if He took her now, she would be content and she continued to look at George as if she had only just recovered her sight and he was her first view of heaven.

George was almost beyond words. He had always felt that love and marriage were not for him and then, one look at Joan and hearing her laugh and he was lost. Or perhaps he was found. In the end, it was all so easy; he loved and was loved. *Our souls have found each other.*

Their vows complete, the new couple with their friends and family entered the church for Mass. George had equipped the children with a few flowers and now bent down to Elizabeth and spoke to her. She nodded and led her sisters and brother into the Legh chapel where they laid their posies on their father's tomb. Joan stared at the tiny offerings, the stems crushed by their little hands and yet again felt her eyes fill with tears. She stepped forward to join the children and found herself on her knees by George. Elizabeth slipped her arm around her mother's shoulders and leaned against her, comforting her as Joan prayed. Her husband had loved her and she was certain that he would want her to have happiness and security but yet again she begged his forgiveness and prayed for his peaceful rest.

In the church, their friends found themselves silent and even the priest forbore to sigh impatiently, especially when he saw the emotion in Joan's eyes. Of course, later he realised what an excellent actress she was, but for now he conducted the holy rite of Communion with love and compassion in his heart.

As sweet and joyous as her new state was – and it really was, each day was a flurry of waking to George smiling at her, of feeling him with her both emotionally and physically – yet there were still dark shadows in her life. Joan knew that before long she would return to London with George and that once again her children would not be with her. Sometimes, especially in the darkest and most quiet points of the night, she lay awake feeling that her children were scattered beyond her reach. Tom and Dorothy were already gone; if they met there would be few words, for their common paths had long since parted. And now her babies would stay here in Cheshire. They would grow each day and see things that they could not share with her and the common bonds of memory would not form.

She would never know when baby saw the first butterfly that she would remember. Or be there when Thomas fell from a hayrick or… and Joan would suddenly heave with tears and George would half awaken and clasp her to him. There was no ideal answer – he had to be in the south. The children would be better here. And she had to be with George.

And there was one more trouble which shadowed her days; that of Thomas Wolsey. George's frequent letters from William carried their usual business news and requests for George's advice or presence. But they also carried news. Thomas had been so sick since Christmas, almost unto death and Joan daily fought with her impulse to worry and grieve. He was no longer hers to fret over and she certainly had no right to think of another man when so happily married to a good man of her own. Wolsey was the concern of God and the King although she rather doubted that either of them would care enough for him.

Each day that spring she walked around Adlington and the grounds. She trod once more the paths of those unhappy first months and saw the places where she had stopped to try and expel her grief. She thought she would be here forever and yet with just a snap of her fingers her time was almost over. Never again would this be her permanent home. Her gardens would continue without her; the children and their aunts and cousins would change things to their own liking. It would seem like no change at all to them, yet when she came again it would be as a thick line through a favourite painting.

George could see his darling suffering through her turmoil. He laughed gently when she asked if William, who could after all do almost anything, could arrange to have Cheshire and London moved closer together. He knew how he filled the loneliness in her, but in doing so he created a grief which was almost equal in depth and like Joan, could see no real answer. To leave her here was unthinkable and he could only hope that she would soon bear a child of his and once settled safely at Basing would grow accustomed to her new life.

Now here was the moment of departure. Her Legh family stood waving, the children running and shrieking as cousins and siblings do. It felt as if she had already left and they were just waiting for her to go before getting on with their lives. In the kitchens, the servants were cooking dinner but she wouldn't eat it. One of her sisters-in-law had some flowers in her hands which Joan would not see fade. She wouldn't eat the new eggs brought in from the hens that morning. Here she shook herself and laughed; neither would she see that fly eat some rotten meat and bring up its new brood.

She grinned at George and he smiled back, surprised at the sudden lifting of her spirits.

'Let's away then! Goodbye, my loves, be good! I'll see you in the summer. Goodbye… goodbye.'

She could still hear their voices, long after they were out of sight and hearing but George didn't see the tearing of her heart behind her bright smile.

Joan determined that the route to London would no longer be a road of deep sorrow. She would likely never travel abroad so she should enjoy this journey and it turned out that George knew where to lodge. Each night turned into a new adventure. Sometimes they lodged at a pleasant inn, warm and dry with good food and ale, and occasionally their party would leave the main road and head towards a house where they would be the honoured guests of friends. The Paulet family knew many families and in turn, these families were happy to accommodate the brother of William Paulet. He was already a man of influence and it would pay to be in his favour.

Some mornings, Joan struggled to remember where she was, but always George was there. His hand was warm and firm around hers, his eyes creasing in a smile as he looked at her. Every time she looked at him, she was surprised by his eyes; she could never quite pin down the shade of them. Were they green-blue or just pale blue or…?

He laughed when she told him about her terrible indecision, 'Well, I'll give you another forty years to decide, shall I?' And more often than not, he would loom over her, eyes wide, and she would giggle before pulling him down for a kiss and the joy of his solid warmth pressing into her.

When they finally reached William's London house, he was away and George read the note he had left.

'Hmm. He wants me at Basing.' He looked at Joan, who was drooping after their long day.

'You're not setting off tonight, are you?' These Paulets were full of energy. Was it always the way with these self-made men, she wondered? Was it their method of getting ahead of their more noble competitors? Mind you, the Paulets were not entirely self-made; some of their ancestors got their feet wet in 1066, landing with William the Bastard and were rewarded by him as many of his fellow invaders were. But she oughtn't to think that. She was part of the family now and may in time bear a child who would carry that bloodline.

'No. Not tonight and you don't have to come...' his voice tailed off and Joan knew that she really did have to go. And she certainly didn't want to remain behind in the empty London house.

'Well, think about it. I'll go and see if they've gathered anything for supper. Knowing Elizabeth's housekeeping, she's sure to have left them well provided for. If I can get them to share it with us...'

Joan heard his feet clattering downstairs to the kitchens and wearily pulled herself together and headed up to the bed chambers. When she reached the top of the stairs, she realised that she had no idea which was George's and started a small voyage of discovery before finding a well-appointed room free of the clothes of children or women. She yawned and sat on the bed before falling sideways and closing her eyes just for a moment.

She didn't awaken when George, hunting for her, carried her to his own bed. She didn't stir when he undressed her or when with a certain amount of hope kissed her. And she didn't open her eyes when placed between the rather chilly sheets.

As a last resort, George waved some freshly cooked food under her nose and laughed when at last she reacted. Her nostrils widened and her eyes opened.

'Oh, I'm so hungry,' she declared, then realised that she was in bed and naked and it wasn't even the room in which she'd closed her eyes.

George sat back out of her reach and took a huge bite of meat and bread and Joan gave a sigh of longing. 'Oh, come on, please… George.' Her mouth was watering and she scissored her legs to get to the edge of the bed and lunge at him. Laughing, he stood up and took several steps away.

'Oh no. You don't deserve anything. What sort of wife are you? You lay yourself in another man's bed and leave me to find my own supper. Pfff.'

Her stomach rumbled and they both burst out laughing and Joan leapt from the bed and grabbed the plate from George, cramming some meat into her mouth before he could take it back.

'Oh,' she mumbled, 'that's so good.'

George chased her and grabbed her around the waist. 'No no, no!' she squeaked but laughing, he flung her on the bed. She was still laughing and stuffing food into her mouth when she suddenly lost interest in eating and remembered where her real passions lay.

They spent two days in London and barely left the house, sated with sleep and love and Joan could barely encompass such happiness. On their final evening, George read more of the documents left by William, and Joan wrote to her children. She had wondered if she would be able to catch a sight of Tom or Dorothy but her daughter was in Shaftesbury Abbey and Tom, now the Archdeacon of York was not currently in London. *Archdeacon of York* – Joan had blinked when she heard that news. It was difficult to imagine her naughty, grinning little boy ever summoning enough gravity to hold such a post or any of the other positions which he'd been granted. But Thomas had been correct; better to call him nephew and allow him a prosperous life in the church.

The journey down to Basing was very easy and they reached it in two days although the final few miles were on rough roads, made worse by the soggy spring.

'It seems forever since the sun warmed my bones.' Joan was tired and slightly grumpy but George was excited. At last, he could bring the two parts of life together. William and Elizabeth had only seen Joan whilst she was distressed. He longed to show them his beautiful wife and let them understand why she was the prize worth waiting for, the soul that was half of his.

Joan looked at him and he seemed like a boy, so keen to get home to his family and his adored elder brother and she longed for him once again. How funny she thought, to yearn for him even though he's mine and right here beside me. She spoke his name almost silently, yet he looked at her, grinned and looked back with utmost seriousness and she felt her soul glow with pleasure.

'Look! There's the house.' George pointed and at the bottom of the gentle slope which ran from the road to their right she could see what looked like a sharply defined hill with its top cut off and just peeping over the top of the hill were the tops of a couple of chimneys.

They turned down a sunken road and soon everything was out of sight. At the end, the road continued, but they turned up a track and swung right and soon a small gatehouse came into view.

George hallooed and the wicket gate opened. 'Matthew Thomas!' he bellowed and the man squinted into the setting sun.

'Master George?'

'Indeed! Open wide the gates! We are here.'

George was so excited and Joan smiled. She lifted her hands and tidied her bonnet. Her heart beat a little faster. William and Elizabeth had seen her at her worst and now she wanted them to know that she was worthy of their beloved George. Her mare followed George's mount through the simple gate and along the cobbled path. There George stopped and a couple of grooms appeared. One held her bridle as George jumped down and ran around to lift her down. She paused for a second and looked at his dear face. Yes, his eyes were blue. Mostly... oh for goodness sake. Then his hands were around her waist and her feet touching the ground. He took her hand and strode towards the large hill on her right. It wasn't a hill and she knew that. It was a Norman castle, a ring of earth constructed from the top of the hill on which it stood and inside was Basing Castle. They turned right once more and faced another gatehouse, this one a little more impressive than the first, but still flint and wood with a few soft red bricks.

My new home, she thought. George was considering a house of their own but for now, they would live here. All manner of people surrounded them and congratulations were coming from every direction. She could only smile and say thank you. The faces were barely distinguishable from one another, and the Hampshire burr was quite different from the Cheshire tones she'd grown accustomed to. But that too had been a challenge after a childhood in Yarmouth. For a moment, she wished Margery was here to share a glance, and then as the second pair of gates opened, her friend fled from her thoughts and William and Elizabeth stood before her.

Elizabeth beamed and clasped her hands under her chin. 'Oh, Joan. Every day I have looked for you and now you're here.' She held out her hands to her new sister and Joan took them gratefully. She had liked this small tidy woman from their first meeting. *Just as well*, she thought wryly, *I'd just have to put up with it if I didn't like her.*

William came forward and kissing her hand executed a gracious bow. For a moment she almost – so nearly it chilled her – said, *what news of the Cardinal?* Then she slightly shook her head and smiled at him. 'Sir William. Thank you. I am very happy to be here at last.'

Elizabeth hurried them in, 'Come and get warm. The fire is lit in my solar. Will this poor weather ever pass? I really don't know how we shall bake bread this coming year.' She slipped her arm through Joan's and they passed through into a small courtyard. Ahead of them was a pleasing, if slightly old-fashioned half-timbered house. Its wings were to their left and right and ahead was a range of glittering window glass. Elizabeth led them to a door on the right-hand side and up a staircase.

Elizabeth waved her hand vaguely in the air, 'This is a funny area; once the wind comes or a storm, it sits in the valley for hours, so being inside this hill is such a protection. But it's so old. I wonder if you'll feel that?'

Joan looked at her, 'Are there spirits?'

'Not so much spirits, as a spirit of the place. It is very peaceful. But yes, there is a presence here.' She gave a half-embarrassed shrug. 'Oh, don't mind me. I grow fanciful in my old age.'

At the top of the stairs, Elizabeth went ahead into a pleasant chamber. 'My solar. And just above the boiling house,' she grinned, 'so if one forgets the smells, it's always beautifully warm in here. And look.' Pointing out a square block of chalk, Joan realised that there were small holes in the stone. 'Look through.'

Joan did so and found that she was looking the length of the Great Hall towards the dais. Elizabeth chuckled, 'The other side is a mask. I've never been able to tell if anyone was looking though. My children certainly used to do so. Your children will love it too.' Her glance slid over Joan's stomach but the question was not spoken and Joan did not answer.

George and William seem to have disappeared, so Elizabeth showed Joan around her new home and finally to her bed chamber.

'My boxes should arrive soon. I do hope so, for I have been wearing the same few clothes for what feels like months.'

Elizabeth smiled sympathetically. 'I don't suppose George has given much thought to such things.'

Again, and Joan thought she must be far too tired, once again inappropriate words nearly fell from her tongue: *To be honest he prefers me naked and in bed.* But she caught them in time, 'No, I think you're right. I'd probably be in filthy rags before he noticed.'

Elizabeth smiled and turned to leave, 'Hot water will be brought to you and when George and William reappear, we will have supper.' Then she hesitated and drew breath and again paused.

'Joan... you must know that we know and understand your past. But George is very dear to us and you were his choice. His choice from so long ago. I felt that he would never marry but I never realised that it was because of you.'

She returned to Joan and stood close to her. 'I love him and for his sake, I love you and I understand. And I think that you will make each other very happy.' Then she gave a little laugh. 'Be patient. He's such an old bachelor.'

Her old bachelor appeared before too long and with great delight bedded his new wife in his old home. Joan found herself responding with the fervour of a girl and wondered if the time would come when this was all too exhausting. Probably not, she thought with the slightest smile to herself.

The hot water was now tepid, so they washed as best they might and with many a description of what Joan could see, George led her through the old house back to Elizabeth's solar. There were countless hidden passages and invisible doors, each with a tale of his childhood attached, telling of this chunk out of the panelling – *probably better than a lump out of my brother's head* – or where they'd hidden and heard this or that from the grown-ups. Or where they'd held a candle against a screen because the burn mark would keep the devil out. Poor Joan was quite lost when they reached William and Elizabeth, who laughed and jumped up to brush cobwebs from Joan's clothes.

'Really George. That was hardly a shortcut, was it?'

'No, but I want to show her everything.' He smiled at Joan. 'I want her to see everything I have seen so that she understands when I tell her things. And when William sweeps it all away it'll still be in her mind.'

Joan widened her eyes, what did he mean? She looked between the two brothers. Here was a rare disagreement between them.

'Joan,' William paused, 'I hope before long to have a licence from the King to crenellate, to place walls about and towers on the house. And this building is too small. I wish to have a great castle to suit a great family.'

Oh, thought Joan. *Great ambition. I see. But doubtless, William Paulet will achieve what he intends.* And now she understood George's enthusiasm, his wish to share it all with her before it disappeared.

And helpfully, as if to smooth over the awkward

moment, her stomach gave one of its spectacular grumbles and everyone laughed and the moment eased.

Over the next half year or so, Joan too grew to love Basing. As Elizabeth had suggested, there was a presence here. Not a spirit, Joan thought, just the layering of generations of people leading happy and peaceful lives.

She remained at Basing for most of the time, only occasionally accompanying George on his travels or his brief visits to London. It was another chilly summer, but not quite as catastrophically wet as the previous two and their promised trip to Cheshire was easy and pleasant.

As they rode the final mile to Adlington, Joan gripped her reins. Anything could have happened since the last letter. She well knew the old family tale of the two messengers who had crossed each other whilst carrying the news of the loss of George's parents, and every man who had passed them on their journey was surely carrying such news south to her. It was with difficulty that George had dissuaded her from hailing every traveller and interrogating him. She calmed as they approached Adlington for news of such wholesale slaughter as she dreaded would surely have spread.

Then at last, the Great Hall of the house was before them and a groom was shouting over his shoulder and within moments the children were there. Joan jumped from her horse and ran the last little way, crouching low and with her arms held out. The children thumped into her and she fell over backwards, laughing and holding them so closely.

They smelt of lavender and it was in their hair and in

the creases of their clothing and underneath it, Joan sniffed to recall the smell of her babies. They rolled over her and all George could see were little arms and legs clutching his wife. They laughed and chattered and he was reminded of summer swallows chittering and telling each other their news all at the same time.

After a moment, the face of Thomas could be seen and he met George's eye. The boy extracted himself and walked over to his stepfather. He brought his feet smartly together before dropping one back and bowing with graceful hands swooping in front of him.

'Your servant, sir.'

Then he slightly spoiled the effect by losing his balance as he looked up, but George pretended not to see and swept an equally impressive bow.

'Master Legh.'

Thomas beamed. At home, he was still Thomas or other variants uttered as a grunt or screaming complaint and his step-father was the first to thus address him.

'My cousins showed me and I've been doing it for months and months for when you came.'

George made an impressed face. 'Really? It looked so effortless that I thought it was as nature taught it to you.'

Thomas might not quite understand, but he knew a compliment when he heard it and was satisfied and delighted his stepfather by flinging his arms around him.

That evening and all the days of their visit passed so quickly. William, it seemed, employed the speediest messengers and not a day passed without news from London. One would bring news, only to be swiftly followed by another entreating George to return, but he placed them all in the fire. William knew when they would return and he refused to cut Joan's time with the children any shorter than it needed to be. The King will still be conducting his Secret Matter when we return, he thought. All the pieces will still be on the chess board and moving to and fro. He knew that his ambition would never match that of his brother's and his glance fell on Joan, dozing with three-year-old Ellen in her arms. *There's my ambition*, he thought, *my prize. Could it really be so simple? One person whose face becomes inexpressibly dear can provide all one wants from life? Ask me on my deathbed and I'll wager I'll say yes.*

And he also didn't tell Joan of the news about Wolsey, how his beloved school in Ipswich had been dissolved. That seemed unnecessarily cruel to him; for together with the Cardinal, he shared a belief in education and the importance of granting it to as many boys as possible. The King could have renamed it and claimed the credit for it as he did for so many other projects. He could even have named it for Anne Bullen which would have surely pleased the wretched woman, he thought, to place her name above Wolsey's.

But the time did pass and once again Joan set off on her road of tears. Gifts were left behind for birthdays and Christmas and Joan had thanked everyone a dozen times for the care of the children. There was one last detour to see Margery and kiss the new baby, Joan's namesake and they left Cheshire through fields ready for harvest.

Joan was quiet for several hours, smiling vacantly at

George when he caught her eye and he let her be. She would return to him when she had worked through her trouble. But this time she brought her horse close beside his and reached over to clasp his hand.

'George?'

'Mmm?'

'What shall we call our baby if she is a girl?'

George jolted and his horse sidestepped uneasily. He peered into Joan's face and she smiled peacefully at him. Then he seemed to reach inside her in that fashion that first touched her heart so many years before and her smile broke into pure sunshine.

'Really?'

'I think so. My courses are three months overdue. Had you not noticed?' And without any regard for the horses, George reached over and gave his wife a resounding kiss.

The rest of their journey passed in almost complete silence. George's head was full of thoughts of his son and he saw every sight as though he was showing it to his new child. It was almost as if he had been born anew and the world was so bright and glorious.

Joan was filled with the joy his delight had brought her and before her she constantly saw the sweet head of her new baby and beyond it, George, looking at them with such love and pleasure that she blasphemously thought that heaven could not be so bright.

The peace and happiness took them all the way home and lasted through the summer and into the autumn.

After another chill summer, autumn was proving to be a gentle season, almost as if, Joan felt, the weather was apologising for the lack of warmth. George was reluctantly from home, although due back any moment when Joan was walking in the orchard with Elizabeth.

The apples were close to being ready to be cropped and Joan's mouth watered at the thought of a crisp new apple; she hated the soft wrinkled ones which must be finished before they could start on the new harvest and every year, as long as she could remember and wherever she had been, she had managed to steal a few apples. She reached up and gently twisted one but it didn't come free and Elizabeth laughed at her glum face.

'It's all right, I'll see you have a couple.'

Then the apple suddenly fell at Joan's feet and she bent to pick it up. But she didn't straighten and Elizabeth looked at her in concern.

'Joan? What's wrong? Is it your back again? Here,' holding out her arm, 'pull on me.'

But Joan didn't take Elizabeth's arm. Instead, she leaned backwards slightly and pulled her skirts aside to show what was causing her such concern. Elizabeth looked and drew her breath in sharply.

'Oh. I see. Listen. It's perfectly all right. I often bled but I never lost one before it's time. Come along.'

She helped Joan to stand up and slipped an arm around her. *My poor girl*, she thought, looking back at the bloody marks Joan was leaving.

Joan remained silent all the interminable way back to the house. Through the gatehouses where they left servants in silent sadness as they passed, then up to her chamber where she barely reached the door before crumpling in a faint.

Elizabeth called for assistance and helping hands arrived but there was nothing to be done. Joan was only gone for a few moments and awoke to find herself on the bed with a cloth between her legs.

She gave a small smile, 'It's too late isn't it?' She could feel the blood seeping from her as her body heaved against her will to rid itself of her child. Was it her imagination or did it really feel so dreadfully solid and flesh-like? She pressed the material closer into herself to soak up the poor failure of her womb.

'Could you see what it was?'

Elizabeth shook her head, hardly trusting herself to speak. 'No.' she whispered, 'I'm sorry, I couldn't.'

She sat all night beside Joan holding her hand and soothing her. At last, Joan accepted a little drowsy syrup from Elizabeth and slept. By morning all was over and Joan was pale but well.

'How shall I tell George? The baby made him so happy.'

'Joan. *You* have made him happy. He will still be happy and you will have another child. I am sure. You have had six healthy children. And I don't see why you shouldn't have another.'

She looked at Joan who seemed so ridiculously young tucked up in bed with her eyes looking especially blue in her tear-reddened face. Joan nodded and closed her eyes.

'Don't tell him unless you have to. Someone might tell him when he arrives, but I would prefer it to be me.'

But George guessed something was wrong as soon as

the first gate was opened to him. There was no cheery greeting but a hat pulled off and clasped to the man's chest above a tragically solemn face. He stayed for no words but ran in as fast as he could, his legs so heavy that he felt he was dragging a great stone. The stairs to his chamber were never longer or steeper and he thought he might die until he saw Joan's face and her tremulous smile.

Elizabeth closed the door and left them alone. She heard only Joan's simple phrase, 'I'm sorry.' And George's sob before she swallowed her own tears and headed to the small chapel to pray.

Chapter 26

November 1530

In his bed at Leicester Abbey, Thomas Wolsey was growing annoyed with the tiptoeing behaviour of his attendants; they asked him about money, he who could buy an army was now reduced to accounting for the least amount. It belonged to the King anyway and was loaned to Thomas to increase the King's glory and influence. Their candles bothered him and he asked for the shutters to be opened; he longed for pure clean daylight but they wouldn't and instead, they persisted with holding their hands in front of candles so that all was a disturbing frieze of flickering shadows and reddened flesh and the maddening whisper of their voices. He couldn't even be sure if they spoke to him or each other.

Always, even now, someone wanted something. He had never been a hunting man; in all those years spent making it possible for Henry to enjoy his favourite pursuit, Thomas had never joined the King. Never wanted to. People thought it was because he was no gentleman and perhaps it was. But in all honesty, he found it distasteful. To him, there was no sport in pursuing terrified animals with shouting laughter and baying hounds. And here, at the last, he was the prey and he was correct, it was utterly dreadful.

Thomas groaned and George Cavendish and another whose name he had had forgotten came and helped him to his stool. He voided his bowels and knew from their reactions that once again it was red with bright blood. Still seated, he felt himself start to vomit and closed his eyes against the sight of his life's blood spattering into the bowl. The taste alone was enough to make his poor empty stomach heave once more.

Once back in bed, he rinsed his mouth with a little wine and sank exhausted into his pillows. His mind wandered and his hand rose unbidden to his neck. Under his night-rail, he wore a hair shirt that irritated his skin almost beyond endurance. His fingers were cold and when he placed his hand between the shirt and his skin, it brought a moment of relief and he stirred slightly and smiled. His chaplain knew of the shirt but what he didn't know – what nobody knew – was that when Thomas commissioned the shirt from the monks, he had taken the lock of Joan's hair and instructed them to include it. They would bury him in the shirt.

He made a wry face and George bent over him, 'My Lord?' but Thomas was drifting away once again. The hunting dogs were close on his heels. They had chased him for many years and sometimes he wondered how he had evaded them but now their breath was hot on his neck and their slobber would soon cover him as they seized him and shook him to death.

Had he given his final speech? He thought so but, in any case, it was written down and in George's hands to pass it to the King. Henry. What trouble the boy was in now and he could do nothing to help him. Not lying uselessly here, caught on the piercing prongs of pain and death. His mind wandered and he thought of Saint Eustace and his vision of the cross between the sharp horns of a stag.

As panteth the hart, he thought and against the window, he saw the tiny lines of light resolve into a white stag. But that faded and something else took its place. A woman in a deep blue robe with hands outstretched to him. Her hair was once again long and beautiful and her dear face lit up with the joy of seeing him. Thomas dared not close his eyes in case the lovely figure of Joan faded as the deer had done, but she really was here. He wanted to rest his head against her and feel her cool hands on his forehead – she would make him feel better. When she reached the bed and clasped his hands, their eyes met and he spoke her name clearly and distinctly and, in the distance, he could hear the abbey bell chime the eighth hour of the morning.

George and the chaplain looked at each other across the bed. Thomas's eyes were slightly open and his mouth was slack. The pulse in his neck was still.

'Master Palmes?' George's voice was soft, 'Did you hear his final words?' The name of Joan rang in his ears and he could still see the rapture on his master's face.

The chaplain coughed. 'Why no. I don't think I did. His voice was very weak. He may have just been clearing his throat.'

George nodded. 'That is my belief too. May God rest his soul.'

Chapter 27

Basing, December 1530

Joan had recovered well from the loss of the child but George had been deeply shaken. It frightened him that his wife was not the solid and robust person he'd thought and he feared further damage to her. He had not lain with her since and treated her with tentative care, almost as if, she thought, she was a stranger.

Before dawn, she had been woken by the arrival of a messenger for William. His letters were clearly of great import to her brother-in-law and she hoped that he had not been called to court, for that invariably meant that George would go too.

It was a fresh morning and she was walking in the privy garden when William appeared and spoke her name.

'May I join you?'

She smiled, William was good company; witty and amusing and she was pleased to have him with her. But then, she saw his expression and turned to face him.

'The children?'

He shook his head and she knew. With the sensation of the world falling away from her, she said a single word, 'Thomas.'

William nodded and took her hands. His sister-in-law

was a sensible woman and he had no fear of hysterics.

'Yes. I have had word. He died a week ago whilst in the care of the Abbey at Leicester. When he arrived, he told them that he was come to lay his bones amongst them. And he did.'

And to his surprise, Joan smiled, 'Then he is at last safe. From intrigue and courtiers and the King. He loved the King more than he loved God but he never understood that the King was his most pressing danger.'

These were perilous words, although William could not deny their truth and it was with relief that over her shoulder, he could see George approaching to attend to his wife in her sadness. But yet again Joan surprised herself and her family. She greeted George with a gentle smile. 'My dear. It seems I am now doubly a widow.'

The news seemed to enliven Joan. She was tired of George treating her as if she were broken. That night she called him to her chamber and told him briskly that enough was enough. She was healed and whole and she missed him in her bed. God would take care of her and George needed to carry out his husbandly duties.

As she spoke, she undressed and he found himself desiring her beyond endurance. He gazed into her bright eyes and saw her spirit challenging him. He forgot his fear of hurting her and seized her by the arms. His fingers dug into her flesh and he kissed her as if he was starved and they made love that was fierce and far removed from their usual laughing conspiracy.

In 1531, the new year brought welcome news to William Paulet; his licence to crenellate was issued and at last, he could begin to plan in earnest his great house at Basing. The news was less welcome to George who was once more heartbroken at the thought of the loss of his childhood home. The two brothers would never agree on this, although William was careful never to point out that he owned Basing and George's consent was not needed. But Joan was certainly aware of it and began to suggest that she and George might seek to make their home elsewhere.

She had always found it amusing that the moments before making love to George were the most propitious ones for asking a favour and the irony was not lost on her that she had to work hard to remember, amid her own lust, what she had intended to say. This morning as she wriggled over to George and kissed him awake, she had almost forgotten her idea of a house at Crondall. Thirteen miles away, it was close enough for easy contact but far enough that George could concentrate on building their own home and avoid seeing the destruction and rebuilding at Basing. But between kisses, she had managed to murmur her thoughts to him before leaving them to take root.

George did indeed like the idea and throughout the summer whenever he was at Basing, he and Joan would ride out from Basing to the surrounding areas. Crondall remained their favourite and one day it was his turn to surprise Joan with his ideas.

They lay in their bed, in fact, the Wolsey bed which they had brought to Hampshire after their last visit to Cheshire. The moon was bright and their bed curtains were open to allow the warm summer air to pass over them.

George lay his splayed hand on Joan's stomach. 'Shall we have the child in our own home?'

Joan propped herself on one elbow to look at him. 'How did you know?' she demanded.

George tucked one arm behind his head and looked smug. 'Of course, I knew. I know your body as an explorer knows a foreign land he has conquered and fallen in love with. The new year I think…'

She gave her puffy laugh which she used whenever George confounded her. 'Well done, Master Paulet. Yes, I believe that by March we shall be proud parents of a boy.'

George felt the familiar dread pluck at his heart and Joan smiled at him. 'Oh my love, I know. I fear the loss of you when you leave to use the piss pot. When you go on one of William's missions, I know for certain that you will die having been thrown from your horse or having been set upon by vagabonds. Whenever I close my eyes, I fear that you will pass from me.' She kissed his forehead and nose.

'It's part of the joy of loving someone,' she kissed his eyelids, 'and that deadly fear is because we are mortal,' and her lips fell on his mouth. 'It's our reward and our curse and we must accommodate it.'

December found them still at Basing, but George had firm plans for a site at Crondall. Building work had not yet commenced on the old house and it was both sweet and poignant to spend a last Christmas there. Elizabeth was pleased to see all the children at home once more and the house was cheerful though uncomfortably crammed. William constantly paced around telling anyone who would listen how roomy his new house would be and behind his back his wife would lift her eyebrows and mouth silent words at him. It would be, she privately believed, decades before his great ideas were realised and she foresaw years of life in London interspersed by episodes of dust and inconvenience in Hampshire. But there was laughter and joy and Joan delighted in the Paulet family and their clever conversations. She was content and calm. If she could have every wish granted, her children would be here too, but they were well and happy and if she placed her hand on her swelling belly, she felt that her unborn child was also healthy and she faced 1532 with a brave heart and armoured with love.

As expected, her birth pangs started in mid-February. The day was blowy and William's physician arrived looking very windswept. Master Owen felt the calm of the chamber and was reassured. He knew that Master George's wife had safely delivered many children as had Mistress Elizabeth and he had no concerns. His hands were dirty from removing a stone from his horse's hoof as he travelled and courteously, he wiped them on his doublet before examining Joan. What he found satisfied him—all was progressing as it ought. Moving to the corner of the room, he conferred with the midwife. He was known as a progressive thinker and happy to speak to a fellow professional, even if she had the misfortune to be a woman and if her opinion agreed with his, then all the better.

He left the chamber and returned to the study where William and George waited. His smile reassured them and the three men sat around the fire to pass the time. They were old friends; they had grown up together and the doctor had delivered most of William's children and successfully seen them through their childhood illnesses and injuries.

In an admirably short time, Joan was easily delivered of her third son and George could barely wait to greet his first child. His Joan looked so well as he entered their room. She was sitting up and leaning against pillows positioned to cushion her against the knobs and hard parts of the carvings behind her. It had been such a calm delivery and now George was here, just as she had imagined, looking at her over the head of their child.

How extraordinary, George thought, *so simple, yet it is everything. There she is. There he is; our boy. Now I understand.* And in his overflowing heart, he even felt room to pity the King for not yet having felt this joy.

Joan had proved a popular addition to the Paulet family and in Basing town the news was greeted with much joy. The news that Mistress Joan has a boy was happily passed along the Street, from person to person and many a toast was drunk that night.

The next morning Joan felt terribly tired. She kept squeezing her eyes tightly closed and telling herself that of course she felt tired; she was no longer young and giving birth was hard work. But each time she reopened them the room shook slightly before steadying. When she held out her arms for the baby her eyes showed four arms and hands in front of her before she could uncross her eyes and see only two. She was tired. It was fine.

It was mid-afternoon before anyone else noticed.

Elizabeth had brought dinner to Joan and they had eaten together, laughing as they often did at some small household drama, then without warning, Joan was neatly sick onto her plate.

'Well,' she said in surprise, before staring wide-eyed at Elizabeth, 'Oh, I am sorry.' And was promptly sick again.

Elizabeth felt sick herself. She looked at Joan and could see that she was very unwell. The bright cheeks did not show health but fever and Joan's hands were fluttering around her stomach before she suddenly sat up and clutched her knees.

'It's really sore.' Joan muttered then grinned up at Elizabeth. 'I'll wager it's wind.' She laughed then winced again.

Elizabeth closed her eyes. *When I open them*, she thought, *Joan will be fine.* In her memory, she saw the doctor wiping his hands on his doublet and heard the midwife's intake of breath. She was a great one for washing her hands and believed dirt to be a spreader of contagion. Perhaps she was right.

By nightfall, it was clear that Joan was suffering from childbed fever. George paced and sat and paced again. He wore a path to the house chapel and constantly besieged God with frantic prayer but Joan did not improve. The baby cried and cried, fretting everyone's nerves. They took him from Joan to the other side of the house and a wet nurse was found.

In the still hours before dawn, George lay on the bed beside Joan. She was completely rational and clear and they spoke together.

'What shall we call him?'

'Oh, George or Thomas, I think. There really aren't enough Georges or Thomases in the world.'

George could hear the humour in her voice and smiled, but his smile was resting on an ocean of tears.

'William perhaps? Your brother has been so kind to me…' her voice faded and once more she stood in London calling out after the wrong Paulet brother. 'Mmm. Yes, William.' And Joan drifted back towards George.

Towards dawn, the birds started to sing. Joan smiled, 'They always want spring before it's here, don't they? Just like us really. George, I'm sorry. And thank you. It's been rather lovely. I should so like to grow old with you and worry about the children and laugh and…' she sighed and looked ruefully at him, 'Ah, well.'

Then she turned her head. The sunlight through the window made her eyes close slightly but the warmth was delightful. Over the birdsong, she should hear children laughing, and over that again, she heard grown-up voices. Was it Thomas? Yes, Thomas called her name, and she found herself leaning on the window sill and looking through the glass. There he was, in shirt sleeves, his hated tonsure all grown out, charging around with the children. As usual, George was covered with the babies, who rode him like a good-natured pony, and her own, her very own darling husband George cradled his brand-new son, lifted him towards the window and beckoned to her. Joan lifted her hand in a wave and turned to race down and join them.

Select Bibliography.

Anon. (1950). *Adlington Hall, Cheshire.* Privately printed.

Anon. (1706). *The Memoirs of that Great Favourite Cardinal Woolsey.* London. B Bragg.

Barksfield, J. (2003) *The Wolsey Altar, Hambledon Parish Church.* Henley Archaeological & Historical Group.

Butterfield, R. (1948). *Monastery and Manor.* Farnham. E W Langham.

Cardinal, E. (1935). *Cardinal Lorenzo Campeggio Legate to the Courts of Henry VIII and Charles V.* America. Mount Vernon Press.

Castiglione, B. (1528) (Translated 1967). Translated by Bull, G. *The Book of the Courtier.* London. Penguin Books.

Cavendish, G. (1962). *Thomas Wolsey late Cardinal his Life and Death.* London. The Folio Society.

Colvin, H & Foister, S (Editors). (1996). *The Panorama of London circa 1544 by Anthonis*

Copeland, A. (1888). *Bridewell Royal Hospital Past and Present.* London. Wells, Gardner, Darton & Co.

Davies, D. (2018). *Yarmouth: a Sand in the Sea.* Lowestoft. Poppyland Publishing.

Fiddes, R. (1726). *The Life of Cardinal Wolsey.* London. Knapton, Knaplock, Midwinter, Imys, Robinson, Osborn, Longman.

Gwynne, P. (1990). *The King's Cardinal.* London. Pimlico.

Karras, R. (2012). *Unmarriages: women, men, and*

sexual unions in the Middle Ages. Pennsylvania. University of Pennsylvania Press.

Loades, D. (1992) *The Tudor Court.* Bangor. Headstart History.

Loades, D. (2008). *Cardinal Wolsey.* Burford. The Davenant Press (Oxford).

MacCulloch, D. *Thomas Cromwell: A Life.* London. Penguin Random House UK.

Malcolm-Davis, J. & Mikhaila, N. (2022). *The Typical Tudor.* Lightwater. Fat Goose Press.

Mikhaila, N & Malcolm-Davis, J. (2006). *The Tudor Tailor.* London. B T Batsford.

Mikhaila, N & Huggett, J. (2016). *The Tudor Child.* London. The British Library.

Moorhouse, G. (2005). *Great Harry's Navy: How Henry VIII Gave England Seapower.* London. Phoenix.

Mumby, F. (1913). *The Youth of Henry VIII.* London. Constable & Company Ltd.

O'Hara, D. (2000). *Courtship and Constraint: Rethinking the Making of Marriage in Tudor England.* Manchester. Manchester University Press.

Penn, T. *Winter King: the Dawn of Tudor England.* London. Penguin Books.

Richards, R. (1947). *Old Cheshire Churches.* London. B T Batsford, Ltd.

Richardson, G. (2020). *Wolsey.* Abingdon. Routledge.

Sparkes, I. (1990). *Four Poster and Tester Beds.* Haverford West, Dafyd. C I Thomas & Sons.

Stanley, A. (1868). *Historical Memorials of Westminster Abbey.* London. John Murray.

Starkey, D. (2009). *Henry VIII: The Mind of a Tyrant.* London. Harper Perennial.

Twinch, C. (2008). *The History of Ipswich.* Derby. The Breedon Books Publishing Company Limited.

Weir, A & Clarke, S. (2018). *A Tudor Christmas.* London. Jonathan Cape.